P9-CNE-097

Edward Lear's Tennyson

The Campagna as seen through an Arch on the Appian Way
from the collection of Roger Ebert, Chicago

EDWARD LEAR'S TENNYSON

with an introduction and commentaries
by Ruth Pitman

CARCANET

Published in 1988 by
Carcanet Press Limited
208-212 Corn Exchange Buildings
Manchester M4 3BQ
and
Carcanet
198 Sixth Avenue, New York
New York 10013

Selection, introduction and commentaries
copyright © 1988 Ruth Pitman
All rights reserved

British Library Cataloguing in Publication Data

Lear, Edward
    Edward Lear's Tennyson.
    1. Lear, Edward – Catalogs
    I. Title   II. Pitman, Ruth
    759.2   ND1942.L37

    ISBN 0-85635-738-3

The publisher acknowledges financial assistance
from the Arts Council of Great Britain

Typeset in 10pt Times Roman & Goudy Old Style by Bryan Williamson, Manchester
Printed in England by SRP Ltd, Exeter

CONTENTS

[1] 83, 84 and 150 not in this set. 3 inserted drawings 115, 125a, 142a make this 'egg' set up to 200.

Editorial Note

All quotations from Lear's writing follow his own spellings and punctuation. Where his spellings of place names vary, they have not been made consistent, with the exception that all accents have been removed. Lear's quotations from Tennyson have not been corrected where they deviate slightly from the printed poem, but where his misquotations are significant, they have been noted.

Numbers and place-name references for Lear's Illustrations are printed after each Tennyson poem or extract. Roman type indicates that the Illustration is reproduced full size, bold numbers and italic text that the Illustration is reproduced in miniature (pp. 197-210).

The texts of Tennyson's poems have been taken from editions as follows, all of them published in London by the firm of Edward Moxon: *Poems*, in two volumes, 1842; *The Princess*, (11th edition) 1851); *In Memoriam*, (4th edition) 1851; 'The Sea-Fairies' and 'To E.L.' from *Poems* (10th edition) 1855; 'The Daisy' and 'Will' from *Maud, and Other Poems*, 1855; 'Lancelot and Elaine' and 'Guinevere' from *Idylls of the King*, 1859; *Enoch Arden, etc.*, 1864. I should like to record my indebtedness to Professor Christopher Ricks, both for pointing out the connections between Edward Lear and the Tennysons, and for his first authoritative edition of *The Poems of Tennyson* (Longmans, 1969).

Published and unpublished sources referred to throughout the book have been abbreviated as follows:

Albanian Journal	Edward Lear, *Journals of a Landscape Painter in Albania, &c.*, London: Richard Bentley, 1851.
A.T. Illustrations	Alfred Tennyson Illustrations: Lear wrote the Laureate's name thus: A.
Calabrian Journal	Edward Lear, *Journals of a Landscape Painter in Southern Calabria, &c.*, London: Richard Bentley, 1852.
Corsican Journal	Edward Lear, *Journal of a Landscape Painter in Corsica*, London: Robert John Bush, 1870.
D.	Diary of Edward Lear, 1858-1887 inclusive. The manuscript volumes are all held by the Houghton Library, Harvard University.
EL Drawing	The quotation from Tennyson written by Lear under each A.T. Illustration.
EL List	Printed list, c.1885/6, of Tennyson poem titles and quotations with places depicted in Lear's Illustrations. This list was kept with the 'egg' (i.e. smallest) size Illustrations which belonged to the Tennyson family after Lear's death. There are some inaccuracies, misquotations and misnumberings on the list. Lear 'corrected' at least three printed lists, but the task of keeping two hundred titles, quotations and place names in order, and without error, was beyond him.
EL to Ann	Letter from Edward Lear to his sister, Ann Lear. The original letters disappeared in the 1930s, but they had been transcribed and are now preserved in typescript in the collection of Dr David Michell. Two ms letters to Ann are in the collection of Mr Donald Gallup.

EL to Emily Tennyson	Letter from Edward Lear to the poet's wife. Part of the original collection has been dispersed, but most of these letters are held by the Tennyson Research Centre, Lincoln. The dedicatory letter is in the collection of the Ruskin Galleries, Bembridge School, Isle of Wight Note: other letters mentioned in the text between Lear and the Tennysons and from Mr Estes to Hallam are in the Tennyson Research Centre.
EL to Hallam Tennyson	Letter from Edward Lear to Hallam Tennyson. The ms is in the collection of Mr Donald Gallup.
EL to Fortescue	Letter from Edward Lear to Chichester Fortescue, later Lord Carlingford. Letters edited and printed in LEL and LLEL; further material, including Fortescue's journal which refers to Lear, in the Somerset Record Office, Taunton (Carlingford MSS).
EL to Underhill	Letter from Edward Lear to Frederick Underhill; the ms was formerly in the collection of Mr Justin G. Schiller.
Hoge	*Lady Tennyson's Journal*, ed. James O. Hoge, Charlottesville: University Press of Virginia, 1981.
Indian Journal	Manuscript of Edward Lear's Indian Journal (1873-75) held in the Houghton Library, Harvard University.
LEL	*Letters of Edward Lear, Author of the 'Book of Nonsense', to Chichester Fortescue (Lord Carlingford), Frances, Countess Waldegrave and others*, ed. Lady Strachey, London: T. Fisher Unwin, 1907.
LLEL	*Later Letters of Edward Lear . . .*, ed. Lady Strachey, London: T. Fisher Unwin, 1911.
Mem. I and II	Hallam, Lord Tennyson, *Alfred, Lord Tennyson. A Memoir by his son*, 2 volumes, London: Macmillan and Co., 1897.
Noakes	Vivien Noakes, *Edward Lear, the Life of a Wanderer*, London: Collins, 1968. The first edition of the standard biography.

Acknowledgements

I am grateful to the National Art-Collections Fund, The Victoria and Albert Museum Purchase Grant Fund and The British Academy for financial help in acquiring Lear material for the University of Bristol; also to Thos. Agnew and Sons and to Spink and Son for their help and co-operation.

I would like to thank: Miss Eleanor Garvey and the Houghton Library, Harvard University, for permission to quote from Lear's Diary and his Indian Journal; the Lincolnshire Library Service for permission to quote from material in the Tennyson Research Centre, Lincoln; Mr Donald Gallup, Mr Justin G. Schiller, Dr David Michell and the Curator, Ruskin Galleries, Bembridge School, Isle of Wight, for permission to quote from unpublished letters and other material.

My thanks are due to: Norman Higham, the Librarian, University of Bristol and particularly to Gordon Kelsey, The Arts Faculty Photographic Unit, who took photographs of Lear's Tennyson Illustrations.

My personal thanks for help and encouragement go to: Vivien Noakes for generously offering me access to her unparalleled knowledge of Edward Lear; to Jean and Stephen Pasmore, Eileen Pitman; to Florence Axford and Beatrice Jenkins; to Penelope Fielding, Rowena Fowler, John Lyon; to Jan Tarling and Tracey James; to Michael Abbott and to my editor, Robyn Marsack. For his knowledge of Amstrad and Autotype &c. I would particularly like to thank Mark Pitman.

By Way of Preface

Edward Lear died at his home, the Villa Tennyson, San Remo, on 29 January 1888. He wanted his memorial stone to give the simplest details: dates of birth and death. His friend and executor, Franklin Lushington, gave rather different instructions. He did not invent a fulsome epitaph but added 'Landscape painter and traveller in many lands' and a reference to Lear's 'many gifts to many souls'. The inscription ended with a few lines of poetry. The choice of poem was obvious, but one which Lear would have been too modest to suggest: a verse from Tennyson's tribute to Lear, 'To E.L. on his Travels in Greece':

> – all things fair
> With such a pencil such a pen
> You shadow'd forth to distant men
> I read and felt that I was there.

So, to all passers by, the artist was linked with his most admired poet, and the suggestion of both painting and writing hint at the imaginative approach to landscape which led to Lear's great unfulfilled plan for Tennyson Illustrations.

In 1887, Lear was seventy-five and in poor health. Sometimes he hardly slept, and found 'the slowness of the night hours...truly dreadful' (D. 18 April 1887). He was often too ill to get up, suffered from acute rheumatic pain, breathlessness, wretched digestion and sore, swollen feet. Each night he was free of pain he wished he could thank God more. And he fought not to give in, either to physical ailments, or to hopelessness and depression – 'the morbids', as he called them, part of his experience from early days. Lear was determined, if possible, to dress, to move about the house, to greet visitors and welcome old friends. He wrote letters, read numbers of books, enjoyed Dickens's Pickwick, and was cheered by Trollope's novels. Even if 'his shoes were far too tight', like those of his own last Nonsense self, Uncle Arly, he managed to travel up to Andorno in the summer. It was a difficult journey for a man who was old and ill, but it took him away from the heat and flies of San Remo. Even then he did not rest. He began work, yet again, on some new large-size Tennyson drawings.

In San Remo during that last year, Lear still delighted in the brilliant weather before the oppressive summer heat. With the window open he watched the pigeons strutting below or flying like shafts of gold and silver. He could see his pink and red roses and below his sloping garden, the blue and sparkling sea. Lear's world had become circumscribed: once he had travelled intrepidly to Albania or Egypt; now it was journey enough to negotiate the steps in the garden, to sit down and admire his carnations and roses, to reach the landmark of a purple clematis by the stairs. In this small landscape, he could enjoy a 'perfect blaze of flowers', pause at the end of a terrace 'where the roses & scarlet Passion flowers are a sight', and list, in his diary, the Latin names of his carefully imported and tended plants. The garden was a world – an island, almost – of growth and colour. One day, feeling stronger, Lear went into the little garden

'first by the Arches walk...Then down – passing the Serbolini Ipomæa to the 2nd Terrace, & then to the Giardinello which was delicious, being all in the shade – yet quite sheltered'. He noted the way the light filtered through the shrubs, and read the paper (sadly there were no letters), sitting on the garden seat, before eight o'clock in the morning (from D. 28 May and 18 June 1887). This was a venture greatly enjoyed, but not lightly undertaken by a man who could scarcely walk. The garden of the Villa Tennyson brought back memories of Lear's first house, the Villa Emily, and of earlier years in San Remo. He always missed the olives in his first garden, but the mandarin orange trees had been transplanted by an enthusiastic gardener although, alas, they never produced the loads of fruit which Lear had loved to give away to friends. To his own surprise, the artist had become fascinated with making a garden. He stuffed cuttings in his pockets when he went on expeditions, and he hid plants and seeds, hoping his trunk would not be searched at the Italian border. Some exotic plants had grown from seeds collected or sent from India: they brought memories of that last great journey, flowerings for the mind, as Lear travelled slowly round his Villa Tennyson domain.

By 1887 Lear's main artistic concern was how to reproduce his Tennyson Illustrations. He could no longer seriously attempt to work on his huge, unfinished oil paintings. But a large Athos and an enormous imaginary scene, Enoch Arden's Island, were advanced far beyond mere outline on canvas. After Lear's death these went to the Tennyson family and were hung at Aldworth, the Laureate's main home. By Lear's meticulous standards, neither painting had been brought to anything like a conclusion. If he could not manage full-scale painting, the artist could keep himself working and occupied in many other ways. He sorted out sketches and drawings to be given to particular friends; he kept at his own Tennyson work, at his letters, his diaries, his garden visits, his reading. He wrote frequently to his lasting friends, who remained a great support. At least he could reach them in letters, and he scanned every post hoping for a reply. The social whirl of acquaintances and invitations had long whirled past him. He was fortunate in having good and capable servants, but no one made up for the Suliot, Giorgio Kokali, who served Lear faithfully for twenty-seven years until he died in 1883. Giorgio was both servant and friend: he had accompanied Lear on many of his journeys. His master knew just what he meant when they both looked at a sunrise and Giorgio said 'Il Nilo, Signore' – they shared Egyptian memories of 1867. While the servant had looked after the master in earlier years, as the servant neared death no master could have tended him more carefully than Lear. By 1887 there was no Giorgio; now Lear was dependent on new servants. One creature remained as a lasting companion and support: the old cat Foss, who had joined the household in 1872. Foss got his name from 'Adelphos' (brother) because he was the twin brother of a cat called Potiphar who ran away. In the winter, once, Lear wrote: 'Foss & the fire make a kind of dim happiness' (D. 25 November 1879). And this striped and stumpy-tailed beast was Lear's last companion. Foss had been in Lear's first home, the Villa Emily. Foss had lived through, with much less interest and agony than his master, the building of the new hotel which ruined Lear's view and painting light. The cat finally moved into the Villa Tennyson, even if he then disappeared, only to rush out of the chimney 'to general applause'. That was in 1881; as far back as 1873 to 1875 Foss stayed with Lear's San Remo neighbours, and sur-

vived to return after Lear's journey to India. Through the illness and death of Giorgio and the problems of his family, Foss was always about. He had to be fed and looked after whatever the human crises.

Writing to Ann, as early as 1847, Lear described his current Roman cat as 'very well bred and amiable'. He hated dogs, unless he knew them very well. When he established a home, a cat was clearly necessary. 'Foss the cat is a good addition to ones lonely lonely life – & is highly absurd this evening,' wrote Lear in his diary, 23 February 1873. For years Foss came in to 'eat his biscuit in tranquillity' after dinner. When the fire was first lit in winter the cat returned at once to his old basket or to the hearthrug. Sometimes Foss was in disgrace: he chewed up letters, ate a new cream cheese, pulled the tablecloth off: 'he' was then demoted to 'it' and banished to the kitchen. 'Oh dear, dear, dear,' wrote Lear on the ink-blotted fly leaf of a copy of his Corsican Journal, 'Foss did it', and he drew a small caricature of the cat and autographed the book. Latterly Foss – 'poor old Foss' – spent much of his time with Lear. He shared meals, finished up roast fowl Lear could not manage, sat in his own chair and was always 'gentle and good'. He needed a new set of bells (to protect the birds) and found them difficult to get used to. Lear drew a minute picture in his diary of Foss curled up with the bells round his neck. 'Foss assisting' or sometimes 'Foss intervening' was Lear's usual phrase for a meal taken downstairs. In letters, in Nonsense Alphabets, in heraldic poses – Lear drew endless caricatures of Foss. He drew himself as well: rotund, with large spectacles and a cane, Foss following along behind. Lear's early love of birds and animals in the Zoological Gardens, his late enthusiasm for camels and 'duskily shuffling' elephants, were focused, in the end, on the surprisingly fierce looking, aggressively striped and almost tail-less cat. More perhaps than the efficient servants, Foss gave a continuing feeling of 'home'. The much cherished, much caricatured cat died in September 1887. He merited a grave stone in Lear's garden: *Qui sotto sta sepolto il mio buon Gatto Foss.* The inscription greatly extended Foss's age – a mistake which suggests how long, in Lear's memory, his cat had been part of everyday life.

Lear lived the last days of his life, calling up, recreating, and looking over memories of the past. As a young man he had remembered significant details of his childhood: as an old man he looked back over all his earlier years. The present and the future he often considered in the light of past experience. Thinking, once, of places and people he might never see again, Lear wrote of his life as 'a series of pictures seen through "Memory's Arch"' (D. 4 August 1880). In his list of Tennyson Illustrations he misquoted a line from 'Ulysses' and turned 'For all experience...' into 'for all remembrance is an Arch'. Through such an arch of memory he looked back on the 'pictures' of his past life. His Tennyson Illustrations were to have been a composite picture of his travels and his achievements as a landscape artist. They were undoubtedly meant as a tribute to the poet, but also as a record of all Lear's 'poetical topography'.[1] They were to have been his *Liber Studiorum* – the book in which Turner brilliantly categorized landscape designs and popularized some of his own work through engravings. Much earlier, Claude's *Liber Veritatis* had been a catalogue which gave visual proof of his own paintings. Lear knew both works, possessed two copies of the Turner – in mezzotint and autotype – and referred to Claude's book as a *Liber Studiorum*. A very early oil, done in Rome, had been a picture of Claude's house. Thus Claude and Turner – great artists from past and present – seemed, in a sense, to preside over Lear's Tennyson project. These illustrations were never a scheme carried out for immediately needed money. They were Lear's own imaginative scheme, and never part of a commission. Individual oil paintings, the 'Bassae', the 'Argos' and various watercolours were very much part of Lear's œuvre, but the Tennyson Illustrations were a picture, in miniature, of his whole artistic past.

Looking further back at the 'pictures' through 'Memory's Arch', the first are those of Lear's childhood. Born in 1812, the twentieth of twenty-one children, Lear had a strange upbringing. His father, Jeremiah Lear, was a well-to-do stockbroker, who lived with his large family, in a comfortable house, Bowman's Lodge, in Holloway, London. But the stockbroker got into financial difficulties; the family had to split up, some of the girls became governesses, and everyone had to leave their home. Edward was a bewildered small boy at the time, and his mother seems to have been too busy and anxious for her husband to take much notice of him. He was more or less relegated to the care of a sister Ann, fifteen years older than her rather sensitive, short-sighted brother, who suffered from asthma and, much worse, the 'demon' epilepsy. Luckily Ann was steady, cheerful and ready to prove a mother to Edward. She looked after him, consoled him for the frequent, but fairly mild, epileptic attacks, and gave him lessons until, for a short time, he went to school. She and another sister also taught him to draw, and encouraged his interest. Very early studies of a bird and a flower show a neat and competent technique which was to stand the aspiring artist in good stead. Edward was never to forget his sister's devotion. On his early travels he wrote her long marvellous letters and always brought back little presents: a shawl, a length of silk, a carved cross, some beads, a small Egyptian scarab. These mementoes, his detailed letters, and his diary entries, reveal his deep affection for Ann. When she lay dying, she longed to see 'darling Edward', but did not wish to put him to any trouble. He could not watch the final moments, but stood in the street until the blinds were drawn down.

Ann died in 1861, so that last sad 'picture', was preceded by many comfortable and even happy memories. The family were never destitute and, when Jeremiah Lear's debts and difficulties were sorted out, they all returned to Bowman's Lodge. Several daughters – it was difficult to keep numbers and identities clear among so many – had succumbed to ill-health and died after a few years of work. But even with a smaller family, Mrs Lear seems to have taken no interest in Edward. He remained in the care of Ann. A married sister, Sarah, lived in Sussex, so Edward was taken to stay in the country, and at some stage visited Petworth and saw Lord Egremont's Turner collection. When Jeremiah decided to retire to Gravesend with his exhausted wife and just one daughter, Ann and Edward took lodgings in Gray's Inn Road. Ann had a little money; Edward now fifteen or sixteen, set about to earn something to help his sister. He began, as he says in 'By Way of Preface', printed in *Nonsense Songs and Stories* (Seventh edition, 1889): '...to draw, for bread and cheese, about 1827, but only did uncommon queer shop-sketches, selling them for prices from ninepence to four shillings: colouring prints, screens, fans, awhile making morbid disease drawings, for hospitals and certain doctors of physic.'

His sister's drawing lessons and his own growing skill allowed Lear to get on to the very bottom rung of the art world ladder. He began to show a talent for drawing birds and animals from life, was noticed working at the Zoological Gardens, and between 1828 and 1830 he began to draw birds for the well-known ornithologists, Prideaux Selby and William Jardine. He contributed to many important books on birds and seems to have drawn monkeys and 'some cats' for William Jardine's *Naturalist's Library*. He made lithographs (a few from his own designs) of wonderfully characterful tortoises for Thomas Bell's *Testudinata*, (1836-42, enlarged in a new edition, *Tortoises, Terrapins, & Turtles*, 1872). But birds, especially parrots, were the young artist's main speciality. He worked for John Gould on a number of volumes – often not being credited with his name on plates he had done. Gould's massive *Birds of Europe* contained some fine work by Lear, and a great deal of help on foregrounds was given by the artist to Gould's wife who also contributed plates. Lear was certainly exploited in this and other ventures, such as the impressive *Ramphastidae or Family of Toucans* (1834). By now he had determined to launch out on his own and, by the time he was twenty, he had produced *The Family of the Psittacidae or Parrots* (1832), 'the first complete volume of coloured drawings of birds on so large a scale, published in England, as far as I know', he wrote, looking back in 'By Way of Preface'.

The *Psittacidae* is a superb production. Lear did not draw from dead and stuffed birds – he preferred to ask a keeper to hold the living struggling parrot for a short time. He saw the bird's wing feathers, muscles, back and tail structure in close up and in life. He lithographed his designs with the bird perched or caught in movement, in a setting of foliage, branch and tree. He supervised the hand-colouring and noted the exact shading of brilliant yellows, greens, blues and reds. It was an expensive outlay and Lear did not finish all the folios he planned. But he got subscriptions for his fine work, and designs for the red and yellow macaw, among others, are still considered masterpieces of ornithological lithography.

The young Edward Lear, who caricatured himself as sober, bespectacled and with a parrot on his top hat, had moved from trivia to skilled lithography. But even the leaves round his parrots, the branches they cling to, begin to show an as yet undeveloped interest in landscape. Gould took Lear to Switzerland, Germany and Amsterdam, entirely in pursuit of birds. Lear mentions a tour of Ireland and the Lakes in 1835 or 1836 during which he leaned more and more towards landscape. But before this he was to go on drawing animals and birds in a completely different environment.

The Right Hon. Lord Stanley, heir to the Earl of Derby, was President of the Zoological Society. He had subscribed to Lear's *Psittacidae* and knew his talents. He invited the artist to Knowsley, seat of the Earl of Derby, a great house which rejoiced in a fashionable private menagerie. Lear was to record its contents, both birds and small animals. He had to part from Ann, but was now more than ready for independence. And the invitation to Knowsley gave him a glimpse of a new world and new possibilities. He was rather awkward and shy, overawed by the Earl's entourage and some of his overdressed guests. His natural habitat was not the kitchen, or housekeeper's room, and yet he had no entrée into drawing-room society. The solution came through the children to whom Lear had always been able to talk quite easily; he invented Nonsense verses and pictures for the grandchildren of the house and soon they were rushing off to visit the amusing young man immediately after dinner. Rather than lose the children, the old Earl asked what they had discovered which was so intriguing; he then promptly invited Lear to join the party in the drawing-room. The artist thus began to learn about the English aristocratic and upper classes. He got used to their snobbery, their inability to imagine any life but their own, yet also to their generosity and patronage of a struggling young painter. He quickly picked up the way of drawing-room society and was ever afterwards a welcome country house weekend guest. In his diary, with pleasure rather than sarcasm, he notes time and time again the exact guest-plan of a dinner-table.

From Knowsley Lear made some forays, into the English countryside, to Ireland and to the Lake District: his feeling for landscape became more distinct. This is what he wanted to draw and paint. He was not always at Knowsley, and he continued work for Gould and others. Soon the close attention to bird and animal detail began to tire his eyes, and the English winters had an increasingly bad effect on his asthmatic and bronchial troubles. He began to wonder if he could cope with drawing *any* bird smaller than an ostrich. Again he was fortunate. Lord Stanley and a friend, Robert Hornby, decided to send Lear to Rome – goal of all young artists – to recover his health, and to paint.

It was in Italy that Lear settled into his chosen profession of topographic artist and landscape painter. For the first time he saw the great antiquities of the Eternal City, tangible memories of the classical past. He joined a community of young artists and sculptors – all living, more or less, on sun and southern air. They were all recording great monuments, watching the bright, warm light change on the stones of the Colosseum or the Arches of Constantine and Severus. And against such backgrounds they painted the Roman day-to-day street scenes, wonderfully un-English in liveliness, colour, costume and equipage. Lear was delighted with the variety of the peasant costumes seen just outside the city and, within, he described the priests:

they are innumerable – white – black – piebald – scarlet – cinnamon – purple: round hats – shovel hats – cocked hats – hoods and caps – cardinals with their 3 footman (for cardinals never walk) – white friars with masks, bishops and Monsignori with lilac and red stockings – and indeed thousands on thousands of every description of religious orders. (EL to Ann, 14 December 1837)

Then there were Neapolitan pipers, who came at Christmas to play for the Virgin. They wore 'tall black hats, with peacock's feathers in them – blue or brown cloaks – red waistcoats.' Even the animals seemed brighter, more picturesque than in England. The cattle Lear saw as 'beautiful gray sleek monsters! with enormous horns, all tied about with bells and ribbands'. And there were the great open tracts of the Campagna with its long lines of ancient aqueducts, its dark buffaloes, its foxes, hedgehogs, butterflies and, above, calm pink and purple-fading sunsets. Lear was amazed, enthusiastic, quite bewildered: '. . . you stumble on pillars – temples – circuses & tombs – all more or less mixed up with modern buildings!' He found lodgings in the Via del Babuino 'close to the church and the Piazza di Spagna – The Academy – the eating and coffee houses – all the English and all the artists!' (EL to Ann, 14 December 1837). He had a few watercolour commissions and gave a few lessons: it was enough. He was an independent artist among artists.

Lear's time in Rome stretched well beyond a year. He travelled in Italy, Sicily and elsewhere; he returned to England to see Ann, to sell pictures, to do the rounds of country visits and set up London gallery exhibitions. But Rome was a centre for about ten years. During that time Lear met numbers of artists, some of whom he remembered, and even encountered, in the years right up to his death. He went travelling and sketching with James Uwins; he knew Frederick Thrupp, mainly a sculptor, who did some painting and illustrating, and was called on in the late 1880s to help Lear with designs for a huge painting of 'Enoch Arden's Island'. Then there was a group of Danish artists, including a particular friend, Wilhelm Marstrand, who left a very sensitive drawing of Lear as a young artist. Richard Wyatt, John Gibson, Penry Williams: these were not to become famous names, but they were all, like Lear, young artists bent on absorbing all they could of Rome, city of arts. They were following in the footsteps of artists such as Richard Wilson, and of Englishmen who had taken the Grand Tour, who had discovered the architecture and classical treasures known from prints, who had gone to see the originals of Palladio's designs or of Piranesi's mysterious, weed-covered monuments and arches.

Lear was happily part of this artistic, Italy-worshipping community. He seems to have played the flute: or so Samuel Palmer remembered, as he and his new wife Hannah passed through Rome on their own Italian tour.[2] Lear drew in Rome; he travelled outside, and he produced two impressive books of lithographs: *Views in Rome and its Environs* (1841) and *Illustrated Excursions in Italy* (2 vols. 1846). The young artist could work on the lithographic stone himself and, with the new straw-coloured tint and white highlights produced by the talented lithographer, Hullmandel, Lear created some fine designs. Many were influenced by Claude whose pictures Lear recommended to Ann as giving an idea of the scenery he drew for his lithographs – variations on framing trees or vines and bright receding distances. But Lear's close observation of the lie of the land, of geological structure, of the relation of vertical tree growth, and of different buildings, to horizontal earth – all these give a sense of his own developing style. Many of his subjects were unusual; rather than obvious sites, the small, high, unknown hill towns of the Abruzzi, and unvisited rocks, plains and rivers were Lear's own choice for drawings and lithographs.

In 1846, Lear's designs brought him a great honour. Impressed with one of his books, Queen Victoria invited the artist to give her some drawing lessons. Lear enjoyed his new role, but remained very much his down-to-earth self. The story goes that he admired some treasures in a cabinet and asked the Queen where she had got them. The answer was regal: 'I inherited them, Mr Lear'. The Queen remembered her drawing-master and later sent him an engraving of his drawing of Osborne House.

When in Rome with his tutor, the young Prince of Wales visited Lear's studio; years later, on 14 June 1865, he bought ten drawings and paid £91.15. Lear had one or two other meetings with royalty, but never attempted to use them to curry favour in the art world.

Rome, Italian travel, lithographs and lessons to the Queen: 1846 was a year of success. Lear added to it by publishing, anonymously, his first *Book of Nonsense* and the clear-lined, eccentric, limerick characters were immediately popular. They were, after all, a great relief from the ordinary social world. They banged and bashed each other; they hopped, ran, jumped and got squashed flat; they ate extraordinary concoctions and fed their relations with vast spoonfuls of fearful mixtures; they turned into birds huddled on branches or extended a nose long enough to accommodate most of the birds of the air. In public Lear, the landscape artist, had to conform. In his Nonsense he could be as wild, irascible, rude and unconventional as he liked, as long as his characters remained within the bounds of comedy.

Lear, then, could look back through 'Memory's Arch' to experience and some success. He still felt the urge to travel much further, to draw, paint and write his impressions of places which were not the usual haunts of artists or even of travellers. He was concerned, too, about his painting technique and his lack of artistic training. His figures were poor: he had never done any anatomical drawings. He was uncertain about aspects of oil painting and felt he needed some guidance. His own free pencil sketches, penned out in the evening and sometimes colour-washed, were far more than quick, unsubtle impressions of landscape. Presumably unworried by drawing 'technique', Lear could produce a record of place, of mountain outline, rock layer, slope of hill, curve of river or ripples of water. Distant sea, mountain or trees were matched with touched-in foregrounds. The structure of the actual land is always clear; the colours, lights, plants, even trees or houses, are sometimes drawn in, sometimes left as annotation; but when Lear wrote on his sketches, his very writing often became part of his drawing. 'Rox' on rocks, 'flox' on a few vestigial sheep are a mild joke. 'Olive' defining the branches of an olive tree, 'O Path' leading the view along a path, 'River' written flat so that the word forms, in itself, another ripple of water – even these few examples show how close landscape drawing and landscape description could become for Lear. And words could bring in the undrawable sounds, of water or bird-song, and, occasionally, the name of a place seen in the past and remembered, for some likeness, in the present landscape. These sketches, large and small, often achieve an imaginative unity, a vitality which eludes the artist in his carefully finished watercolours and rarely lightens his large, 'important' oil paintings.

Lear's unworried and unselfconscious technique was described by a pupil. In the 1870s, in San Remo, Lear gave some drawing lessons to Arny and Hubert Congreve, sons of a neighbour. The elder boy, Hubert, worked hard and, as an adult, remembered the lessons as 'most delightful experiences...accompanied with running comments on art, drawing, nature, scenery and travels', as well as instruction. Lear hoped very much that Hubert might become an artist, but instead he took up engineering. He remained a life-long friend and correspondent of the artist. It was Hubert who described a sketching expedition with Lear. Off they went with 'Lear plodding slowly along, old George following behind, laden with lunch and drawing materials'.

> When we came to a good subject, Lear would sit down, and taking his block from George, would lift his spectacles, and gaze for several minutes at the scene through a monocular glass he always carried; then, laying down the glass, and adjusting his spectacles, he would put on paper the view before us, mountain range, villages and foreground, with a rapidity and accuracy that inspired me with awestruck admiration.
> (LLEL, Preface, pp. 15-16)

These sketches were done 'in pencil on the ground, and then inked in in sepia and brush washed with colour in the winter evenings'. Lear was, as Hubert acknowledges, an indefatigable worker: '10,000 large cardboard sheets of sketches' may be an exaggeration, but at his death he certainly left several thousand drawings.

Hubert Congreve was Lear's pupil in the early 1870s, when the artist had settled down into the Villa Emily in San Remo, but had not yet taken his last voyage – to India and Ceylon (1873-75). Lear used to sketch just as rapidly on some of his early travels and in conditions far less tranquil than those Hubert describes. In Albania (1848-49) the artist often needed an armed guard to keep off the curious and furious. The people of towns and villages alike crowded round in amazement at this extraordinary Englishman who could put down their houses and even themselves on paper. Such images were devilish to the good Muslim who shrieked and protested until the powers above arranged a guard. 'Shaitan, shaitan', they howled, 'the Devil, the Devil': 'Scroo! Scroo!', 'he writes us down!' Lear was quite unperturbed and once managed to get a whole crowd shrieking with laughter, rather than fury, until they were dispersed by scolding dervishes. All these tales are to be found in Lear's Albanian Journal in which his delight in strange landscapes, colourful costumes, local history – everything to do with his journey – is combined with his wonderfully self-observing and non-pompous sense of humour. Picnicking one day by a stream, he picked and ate some delicious fresh watercress. The local children found this hilarious and immediately offered Lear a fat grasshopper, a thistle and a collection of sticks to eat. Much laughter followed; and Lear went on his way saying that the 'wits of Episkopi will long remember the Frank who fed on weeds out of the water' (Albanian Journal, p. 321). Lear knew how to prepare himself for travel and how to deal with the unexpected: he rarely ran into danger. And he never gave up his search for landscapes, antiquities, mountains, unvisited towns until the last possible moment. Whispers of revolution in Italy made him cut short his Calabrian tour (1847), but not before he had drawn his way down to the southernmost shore of all. Marauding Arabs disturbed his visit to Petra (1858), but he left all the money-grabbing parties arguing, and climbed quickly to the heights which would give him a last good view of the amphitheatre (see his account in *Macmillan's Magazine*, April 1897). The detail of his drawing was exact, though he sometimes moved a monument or added to a piece of architecture to give a more satisfying design. But where his views in Calabria, for instance, still exist unspoiled, they can easily be identified from his lithographs. Lear's topography is, ultimately, 'poetical topography' and his finest pictures, however quickly sketched, match detail with an imaginative power which gives us the inner life of the landscape and, as 'To E.L.' suggests, makes us feel that we were 'there'.

The free sketches, now so valued, did not give Lear any importance as an artist. He felt, early on, his lack of sufficient formal training. He was never an establishment artist, and never became a member of the Royal Academy or either of the Watercolour Societies. He was dependent on commissions and on producing enough low-priced watercolours for sale from his studio or from a hired gallery. He had oils to show, too, and some of these were accepted for exhibition at the Royal Academy. But Lear was never free to paint exactly as he liked. He was always short of money and did himself no service by producing, from time to time, competent pictures painted as a series of 'Tyrants', each one outlined, skied and put through the various processes of colour as part of a mass production of sixty or even one hundred and twenty watercolours. The fashionable world often looked in at an exhibition, talked, and walked out. Pictures at £5.00 to £8.00 did not make much money and detracted from Lear's serious work. Friends knew of the artist's dilemma and bought or commissioned pictures; occasionally they were almost bullied into buying. Lear's early gratitude and rather subservient attitude to buyers became hard to maintain. Yet he always undervalued his ability and his work while remaining dependent on more or less the same group of English aristocratic and upper class families. Later in life he grew irascible, shut his doors on an 'exhibition' day, said he was ill or expressed his exasperation in a splendid piece of Nonsense: in one of his oil paintings there was a large beech tree, 'at which all intelligent huming beans say – "Beech!" – when they see it. For all that one forlorn ijiot said – "Is that a *Palm*=tree Sir" – "No", replied I quietly, "it is a Peruvian Brocoli"' (EL to Fortescue, LLEL p. 145).

Lear felt some bitterness when he compared a painting he had worked at for years with one offered at a very high price by a popular artist such as Millais. Sometimes he put his own price up, as with his 'Cedars of Lebanon', only to find that the picture did not sell. 'The Cedars' had had some success on exhibition in Liverpool, but in London it was 'hung high' at the Great International Exhibition (1862) and no one was interested. Eventually Lear had to lower his price and sell to someone he knew. There was no doubt: Lear did not 'belong'; he was out of England too much; his pure landscape was less sought after than narrative and genre painting. Even Lear's ideal painter, the earlier Turner, although a greater genius and innovator, and although an accepted academician, had had a very mixed reception.

Lear had made a spirited attempt to improve his artistic technique by further study. He tried to solve some of his problems by going back to Sass's school to work at figure drawing, and he did a caricature of himself among the 'little boys'. From there he gained entry to the Royal Academy Schools, and spent some months drawing from the antique among a class of young stu-

dents. This was in 1850, when he was in his late thirties. Perhaps this did something for Lear's figure drawing (it was not a life class), or his morale, but his next effort at self-improvement was in quite another direction. He came under the influence of the new school of Pre-Raphaelites. He met Holman Hunt, who insisted that on one could paint in oil from Lear's sketches and in 1852 invited him down to Clive Vale Farm, near Hastings, to observe stone formation and fig trees for Lear's large painting, 'The Quarries of Syracuse'. Lear was fascinated by Hunt's personality and artistic theory: he was also eager for advice. Hunt became 'Daddy' and remained one of Lear's long-term correspondents. Later on, Lear was somewhat disturbed by Hunt's strong religious leanings and wrote to Ann about the strange subject matter of 'The Scapegoat' which he did not like, but which he thought beautifully painted. Many of Lear's oils show hints of the brilliant colour, exact detail and high finish favoured by the Pre-Raphaelites. His originality as a landscape painter, however, lies in his clear-lined watercolours which suggest the influence of Dürer, whom Lear greatly admired. His greatest gifts never seemed to Lear to be his greatest asset; it did not bring public acceptance within his own time.

Of his love of landscape, from Nubian desert to San Remo garden, Lear was completely sure. He painted quiet and rugged scenes and had a preference for calm sea, 'the endless brightness of foliage', the lines and chasms of rock, the 'brusque original independent fig, – dependent vine, – tremulous olive' (D. 17 May 1860). He delighted in sunrise and sunset, southern light and dark shadow, the warmth of apricot-coloured sand, the shapes of palm leaves or twisted olive, the orange trees of Corfu. The range of his landscape interests is enormous. Lear would travel, however hard the journey, to see Athos, Mount Sinai, Jerusalem. Yet he hated a rough sea and was often sea-sick; he disliked crowded trains, bumpy carriages, difficult mules and camels. Curious, restless, fascinated by distant places, Lear

would quite cheerfully come to terms with the burning heat of Calabria, the drenching rains in Thessaly, the humidity of India. Sometimes letters of introduction produced kind hospitality, sometimes Lear had to put up with a filthy, insect-ridden inn. Strange noises one night caused him to strike a light – only to find he was sharing his sleeping space with a huge, dirty, tame sheep. But the landscapes, the light, the sunrises, sunsets, local people, animals, birds – these were worth anything. Wherever he went, he drew, and he wrote – in diaries, letters, published and unpublished journals (see Bibliography). Apart from the Italian lithographs, Lear published journals on Albania, Calabria and Corsica. A third book of lithographs covers the Ionian Islands. Travel description and short journals, such as the Nile journey of 1867, appear in Lear's diaries. Franklin Lushington published the account of the Petra expedition in *Macmillan's Magazine*, April 1897. An expert observer, Lear's writing is extremely perceptive. He moves easily from an outward scene – 'the pinknesses & pearlinesses all so soft and shadowy of Egyptian coloring' (D. 23 February 1867) – to inward thought: 'The desert, tho' here perfect loneliness, is nowise sad to me: – its simplicity & silence give place for memory I thought – past & future – to act' (D. 30 March 1867). And, after the last desert days, the relief of the bright, deep greens and luxuriant vegetation is somehow enhanced by Lear's cheerful and practical note: 'Fed my camel, principally with daisies & dandelion, or marigolds, wh. he appreciates' (D. 2 April 1867).

On 17 October 1876 Lear looked back on his own journeys as he went through, quite literally, 'a series of pictures'.

Worked all day long in looking over sketches – more than three cabinets full, so that today & yesterday I seem to have lived over again every year of my life from 1824 – Sussex – Lancashire, the Rhine – Rome – Naples – Campagna, Abruzzi – Sicily, Calabria – Sicily again – Apulia – Corfu – Greece, Constanty[z]a, Albania,

Greece & Thessaly – Egypt – Ionian Isles, Athos, Palestine, Malta, Cornice, Venice, the Lakes, Dalmatia, Crete, Corsica, India.

Lear himself forgot Sinai, and added it to his diary entry between Thessaly and Egypt. Visits to England and most second or third visits to the same place are not mentioned. But to look over the sketches of fifty years' journeys was indeed to live through a lifetime of landscape and experience.

Travel and return to England formed the pattern of Lear's life from his first long stay in Rome until 1871. He spent a winter in Malta; he had a house on Corfu for a while; mostly he visited England once a year and took rooms usually in Stratford Place. He would set up an exhibition in his room or a gallery, and visit everyone he knew in London and on the country house circuit. After a few months Lear fled the English winter and the need to pander to gallery visitors. His health depended on sun and warmth: he found both in Malta and Corfu, but fled again from routine painting and from loneliness. In the end he decided to find a house of his own, and tried out a villa in Cannes for a disastrous season when he found no friends and sold no pictures. His final choice was San Remo: a small resort, with two hotels, English visitors, but as yet without crowds and with a friendly, gossipy local population. The climate was excellent and surrounding mountains offered Taggia, Certosa del Pesio, nearby Brianza, distant Monte Generoso, for retreat from the worst heat of summer. Lear managed to buy some land and plan the building and garden of his first home, the Villa Emily (named after, he maintained, his niece in New Zealand). He was pleased to be a householder and, looked after mainly by Giorgio, he travelled far less, entertained friends who stayed in the large hotels, and brought his love of flowers and exotic plants to the cultivation of his beautiful garden. On Wednesdays, in season, he opened his studio to visitors. Friends passed through San Remo, and Lear still went to England but, by 1877, he seemed almost to be taking leave of the country houses he felt he would never see again. Of Ashstead Park, once presided over by Mrs Greville Howard, now a frail ninety-two, Lear wrote: 'Walked in the garden – & sate in the beautiful upstairs room – the gold green grass – deep green trees – long shadows – & the Deer! – all as of old – yet this is the last time' (D. 21 July 1877). The same year Tennyson's sons, Hallam and Lionel, greeted Lear in Regent Street. He thought them delightful, but looked back to the past 'O days of Farringford! Giorni passate – perche non retorni!' (D. 19 June 1877). Lear even went back to look at the old house in Gray's Inn Road where he and Ann had begun their 'Art Life' in 1828-9. It was a year full of memories and it had begun with Lear sending Giorgio back to Corfu for his health. He knew he would return from England to a loneliness he felt as 'the extremity of horror – worse than many deaths' (D. of May 1877). In April, he had walked 'toward the West Cape: one of the loveliest possible of Sanremo spring evenings – with a half full moon: – but…all was black as the valley of olives in Corfu – 1855. – Tears, idle tears. –' To express the misery of 1877 Lear looked back to the time when he stayed on Corfu, and felt almost abandoned by his

friend Franklin Lushington who was always busy with official duties. Lear often experienced the present in terms of the past. Before the end of 1878 Giorgio had, in fact, returned to San Remo. Lear's loneliness and depression had lifted: his old servant and friend 'came in & sate some time – we two talking of various long ago visited places, & of incidents – all of which G. remembers minutely for 24 years' (D. 30 December 1878).

One long and difficult struggle marred the peace of the Villa Emily. The angry and almost obsessional tale in the diary explains that Lear had no control over building on the next plot of land. To his horror, a large hotel was erected and his view and painting light were ruined. Blinds and shutters were temporary expedients: the artist felt shut in by a great, bright wall. His home was no longer his home, but he could do little except write miserably and furiously to his friends. In the end he borrowed money, bought more land which went right down to the sea, and built an almost exactly similar home, the Villa Tennyson. He moved in 1881, created a new painting studio and gallery, and started another garden.

The picture of the Villa Tennyson, seen in old photographs, is a memory which outlived Lear himself; for the artist the house was a memory of the Villa Emily. Before moving, worried about money and selling no pictures, Lear looked over his original sketches, those rapid, often lovely, drawings and watercolours which he kept for his own reference. He picked out five hundred and eighty for possible sale, took back one hundred and eighty and prepared to send four hundred to London. Soon, he felt, he would no longer be able to journey even among his pictures, his visible memories: 'I seem by doing this to be cutting out parts of my own flesh, for I can never see them again' (D. 24 February 1880).

For Lear all remembrance *was* an arch through which he looked back at pictures of the past and sought glimpses of the future. In 1880 on his way back from England, he was momentarily delighted that the Italian Customs had not noticed three tin cases of flowers, wrapped in flannel shirts and placed underneath a large folio of sketches and several linen sheets (D. 28 August). He had reflected, 'So far, I ought to be very thankful, but – but – but – the past & the future often will outweigh the present. Leatherhead, Stratton, Aldworth, Compton, Dudbrook, Guy's Cliffe, Oxford & Templehurst, – for the past: – Sanremo the future' (D. 25 August 1880). All these English places were the homes, or country houses, of Lear's closest friends and patrons. He was never to see these places again. He never went back to England and relied on friends coming to see him in the Villa Tennyson. He always remembered Ann, but she and other favourite sisters were dead. In the 1880s Lear was always sadly recording the death of friends, acquaintances, artists, in his diary.

His own old friends did not abandon him. As late as 1887 Lord Northbrook, and his charming, unaffected daughter, Lady Emma, came to visit Lear. It was Lord Northbrook, as Viceroy, who had invited and encouraged Lear to go to India and had commissioned him to paint. The same year Lear was both consoled and regretful to see the gentle Augusta Parker, 'Gussie' Bethell, daughter of Lord Westbury, and a widow since the death of her elderly husband in 1883. Even before that marriage, Lear had never felt quite able to propose to 'Gussie'. Yet she remained the only woman he ever seriously thought of marrying. He wondered about his age, his health, the possibilities of rejection – and never made a move. In 1883 'Gussie' had come to San Remo with two nieces; Lear thrust nosegays of his garden flowers into their hands as they left. And he wept when 'Gussie' was gone. She came back, kind and understanding, to sit with the old artist again, in 1887. Even then Lear wondered if he should propose, but the moment slipped by.

Another visitor was Chichester Fortescue, a long-standing friend and art-lover whom Lear had known since 1848. A Member of Parliament, he had married the much admired Lady Waldegrave, became Lord Carlingford, and under Gladstone, Keeper of the Privy Seal and President of the Council. Lear wrote numerous letters to '40scue' and later, much nonsense about the visit of the 'phoca' or 'seal'. Lady Waldegrave commissioned paintings and Lear remembered the round of gaiety and entertainment, the huge dinner parties at one of 'my Lady's' houses: Strawberry Hill. Fortescue – or rather Carlingford – was heartbroken when his wife suddenly

died, in 1879. He came and sat sadly and silently in Lear's villa, while Lear, sad himself, tried to comfort him. '40scue' who had found the artist a delightful companion in the Roman days of 1848, remained a steady life-long friend.

Late in 1886 Lear had a visit from the friend he was probably most attached to, Franklin Lushington. One of three brilliant brothers, Lushington came of a family who had known the Tennysons well. He was himself a lawyer and had spent some time as head of the British Judiciary in Corfu while the island was still under British rule. Lear spent one idyllic Greek spring, starting from Patras in 1849, with Lushington as a companion. Although Lear's emotional involvement was greater than Lushington's, the friendship survived. After Lushington's marriage Lear grew to like his wife and became godfather to one of 'Frank's' children. 'The Judge', as Lear sometimes called him, was not particularly outgoing or volatile: he was always in a hurry to get back to work. Lear wished he could lengthen the short visits, but over the years had written many letters to Lushington and cherished the idea of his 'A No 1 friend'. The very last entry in the final diary for 1887 is 'wrote to Franklin Lushington – 6 January 1888'.

None of his friends saw Lear as he saw himself, like an old, unfinished painting of which he wrote: 'Its dogged persistence of life, & its incompleteness after all, is no bad type of my own poor & sad existence'. No 'series of pictures' should end with Lear as a persistent but unfinished painting. His personality and achievements are subtle and difficult to summarise. His self-deprecation and depression are part of his life: if they dragged him down, they also added to his sensitivity both to people and to landscape. A wish to express himself in some kind of poetic language, as well as painting, seems to surface in verses, in parody (of Clough, for example), in the gloomy 'Eclogue' written with J.A. Symonds, and in many of his descriptions – as of the olive trees weeping, and of hearing their thin, sad voices, 'songs of a time long past' (D. 13 March 1877, 17 March 1870). His Nonsense verses are full of 'serious' lines, and yet Lear's seriousness must always be balanced with his sense of the comic. Once he passed a well-known place on the coast near San Remo and cheerily turned the scene into a person, and both into verse (D. 13 September 1877):

Finale Marina! if ever you'd seen her!
Your heart had been quickly enslaved.
Her eyes were pea green, & her bonnet was greener.
And wonderful fine she behav'd!

A sudden lightheartedness went with geniality and generosity to friends. Lear, unless worried, angry or ill, was very good company. What he left was a wealth of letters, writings, drawings, paintings which take us back through his life and, as we read and see, make us feel that we were 'there'.

To end at the beginning, we should consider the verse on Lear's tombstone. 'All things fair' pointed, for Lear, to a 'series of pictures', two hundred chosen scenes which were part of a plan to link poetry and topography. Lear's last years were filled with work on one project: his unfulfilled dream of publishing two hundred illustrations for lines from Tennyson's poems. These drawings were to be a tribute to Tennyson and his landscape descrip-tion; they were to bring together all Lear's work as an artist. The Tennyson Illustrations, spanning the whole of Lear's past, were the last pictures he saw 'thro' "Memory's Arch".'

Notes

1 Lear often linked poetry and topography when referring to his own work, for instance in a letter to Fortescue '...*totally* unbroken application to poetical-topographical painting and drawing is my universal panacea for the ills of life' (26 May 1872, LLEL, p. 150).

2 Edward Malins, *Samuel Palmer's Italian Honeymoon* (Oxford University Press, 1968), pp. 62-3, 109-10.

'Mr Lear a carrying of his 6 prints to Mr Eatons, March 15th 1871

The Tennyson Illustrations

Edward Lear read and admired Tennyson's 1842 *Poems* long before he met the poet himself. He knew them so well that he quoted and misquoted them from memory, used phrases as titles for paintings, and echoed their rhythms in some of his own Nonsense verse. It was in the Lushingtons' house at Maidstone, about 1850, that the artist finally encountered the poet.[1] In 1850 Tennyson had, after long waiting, married the gentle Emily Sellwood who was to respond with kindness and understanding to Lear's problems over the years. For the poet, 1850 held another great event: he became Poet Laureate. Recognition and fame emphasized the complex and often opposing traits in his personality. He was both charismatic and withdrawn, relaxed and eccentric, self-critical and darkly aloof – an intimidating figure to all but his oldest and closest friends. Lear did not belong to that inner circle: he never knew Tennyson well.

After their initial meetings Lear became a friendly acquaintance who sometimes stayed for a few days at Farringford, the Tennysons' house on the Isle of Wight. He was enchanted when the great poet walked and talked with him along the cliff-tops near the house or when Tennyson, in a deep, distinctive voice, recited one of his recent poems. The poet showed no particular interest in Lear's pictures, but he approved the artist's musical settings of some of his lyrics: they seem to throw 'a diaphanous veil over the words – nothing more'.[2] Lear was an entirely amateur musician who sang Tennyson's verses movingly to an unobtrusive piano accompaniment.

When Lear went abroad, and eventually settled in San Remo, he kept up with the Tennyson family by letter, and by visits whenever he came back to England. He was delighted with the announcements of the births of Hallam and Lionel, sent congratulations and Nonsense books at appropriate moments, and met both sons as they grew up. He came to know Hallam well and was shocked at Lionel's early death, from illness, in India. Lear revered Tennyson for his poetry, and particularly for the early work. Every new volume was ordered as it came out and Lear was very pleased if Tennyson also sent him a signed copy. *In Memoriam* made a deep impression, as did the four *Idylls of the King* published in 1859 and the tale of 'Enoch Arden', 1864. Of poems published in the 1870s and 1880s Lear says little: of one volume he simply notes 'much of the contents curious & interesting' (D. 11 December 1885). It was the *Poems* of 1842 and a few others, none published later than 1864, which remained an inspiration for Lear and for his art.

The most immediately accessible of the Tennysons was Emily, to whom Lear wrote on 5 October 1852 asking if she liked the idea of landscape illustrations. Lear hoped to gain the poet's approval and felt he could most easily approach him through his wife. The subject had been mentioned before and Lear began:

> I think I once said something about illustrating Tennyson's poems – so far as the Landscape therein set forth admit of –. Many of the subjects I have arranged, though none as yet have I thoroughly carried out, which indeed it would require great time and labour thoroughly to do. But I have latterly extracted and placed in a sort of order all the lines which convey to me in the most decided manner his genius for the perception of the beautiful in landscape, and I have divided them into "suggestions" and "Positive" and altogether there are 124 subjects in the 2 volumes (I have not included the Princess or In Memoriam). By "suggestions" I mean such lines as "vast images in glittering dawn" – "Hateful is the dark blue sky" – and so on – which are adaptable to any country or a wide scope of scenery.
>
> By "positive" – such as "the long moated grange" – "They cut away my tallest pines" – "A huge crag platform" – "the balmy moon of blessed Israel", and so on – which indicate perforce certain limits of landscape and which I am possibly more than most in my profession able to illustrate – not, pray understand me – from any other reason than that I possess a very remarkable collection of sketches from Nature in such widely separated districts of Europe – not to say Asia and Africa.
>
> It may seem rather impertinent that I can't help thinking "No-one could illustrate Tennyson's landscape lines and feelings more aptly than I could do" – but this very modest assertion may after all turn out to be groundless inasmuch as my powers of execution do not at all equal my wishes, or my understanding of the passages I have alluded to.
>
> My desire has been to show that Alfred Tennyson's poetry (with regard to scenes –) is as real and exquisite as it is relatively to higher and deeper matters – that his descriptions of certain spots are as positively true as if drawn from the places themselves, and that his words have the power of calling up images as distinct and correct as if they were written from those images, instead of giving rise to them.

Lear wanted to 'carry out 2 or 3' designs and then, with Tennyson's permission, 'fill up the whole'. 'Engravings from such a work', he added hopefully, 'would make a beautiful edition'.

This letter to Emily was crucial to Lear's Tennyson Illustration project. She reacted favourably and Tennyson himself, who had been reading Lear's present of his Albanian Journal, composed 'To E.L. on his Travels in Greece' which was to form the cherished centrepiece for Lear's Illustrations. It was difficult for the sensitive, self-critical and largely unrecognized artist to communicate with such a daunting character as Tennyson. Lear sometimes lamented, on Farringford visits, that the Laureate had been 'snubby & cross' (D. 17 June 1860), or that he had been egotistical and selfish with his family. Lear felt that despite Tennyson's dark moods, the poet was still unforgivably harsh with the frail Emily and, later, with both Hallam and Lionel. There was a moment in summer 1855, when Lear, with his half-longing for stability, wondered if he should settle near the Tennysons, but the idea faded. It was Emily, always called an 'angel', he felt for, and she perhaps offered the motherly affection which Lear needed, particularly after the death of his sister, Ann. As for Tennyson, Lear responded to the poet rather than the man.

The Tennyson Illustrations were a tribute to the poet, and to his perception of landscape. They became, over the years, very personal to Lear, to his concern with 'poetical topography', to his interpretation of an 'illustration' and, finally, to his idea of a record of his own artistic endeavour. More orthodox illustrators included landscape backgrounds or vignettes in their work for Tennyson's poems. Examples include Gustave Doré's plates for the Idyll 'Vivien' (1867) and Arthur Hughes's 'Enoch Arden' (1866). As with the 'Pre-Raphaelite' illustrated Moxon edition of 1857, both Doré and Hughes in their quite different styles focused mainly on the characters in the poems. This was true, too, of Daniel Maclise's illustrations for 'The Princess' (1866). Lear avoided depicting Tennyson's characters and their interactions completely. He chose a line, or several, describing landscape and delved into his own journeys for an illustration which might relate to that line, but not necessarily to the rest of the poem. His drawing might include a few peasants, monks or other small figures, but these were brought in only to suggest the scale and strangeness of some exotic, distant place.

When Lear began choosing illustrations before and during the 1850s he already had an extensive collection of travel drawings. By the time the project continued into the 1870s and 1880s he had new material from many more journeys – from Athos, Malta, Corsica and from Egypt, India and Ceylon. He had returned to many places, such as the Nile, Corfu and Rome several times, made new sketches and relived past memories. He had, in 1871, settled into the Villa Emily in San Remo. Quickly, he became familiar with the coastline his house overlooked, and with cooler, higher places such as Taggia and the Sanctuary of Lampedusa. He visited again the Lakes of Como, Lugano and the smaller Orta and Iseo: he knew all the nearby mountainous places, the little towns by lakes and the cool retreats of the region. All this material – thousands of sketches – was to provide a wealth of choice for Tennyson landscapes. Each scene finally selected had, for Lear, its own significance and each contributed to a summary of his life's experiences. Some designs were based on landscape seen years before, in the 1840s: for instance, the mysterious 'Someone pacing there alone' (unusual for its important, anonymous figure) included Pentedatelo, the five-fingered rock of Lear's Calabrian journey. The earliest scene is probably that of the Mill at Arundel, Sussex, which Lear saw as a child when he visited his sister, Sarah. But Lear revisited old landmarks when he went

to England: 'Arundel', like many other illustrations, represents not a single experience of landscape, but an accumulation of memories. All the Tennyson drawings were chosen or adapted from existing sketches, even the one which was probably the last to be drawn. In his diary for 12 June 1885 Lear talks of the view from the garden and steps of the Villa Tennyson. He draws from his studio balcony, from the terrace and from several places in the garden for his second San Remo view, no. 160.

Lear had always reworked his drawings for sale, or for a particular commission. He kept his original sketches, mostly done on the spot in pencil and later 'penned out', given a pen outline, and often, watercolour washes. Pencil notes about colours, contours, tree forms, high lights, shadow, foreground plants etc. were 'penned' over too. From these sketches Lear could re-create a finished scene. This method meant that his endless reconsidering and reworking of the Tennyson Illustrations was part of a usual pattern for the artist. It was part, too, of his preoccupation with the past, a passion he shared with Tennyson. His feeling for the importance of memory, and of the need to bring the past to bear on the present, perhaps helped to give some of his re-drawn designs an atmosphere and life of their own. Lear may have copied his own sketches with great competence, but he also relived and re-created his impressions of a landscape.

In March 1871 all Lear's drawings and papers had to be packed and unpacked. Surrounded by people planting fig trees, painting gates, fitting locks and hanging curtains, Lear found himself 'bothering in all places'. He was in the middle of moving into the Villa Emily. Lear had worked at his Tennyson Illustrations on and off over the years since 1852, but now he positively 'searched for A.T. mss.' On 24 March he wrote in his diary: 'Looked over, and make notes from the old A.T. book of 1852. – I am really such a fool as to think of beginning 100 of these subjects, all at onst!' Yet he was to make a renewed and serious attempt on the great scheme now that he was settling into his first home. He began with a charcoal outline of the Philae design 'Moonlight on still waters' and planned work on what proved to be a very difficult oil painting. On 6 April 1871 he 'wrote out A.T. illustrations', presumably as a list. By the end of the year, in spite of all other work, Lear had begun three Tennyson oils: 'Moonlight on still waters' (Philae), 'The Crag that fronts the Even' (Kasr es Saad), and 'Acroceraunian Walls' (one of the Albanian subjects). These large oils would have been important to Lear as achievements in the high art of painting. His real talent was for the quick sketch, penned out with fine detail and delicate colour wash – his characteristic original watercolours. But it was hard to be excluded, as he was, from both the Watercolour Societies and from the Royal Academy. Oil paintings were exhibited in the Academy and these were what really made a painter's reputation, especially if he was accepted as an Academician. The status of oil painting perhaps explains why Lear began his Tennyson Illustrations on this large scale and in a medium to which he was never really suited.

On 17 June 1871 Lear set to work on some small drawings and 'outlined 6 of them on small [wooden] prepared surfaces'. These are 'first stages', '... the small initiative preliminary pestilential pseudo perry derry pumpkinious beginnings for the Tennyson work' (D. 23 June 1871). The number of designs varies from one hundred to one hundred and twenty; at times the number swells to three hundred before settling, eventually at two hundred. Were these small illustrations meant to stand on their own, to complement the oil paintings? Or were they designs destined to be enlarged into watercolour or oil? When Lear thought about the Tennyson Illustrations he had more than one idea in mind. He imagined a gallery designed to show off large oil paintings, and perhaps some watercolours, of mainly Tennyson subjects. The Villa Tennyson was built with a gallery of this kind. Yet for single plates or book illustration any painting would have to be scaled down, engraved on wood or copied by some process which would make it available in multiple copies. Perhaps with this different idea – of small designs – and remembering his own early lithographic skills, Lear began scaled-down drawings which could be worked up to a larger size, but which were, as they stood, a suitable size for reproduction.

For a time Lear worked on five oils, on outlines for watercolours and on small-scale designs. The 'Morn Broadens' oil, with its Tennyson title, had been sold long before 1871. The present five were 'The Crag that fronts...', 'To watch the crisping ripples...' (Parga), 'Tomohrit', 'Acroceraunian Walls' and 'Moonlight on still waters'. Lear could remember them only by some 'mysterious and beautiful verses', or so he wrote jokingly to Fortescue (12 September 1873, LLEL p. 161).

'Crag'	1)	*Like the Wag who jumps at evening* *All along the sanded floor.*
'Parga'	2)	*To watch the tipsy cripples on the beach* *With topsy turvy signs of screamy play.*
'Tomohrit'	3)	*Tom-Moory Pathos; – all things bare, – . . .*
'Walls'	4)	*Delirious Bulldogs; – echoing, calls* *My daughter, – green as summer grass: –* *The long supine Plebeian ass,* *The nasty crockery boring falls; –*
'Moonlight'	5)	*Spoonmeat at Bill Porter's in the Hall,* *With green pomegranates, and no end of Bass.*

The Illustrations were certainly not meant to be publicly labelled with his Nonsense lines, but they ward off over-serious comment and perhaps helped Lear in the wearisome, 'important' task of oil-painting. He later mentions a plan to write a serious description of each Tennyson Illustration: none seems to have survived, unless Lear's description of 'Civitella di Subiaco' for 'Morn Broadens' suggests something of what he meant to do. (See 'A Dream of Fair Women', p.97). Lear carried out, and embarked on, several other Tennyson oils, including a 'Bavella' and a 'Beachy Head'. A huge unfinished 'Enoch Arden' canvas, and one version – with 'a red man' – of 'Someone pacing there alone' ended up, after Lear's death, in Tennyson's last home at Aldworth.

As far back as 1867 Lear had made a list of Tennyson designs to be done in watercolour. In 1878 he subjected thirty drawings to his 'Tyrant' colour processes, but was not satisfied with the result. In 1879 he chose fifty subjects to be traced, enlarged, outlined in pen and ink, and fully finished in watercolour. The whole process was self-perpetuating: Lear could not bring himself to accept any designs, in any medium, as perfect. He re-drew early designs and complained that he had to use a thick black outline because of his increasingly bad eyesight. He imagined finer and finer drawings, but by the 1880s, began to produce or work over designs he found coarse and which he then disliked. He knew, before he noted in his diary for 1 May 1885, that the labour of colour for small illustrations was useless. For the last few years of his life he devoted himself to the labour of monochrome.

This was by no means a simple process. Lear was prepared to draw his illustrations any number of times. He had, apart from the oil paintings, very little commissioned work and his gallery watercolours hardly sold. Yet work helped him to survive and the Tennyson Illustrations were the work which reflected his whole lifetime's experience of travel and of landscape. He needed to finish them, and at the same time, he needed not to finish them. What could come afterwards? In his diary he sets out what seem to be exact details of the progress of these drawings. In 1879, for instance, he went up on a 'summer migration' to Varese. He needed 'five huge folios of original sketches to help him work at fifty Tennyson drawings. He tried tracing some of the sketches, tired his eyes, and put all five folios into his black trunk. Once up in Varese he began outlining twenty-five drawings and finishing them in blue. (That process usually suggests he intended to put some colour on the designs.) Then he put them aside and began some 'longer size' drawings in pencil outline. In spite of this apparently detailed evidence from Lear's diary, there are never quite enough facts about number, size, mount or type of monochrome, for the reader to form a coherent view of the progress of the illustrations. The artist, in his diary, does not need to explain exactly what he means by 'narrow' or 'longer' or 'broad'. Similarly a series of numbers – 'eight' or 'twenty-five' or 'fifty' – does not reveal what any single drawing actually looked like. Tracings, thin paper, panel boards with paper laid down, mounting, de-mounting – what does all this infinity of detail tell us? We are given a mass of information, but little of it takes us beyond generalization: 'by hard work, actually finished the last of the long set of 25 A.T.s...' (D. 8 July 1879). This is followed by a list of places, mostly familiar from Lear's printed list, and the time of day when groups of drawings were completed. Sometimes it becomes clear that a number of illustrations have been done in a particular type of monochrome for a discernible reason, usually a specific effort to meet the needs of reproduction: '...new idea of doing the large outlines of the A.T. illustrations, roughly – with lampblack – for Photography...' (D. 20 November 1883). Lear was extremely interested in Turner's *Liber Studiorum* and both mezzotint and autotype could give the prints a brown tone suggesting the original drawings. Without comment, Lear began a series of sepia and umber outlines and brown washes after studying the *Liber*. By September 1882 Lear had finished '60 brown A.T. designs' and by December 1883, his diary refers to 'the Umber set of A.T. Illustrations – some 180 or 200.' Later, in 1885, friends advised a 'brown' tint, but no 'brown' set seems to have remained complete. Grey wash with white highlights, umber, sepia, pen, ink, pencil, lamp-black – Lear used all kinds of variations, sometimes for experiment, sometimes by request for 'darker' or 'larger' originals, often in conjunction with a particular method of reproduction. Some of Lear's many Tennyson Illustration monochrome drawings may be recognized in exhibitions, galleries or auction rooms. They can be found in private or public collections, especially in American Lear holdings. Lear's final list of two hundred includes designs made early, designs added late, and he tried out a large number of these in a variety of sizes and monochrome effects. All that can be added, now, is that unnamed Tennyson Illustrations, in oil, watercolour or any form of monochrome, are usually identifiable from the two sets of two hundred designs which have survived.

Lear cheered himself up, during the endless experiments, by giving his Tennyson Illustrations a set of Nonsense names. Thus as well as the various categories of 'long', 'broad', 'larger', the reader of Lear's diary encounters 'eggs', 'caterpillars', 'chrysalisses' and 'perfect insects'. The last creatures were to have been large, finished watercolours and they soon crawled, or flew, away as quite unattainable. Leaving aside the question of 'new-born caterpillars', and the fact that the 'caterpillar' size seems to have been merged eventually with the 'chrysalisses' – what can we determine? It is clear from diary entries, and from letters, that the 'eggs' were the smallest size drawings. They were three or four inches long and, in the end, they were all 'underwritten' with Tennyson quotations and with place-names. 'Eggs' are mentioned in 1881 in the diary, and a year earlier in a letter to Tennyson, but it is not clear that they existed, then, as a complete and finished set. Lear worked on his 'eggs' from November 1884 to March 1885; he finally mounted them, drew frame lines round all but a few and wrote out the lines of poetry and details of place. He signed many with his E.L. monogram. On 14 October 1885 (D.) he found the large number of small 'eggs' mounted together made an unwieldy sheet of drawings. He cut them up so that two 'eggs' were mounted on one piece of card. All this evidence points to the fact that the set of drawings described and illustrated in this book are Lear's 'eggs'. He may have taken earlier 'egg' drawings and matched them into his final set: this could account for the great variety of technique.

This set of 'eggs' has the distinction and authority of having belonged to the Tennyson family. It remained in the collection at the Tennyson Research Centre, Lincoln, intact, with card mounts, Lear's frame-lines and handwriting, until 1980 when the set was cut up and dispersed. At the time of the dispersal an archive of two hundred photographs was made for the University of Bristol, and this is now the only known complete record of Lear's smallest Tennyson drawings. The pictures (approximately 3 3/4″ x 5 3/4″) are in pencil, ink and grey wash with occasional white heightening; some drawings have no frame lines and a few lack quotations. Lear's handwriting shows considerable changes through the set, but no change is incompatible with varieties of his writing to be found in his diaries. Many are signed with Lear's monogram.

The other known set of Tennyson drawings is still complete and part of the Lear Collection in the Houghton Library, Harvard. Many of the Houghton set have '1885' on the actual illustration as well as the A.T. cipher and E.L. monogram. These drawings (approximately 6 5/8 x 10 1/4 inches) are larger than the 'eggs', in grey wash with some variety in drawing technique. It is usually accepted that they are the final 'chrysalis' set. Almost all the pictures are identified by a printed slip pasted on the mount: the slips are taken from one of Lear's printed lists, but not the one which remained with the 'egg' set. Lear notes finishing the writing of poetry and titles for two hundred 'chrysalisses' in his diary on 20 November 1885. This suggests that he may have done another set in the 'chrysalis' size, but evidence from the diary does not make the matter clear.

Lear was always pleased to show his finished Tennyson drawings to friends. He seems to have had a 'showable' set of 'eggs' finished before any other large number of these designs. He often had difficulty in keeping track of his two hundred drawings, particularly when he had two major sets and a vast proliferation of contributory and experimental material. His smallest set is remarkable for variety of drawing. Some pictures are intricately detailed and show the delicate line of Lear's best period; some are over-drawn, with thick outline and generalized dark foregrounds. The latter may be the result of poor eye-sight and also of Lear's persistence in trying to improve certain drawings for reproduction. The fact that Lear drew these 'eggs' at all suggests a relationship between them and his other miniature drawings in diary, letters and Nonsense books. Tiny landscapes appear in the diary – in 1871 and 1881 several sketches for 'Someone pacing there alone' – and, elsewhere, minute, rough, but recognizable outlines of current picture designs in place on a studio wall. A few Nonsense self-portraits and other pictures occasionally make their way into the text. Nonsense pictures and caricatures in letters are, of course, also very small. It is as though Lear had a need to create and dominate a world in miniature, even while he was working, with difficulty, on large oils or large drawings. 'Smallness' both attracted and repelled. Lear's short sight made it trying for him to work on a small scale, his early ornithological and zoological work, with its mass of detail, had been essential to his career and yet ultimately very bad for his eyes. Perhaps the small 'egg' set of Tennyson Illustrations fulfilled Lear's need to complete the project in some way: here, on a small and manageable scale, he had achieved two hundred designs. Yet it left open the possibility of going on, of enlarging, of creating a bigger, better, more satisfying set of drawings.

The 'eggs' were 'beginnings': they need not attract criticism. They were also notes for an as yet uncompleted text. In this connection it is interesting that Tennyson, too, copied, revised and re-used his earlier verse. He found it difficult to publish, at first, because no poem seemed in a suitably perfect state. And, rather in the way that Lear put down small sketches, quick visual notes, miniature scenes for later use, so Tennyson wrote down lines in response to a landscape, 'suggestions' to be hoarded for inclusion in some unwritten or uncompleted poem. Hallam Tennyson (*Mem* I, pp. 257-8) prints a letter of 1882 in which the poet describes a period in his life when: '...as an artist, Turner for instance, takes rough sketches of Landskip, etc, in order to work them eventually into some great picture, so I was in the habit of chronicling, in four or five words or more, whatever might strike me as picturesque in Nature.' Examples follow, including:

A great black cloud
Drags inward from the deep.

Suggestion
A coming storm seen from the top of Snowdon.

These lines, like the small sketches, are both ways of recording a passing moment and retaining that past for present and future artistic creation.

Lear's 'eggs', then, although his smallest set of Tennyson Illustrations, represented, in miniature, the complete project and the artist's *Liber Studiorum*. Each landscape was important to Lear, and the whole set recorded his life from childhood to age, from England to the years in San Remo, with many journeys in between. The inveterate traveller had journeyed through and through his folios of drawings to match the Tennyson quotations and display the scenery of a lifetime's experience. The next stage was reproduction, and at this point Lear's efforts ended only in frustration and despair. As with the size and type of monochrome, the diary shows a series of problems, experiments, trials and failures. Lear had tried the Autotype process (for all Processes see Appendix) for some Nile drawings, in July 1871, but did not much like the results. He had found out more about Autotype by 1882 and sent a few Illustrations – first 'eggs', then other sizes – for trial. As with almost all the other processes he tried, he liked one or two proofs, disliked others and gave the whole experiment up. At one stage he sent all the 'eggs' and the proofs were useless: the Autotype Company suggested Lear should send larger drawings. Lear was very disappointed and, as he often did, decided he would give up the Illustrations completely. He did not do so, of course, and he later returned to Autotype. First he tried out other processes. Commercial lithography in San Remo bore little relation to Lear's own delicate, early work on the stone. He wrote to the young artist and lithographer, Frederick Underhill, who had helped him before, and complained that the commercial proofs did not represent his art or his way of looking at landscape: 'the trees might all be made of wool, or butter, or sponge'. Underhill, Lear points out, understood the artist's 'particular sharp individual style of drawing' and might be able to try some lithographs for him. 'Delicate sharpness' – Lear could no longer produce it, yet imagined his drawings reproduced with this perfection of line (EL to Underhill, 2 July 1885). Underhill came to San Remo and made one or two successful lithographs, but soon Lear found the work lacking in force. In the end Underhill was kindly dismissed. The real answer was that nothing could have reached the perfection Lear dreamed of and some of his drawings, whatever the size, were overworked and not at all amenable to good reproduction. Lear tried photography, usually too dark; he tried autotype again, lacking in tone. He went on to chromolithography and the expensive, but still unsatisfactory platinotype. Aquatint engraving claimed a drawing or two as did various combined processes. In February 1886, Lear thought desperately he could work on a photograph and then have that autotyped. Every process took up time and diminished Lear's £500 legacy (from a sister) which had given him means with which to experiment. Waiting for proofs was, at least, something to wait for. The frustration of these experiments made Lear despair, and yet they kept him at work on the Tennyson Illustrations. He still felt he had something to work at and strive for.

By 1887 Lear announced, yet again, that he had given up. The great A.T. work had come to grief (EL to Fortescue, 2 December 1886, LLEL pp. 323-4). At one point he ordered all his drawings to be sent back from the Autotype Company who were beginning to wonder what they were supposed to do with them. Lear was pleased to show the Tennyson originals to friends, and that an American publisher, Mr Dana Estes, showed an interest. Estes wrote to Hallam Tennyson to say that the designs would need very careful treatment by etcher and engraver, that some were not finished, and that he felt he could not undertake the work, which he thought most interesting, because of the uncertainty and expense involved (Estes to H. Tennyson, 8 May 1887). Lear sold Estes a Tennyson drawing (one perhaps of the many monochrome variations) and was pleased with his courtesy. When Underhill was working for him, Lear thought of issuing single Illustrations with descriptive texts, and showing them in some gallery window. He began a few descriptions; he wrote and revised a Dedication to Emily Tennyson; he had printed several rather inaccurate lists of his Tennyson designs. He sent lists and sometimes photographs to friends at moments when he felt hopeful about a particular process. Such hopes continued in the 1880s, particularly in 1885 and 1886. The Tennyson Illustrations, long before, had become both a lasting interest and something of an obsession. In October 1887 Lear thought he would try yet again: perhaps large size drawings in charcoal outline would be the answer. Before the end of the year the artist was ill and incapable of work. In his last diary reference to the Illustrations, Lear thought he would look over the two hundred A.T.s again.[3] He could do nothing with them any more, but he might still journey through them and review, once again, the landscapes of his past.

Notes

[1] There is a reference in Hoge, p.19, to the Tennysons meeting Lear, with other guests, at the Lushingtons' house in the summer of 1850.

[2] Charles Tennyson, *Alfred Tennyson* (Macmillan, 1949; reissued with alterations, 1968), p. 441.

[3] In 1889 Boussod, Valadon & Co., London, published a small book containing sixteen full-page illustrations and six vignettes, with three poems by Tennyson. One hundred copies were issued and each was signed by the Laureate, 'for the sake of' his old friend, Edward Lear. The drawings used were from the 1885 set. This rare memento could never have suggested the scale of the artist's A.T. project.

Preparing for Publication, by Edward Lear
Landscape Illustrations of Poems by Lord Tennyson
Dedicated to Lady Tennyson

Dear Lady Tennyson,

It is more than 40 years since I first read "Poems by Alfred Tennyson", in the Edition published by E. Moxon in 1842.

At that time, (1843) I was studying Landscape in the neighbourhood of Rome, and it was not till some years later that I began to visit so many other places. But, even in 1843 I thought that if I tried to illustrate portions of the Tennyson Poetry by combining Poetical treatment with Topographical accuracy, I might eventually produce an original & beautiful work.

Thenceforward, the accomplishment of this scheme has been the unceasing occupation of my life, and in 1852, when I was staying with you and Alfred at Seaford, I had already formed an extended plan for the illustration of numerous passages, the united musical charm, vivid imagination, terse and descriptive power of which, – I in vain sought for in the writings of other Poets. Afterwards, in Greece and Albania, in Italy and Sicily, in Macedonia Bulgaria and Thrace, in Crete, Malta, Dalmatia, Egypt and Nubia, Syria & Palestine, & lastly in India & Ceylon, – my poetical=topographical work went continually forward, until from the great collection of drawings thus made, I was able to select three or four hundred subjects towards the completion of my labour. – Of these subjects, only 200 have been finally carried out as finished drawings, and the present series of 10 (which I hope are also to be published singly,) is to be considered as the first instalment of [illustration] to be more or less prolonged according to its success.

The subjects are not equally connected with, or parallel to the quotations they illustrate: – some being simply literal portraits, (as Cannes, Mar Sabbas &c.) while others, (as the Lotos Eaters, Enoch Arden &c, – although mostly drawn from real scenes are by no means to be looked on as correct Topographical likenesses. Again, – other subjects represent scenes widely separated from the places described in the Poems, though in full accord with the quotations, – such as – "the sun fell & all the land was dark," – "Rosy blossom in hot ravine" – &c, &c. In general, only one or two subjects have been taken from a Poem. But some portions of Lord Tennyson's Poetry seemed to me to claim much fuller representation than others, as for example, the pictures described in "The Palace of Art," – and the line "I will see before I die – the Palms & Temples of the South". The beautiful lines addressed to myself "To E.L. on his travels in Greece", appeared to me to call for abundant illustration, whether as to the Monasteries of Mt. Athos – so singularly interesting for situation & picturesqueness, – or for the words "all things fair" – which I have chosen partly to interpret by 4 of the most strikingly beautiful scenes I know. "Tropic Shades" are set forth by views made in India; while the "Daisy" – more than any other poem, – presents an unbroken series of Landscape Portraits. All these in different ways will show that the aim of this work has been to prove how perfectly the Poet's words adapt themselves to the description of Landscapes expressly sought out by me for the purpose already named. And in as much as during these 40 years of labour in a single direction, a wonderful amount of interest and gratification has arisen from so sustained and regular an occupation, I may well add my testimony of gratitude to the writer who has done so much for all of us. As for yourself and Lord Tennyson – as well as Hallam & Lionel, I well know how much kind interest you have taken in these joint records of Poetry and Landscape. And if it shall be found that I have been able to bring ever so little an addition to the reputation of one of the greatest and most beautiful of writers, to whose thoughts and to whose expression of those thoughts, English=speaking Peoples of all future generations, will owe an untold amount of thankfulness, – I may well leave this world with a satisfaction I might not have attained to, had I not resolved to make & to publish this Collection of Poetical Topographical Tennysoniana.

I remain,
Dear Lady Tennyson,
Yours affectionately
Edward Lear

Villa Tennyson, Sanremo,
24 Novbr 1885

MARIANA

'Mariana in the moated grange.'
Measure for Measure

I

With blackest moss the flower-plots
    Were thickly crusted, one and all,
The rusted nails fell from the knots
    That held the peach to the garden-wall.
The broken sheds look'd sad and strange:
    Unlifted was the clinking latch;
    Weeded and worn the ancient thatch
Upon the lonely moated grange.
      She only said, 'My life is dreary,
        He cometh not,' she said;
      She said, 'I am aweary, aweary,
        I would that I were dead!'

II

Her tears fell with the dews at even;
    Her tears fell ere the dews were dried;
She could not look on the sweet heaven,
    Either at morn or eventide.
After the flitting of the bats,
    When thickest dark did trance the sky,
    She drew her casement-curtain by,
And glanced athwart the glooming flats.
      She only said, 'The night is dreary,
        He cometh not,' she said;
      She said, 'I am aweary, aweary,
        I would that I were dead!'

III

Upon the middle of the night,
    Waking she heard the night-fowl crow:
The cock sung out an hour ere light:
    From the dark fen the oxen's low
Came to her: without hope of change,
    In sleep she seem'd to walk forlorn,
    Till cold winds woke the gray-eyed morn
About the lonely moated grange.
      She only said, 'The day is dreary,
        He cometh not,' she said;
      She said, 'I am aweary, aweary,
        I would that I were dead!'

IV

About a stone-cast from the wall
    A sluice with blacken'd waters slept,
And o'er it many, round and small,
    The cluster'd marish-mosses crept.
Hard by a poplar shook alway,
    All silver-green with gnarled bark,
    For leagues no other tree did dark
The level waste, the rounding gray.
      She only said, 'My life is dreary,
        He cometh not,' she said;
      She said, 'I am aweary, aweary,
        I would that I were dead!'

1

the day
was sloping toward his western bower. (Mariana)

Cannes.
France

V

And ever when the moon was low,
    And the shrill winds were up and away,
In the white curtain, to and fro,
    She saw the gusty shadow sway.
But when the moon was very low,
    And wild winds bound within their cell,
    The shadow of the poplar fell
Upon her bed, across her brow.
      She only said, 'The night is dreary,
        He cometh not,' she said;
      She said, 'I am aweary, aweary,
        I would that I were dead!'

VI

All day within the dreamy house,
    The doors upon their hinges creak'd;
The blue fly sung i' the pane; the mouse
    Behind the mouldering wainscot shriek'd,
Or from the crevice peer'd about.
    Old faces glimmer'd thro' the doors,
    Old footsteps trod the upper floors,
Old voices call'd her from without.
      She only said, 'My life is dreary,
        He cometh not,' she said;
      She said, 'I am aweary, aweary,
        I would that I were dead!'

VII

The sparrow's chirrup on the roof,
    The slow clock ticking, and the sound
Which to the wooing wind aloof
    The poplar made, did all confound
Her sense; but most she loath'd the hour
    When the thick-moted sunbeam lay
    Athwart the chambers, and the day
Was sloping toward his western bower.
      Then, said she, 'I am very dreary,
        He will not come,' she said;
      She wept, 'I am aweary, aweary,
        Oh God, that I were dead!'

1. Cannes, France
2. Albenga, Riviera di Genova, Italy
3. *Sattara, Bombay Presidency, India*
4. Waiee, Bombay Presidency, India

'Mariana' was one of Tennyson's greatest successes in *Poems, Chiefly Lyrical* 1832, and it lost none of its lasting power in the volumes of 1842. Inspiration had come from *Measure for Measure*, from Mariana of the 'moated grange' rejected by her contracted lover Angelo. From that one phrase 'moated grange' Tennyson conjures every detail which could suggest the isolation and slow ruin of a landscape and a house. Mariana seems to live only by articulating her misery – and the four-lined refrain stresses in direct speech her own feeling of loneliness, weariness and a wish for death. Yet, curiously, her repeated lament gives her life and individuality: it stops her merging into the process of decay which surrounds her. Tennyson begins with the powerful image of a ruined garden – 'The rusted nails fell from the knots /

That held the peach to the garden-wall' – a tradition going back to Ben Jonson's 'To Penshurst', and even earlier, immediately suggesting a paradise-place untended, fallen. And throughout the poem, Tennyson complements the scenic details with accumulating, small sounds: 'the clinking door', the night-fowl's crow, the distant lowing of oxen, the shaking of a poplar, shrill winds, creaking hinges, the blue fly singing, and, as the day goes down, the 'slow clock ticking'. Everywhere the sounds emphasize Mariana's isolation; they are heard clearly only in such silence, in such seclusion. No human voices or noises disturb house or landscape. Tennyson reveals Mariana's imagined fears: 'the mouse / Behind the mouldering wainscot shriek'd', and 'Old footsteps trod the upper floors.' The place is live with the light, shadows and sounds of nature: to Mariana all seem menacing, as do old steps and voices from a past which seems to mingle with the present. As each stanza details Mariana's surroundings, so each refrain echoes and re-echoes Mariana's response. Her weariness is so consuming that its enervating power is even stronger than her wish for death. This evocation of mood, with its artistry of description and verse structure, shows Tennyson the mature poet already apparent in an early poem.

Lear, considering the poem's landscapes, chose four sunsets to illustrate one line in the last stanza. The drawings did not lend themselves to minute detail and the many sounds he could hardly hope to encompass. Perhaps his musical setting of 'Mariana', heard by Hallam Tennyson in 1855 (*Mem.* I, p.391), did in some way bring out the poem's sounds in song, accompanied by piano. But the 'thick-moted sunbeam' and the claustrophobic moment of sunset signalled the loneliest and most hopeless hour for Mariana. In the 1880s in San Remo, when darkness fell, Lear could no longer see his beloved garden, and, with Giorgio dead, was often completely friendless and alone. He spent much time reading, and in his diary often quoted the Tennyson lines he had long ago chosen for his illustrations.

This poem frequently echoes both early and late in his diary, 'I am aweary, aweary,' sometimes in vexation or parody, being one of the most quoted Tennysonian phrases. Though the landscapes and sunsets are taken from France, Italy and India, it was Tennyson's evocation of loneliness, of life without meaning, which seems most deeply to have struck the artist. Cannes, where Lear lodged for a while, and nearby Albenga, were places in which a depressed and isolated mood might deepen, as it did in San Remo. Even the new sights of India and the fascination of its landscapes and people sometimes left Lear exhausted and feeling he could hardly bear to go on.

In his diary for 3 October 1865, Lear describes a country house visit, and walking through a glorious park of hanging oaks with his host, going on to view a partly completed house on a magnificent site. Lear did not feel envy, yet he wrote: '...I tire of seeing these gloryglories – & of being idle. And on the way back – by 1.30 – I thought I would roll up the Cedars & Masada, – pack up all the drawings – & give up Stratford Place – next year, – "He only said – I am aweary."' Lear is thinking of giving up the London house, which, in summer, he used for painting, for displaying pictures for sale, and as a base for visiting London and the country.

the day
Was sloping toward his western bower. (Mariana)

Albenga.
Riviera di Genova,
Italy.

On 19 February 1866, staying in Malta, Lear's misery broke out: 'He only said – my life is ugly – / My life's a bore he said.' On 27 September 1870 Lear was waiting to get into his new house – he wrote melodramatically, 'As for me the House weighs heavy on my eyelids & my soul' and Mariana-like, 'But, he only said – my life is weary'. These few examples from his diary show how Lear found Tennyson's poem could exactly articulate his own mood.

1. Cannes

Lear found much to draw in and around Cannes; out of the city he admired 'Claude-like' views with 'pale broad graduations of distances, & the lofty olive breadths which make up the middle of the landscape.' But the city was becoming a crowded summer resort, and Lear, the artistic snob, wrote: 'Could Cannes have been saved from the "VULGAR" – it might have really been Paradise' (D. 11 June 1870).

> *. . . . walked to the Bocca – it is not easy to say why that scene of pines & far hills is so lovely now – except that it really is quiet & one can perceive its beauties.*
>
> *What a mingling of sadness & admiration of landscape botheringly will persist in existing! All the unsought morbid feelings – (certainly unsought – for I knew not what even the meaning of morbid was in those days,) of past years crop up at once – such as the Hornsey fields & Highgate archway, & the sad large Thorn tree at Holloway about 1819 or 1820. . . the Mill at Arundel, or Peppering in 1824 & 5 – the heights above Plymouth in 1836-7 – the*

> *Godesberg – 1837 – Civitella 1839 & Nemi – all were with me at once. How far is it right or wise to get rid of & crush the morbids altogether? – I can't tell. Yet I have tried & do try to do so – tho' I crush a good deal else with them – because I have a feeling that to encourage "morbids" is wrong.* (D. 1 June 1870)

> *Then I walked on to the Bocca, & past all the pines. That landscape is most lovely – hardly any I know is more so – & now as tranquil – & so golden = melting into hazy sky: – it is Ravenna, & the Campagna mixed together. Walked back by the almost deserted road – how gt a contrast to what it was a few weeks back!* (D. 12 June 1870)

Pine woods at Cannes lead Lear back into the past and make very clear, with the first picture, that outward scenes are linked for this artist, as for Tennyson, with inner landscape of heart and mind.

2. Albenga, Riviera di Genova, Italy

On 2 October 1883 the weather was lovely and Lear decided to make an expedition. He arrived at Albenga after a two-hour train journey and he and his servant took two rooms in the old Hotel Vittoria and wondered about the new Hotel Albenga. They arranged for supper, and then went back to the station and looked about for Lear's 'much wanted view'. There were problems, because the railway was high above the plain and they did not have permission to walk on it. The plain was too low and interrupted by trees. Then, down by the shore, after much difficulty, Lear 'succeeded in getting separate positions of the subject'. He thought he might 'patch up the whole' and went back to an uneatable dinner cooked with 'filthily bad oil' (D. 2 October 1883).

Next day it rained; Lear nevertheless got 'some outline of the Albenga towers', but there was no possibility of drawing mountains. He decided to go to Alassio for a day, but the hotel gave him the wrong train time and, although ready about 5.40 a.m., Lear was 'left forlorn' on the station. After a later trip to Alassio he returned to Albenga, lost some original Albenga sketches, but found them in the sheets and blankets on the bed. Changing his mind about going back to San Remo, the artist thought he 'would make the best of being here' and by staying one more day, got another chance at the Albenga view '"day is sloping to his western bower" – all the more that the sky gets clearer'. The hills were clear enough to draw accurately and later he walked round the walls of the 'queer dead town' with its 'narrow streets . . . . interesting church doors & towers' (D. 4 October 1883).

4. Waiee, Bombay Presidency

The plain of Waiee & the mountains round about are exquisitely beautiful, & remind me of some of the very finest Greek or Syrian scenes. At Waiee by 5.20. The many Temples, gleaming out of the Damascus-like band of deep green are delightful, & so are all the forms of the hills beyond. The rain however did come before we got in,

but not heavily: & it soon stopped, as we reached the neat & new-looking Dak Bungalow at 5.20. The lightsome cleanliness of this place is charming after "Hotels". Walked out a while with G, – & surely no place on earth can be more lovely than this! – Not to speak of the Temples, & groves, & the River Kristna, there are Camels & Elephants, & all kinds of living Creatures. (Indian Journal, 28 May 1874)

Slept tolerably. Rose 4.30, & got tea at 5. Went out directly, & drew hard at 2 or 3 subjects till 9.30. Morning quite lovely. Assuredly Waiee is one of the most exquisitely beautiful places I have ever seen. Every spot is a picture, & the colouring is more than usually interesting, owing to the profusion of green, & because the temples are of such rich browns & yellows. When the River is full, all these Temples must stand more or less in the Water. Walked about the place, – one truly Indian in character, – on both sides of the river, till 10 & later; then to breakfast, – which, being good, – viz – mutton chops, stew, & omelette, – & all well & quietly served – was a pleasure. Prowled about to see what I ought to draw, – where, – & when, – & decided to go up a mile & a quarter to draw Waiee on its plain. (29 May 1874)

1-4. EL List: The sun was sloping to his western bower
   EL Drawing: the day
       Was sloping toward his western bower.
On 4 (Waiee), 'to' is crossed out and 'toward' lightly written in above.

From: RECOLLECTIONS OF THE ARABIAN NIGHTS

I

When the breeze of a joyful dawn blew free
In the silken sail of infancy,
The tide of time flow'd back with me,
   The forward-flowing tide of time;
And many a sheeny summer-morn,
Adown the Tigris I was borne,
By Bagdat's shrines of fretted gold,
High-walled gardens green and old;
True Mussulman was I and sworn,
   For it was in the golden prime,
     Of good Haroun Alraschid:

II

Anight my shallop, rustling thro'
The low and bloomed foliage, drove
The fragrant, glistening deeps, and clove
The citron-shadows in the blue:
By garden porches on the brim,
The costly doors flung open wide,
Gold glittering thro' lamplight dim,
And broider'd sophas on each side:
   In sooth it was a goodly time,
   For it was in the golden prime
     Of good Haroun Alraschid....

IV

A motion from the river won
Ridged the smooth level, bearing on
My shallop through the star-strown calm,
Until another night in night
I enter'd, from the clearer light,
Imbower'd vaults of pillar'd palm,
Imprisoning sweets, which, as they clomb,
Heavenward, were stay'd beneath the dome
   Of hollow boughs. – A goodly time,
   For it was in the golden prime
     Of good Haroun Alraschid!...

VII

Far off, and where the lemon-grove
In closest coverture upsprung,
The living airs of middle night
Died round the bulbul as he sung;
Not he: but something which possess'd
The darkness of the world, delight,
Life, anguish, death, immortal love,
Ceasing not, mingled, unrepress'd,
   Apart from place, withholding time,
   But flattering the golden prime
     Of good Haroun Alraschid.

VIII

Black the garden-bowers and grots
Slumber'd: the solemn palms were ranged
Above, unwoo'd of summer wind:
A sudden splendour from behind
Flush'd all the leaves with rich gold-green,
And, flowing rapidly between
Their interspaces, counterchanged
The level lake with diamond-plots
   Of dark and bright. A lovely time,
   For it was in the golden prime
     Of good Haroun Alraschid!

IX

Dark-blue the deep sphere overhead,
Distinct with vivid stars inlaid,
Grew darker from that under-flame:
So, leaping lightly from the boat,
With silver anchor left afloat,
In marvel whence that glory came
Upon me, as in sleep I sank
In cool soft turf upon the bank,
   Entranced with that place and time,
   So worthy of the golden prime
     Of good Haroun Alraschid.

X

Thence thro' the garden I was drawn –
A realm of pleasance, many a mound,
And many a shadow-chequer'd lawn
Full of the city's stilly sound,
And deep myrrh-thickets blowing round
The stately cedar, tamarisks,
Thick roseries of scented thorn,
Tall orient shrubs, and obelisks
   Graven with emblems of the time,
   In honour of the golden prime
     Of good Haroun Alraschid.

XI

With dazed vision unawares
From the long alley's latticed shade
Emerged, I came upon the great
Pavilion of the Caliphat.
Right to the carven cedarn doors,
Flung inward over spangled floors,
Broad-baséd flights of marble stairs
Ran up with golden balustrade,
   After the fashion of the time,
   And humour of the golden prime
     Of good Haroun Alraschid.

7

And where the Lemon Grove
In closest coverture upspring.
(Recollections of the Arabian Nights.)

Corfu. (from Viro.)
Greece.

9

From the long alley's latticed shade
(Recollections of the Arabian Nights.)

Turin.
Palazzo Valentini
Italy

XII

The fourscore windows all alight
As with the quintessence of flame,
A million tapers flaring bright
From twisted silvers look'd to shame
The hollow-vaulted dark, and stream'd
Upon the mooned domes aloof
In inmost Bagdat, till there seem'd
    Hundreds of crescents on the roof
      Of night new-risen, that marvellous time,
      To celebrate the golden prime
      Of good Haroun Alraschid.

XIII

Then stole I up, and trancedly
Gazed on the Persian girl alone,
Serene with argent-lidded eyes
Amorous, and lashes like to rays
Of darkness, and a brow of pearl
Tressed with redolent ebony,
In many a dark delicious curl,
    Flowing beneath her rose-hued zone;
      The sweetest lady of the time,
      Well worthy of the golden prime
      Of good Haroun Alraschid.

XIV

Six columns, three on either side,
Pure silver, underpropp'd a rich
Throne of the massive ore, from which
Down-droop'd, in many a floating fold,
Engarlanded and diaper'd
With inwrought flowers, a cloth of gold.
Thereon, his deep eye laughter-stirr'd
    With merriment of kingly pride,
      Sole star of all that place and time,
      I saw him – in his golden prime,
      THE GOOD HAROUN ALRASCHID!

5. *Near Tel El Kebeer, Egypt*
6. *Wady Feiran, Peninsula of Mt Sinai*
7. Corfu (from Viro), Greece
8. *Philae, Egypt*
9. Turin, Palazzo Valentini, Italy

'Recollections of the Arabian Nights', a series of exotic descriptions in a dream setting, was a popular poem in Tennyson's earliest volume of 1830. Arthur Hallam apparently singled it out as his favourite. Among many more substantial poems in the 1842 volumes, 'Recollections' still earns a place with its distant dream world of 'Bagdat', and its varying perspectives on the 'tide of time'. We recognize yet again in this slight piece, Tennyson's 'passion of the past'. In the poem, time flows back to reveal a perfect retreat: a world amazing enough for a child, sensuous enough for an adult – a fusion of two tales remembered from the distant, but fascinating, *Arabian Nights*. In 1842, time stands still for the poet's Lotos-Eaters, and for the Soul who hopes to retreat for ever, to the delights of the Palace of Art; 'Recollections'

fits a pattern of ideas which Tennyson is concerned to explore. The Soul has to give up its Palace: the Lotos-Eaters succumb to a half-life of fantasy. But in this poem nothing disturbs the Eastern dream: no waking, no pain, no confrontation with day to day reality. The speaker – who is both child and adult, and in that double role, a reader of *The Arabian Nights* – journeys down river in a 'shallop', a small boat, as the wind gently swells the 'sails of silken infancy'. The tide of the past, set flowing in the poem, shows the sights on the banks of the great river Tigris: gardens at night with strange flowers and bulbuls' songs, palaces, lighted doors, fretted windows, golden shrines, great domes. The poem is filled with richly decorative description, and experience of anguish, death and love are kept at a great distance. In *The Arabian Nights* a maiden tells the tales to entertain a King and preserve herself from a cruel death. Tennyson drew on two tales, but not on the suspended violence of the framing scheme. The poem has no complex story and the varied descriptions are given order as each stanza, rhyming on 'time' and 'prime', returns to the soothing refrain which invokes the benevolent Caliph, 'good Haroun Alraschid'; his very name becomes almost a lullaby. The traveller in dream or reverie first casts anchor, and then moves through gardens towards the inmost throne. Tennyson devotes a stanza to the beauteous Persian girl, but tells no story and brings the traveller at last before the Caliph. Smiling, beneficent, this Haroun Alraschid presides over a golden world, an Eastern dream.

Lear knew *The Arabian Nights* and responded to Tennyson's idealized 'Recollections'. In Istanbul, Egypt and on further travels he had seen some of the beauty and squalor of the Arab world. But for this dream poem he chose five landscapes involving foliage. He knew about palms clustered or leaning over the banks of a river, about gardens and trees near water. Tennyson's glimpsed interiors Lear left to such fashionable artists as John Frederick Lewis, who was bringing idealized harem scenes to English drawing-rooms.

In one landscape particularly, Lear drew his recollections of a beauty he had found dream-like; citrus groves on the island of Corfu. His three illustrations of Palestinian and Egyptian palms recall journeys of 1858, 1854 and 1867. The 'latticed shade' brought back the cool air of Turin, welcome after the heat of the coast, or tiring journeys in France or Italy. Lear's illustrations suggest the serenity of Tennyson's poem. Shade, quiet, a long view of purple sea and hills: such visual impressions match the surprisingly tranquil quality of 'Recollections of the Arabian Nights' in which dream never turns to nightmare.

7. Corfu
Yesterday afternoon I walked to find a place called Viro, whence I heard that there were good views of Corfu; & I really think I saw the loveliest of anything one has yet discovered. You see the whole coast & channel, the Citadel, town & lake – immediately above a thick wood of orange trees: – I never saw anything more exquisite, with the millions of oranges glittering in the sun. Won't I paint a large picture from there some day!
(EL to Ann, 10 February 1856)

Today, & hence for several days, I shall hope to be painting at Viro – where there is such a wonderful orange garden! "Oranges & Lemons" as far as one can see. 21st... Good Friday... No letter from you yet! I hear the Trieste steamer just coming in now – so I hope for tomorrow. It is colder now than, except for one or 2 days, it has been here; – & such clear lovely weather! – but I weary sadly for a quiet abode. If one is travelling one can bear anything, but not when settled. Meanwhile, I have had to buy 2 deal tables – & a table cover, & to put up muslin blinds, to keep the sun out. – £2 soon vanished! – but I trust to send Mary £10 in the autumn; let me know how she is. Good-night. What a hodgy podgy letter! 22nd. Another drawing ordered today! – & I went at noon to the "Orange & Lemon Garden" & only came back at 7...
(EL to Ann, 1 March 1856)

... no other spot on earth can be fuller of beauty & variety of beauty. For you may pass your days by gigantic cliffs with breaking foam-waves below them... – or on hills which overlook long seas of foliage backed by snow-covered mountain ridges... or beneath vast olives over-branching dells full of fern & myrtle & soft green fields of bright grass: or in gardens dark with orange & lemon groves, those fruits sparkling golden & yellow against the purple sea & amethyst hills...   (D. 30 March 1863)

9. Turin
Views of Turin from the tree bordered walks are very pleasant. Pale purple alps... poplars & trees beyond – all seen between trunx of trees – delightful enough.
(D. 25 July 1861)

7. EL List: Far down, and where the lemon grove.
   EL Drawing: And where the Lemon Grove
                      In closest coverture upsprung.
9. EL List: From the long alley's latticed shade,
   EL Drawing: From the long alley's latticed shade

10

the Waterfall

— A pillar of white light upon the wall
Of purple cliffs.
(Ode to Memory.)

near Mendrisio
Switzerland.

ODE TO MEMORY

I

Thou who stealest fire,
From the fountains of the past,
To glorify the present; oh, haste,
Visit my low desire!
Strengthen me, enlighten me!
I faint in this obscurity,
Thou dewy dawn of memory.

II

Come not as thou camest of late,
Flinging the gloom of yesternight
On the white day; but robed in soften'd light
Of orient state.
Whilome thou camest with the morning mist,
Even as a maid, whose stately brow
The dew-impearled winds of dawn have kiss'd,
When she, as thou,
Stays on her floating locks the lovely freight
Of overflowing blooms, and earliest shoots
Of orient green, giving safe pledge of fruits,
Which in wintertide shall star
The black earth with brilliance rare.

III

Whilome thou camest with the morning mist,
And with the evening cloud,
Showering thy gleaned wealth into my open breast,
(Those peerless flowers which in the rudest wind
Never grow sere,
When rooted in the garden of the mind,
Because they are the earliest of the year).
Nor was the night thy shroud.
In sweet dreams softer than unbroken rest
Thou leddest by the hand thine infant Hope,
The eddying of her garments caught from thee
The light of thy great presence; and the cope
Of the half-attain'd futurity,
Though deep not fathomless,
Was cloven with the million stars which tremble
O'er the deep mind of dauntless infancy.
Small thought was there of life's distress;
For sure she deem'd no mist of earth could dull
Those spirit-thrilling eyes so keen and beautiful:
Sure she was nigher to heaven's spheres,
Listening the lordly music flowing from
The illimitable years.
O strengthen me, enlighten me!
I faint in this obscurity,
Thou dewy dawn of memory.

IV

Come forth, I charge thee, arise,
Thou of the many tongues, the myriad eyes!
Thou comest not with shows of flaunting vines
Unto mine inner eye,
Divinest Memory!
Thou wert not nursed by the waterfall
Which ever sounds and shines
A pillar of white light upon the wall
Of purple cliffs, aloof descried:
Come from the woods that belt the gray hill-side,
The seven elms, the poplars four
That stand beside my father's door,
And chiefly from the brook that loves
To purl o'er matted cress and ribbed sand,
Or dimple in the dark of rushy coves,
Drawing into his narrow earthen urn,
In every elbow and turn,
The filter'd tribute of the rough woodland.
O! hither lead thy feet!
Pour round mine ears the livelong bleat
Of the thick-fleeced sheep from wattled folds,
Upon the ridged wolds,
When the first matin-song hath waken'd loud
Over the dark dewy earth forlorn,
What time the amber morn
Forth gushes from beneath a low-hung cloud.

V

Large dowries doth the raptured eye
To the young spirit present
When first she is wed;
And like a bride of old
In triumph led,
With music and sweet showers
Of festal flowers,
Unto the dwelling she must sway.
Well hast thou done, great artist Memory,
In setting round thy first experiment
With royal frame-work of wrought gold;
Needs must thou dearly love thy first essay,
And foremost in thy various gallery
Place it, where sweetest sunlight falls
Upon the storied walls,
For the discovery
And newness of thine art so pleased thee,
That all which thou hast drawn of fairest
Or boldest since, but lightly weighs
With thee unto the love thou bearest
The first-born of thy genius. Artist-like,
Ever retiring thou dost gaze
On the prime labour of thine early days:
No matter what the sketch might be;
Whether the high field on the bushless Pike,
Or even a sand-built ridge
Of heaped hills that mound the sea,
Overblown with murmurs harsh,
Or even a lowly cottage whence we see
Stretch'd wide and wild the waste enormous marsh,
Where from the frequent bridge,
Like emblems of infinity,
The trenched waters run from sky to sky;
Or a garden bower'd close
With plaited alleys of the trailing rose,
Long alleys falling down to twilight grots,
Or opening upon level plots

12

Stretch'd wide and wild the waste enormous marsh
(Ode to Memory.)

The Pontine Marshes,
from above Terracina.
Italy

Of crowned lilies, standing near
Purple-spiked lavender:
Whither in after life retired
From brawling storms,
From weary wind,
With youthful fancy reinspired,
We may hold converse with all forms
Of the many-sided mind,
And those whom passion hath not blinded,
Subtle-thoughted, myriad-minded.
My friend, with you to live alone,
Were how much better than to own
A crown, a sceptre, and a throne.
O strengthen me, enlighten me!
I faint in this obscurity,
Thou dewy dawn of memory.

'Ode to Memory', first published in 1830, owes something to Wordsworth's 'Immortality Ode', and the diction often recalls Milton's 'L'Allegro' and 'Il Penseroso' as well as *Comus* and 'Lycidas'. In long stanzas Tennyson invokes a personified Memory who, like Prometheus, steals fire, but only 'From the fountains of the past, / To glorify the present'. Memory has brought night's gloom to 'the white day': both Tennyson and Lear knew the black misery of such times. But now Memory is to come 'rob'd in soften'd light' as a maid, bearing '. . . the lovely freight / Of overflowing blooms, and earliest shoots / Of orient green, giving safe pledge of fruits.' In the next stanza the flowers 'Never grow sere' because they are to be 'rooted in the garden of the mind'. The tone is highly dignified, archaic and distant; the poet does not succeed in giving any immediacy to the next long stanza on Hope, infant of Memory. A new energy and directness enters the poem, however, when Tennyson begins to describe specific landscapes: Memory is not nursed by the shining waterfall, but comes '. . . from the woods that belt the gray hill-side, / The seven elms, the poplars four / That stand beside my father's door'. The details of brook with 'matted cress and ribbed sand', of woodland, and the bleat of 'thick-fleeced sheep from wattled folds', end with a Miltonic 'amber morn', but show the beginning of Tennyson's individual descriptive power. The last stanza moves out to marsh and sea and back to the garden of Somersby, so that scenes from the past may re-inspire and

We may hold converse with all forms
Of the many-sided mind,
And those whom passion hath not blinded,
Subtle-thoughted, myriad-minded.

The whole ode may have echoed Lear's thoughts: he was always strengthened and enlightened by memory. He looked back to early years and sometimes to the difficulties of his childhood. But mostly he cherished memories of his sister, Ann; of friendly relationships and visits to England; of early Italian travels and hints of their landscapes suddenly remembered in much more distant places. Memory, in his last years, held his life together and memory kept up his efforts at the Tennyson illustrations. The last section of the poem talks of 'the great artist Memory' whose first pictures so enrapture the 'young spirit'. And Memory is always attracted to the 'discovery' and 'newness' of her art, 'Artist-like, / Ever retiring thou dost gaze / On the prime labour of thine early days.' Lear loved to look back over sketches and diaries. Many of his oils and watercolours had been sold, but his 'prime labour' was the on-the-spot sketch which he kept for reference. When it looked as though he would have to sell a large number of original sketches he felt, as he looked at them again, that if they went it would be as though flesh had been torn from his own side. Memory 'Artist-like' may have meant more to Lear than, in this ode, it did for Tennyson.

Lear chose, as illustration for this ode, a waterfall seen early at Oeschiner-See, another at Mendrisio where he often stayed towards the end of his life. These are both large mountain scenes and, though seen in miniature in these drawings, suggest a distance and scale very different from Tennyson's landscapes which are mainly culled from the familiar places of his own youth. Lear's 'wide marsh', from Terracina, is a view of the Pontine marshes near Rome which attracted the artist with their receding horizontal space. Mendrisio (10), in the cool mountains below Monte Generoso, was one of the several places not far from San Remo where the artist went to escape the heat in his last years. In 1883 it was also the scene of Giorgio's funeral; Lear's loved and faithful servant and companion was buried there. In his diary Lear drew a picture of the headstone and inscription on Giorgio's grave. For days he could hardly keep back tears, and quoted again and again, the first lines, which he found most consoling, from *In Memoriam*. 'As yet,' he wrote, 'this separation from that dear good man seems like a dream...' and he reflected that he had felt alone before, and now what must he feel?
(D. 12 August 1883).

12. The Pontine Marshes

After this came Terracina – the frontier of the Papal States – & glad was I once more to be in them – luggage searched – & everything settled. Terracina is on the sea, & is stocked with palm trees so as to look quite oriental: it was hereabouts that so many robberies once used to take place: famous brigands abounded about it: – you know there is an Opera – "The Brigand" or "The Inn of Terracina" – Immediately on leaving it, – commences the Pontini Marshes[1] – in other words – part of that enormous plain called near Rome – "The Campagna". These marshes – marshes now no longer – since they are drained all over – are uninhabitable during summer from Malaria – otherwise ague: – & indeed, after great rains are even now impassable from overflowed canals. – For my part, I never could have guessed they were marshes: I should as soon have thought them puddings, or lobsters. What do you think the "Pontini Marshes" are like? – why – one straight road – one everlasting avenue, like an arrow – For 40 miles – all the way bordered with the most beautiful trees imaginable: beyond are vast plains & fine mountains! – I never saw such an avenue in my life: you see a little round hole at the end like a pin's head – hour after hour till you grow sick. Uwins & I walked a long way – & counted 9 vipers & one snake.[2] I had a most narrow escape from one: – walking on – I heard Uwins scream out – which he being usually taciturn, surprised me very much: – I had trodden on one of these creatures – as they bask in the sun – but – on its head! Had I trodden on his tail, I must have been bitten. At sunset we reached Cisterno – & there we slept: a stupid little town – 10 miles from which all the robberies nowadays are committed; fortunately we arrived safely. (EL to Ann, 26 September 1838)

[1] The typed version of this letter has 'marches' throughout.
[2] James Uwins, an artist with whom Lear went on expeditions from Rome, and who remained a friend.

10. EL List: The waterfall, a pillar of white light
  EL Drawing: the Waterfall
         – A pillar of white light upon the wall
         Of purple cliffs.
12. EL List: Wild and wide the waste enormous marsh
  EL Drawing: Stretch'd wide and wild the waste enormous marsh

THE POET

The poet in a golden clime was born,
    With golden stars above;
Dower'd with the hate of hate, the scorn of scorn,
    The love of love.

He saw thro' life and death, thro' good and ill,
    He saw thro' his own soul.
The marvel of the everlasting will,
    An open scroll,

Before him lay: with echoing feet he threaded
    The secret'st walks of fame:
The viewless arrows of his thoughts were headed
    And wing'd with flame,

Like Indian reeds blown from his silver tongue,
    And of so fierce a flight,
From Calpe unto Caucasus they sung,
    Filling with light

And vagrant melodies the winds which bore
    Them earthward till they lit;
Then, like the arrow-seeds of the field flower,
    The fruitful wit

Cleaving, took root, and springing forth anew
    Where'er they fell, behold,
Like to the mother plant in semblance, grew
    A flower all gold,

And bravely furnish'd all abroad to fling
    The winged shafts of truth,
To throng with stately blooms the breathing spring
    Of Hope and Youth.

So many minds did gird their orbs with beams,
    Though one did fling the fire.
Heaven flow'd upon the soul in many dreams
    Of high desire.

13

And thro' the wraths of floating dark uprear'd
Rare sunrise flow'd.
    (The Poet.)

Amalfi.
Italy

Thus truth was multiplied on truth, the world
    Like one great garden show'd,
And thro' the wreaths of floating dark upcurl'd,
    Rare sunrise flow'd.

And Freedom rear'd in that august sunrise
    Her beautiful bold brow,
When rites and forms before his burning eyes
    Melted like snow.

There was no blood upon her maiden robes
    Sunn'd by those orient skies;
But round about the circles of the globes
    Of her keen eyes

And in her raiment's hem was traced in flame
    WISDOM, a name to shake
All evil dreams of power – a sacred name.
    And when she spake,

Her words did gather thunder as they ran,
    And as the lightning to the thunder
Which follows it; riving the spirit of man,
    Making earth wonder,

So was their meaning to her words. No sword
    Of wrath her right arm whirl'd,
But one poor poet's scroll, and with *his* word
    She shook the world.

13. Amalfi, Italy

Lear visited the Bay of Naples, including Amalfi, in 1838. It was during his first visit to Italy, and he and his friend, James Uwins, were escaping from the summer heat of Rome and the bustle of Naples.

Praise of the poet and his power seems to have given this poem its appeal to Lear. There are no detailed descriptions of landscape, but the artist found one sunrise to illustrate line 36. He remembered the image of a golden flower over the years and, in an early letter to Emily Tennyson (5th October 1852), he used it when mentioning his wish to illustrate Tennyson's poetry:

My desire has been to show that Alfred Tennyson's poetry (with regard to scenes –) is as real and exquisite as it is relatively to higher and deeper matters – that his descriptions of certain spots are as positively true as if drawn from the places themselves, and that his words have the power of calling up images as distinct and correct as if they were written from those images, instead of giving rise to them. If I could prove this at all, it would be a pleasant carrying out and sealing of his own words –

    Cleaving, took root and sprang forth anew,

    Where'er they fell, behold
    Like to the mother plant in semblance grew
    A flower all gold –

– a quotation which if my illustrating can 'come to anything' I would willingly see at the head.

A badly executed project, Lear added, at that early stage, might grow 'a flower all mud – or all cold – or all anything else totally disagreeable'. But if done well, engravings from such designs would make a beautiful edition and might grow – in Victorian slang for the money he was always short of – 'a flower all tin'.

13. EL List: And from the East rare sunrise flow'd
    EL Drawing: And thro' the wreaths of floating dark uprear'd
                   Rare sunrise flow'd
    [*Poems*, 1842: And thro' the wreaths of floating dark upcurl'd,
                   Rare sunrise flow'd.]

Lear often found his Tennyson quotations difficult to remember and write down with complete accuracy. Here the printed list conflates both lines of the quotation and the 'wreaths of floating dark' becomes, simply, 'from the East'. This could have been the result of Lear quoting and writing from memory, or from some mistake compounded by printer's errors. The word 'uprear'd' substituted for 'upcurl'd' is an easily made error of transcription, or of memory.

THE POET'S MIND

I

Vex not thou the poet's mind
   With thy shallow wit:
Vex not thou the poet's mind;
   For thou can'st not fathom it.
Clear and bright it should be ever,
Flowing like a crystal river;
Bright as light, and clear as wind.

II

Dark-brow'd sophist, come not anear;
   All the place is holy ground;
Hollow smile and frozen sneer
     Come not here.
Holy water will I pour
Into every spicy flower
Of the laurel-shrubs that hedge it around.
The flowers would faint at your cruel cheer.
   In your eye there is death,
   There is frost in your breath

Which would blight the plants.
   Where you stand you cannot hear
     From the groves within
     The wild-bird's din.
In the heart of the garden the merry bird chants.
It would fall to the ground if you came in.
   In the middle leaps a fountain
     Like sheet lightning,
     Ever brightening
   With a low melodious thunder;
All day and all night it is ever drawn
   From the brain of the purple mountain
   Which stands in the distance yonder:
It springs on a level of bowery lawn,
And the mountain draws it from Heaven above,
And it sings a song of undying love;
And yet, though its voice be so clear and full,
You never would hear it – your ears are so dull;
So keep where you are: you are foul with sin;
It would shrink to the earth if you came in.

---

14. *Platania, Crete*
15. Mount Olympus, Thessaly, Greece

'The Poet's Mind' is one of several poems which idealize poetic creativity. Tennyson is concerned with the poet's wisdom, clear-mindedness, and vatic power. No shallow wit – and that includes the reader's – should vex the poet's unfathomable mind, which is imagined: 'Flowing like a crystal river; / Bright as light, and clear as wind.' The brief opening strophe gave Lear the first of his two illustrations to the poem. He remembered a landscape with a 'crystal river' at Platania, one of the places he visited on his extensive tour of Crete in 1864.

In the long second strophe, Tennyson imagines a 'Dark-brow'd sophist' who must not approach and annihilate the poet's ideal garden and 'holy ground'. Apollonius in Keats's 'Lamia' has a similar threatening effect. And when Tennyson describes the fountain in the garden he may have had Coleridge's 'Kubla Khan' in mind. Like Coleridge, Tennyson suggests a powerful, almost frightening creativity, 'In the middle leaps a fountain / Like sheet lightning...'. The fountain, with its light and sound that warn of thunder, is mysteriously drawn from the 'brain' of the distant mountain. 'The Poet's Mind' is far from being an abstract statement: river, garden, 'bowery lawn' all suggest pictorial landscape with the fountain as centre, and in the far distance the 'purple mountain'.

Lear, in his list, though not on the drawing, conflates two lines of the poem: 'From the brain of the purple mountain / Which stands in the distance yonder' becomes simply, 'The purple mountain yonder'. The artist concentrates on the main features of the landscape. The mountain, in the poem, is the ultimate source of unknowable creative power and Lear chose Mount Olympus, dwelling of the Gods. This accords well with Tennyson's insistence that the poet, unlike the sophist, reaches upwards to the divine.

15. Mount Olympus, Thessaly

Larissa, and even Olympus, except now and then in its highest peaks, are soon lost to sight, from the comparatively uneven nature of the ground; and it is only from some eminence where a village is planted . . . that anything like a satisfactory drawing can be made.

Yet the very simplicity, the extreme exaggeration of the character of a plain, is not without its fascination; and the vast lines of Thessaly have a wild and dream-like charm of poetry about them, of which it is impossible for pen or pencil to give a fully adequate idea.
(Albanian Journal, 21 May 1849, pp.416-7)

15. EL List: The purple mountain yonder
    EL Drawing: the purple mountain
                 Which stands in the distance yonder;

the purple Mountain
Which stands in the distance Yonder;
(The Poets' mind.)

Mount Olympus.
Thessaly.
Greece

Slow sail'd the weary mariners and saw,
Betwixt the green brink and the running foam,
Sweet faces, rounded arms, and bosoms prest
To little harps of gold; and while they mused
Whispering to each other half in fear,
Shrill music reach'd them on the middle sea.

Whither away, whither away, whither away? fly no more.
Whither away from the high green field, and the happy
    blossoming shore?
Day and night to the billow the fountain calls;
Down shower the gambolling waterfalls
From wandering over the lea;
Out of the live-green heart of the dells
They freshen the silvery-crimson shells,
And thick with white bells the clover-hill swells
High over the full-toned sea:
O hither, come hither and furl your sails,
Come hither to me and to me:
Hither, come hither and frolic and play;
Here it is only the mew that wails;
We will sing to you all the day:

Mariner, mariner, furl your sails,
For here are the blissful downs and dales,
And merrily merrily carol the gales,
And the spangle dances in bight and bay,
And the rainbow forms and flies on the land
Over the islands free;
And the rainbow lives in the curve of the sand;
Hither, come hither and see;
And the rainbow hangs on the poising wave,
And sweet is the colour of cove and cave,
And sweet shall your welcome be:
O hither, come hither, and be our lords
For merry brides are we:
We will kiss sweet kisses, and speak sweet words:
O listen, listen, your eyes shall glisten
With pleasure and love and jubilee:
O listen, listen, your eyes shall glisten
When the sharp clear twang of the golden chords
Runs up the ridged sea.
Who can light on as happy a shore
All the world o'er, all the world o'er?
Whither away? listen and stay: mariner, mariner, fly no more.

16. Palaiokastritza, Corfu, Greece

For Lear, Corfu was always remembered as an enchanted island. He visited it first in 1848 after a decade of travel which began with his journey to Rome in 1837. He had seen Germany, Switzerland, the Alps; he had walked and sketched by the lakes of Lugano and Como; he had crossed the Apennines and delighted in Florence, Rome, the Campagna, unknown hill towns, hidden lakes, cypresses, vineyards – he had drawn a variety of Italian scenery, and used many sketches for his early books of lithographs. Most recently, in 1847, he had gone South to Sicily and to the parched and mountainous region of Calabria. Hints of revolution forced him back to Naples: fear and silence had begun to spread among his hosts, and Lear's half-joking references to scenes of gothic horror seemed all too likely to turn into sober fact.

After Calabrian landscapes Corfu seemed, by contrast, a peaceful paradise. From a calm blue sea rose slopes covered with cypress, olive, orange, almond; white convents and white villages showed up the varying tints of green. In places, lower hills looked up to the central mountains, so the island offered all kinds of views to an artist. Nearby lay the tiny islands of Zante, Cephalonia, and Ulysses' Ithaca; in the far distance, across the water, it was often possible to see the mountains of Albania. Of all the Ionian islands, Lear most loved Corfu. He drew it, painted it and, for a while, tried living on it. It was the scene of great happiness and creative work. It also saw Lear's despairing lethargy in 1855, when he felt himself abandoned by his friend Franklin Lushington. who had been made head of the island's Judiciary. Once, with Lear, he had revelled in the spring beauty of Greece, but now he seemed to have turned away into a cold and remote public figure.

All these events belonged to the distant past. Lushington had married; Lear's attachment had settled into quiet friendship. For Lear, working at the Tennyson Illustrations in the 1880s, Corfu remained in memory an ideal place and the threshold of his beloved Greece. The bay of Palaiokastritza was a design he repeated again and again: the calm sea and high encircling rocks are gently contoured and yet unrestricting to the eye. The place as Lear saw it was familiar, safe: 'giant rocks,' he said, 'rise perpendicularly from the sea', but the scene holds no horror, the 'sea, perfectly calm and blue stretches right out westward unbrokenly to the sky, cloudless . . . . save a streak of lilac cloud on the horizon.' Lear wrote this on Easter Sunday, 20 April 1862, to Chichester Fortescue, trying to find words for the quietness of the scene with the Convent of Palaiokastritza – at a time when the monks were asleep and he could see the 'many peacocktail-hued bays' as he stood high above the shore. The quiet half-circling bay, with cliff, cave and smooth water perhaps suggested the elusive perspective of a landscape which imaged for Lear the unattainable close relationship with another human being.

Lear might have been lured by the siren-song of Corfu, and in Tennyson's light and easy poem sea-fairies tempt the passing mariner to stay. This piece did not appear in the 1842 edition; it was published in 1830, and revised and reprinted in the *Poems*, 8th edition, 1853. Lear might have seen either version, but 1853 is likely because his serious interest in Tennyson illustration began in 1852.

The fairies in a Victorian vignette of 'Sweet faces, rounded arms, and bosoms prest / To little harps of gold' urge the weary mariners to remain in a flowery, paradise land. They offer to become merry brides, bringing pleasure and love: 'Who can light on as happy a shore / All the world o'er, all the world o'er?' Lear often longed to listen to such a refrain in his travelling life, but he always moved on. 'The color of cove and cave' in Lear's quotation points to the original intention of producing these drawings in colour. This cherished design is badly overdrawn, far better seen in the lithograph in the *Ionian Islands* book. The half-circle of the bay is heavily scored in; Lear's failing sight has left him unable to show the detail in cliff and cave. The picture has become the mere outline of a memory.

16. Corfu

Oh! I never told you about the fireflies: they are here by millions now from 8 to 10 every night, & are certainly better animals than the frogs. The whole land is like a fairy scene lit up with myriads of tiny lamps – At present the weather is mild, but very rainy again, that is – morning showers for an hour or two: these do a great deal of good, & the fig trees & others are already out in full leaf. – As for the flowers, they are more & more & more & more – & every place is like Covent Garden Market. Only think of streets of crimson Gladiolus – hills white & pink with large rose cistus, or yellow with bright asphodels & tulips! Except the fern & myrtle the flowers have swallowed up

all the leaves. Some beautiful birds are come too. Hoopoes, & yellow orioles are quite common: blue rollers & turtledoves & quails: –   (EL to Ann, 18 April 1856)

The weather, it has been simply cloudless glory, for 7 long days & nights. Anything like the splendour of olive-grove & orange-garden, the blue of sky & ivory of church & chapel, the violet of mountain, rising from peacockwing-hued sea, & tipped with lines of silver snow, can hardly be imagined.
(EL to Fortescue, 6 December 1857, LEL, p.68)

Palaiokastritza, Corfu

[The] sea perfectly calm and blue stretches right out westward unbrokenly to the sky, cloudless.... save a streak of lilac cloud on the horizon. On my left is the convent of Paleokastrizza, and happily, as the monkery had functions at 2 a.m. they are all fast asleep now and to my left is one of the many peacocktail-hued bays here, reflecting the vast red cliffs and their crowning roofs of Lentisk Prinari, myrtle and sage –
(EL to Fortescue, 20 April 1862, LEL, p.234)

16. EL List: Sweet is the colour of cove and cave
     EL Drawing: Sweet is the color of cove and cave,

16

Sweet is the Color of cove and cave,
(The sea Faires.)

Palaio Kastritza
Corfu:
Greece

THE DYING SWAN

The plain was grassy, wild and bare,
Wide, wild, and open to the air,
Which had built up everywhere
    An under-roof of doleful gray.
With an inner voice the river ran,
Adown it floated a dying swan,
      Which loudly did lament.
   It was the middle of the day.
       Ever the weary wind went on,
    And took the reed-tops as it went.
Some blue peaks in the distance rose,
And white against the cold-white sky,
Shone out their crowning snows.
   One willow over the river wept,
And shook the wave as the wind did sigh;
Above in the wind was the swallow,
Chasing itself at its own wild will,
And far thro' the marish green and still
    The tangled water-courses slept,
Shot over with purple, and green, and yellow.

The wild swan's death-hymn took the soul
Of that waste place with joy
Hidden in sorrow: at first to the ear
The warble was low, and full and clear;
And floating about the under-sky,
Prevailing in weakness, the coronach stole
Sometimes afar, and sometimes anear;
But anon her awful jubilant voice,
With a music strange and manifold,
Flow'd forth on a carol free and bold;
As when a mighty people rejoice
With shawms, and with cymbals, and harps of gold,
And the tumult of their acclaim is roll'd
Thro' the open gates of the city afar,
To the shepherd who watcheth the evening star.
And the creeping mosses and clambering weeds,
And the willow-branches hoar and dank,
And the wavy swell of the soughing reeds,
And the wave-worn horns of the echoing bank,
And silvery marish-flowers that throng
The desolate creeks and pools among,
Were flooded over with eddying song.

17

The plain — *sun* — ——

  (The Dying Swan.)

one willow over the river hung

River Anio.
Campagna di Roma.

Italy

52

17. River Anio, Campagna di Roma, Italy

Tennyson is very much the 'landscape poet' as he creates a setting for the dying swan. He works slowly, with a desolate landscape, towards giving the legendary song its greatest impact on the reader. The poem opens with a wide, wild plain open to an 'under-roof' of grey-clouded air. Horizontal freedom is balanced with vertical restraint: the scene is oddly claustrophobic even with the quietly moving river, the loud lament of the swan, and the 'weary wind' in the reed-tops. In the second stanza blue and snowy mountain peaks rise upwards, breaking the prevailing horizontal line. Coloured marsh plants brighten the ground and, high above, the swallow follows its own wild will, escaping the weeping and sighing of willow and wind. Yet the bird is seen as wilful rather than carefree: the swallow's freedom is not celebrated, but given merely as a contrast to the swan's solemn and ritualistic death.

The minutely detailed scenery becomes, in the last stanza, a backdrop for the amazing song: the 'death-hymn' of the swan. The sound takes '...the soul / Of that waste place with joy / Hidden in sorrow.' The music, low at first, becomes 'awful jubilant' and the landscape is suddenly filled with an almost Biblical image of a 'mighty people' rejoicing, 'With shawms, and with cymbals, and harps of gold.' From their city gates the sound reaches the shepherd and takes over the mosses, weeds, willow-branches, the river, the reeds, the 'marish-flowers' – the whole desolate plain and marsh. Tennyson's strategy at last becomes clear: his bleak unpromising landscape is to be 'flooded over with eddying song'. The scene becomes not beautiful, but renewed, given distinctive life by the swan's last and only song. And that song is in itself a figure for the poet's creativity. He, too, can rouse the music of a 'mighty people' to enliven a desolate scene. But such art asks sacrifices, asks dedication: the swan's eddying song is, in some ways, analogous to the poem in which it appears.

For Lear, the wide plain of the 'dying swan' was the Roman Campagna. From his first visit to Rome in 1837 he loved this strange desolate place with its long line of aqueducts, its tombs, its marshes, its goats and dark buffaloes. The legend of the dying swan's song was immediately comprehensible, and, in his picture, Lear concentrated on the tree and the river, but drew a rather unconvincing swan. His Nonsense is full of birds, sometimes realistic, sometimes in deliberately naïve outline, but after his detailed ornithological work he rarely drew birds in close-up within a scene. His interest may have been caught by the poet's whole landscape, strange as the Campagna, suddenly flooded by undrawable song. And yet the metamorphic song may have seemed an image of Lear's wish to create great and accepted art. He had, of course, set several of Tennyson's poems as songs, and perhaps his own tribute to music gave him immediate insight into the 'eddying song' of the poet's art, which is central to this poem.

17. River Anio, Campagna di Roma

After this about 10 miles of up & down all over the Campagna, I have so often talked of, & which you must cross to get away from Rome. All the while you are getting nearer to the blue mountains, & you see Tivoli perched on a rock a great way up. By degrees the buildings become more distinct & you see quantities of cypress trees – so black – sprinkled about the town. Nearer still – the Campagna is very rugged & dreary, & you cross a queer sulphur stream as white as milk – & of a hideous smell; but shortly afterwards the country becomes cultivated – & you drive through plantations of olives & figs – & all kinds of grain. Then you reach the Anio or Teverone, – the river which runs through Tivoli, & you cross it on a Roman bridge – with a fine tomb; you know the old Romans always built their tombs by the roadside.
(EL to Ann, 3 May 1838)

Very clear and lovely early – resolved to go into the Campagna if possible. Hired a car, 1. horse – : 18 franks the day. G. and I went – to the Alexdre Acqueduct, & then, leaving the carriage – went towards the Appian way, & I drew various times: – but it became cloudy and cold – & it was not easy to draw. – The gloomy = bright width of the Campagna was strangely beautiful: – the silver lit snow of the Lionessa hill when all else so dark, or so deeply blue! – so simple these foregrounds – thistles – brambles – arums: & stones. (D. 11 January 1860)

Nothing could be more lovely than the green green green of the Campagna, & the bright hills, & river, & cattle & trees. (D. 8 May 1860)

17. EL List: One willow over the river hung
    EL Drawing: One willow over the river hung

On the mount, above this line and the title, Lear has written 'The plain – & & – – ' from the first line of the poem.

LOVE AND DEATH

What time the mighty moon was gathering light
Love paced the thymy plots of Paradise,
And all about him roll'd his lustrous eyes;
When turning round a cassia, full in view
Death, walking all alone beneath a yew,
And talking to himself, first met his sight:
'You must begone,' said Death, 'these walks are mine.'
Love wept and spread his sheeny vans for flight;
Yet ere he parted said, 'This hour is thine:
Thou art the shadow of life, and as the tree
Stands in the sun and shadows all beneath,
So in the light of great eternity
Life eminent creates the shade of death;
The shadow passeth when the tree shall fall,
But I shall reign for ever over all.'

as the tree
Stands in the sun, and shadows all beneath,
(Love and Death.)

Barrackpore
Calcutta. India.

18. Barrackpore, Calcutta, India
19. *The Dead Sea, Palestine*

This quasi-sonnet, in Miltonic blank verse, is a contest between Love and Death. There is little description of the Paradise setting – a 'mighty moon', 'thymy plots', a 'cassia' – but in fifteen lines Tennyson clearly reminds us of *Paradise Lost* and Satan lurking in the garden of Eden. The whole anecdote is set in the past, but action and dialogue are given in the present and the poem's resolution looks towards a distant future. Love, walking in Paradise, encounters Death. And Death by his yew, claims the present hours and banishes Love. This is the poem's 'turn': Love weeps, prepares to go, but then begins his counter-claim, his prophecy. He concedes only that Death is the 'shadow of life', like a great tree which keeps the sun from everything beneath it. But in the great light of eternity the shade of Death will finally pass, like the fallen tree which loses all its shadow in the sun. The future belongs to Love whose banishment becomes a triumph in the last line of the poem: 'But I shall reign for ever over all.'

Avoiding any suggestion of Paradise, Lear takes up Love's simile of Death as a shadow and chooses a huge banyan tree, with its great self-rooting branches, from the sketches of his Indian journey. His voyage began late in 1873, and he returned early in 1875. His sight was bad, and his health indifferent: at times the shadow seemed near. Yet in this picture, near the great down-drooping tree, Lear has drawn a couple of elephants; for them the shadow is not sinister, but offers relief from the heat. For the British the tree's shade was a favourite picnicking place. Lear was amazed and enlivened by India: the colour, the foliage, the people, the rivers, the temples, the Taj Mahal. He responded eagerly to Indian contrasts of cold and heat, of crowds and calm places, of varieties of costume and picturesque activity. He watched birds and animals and loved to draw those 'majestikle beastses', the elephants. The ageing artist came back to San Remo with, he claimed, 2,300 drawings. The second illustration, of the Dead Sea, goes back to an earlier journey in 1858. Lear had very much wanted to visit the Holy Land, and the Dead Sea from the Mount of Olives: '...clear pale milky far blue, into farther pale rosy mountains...' (D. 28 March 1858) was a particu-

larly beautiful sight. Was Lear aware of the two contrasting voices which spoke of Death and Love? He knew Tennyson's 'Two Voices' and the poet's usual oscillation between hope and despair. The Dead Sea may have been suggested by 'Death' in the poem, but its beauty associates it with the 'Love' which will reign over all. In the other design, the banyan tree casts a shadow, but far from being deadly, it suggests the vitality of India, and Lear's delighted response to the new exploration which was to be his last.

18. Barrackpore, Calcutta

At 3.30 – State carriages to Ghat – 1st. Viceroy, Miss B. & Hope. – 2nd. I & Miss Foulkes &c. Gorgeous boat, & gorgeous steamer! Immense Commerce & population of Calcutta Ghats – for wh. I was not prepared. Start at 4PM – 4.45. River pretty, later quite lovely, with "Palms & Temples." Exquisite at sunset. Barrackpore by 6. Darky. Evelyn B helps up steps.
(Indian Journal, 27 December 1873)

Make drawing of Banyan till 9. Walk back, pass – apparently a summer house, or picnic place. Nothing to draw here but studies of trees, – but those would be perfect, were study possible. Bkft. Afterwards walk to the supposed Summerhouse, – which is really Lady Canning's tomb, very beautiful, but a sad & strange dream to one who saw so much of her years ago. Talk, & dawdle. Walk to riverside – vultures. Dawdle till 2. Tiffin . . . . At 4, began a drawing of another Banyan. Viceroy says, "Go to Menagerie?" And red men come to lay cloth for tea under tree. So I give up.   (28 December 1873)

Rose before 6. Packed. Off with G. to Banyan tree. Then to the Zoological, & afterwards to the tree close to the house.
    [Many messages about arrangements for breakfast and lunch – the Viceroy and his suite had left at 9.0 a.m.]
    "Good Lord" (as dear Aunt P used to say,) the fuss of Viceregal life!! Then I drew another Banyan tree, & selected other matter, & back to the house at 11, when Bkft.   (29 December 1873)

18. EL List: Stands in the sun, and shadows all beneath
    EL Drawing: as the tree
                   Stands in the sun, and shadows all beneath,

THE BALLAD OF ORIANA

My heart is wasted with my woe,
    Oriana.
There is no rest for me below,
    Oriana.
When the long dun wolds are ribb'd with snow,
And loud the Norland whirlwinds blow,
    Oriana,
Alone I wander to and fro,
    Oriana.

Ere the light on dark was growing,
    Oriana,
At midnight the cock was crowing,
    Oriana:
Winds were blowing, waters flowing,
We heard the steeds to battle going,
    Oriana;
Aloud the hollow bugle blowing,
    Oriana.

In the yew-wood black as night,
    Oriana,
Ere I rode into the fight,
    Oriana,
While blissful tears blinded my sight
By star-shine and by moonlight,
    Oriana,
I to thee my troth did plight,
    Oriana.

She stood upon the castle wall,
    Oriana:
She watch'd my crest among them all,
    Oriana:
She saw me fight, she heard me call,
When forth there stept a foeman tall,
    Oriana,
Atween me and the castle wall,
    Oriana.

The bitter arrow went aside,
    Oriana:
The false, false arrow went aside,
    Oriana:
The damned arrow glanced aside,
And pierced thy heart, my love, my bride,
    Oriana!
Thy heart, my life, my love, my bride,
    Oriana!

Oh! narrow, narrow was the space,
    Oriana.
Loud, loud rung out the bugle's brays,
    Oriana.
Oh! deathful stabs were dealt apace,
The battle deepen'd in its place,
    Oriana;
But I was down upon my face,
    Oriana.

They should have stabb'd me where I lay,
    Oriana!
How could I rise and come away,
    Oriana?
How could I look upon the day?
They should have stabb'd me where I lay,
    Oriana –
They should have trod me into clay,
    Oriana.

Oh! breaking heart that will not break,
    Oriana;
Oh! pale, pale face so sweet and meek,
    Oriana.
Thou smilest, but thou dost not speak,
And then the tears run down my cheek,
    Oriana:
What wantest thou? whom dost thou seek,
    Oriana?

I cry aloud: none hear my cries,
    Oriana.
Thou comest atween me and the skies,
    Oriana.
I feel the tears of blood arise
Up from my heart unto my eyes,
    Oriana.
Within thy heart my arrow lies,
    Oriana.

O cursed hand! O cursed blow!
    Oriana!
O happy thou that liest low,
    Oriana!
All night the silence seems to flow
Beside me in my utter woe,
    Oriana.
A weary, weary way I go,
    Oriana.

When Norland winds pipe down the sea,
    Oriana,
I walk, I dare not think of thee,
    Oriana.
Thou liest beneath the greenwood tree,
I dare not die and come to thee,
    Oriana.
I hear the roaring of the sea,
    Oriana.

20. Kingly Vale, Chichester, England

The background of this poem is Northern darkness, wind and sea. Whatever ballads Tennyson remembered, he created a subtle version of the form. Each stanza has nine lines bisected by a couplet, and five of these lines enclose, with one rhyme, the lamenting refrain of the single name: 'Oriana'. This emphasizes the speaker's misery, his obsessive introspection. The tale begins boldly enough, Oriana and her lover plight their troth in the dark yew wood immediately before he rides into battle. White snow and hints of star- and moon-light bring little relief to the ominous blackness. As the fight rages Oriana watches from the castle wall and her lover's own fatal arrow, meant for a swift foe, glances aside and pierces her heart. The lover, fighting and calling out, seems to have seen Oriana's death, but, struggling towards her, he falls, not dead, but wishing only that he might be trampled on or stabbed. Guilt, weariness, 'utter woe': within the strict pattern of the poem Tennyson acutely circles and probes the feelings of the man who now dare not die. Oriana, under the greenwood tree, is at least allowed to rest.

Lear chose one illustration for this poem, and it is the darkest in the whole set. He reacted to the utterly enclosed blackness of the yew wood where the lovers meet before the battle. In trying to render that ominous darkness Lear's artistic technique failed. The emphatic blackness without a hint of relief in lighter branches, suggests that Lear, trying to achieve a picture which would appear dark enough for monochrome reproduction, ended by eliminating contrasting detail. The result, possibly much overdrawn, is little more than a black rectangle. On the whole Lear is very interested in foliage, and some fine drawing of dark and light branches and leaves survives even into this late set of small illustrations. But his 'Oriana' yew-wood could never have provided a good reproduction: seen here, it emphasizes one of the problems of the set.

20. Kingly Vale, Chichester

At 10.30 walked out to Stoke – & Kingly Vale. There is no prettier walk in England methinx. Those old grand trees – & the subtle = delicate slopes of the down hollowed into shade, & shrubstudded – the 2 kings tombs crowning. – Those yews! – something unearthly of feeling used to pervade this place years ago – but now there are rifle butts – & various signs of modern life. Nevertheless the trees are much the same as when J. Sayers took me there from Midhurst in 1832 or thereabouts.
(D. 16 September 1860)

In 1888, some months after Lear's death, Tennyson saw the yew wood and Hallam wrote:

In August my father and I visited Chichester and Kingly Vale, where is a grove of yews which Mr Lear had sketched for "Oriana"; and we wandered far by the side of the Lavant, and among the beech-feathered coombs in the Downs. Leaning over a gate and looking over the wood he repeated his "Vastness", and "Far, far away," without hesitating for a moment. (*Mem*. II, p.346)

The old Laureate still responded to landscape and started to recite, as Lear would once have started to sketch.

20. EL List: In the yew-wood black as night
     EL Drawing: In the yew=wood black as night,

In the Yew=wood black as night,
(Ballad of Oriana .)

Kingly Vale . Chichester
England.

MARIANA IN THE SOUTH

I

With one black shadow at its feet,
  The house thro' all the level shines,
Close-latticed to the brooding heat,
  And silent in its dusty vines:
A faint-blue ridge upon the right,
  An empty river-bed before,
  And shallows on a distant shore,
In glaring sand and inlets bright.
    But 'Ave Mary,' made she moan,
      And 'Ave Mary,' night and morn,
    And 'Ah,' she sang, 'to be alone,
      To live forgotten, and love forlorn.'

II

She, as her carol sadder grew,
  From brow and bosom slowly down
Thro' rosy taper fingers drew
  Her streaming curls of deepest brown
To left and right, and made appear,
  Still-lighted in a secret shrine,
  Her melancholy eyes divine,
The home of woe without a tear.
    And 'Ave Mary' was her moan,
      'Madonna, sad is night and morn,'
    And 'Ah,' she sang, 'to be all alone,
      To live forgotten, and love forlorn.'

III

Till all the crimson changed, and past
  Into deep orange o'er the sea,
Low on her knees herself she cast,
  Before Our Lady murmur'd she;
Complaining, 'Mother, give me grace
  To help me of my weary load.'
  And on the liquid mirror glow'd
The clear perfection of her face.
    'Is this the form,' she made her moan,
      'That won his praises night and morn?'
    And 'Ah,' she said, 'but I wake alone,
      I sleep forgotten, I wake forlorn.'

IV

Nor bird would sing, nor lamb would bleat,
  Nor any cloud would cross the vault,
But day increased from heat to heat,
  On stony drought and steaming salt;
Till now at noon she slept again,
  And seem'd knee-deep in mountain grass,
  And heard her native breezes pass,
And runlets babbling down the glen.
    She breathed in sleep a lower moan,
      And murmuring, as at night and morn,
    She thought, 'My spirit is here alone,
      Walks forgotten, and is forlorn.'

V

Dreaming, she knew it was a dream:
  She felt he was and was not there.
She woke: the babble of the stream
  Fell, and without the steady glare
Shrank the sick olive sere and small.
  The river-bed was dusty-white;
  And all the furnace of the light
Struck up against the blinding wall.
    She whisper'd, with a stifled moan
      More inward than at night or morn,
    'Sweet Mother, let me not here alone
      Live forgotten and die forlorn.'

VI

And, rising, from her bosom drew
  Old letters, breathing of her worth,
For 'Love,' they said, 'must needs be true,
  To what is loveliest upon earth.'
An image seem'd to pass the door,
  To look at her with slight, and say,
  'But now thy beauty flows away,
So be alone for evermore.'
    'O cruel heart,' she changed her tone,
      'And cruel love, whose end is scorn,
    Is this the end to be left alone,
      To live forgotten, and die forlorn!'

VII

But sometimes in the falling day
  An image seem'd to pass the door,
To look into her eyes and say,
  'But thou shalt be alone no more.'
And flaming downward over all
  From heat to heat the day decreased,
  And slowly rounded to the east
The one black shadow from the wall.
    'The day to night,' she made her moan,
      'The day to night, the night to morn,
    And day and night I am left alone
      To live forgotten, and love forlorn.'

VIII

At eve a dry cicala sung,
  There came a sound as of the sea,
Backward the lattice-blind she flung,
  And lean'd upon the balcony.
There all in spaces rosy-bright
  Large Hesper glitter'd on her tears,
  And deepening thro' the silent spheres
Heaven over Heaven rose the night.
And weeping then she made her moan,
    'The night comes on that knows not morn,
When I shall cease to be all alone,
    To live forgotten, and love forlorn.'

21

Till all the Crimson changed, and past
Into deep orange o'er the sea.
　　(Mariana in the South.)

Pentedátelo · Calabria
　　Italy

22

Till all the Crimson ~~changed~~, & past
Into deep orange o'er the sea.
　(Mariana in the South.)

Calicut. Malabar.
　India

21. Pentedatelo, Calabria, Italy
22. Calicut, Malabar, India

'Mariana in the South' offers another setting for an abandoned and lovesick Mariana. 'It is intended,' wrote Arthur Hallam 'as a kind of pendant to his former poem of "Mariana", the idea of both being the expression of desolate loneliness, but with this distinctive variety in the second, that it paints the forlorn feeling as it would exist under the influence of different impressions of sense'. There is 'a greater lingering on the outward circumstances' than in the former poem, but this does not necessarily make the poem 'too picturesque' (*Mem.* I, pp.500-01). He mounts a complex argument, or tries to, and reaches out to fragments of Greek poetry: it seems that he is trying to still his own doubts about the poem, written in 1830-31 and revised for 1842, which brilliantly evokes the heat and dust between Narbonne and Perpignan. (Arthur Hallam and Tennyson had toured Southern France and the Pyrenees in the summer of 1830.) And in this 'brooding heat' a house looms over its own black shadow, 'close-latticed', silent, shut up against the surrounding landscape of 'dusty vines', 'empty river-bed' and 'glaring sand'. Sunset draws crimson and orange over this deadened scene, but the colour brings no new liveliness to the Southern Mariana with her lamenting 'Ave Mary' and her echoing complaint: 'To live forgotten, and love forlorn.' Tennyson uses a stanza ending in four lines which form a slightly changing refrain, but always insist on 'forgotten' and 'forlorn'. As the flame of sunset and the heat of day recede, the reader is given momentary hope of change. But Mariana merely dreams of cooler, Northern scenery, once her home. Old letters, memories, serve to keep forlorn love alive and, as the day moves into night, leaning 'upon the balcony' looking at the stars, Mariana looks to death to end her loneliness. The girl herself, with 'rosy taper fingers' and 'streaming curls of deepest brown' has a rather clichéd Victorian beauty. But the brooding landscape and the play of light follow convincingly the daily pattern of her despair.

Lear's illustrations transpose the poem's sunset to India and Calabria. The dry white river-beds of his journey to Southern Italy, and the heat that keeps houses locked against the light, the view of the menacing rock of Pentedatelo: these make a fitting setting for this Mariana, and reflect Lear's own fears of being forgotten by friends, of dying (as he did) forlorn. In 1847 Lear toured Calabria and published a journal with lithographs in 1852. His last journey, from his arrival in Bombay in 1873, revealed a new world of colour, heat and foliage. Lear's health and eyesight were failing, but he responded to the new exotic scenes, drew pictures, took on commissions and kept a detailed journal which he did not publish. In 'Mariana in the South', Italy and India interpret Tennyson's Southern France.

In Lear's Calabrian Journal he remembered, but misquoted, this poem. He may have jotted down the lines from memory. Thinking of the dry 'fiumara', it is quite possible that he altered 'the blinding wall' of the original to 'our dazzled eyes' simply because there was no house and the glaring light was reflected back from the white stones of the river bed.

Down, therefore, we went into a new scene – ridges and lines beyond lines of chalky-bright heights, town-crowned heights, and glaringly white fiumaras, a great tract from hill to sea of glitter and arid glare. The picking and stealing of some grapes growing near the burning sandy road seemed a light matter to our parched consciences as we pursued this hottest of walks through the plain, towards the first outworks of the steeps, high on which stood the convent of Bianco; the houses of the town of that name being dotted along a narrow ridge of the whitest of chalk – oh how white! how ultra chalky! We became very cross as we crept on in the scorching sun, and passed along the stony fiumara;–

> *'The river-bed was dusty white,*
> *And all the furnace of the light*
> *Struck up against our dazzled eyes.'*

(towards Sta Agata, Calabrian Journal, August 1847 pp.61-2)

21. Pentedatelo

Leaving the carriage we then struck inland, as the sun was getting low, by mule-routes crossing the frequent fiumaras here joining the sea. On advancing, the views of the wondrous crags of Pentedatilo become astonishingly fine and wild, and as the sun set in crimson glory, displayed a truly magnificent and magical scene of romance...
(Calabrian Journal, 1 September 1847, p.185)

22. Calicut

For the last 10 miles, rice aboundeth, & palms, both Cocoa & Palmyra, & there is a river with sandy banks, and low hills, and distant blue mountains, – all beautiful. Clouds however, seem to threaten rain. Paddy birds. 10.23 Woollopollium: very new and pretty, scenery all about, – no end of green, umbrellas innumerable. Train passes – 3d class, all open plantain leaf umbrellas in the train=boxes. In the fields they look like large Mushrooms. 10.45 Shoranoor. Extreme beauty & luxuriance of foliage – My! behold for the first time the naked breasted females of Malabar!! – 11 AM Flat rice, with tracts of lovely foliage now & then, but generally not so interesting. 11.10 Puttamby. Low near woody hills, & often very pretty bits of scenery. Also Sago palms & Creepers up Palmyra stems. 11.40 cloudy & rain. 12.5 Cootipooram; exquisite bits of Palmery foliage, & universal Umbrellaism. 12.55 – 403d mile (from Madras?) 1 PM Beypore. Get luggage & leave it below, & come upstairs to breakfast on cold meat. The Upper room of the Railway Hotel (or station) overlooks the sea, the sight of which is pleasant; calm all but breakers about some bar, or rocks. 1.55 Off in boat; stair; cross river; very beautiful; carried on shore by coolies. 2 carts, & off at 2.5 PM. Wonderful beauty of villages & lanes, & very surprising undressed females! It was, I think, past 4 when at the end of the grandest tree bordered roads I ever saw, – we reached Calicut Station. Roads of such redundant beauty one could hardly dream of! India Indiaissimo! Every foot was a picture, & the naked breasted women wonderful – (& in the case of the old ones by no means pleasant, –) to see! And men with such hats!! Altogether, a new world my masters!
(Indian Journal, 16 October 1874)

21-22. EL List: Till all the crimson passed and changed
    EL Drawing: Till all the crimson changed, and past
            Into deep orange o'er the sea.
Both drawings the same. The version on the drawings is correct.

From: ELEÄNORE

Thy dark eyes open'd not –
   Nor first reveal'd themselves to English air,
     For there is nothing here,
Which, from the outward to the inward brought,
Moulded thy baby thought.
Far off from human neighbourhood,
   Thou wert born, on a summer morn,
A mile beneath the cedar-wood.
Thy bounteous forehead was not fann'd
   With breezes from our oaken glades,   10
But thou wert nursed in some delicious land
   Of lavish lights, and floating shades:
And flattering thy childish thought
   The oriental fairy brought,
     At the moment of thy birth,
From old well-heads of haunted rills,
And the hearts of purple hills,
   And shadow'd coves on a sunny shore,
    The choicest wealth of all the earth,
   Jewel or shell, or starry ore,   20
   To deck thy cradle, Eleänore.

Or the yellow-banded bees,
Through half-open lattices
Coming in the scented breeze,
   Fed thee, a child, lying alone,
    With whitest honey in fairy gardens cull'd –
A glorious child, dreaming alone,
In silk-soft folds, upon yielding down,
With the hum of swarming bees
   Into dreamful slumber lull'd.   30

Who may minister to thee?
Summer herself should minister
   To thee, with fruitage golden-rinded
   On golden salvers, or it may be,
Youngest Autumn, in a bower
Grape-thicken'd from the light, and blinded
   With many a deep-hued bell-like flower
Of fragrant trailers, when the air
   Sleepeth over all the heaven,
   And the crag that fronts the Even,   40
   All along the shadowing shore,
Crimsons over an inland mere,
     Eleänore!

How may full-sail'd verse express,
   How may measured words adore
    The full-flowing harmony
Of thy swan-like stateliness,
     Eleänore?
    The luxuriant symmetry
Of thy floating gracefulness,   50
     Eleänore?
   Every turn and glance of thine,
   Every lineament divine,
     Eleänore,
   And the steady sunset glow,
   That stays upon thee? For in thee
Is nothing sudden, nothing single;
Like two streams of incense free
   From one censer, in one shrine,
   Thought and motion mingle,   60

23

The Crag that fronts the Even,
All along the shadowy shore.
    (Eleänore.)

Kasr es Saad. Nile.

    Egypt.

Mingle ever. Motions flow
To one another, even as though
They were modulated so
    To an unheard melody,
Which lives about thee, and a sweep
Of richest pauses, evermore
Drawn from each other mellow-deep;
    Who may express thee, Eleänore?

I stand before thee, Eleänore;
    I see thy beauty gradually unfold,   70
Daily and hourly, more and more.
I muse, as in a trance, the while
    Slowly, as from a cloud of gold,
Comes out thy deep ambrosial smile.
I muse, as in a trance, whene'er
    The languors of thy love-deep eyes
Float on to me. I would I were
    So tranced, so rapt in ecstacies,
To stand apart, and to adore,
Gazing on thee for evermore,   80
Serene, imperial Eleänore! ...

... As thunder-clouds that, hung on high,
    Roof'd the world with doubt and fear,
Floating thro' an evening atmosphere,   100
Grow golden all about the sky;
In thee all passion becomes passionless,
Touch'd by thy spirit's mellowness,
Losing his fire and active might
    In a silent meditation,
Falling into a still delight,
    And luxury of contemplation:
As waves that up a quiet cove
    Rolling slide, and lying still

Shadow forth the banks at will;
    Or sometimes they swell and move,
        Pressing up against the land,
        With motions of the outer sea:
            And the self-same influence
            Controlleth all the soul and sense
        Of Passion gazing upon thee.
His bow-string slacken'd, languid Love,
Leaning his cheek upon his hand,
Droops both his wings, regarding thee,
    And so would languish evermore,   120
    Serene, imperial Eleänore.

But when I see thee roam, with tresses unconfined,
While the amorous, odorous wind
    Breathes low between the sunset and the moon;
        Or, in a shadowy saloon,
On silken cushions half-reclined;
        I watch thy grace; and in its place
My heart a charmed slumber keeps,
        While I muse upon thy face;
        And a languid fire creeps   130
        Thro' my veins to all my frame,
Dissolvingly and slowly: soon
        From thy rose-red lips MY name
Floweth; then, as in a swoon,
    With dinning sound my ears are rife,
        My tremulous tongue faltereth,
    I lose my colour, I lose my breath,
    I drink the cup of a costly death,
Brimm'd with delirious draughts of warmest life.
        I die with my delight, before   140
        I hear what I would hear from thee;
    Yet tell my name again to me,
I *would* be dying evermore,
So dying ever, Eleänore.

In Eleänore, Tennyson created a child of the 'warm south'. He set her to grow to 'swan-like stateliness' in a 'delicious land' of sun, summer, fruit and flowers. The landscapes are often finely described; the girl herself is quite disembodied; the speaker's feelings in the last verse are those of the idealizing adolescent. 'Eleänore', like 'Lilian' or 'Madeline', is about the worship of beauty, but without the tension of relationship. In 'Mariana' and 'The Lady of Shalott' the sense of frustration and loss shows how deeply Tennyson could write, in 1842, of some of the turmoil of human feeling.

Eleänore, then, watched over by an 'oriental fairy', lives in a magically protected summer scene. Even the 'crag that fronts the Even' offers no boundary, no resistance. The cliff 'crimsons' over an island lake as the sun sets, but darkness never intrudes. In the last stanza, gazed on, and gazing, Eleänore breathes the speaker's name, causing him to die of delight. In this early poem it is not the imagined girl but her surroundings which suggest the sensuous warmth, ease, ripeness which have

moulded beauty. Lear, moved by southern light and warmth, chose as illustrations scenes from Egypt and the gentler landscapes of Albania. The 'crag that fronts the Even' is, paradoxically, a warm scene; it is softened by the evening light and the low 'crag' touched by the colour of sunset. An Egyptian scene, this was one of the first five oil paintings, planned as a group, which Lear began in the first stages of the Tennyson Illustration project. The design was repeated, in oil again, in water-colour, and in monochrome versions. There are no figures, and certainly no Eleänore, as there might have been in the Pre-Raphaelite Illustrated Tennyson of 1857. One oil painting shows a line of cliffs, low, without sharpness, and deep pink in the evening sun. A flight of birds breaks the horizontal line very lightly, and gives the design fluency, linking earth and sky.

Lear gave this short poem three other illustrations, Albanian scenes. Lago Luro, with shadowy trees and soft foliage is contrasted with two views of Joannina. The city, beautifully sited, precise in outline, has tall mosques rising under near impressionistic clearing thunder-clouds. These are all good designs, finely drawn, and copied from similar successful views. Tennyson's description, not his heroine, found a parallel in the sensuousness of Lear's chosen landscapes.

24

The Crag that fronts the Even,
All along the shadowy shore.
(Eleänore)

Lake of Luro. Epirus.
Albania

23. Kasr es Saad

At 11.35 – getting near the Kasr es Saad cliffs: I see the identical spot of palmy boskiness from wh. I made a drawing – afterwards done out at Nice & eventually sold to EW Browne – I think you have generally painted your Doms too green – not baked – dry – dusty enough: the ends of many of the Fans, & many whole ones should be more golden – okery red. – Also there should be more gold in your Date Palm ends. 11.45. – A new & most beastly factory – lo! just in the midst of my Doms & Dates & blocking out the beautiful Gebel!! – "The Crag that fronts the Even". Sit on upper deck... & meditate as I look on the old place of 1854 – Jany 17 & 18 – & Feby 25-26-27. What changes since those days!! – yet all here seems unchanged.... The value of the 2nd Nile Voyage should be 3 fold to me. 1st by the renewing & strengthening of the impressions of 1854. 2nd the being able to mark a mental & moral improvement since then: & 3rd the gain of a set of Nubian subjects.   (D. 14 January 1867)

15 miles from Kenneh. Disnee.
Here we are you see, after all not so far forward as we thought to be. We have had no wind today – or only against us, so that we have been pulled by the rope all day long: – for my part, I find this very pleasant work as I live on shore, walking slowly & sitting on the bank waiting for the boat & there is always something to look at. Last night, we arrived at one of the most beautiful places I ever saw

– Kasr el Saadd. I am quite bewildered when I think how little people talk of the scenery of the Nile – because they pass it while sleeping I believe. Imagine immense cliffs, quite perpendicular about as high as St. Paul's & of yellow stone – rising from the most exquisite meadows all along the river! while below them are villages almost hidden in palms. In returning, I hope to pass a day or 2 at least at Kasr el Saadd – for it is one of the most beautiful spots in the world.   (EL to Ann, 17 January 1854)

24. Lake of Luro

I am off by half-past five. The morning is bright, and the nightingales, who have warbled all night long, are as melodious as ever. In spite of my regret at not having been able to see Zalongo or Cassope, I shall remember the green hills of Kamarina with pleasure.

I descend through woodland glades, with views of the Gulf of Arta ever before me, and the peaks of its fine mountains are wrapped in rolling mist. Lower down, towards the plain, the route winds among groups of oak and walnut trees, and below them are shepherds with their flocks. In about two or three hours we reach Luro, a scattered collection of huts, with one or two better houses at the foot of the hills, and following the track at their base, shortly arrive at clear springs, and a quiet secluded lake, fringed with luxuriant foliage, and resounding with the notes of the nightingale and the cuckoo.

All the country hereabouts resembles the most beautiful

63

25

Thunder clouds that, hung on high,
Roof'd the world with doubt and fear,
(Eleänore.)

Joánnina. Epirus.
Albania

park or woodland scenery in England, excepting that the variety of underwood is greater, and the creepers and flowering shrubs are such as we have not. The tall white stems of the ash and plane shooting out of dark masses of oak foliage, and reflected in the clear water below, form charming pictures.

In the midst of this delightful bosky region, at an hour's distance from Luro, stands Kanza, a hamlet of a few very poor thatched huts; and from hence, keeping always through a thick and shady wood, which skirts the base of the hills, the route passes onward, till it emerges (after two hours' ride from Kanza) on to an elevated pasture land, opposite the Castle of Rogus; and here I halt for mid-day rest.

This fortress, standing on an ancient site, forms a part of one of those beautiful Greek scenes which a painter is never tired of contemplating. Rising on its mound above the thick woods, which here embellish the plain, it is the key of the landscape; the waters of a clear fountain are surrounded by large flocks of goats reposing. The clumps of hanging plane and spreading oak, vary the marshy plain, extending to the shores of the Gulf; while the distant blue mountains rise beyond, and the rock of Zalongo shuts in the northern end of the prospect. All these form so many parts, each beautiful in itself, that combine to make a composition, to which I regretted not being able to devote more time.

After a short repose, I pursued my journey across the plain in the direction of Arta, where I intend to pass the night. We soon cross the Luro, on a narrow bridge, and so unstable as to allow of but one horse passing it at a time,

and then we follow the track across the wide level. During this morning's ride I have seen upwards of twenty large vultures; but now, the ornithological denizens of this wide tract of marshy ground are storks, which are walking about in great numbers, and their nests are built on the roofs of the houses, clustered here and there in the more cultivated part of the district. Snakes and tortoises also were frequent during the morning, concerning which last animals Andrea volunteers some scientific intelligence, assuring me that in Greece it is a well-known fact that they hatch their eggs by the heat of their eyes, looking fixedly at them, until the small tortoises are matured, and break the shell.
(Albanian Journal, 3 May 1849, pp. 348-51)

25. Joannina, Epirus

On Andrea joining me with the horses, we made the best of our way to Ioannina in pouring rain, which never ceased until we were near the lake, when Pindus, glittering in silvery snow, peeped forth from clouds, and all the wide meadows south of the city were flocked with numberless white storks.

Before eleven I reach Ioannina, and am once more at the hospitable vice-consulate, where Signor Damaschino and his family have arrived a few days back from Prevyza.

Three days passed at Ioannina, but with constant interruptions from showers. The mornings are brilliant, but clouds gather on Mitzikeli about nine or ten, and from noon to three or four, thunder and pouring rain ensues. The air is extremely cold, and whereas at Parga I could only bear the lightest clothing, I am here too glad to wear a double capote, and half the night am too cold to sleep.

Apart from the friendly hospitality of the Damaschino family, a sojourn at Ioannina is great pleasure, and were it possible, I would gladly pass a summer here. It is not easy to appreciate the beauty of this scenery in a hasty visit; the outlines of the mountains around are too magnificent to be readily reducible to the rules of art, and the want of foliage on the plain and hills may perhaps at first give a barren air to the landscape. It is only on becoming conversant with the groups of trees and buildings, picturesque in themselves, and which combine exquisitely with small portions of the surrounding hills, plain, or lake, that an artist perceives the inexhaustible store of really beautiful forms with which Ioannina abounds.

During these days time passed rapidly away, for there was full employment for every hour; one moment I would sit on the hill which rises west of the city, whence the great mountain of Mitzikeli on the eastern side of the lake is seen most nobly: at another, I would move with delight from point to point among the southern suburbs, from which the huge ruined fortress of Litharitza, with many a silvery mosque and dark cypress, form exquisite pictures: or watch from the walls of the ruin itself, the varied effects of cloud or sunbeam passing over the blue lake, now shadowing the promontory of the kastron or citadel, now gilding the little island at the foot of majestic Mitzikeli. Then I would linger on the northern outskirts of the town, whence its long line constitutes a small part of a landscape whose sublime horizon is varied by mountain forms of the loftiest and most beautiful character, or by wandering in the lower ground near the lake, I would enjoy the placid solemnity of the dark waters reflecting the great mosque and battlements of the citadel as in a mirror. I was never tired of walking out into the spacious plain on each side of the town, where immense numbers of cattle enlivened the scene, and milk-white storks paraded leisurely in quest of food: or I would take a boat and cross to the little island, and visit the monastery, where that most wondrous man Ali Pasha met his death: or sitting by the edge of the lake near the southern side of the kastron, sketch the massive, mournful ruins of his palace of Litharitza, with the peaks of Olytzika rising beyond. For hours I could loiter on the terrace of the kastron opposite the Pasha's serai, among the ruined fortifications, or near the strange gilded tomb where lies the body of the man who for so long a time made thousands tremble! It was a treat to watch the evening deepen the colours of the beautiful northern hills, or shadows creeping up the furrowed sides of Mitzikeli.
(Albanian Journal, 11, 12, 13 May 1849, pp. 380-83)

23. EL List: Like the crag that fronts the evening
    EL Drawing: The Crag that fronts the Even,
                All along the shadowy shore.
24. EL List: Crimsons over an inland mere
    EL Drawing: The Crag that fronts the Even,
                All along the shadowy shore.
25. EL List: Thunderclouds, that, hung on high,
    EL Drawing: Thunderclouds that, hung on high,
                Roof'd the world with doubt and fear.

From: THE MILLER'S DAUGHTER

... I loved, and love dispell'd the fear
    That I should die an early death: 90
For love possess'd the atmosphere,
    And fill'd the breast with purer breath.
My mother thought, What ails the boy?
    For I was alter'd, and began
To move about the house with joy,
    And with the certain step of man.

I loved the brimming wave that swam
    Thro' quiet meadows round the mill,
The sleepy pool above the dam,
    The pool beneath it never still,   100
The meal-sacks on the whiten'd floor,
    The dark round of the dripping wheel,
The very air about the door
    Made misty with the floating meal.

And oft in ramblings on the wold,
    When April nights began to blow,
And April's crescent glimmer'd cold,
    I saw the village lights below;
I knew your taper far away,
    And full at heart of trembling hope,   110
From off the wold I came, and lay
    Upon the freshly-flower'd slope.

The deep brook groan'd beneath the mill;
    And 'by that lamp,' I thought, 'she sits!'
The white chalk-quarry from the hill
    Gleam'd to the flying moon by fits.
'O that I were beside her now!
    O will she answer if I call?
O would she give me vow for vow,
    Sweet Alice, if I told her all?'   120

Sometimes I saw you sit and spin;
    And, in the pauses of the wind,
Sometimes I heard you sing within;
    Sometimes your shadow cross'd the blind;
At last you rose and moved the light,
    And the long shadow of the chair
Flitted across into the night,
    And all the casement darken'd there.

But when at last I dared to speak,
    The lanes, you know, were white with may,   130
Your ripe lips moved not, but your cheek
    Flush'd like the coming of the day;
And so it was – half-sly, half-shy,
    You would, and would not, little one!
Although I pleaded tenderly,
    And you and I were all alone ....

27

The white chalk quarry from the hill
Gleamed,
    (The Miller's daughter.)

Arundel.
England

... A trifle, sweet! which true love spells –
    True love interprets – right alone.
His light upon the letter dwells,
    For all the spirit is his own.
So, if I waste words now, in truth   190
    You must blame Love. His early rage
Had force to make me rhyme in youth,
    And makes me talk too much in age.

And now those vivid hours are gone,
    Like mine own life to me thou art,
Where Past and Present, wound in one,
    Do make a garland for the heart:
So sing that other song I made,   200
    Half-anger'd with my happy lot,
The day, when in the chestnut shade
    I found the blue Forget-me-not.

        Love that hath us in the net,
        Can he pass, and we forget?
        Many suns arise and set.
        Many a chance the years beget.
        Love the gift is Love the debt.
            Even so.
        Love is hurt with jar and fret.
        Love is made a vague regret.   210
        Eyes with idle tears are wet.
        Idle habit links us yet.
        What is love? for we forget:
            Ah, no! no!

Look thro' mine eyes with thine. True wife,
    Round my true heart thine arms entwine;
My other dearer life in life,
    Look thro' my very soul with thine!
Untouch'd with any shade of years,
    May those kind eyes for ever dwell!   220
They have not shed a many tears,
    Dear eyes, since first I knew them well.

Yet tears they shed: they had their part
    Of sorrow: for when time was ripe,
The still affection of the heart
    Became an outward breathing type,
That into stillness past again,
    And left a want unknown before;
Although the loss had brought us pain,
    That loss but made us love the more,   230

With farther lookings on. The kiss,
    The woven arms, seem but to be
Weak symbols of the settled bliss,
    The comfort, I have found in thee:
But that God bless thee, dear – who wrought
    Two spirits to one equal mind –
With blessings beyond hope or thought,
    With blessings which no words can find.

Arise, and let us wander forth,
    To yon old mill across the wolds;   240
For look, the sunset, south and north,
    Winds all the vale in rosy folds,
And fires your narrow casement glass,
    Touching the sullen pool below:
On the chalk-hill the bearded grass
    Is dry and dewless. Let us go.

27. Arundel, [Sussex], England
28. *Narni, Italy*

'The Miller's Daughter' is one of the so-called 'English Idylls', written in 1832 and much revised for the 1842 volumes. It was admired as a series of familiar, domestic scenes which centred on a happy marriage between the speaker and the charmingly modest English Alice. This was one of the poems which showed Tennyson in touch with ordinary life, not luxuriating in the passion of Fatima, the despair of Œnone, the distant beauties of Lilian or Eleänore. The poem is a recollection which begins with a vignette of the wealthy, genial miller, and places the speaker as socially distinct: the orphan of the squire. But the miller is given 'a slow wise smile', a solid sense of being able to deal with the world and yet retain a soul 'full of summer warmth'. He is a perfect father-figure for Alice and is idealized, as good English yeoman stock, by the speaker who remembers himself as 'the long and listless boy' in the old mansion. Slowly the squire's son tells the tale of his courtship set in an English country scene with mill-dam and pond, stepping-stones, flag-flowers, chestnut trees. The 'dripping wheel' turns; outside the house the would-be lover catches a glimpse of Alice spinning, hears her singing, or watches her shadow as she finally moves her lamp. The details of quiet domestic life fill out the narrative which is given a hint of drama when the suitor's mother (added in 1842) complains he is too young to wed and moreover he might have looked higher. But the timid and ever-charming Alice wins round her future mother-in-law. The idyll continues peacefully, describing, after the nervous feeling of early love, the settled maturity of an ideal marriage partnership: 'Where Past and Present, wound in one, / Do make a garland for the heart'.

Two songs, inserted among the regular stanzas, help to bring out the changing tone of the poem. The first is a weaving song, the second a half angry, half fearful questioning of whether or not love has become idle habit; the answer given is 'no!' The second song has its 'idle tears' which so strangely, in another poem, express feelings, almost unidentifiable, yet shared by Tennyson and Lear. But tears are dismissed, and the past moves smoothly into the present with the couple's decision to visit the mill as sunset colours the valley, the old casement, and the 'sullen pool below'.

The poem is mostly serene and sometimes sentimental, but it may have suggested to Lear the ideal relationship for which he always yearned. His long friendship with Franklin Lushington was never so strong on Lushington's side as it was on Lear's. This made it particularly vulnerable to change (for instance, Lushington's marriage) and absence. Lear's feeling for Augusta (Gussie) Bethell may have been reciprocated, but Lear never found out. He worried about his life, his illness. He was nervous, uncertain, delaying (as well as often travelling), and Gussie finally married Adamson Parker, a man much older than Lear. A fantasy of settled marriage haunts Lear's Nonsense and even in 1887 he wondered, and still wondered, if he should propose to the widowed Gussie. But he did not, and, though he often comments on the marriage of friends and acquaintances, we cannot know why he chose the marriage of 'The Miller's Daughter' for his Tennyson list.

Lear took an Italian sunset for illustration to the poem's last stanza. The 'white chalk quarry', by contrast, is one of the few English scenes among these late Tennyson Illustrations. Lear catches together his own past and present by drawing Arundel Mill, which he visited as a child when he went to stay with his sister, Sarah Street. In a letter to Emily Tennyson in the early 1850s (n.d.) he said he was resolved

> on not *doing anything like "the Moated Grange" or "the 7 elms the poplars 6" from spots near or similar to those said to be the ones T. has described. The Mill I transfer to Sussex, and so on with others – for I don't want to be a sort of pictorial Boswell, but to be able to reproduce lines of poetry in form and color.*

As for Tennyson, he maintained that he did not have any particular mill in mind, but if at all, it was the Mill at Trumpington, near Cambridge (*Mem.* I, pp. 117-18). For Lear, Arundel Mill brought back the past, winding it into the present: as a man he had not lost the enjoyment of the countryside after travel from London, or the melancholy of a weak-sighted, lonely, sensitive boy.

In a fragment of a letter to his future wife, Emily Sellwood, Tennyson claims: 'Dim mystic sympathies with tree and hill reaching far back into childhood. A known landskip is to me an old friend, that continually talks to me of my own youth and half-forgotten things, and indeed does more for me than many an old friend that I know' (*Mem.* I, p. 172). For Lear, too, 'a known landskip' remained in the memory, its associations giving life to drawing and painting or illustration for a Tennyson poem.

27. Arundel

Arundel station at 12.30 – walked thence down the hill – passing J.L. of Lyminster, the old Blake House – & Brookfield – & quite to the old mill by the river, whence I walked all along the old walk – across to "brooks" – & up the chalk pit to Burpham, – & there I saw the church, & the tombs &c. &c. Peppering is green and merry – 4 nice little girls, the youngest a very nice child. Robert in better health than I expected – a sterling good man, as his father before him. Mr R.D.D. [Drewitt] seems to me also much improved. – What an absurd dream of time!
(D. 15 September 1860)

27. EL List: The white chalk quarry from the hill
    EL Drawing: The white chalk quarry from the hill
                Gleamed,

FATIMA

I

O Love, Love, Love! O withering might!
O sun, that from thy noonday height
Shudderest when I strain my sight,
Throbbing thro' all thy heat and light,
  Lo, falling from my constant mind,
  Lo, parch'd and wither'd, deaf and blind,
  I whirl like leaves in roaring wind.

II

Last night I wasted hateful hours
Below the city's eastern towers:
I thirsted for the brooks, the showers:
I roll'd among the tender flowers:
  I crush'd them on my breast, my mouth:
  I look'd athwart the burning drouth
  Of that long desert to the south.

III

Last night, when some one spoke his name,
From my swift blood that went and came
A thousand little shafts of flame
Were shiver'd in my narrow frame.
  O Love, O fire! once he drew
  With one long kiss my whole soul thro'
  My lips, as sunlight drinketh dew.

IV

Before he mounts the hill, I know
He cometh quickly: from below
Sweet gales, as from deep gardens, blow
Before him, striking on my brow.
  In my dry brain my spirit soon,
  Down-deepening from swoon to swoon,
  Faints like a dazzled morning moon.

V

The wind sounds like a silver wire,
And from beyond the noon a fire
Is pour'd upon the hills, and nigher
The skies stoop down in their desire;
  And, isled in sudden seas of light,
  My heart, pierced thro' with fierce delight,
  Bursts into blossom in his sight.

VI

My whole soul waiting silently,
All naked in a sultry sky,
Droops blinded with his shining eye:
I *will* possess him or will die.
  I will grow round him in his place,
  Grow, live, die looking on his face,
  Die, dying clasp'd in his embrace.

Below the city's Eastern towers,
(Fatima.)

Constantinople.
Turkey.

29. Constantinople, Turkey

'Fatima' is a poem of longing. A fragment of Sappho, a tale from Savary's *Letters on Egypt*, and *The Arabian Nights* are among the sources which combined with Tennyson's own adolescent eroticism. In 'Eleänore' for instance, the heroine is worshipped from afar, but in 'Fatima' we hear nothing but Fatima's own words voicing her almost uncontrollable passion. The exotic setting, heat, sultry sky, accentuate her desperate feeling as she waits for her lover, 'I will possess him or will die.' The opposition of passion or death is a wild fantasy suitable to the heroine of an Eastern tale. Fatima is no shy Miller's Daughter or languorous Eleänore; her desire is uninhibitedly active, even predatory:

> I will grow round him in his place,
> Grow, live, die, looking on his face,
> Die, dying clasp'd in his embrace.

Through her, Tennyson can safely express his own youthful love-longing; his own wish to possess.

By the 1880s, when Lear's illustrations were finalized into a set, he had no hopes of passion or possession: he longed only to temper intense loneliness with friendship. In any case, he drew the obvious place for an exotic tale: Constantinople. This archetypal Eastern city, with its secret harems, its mosques, minarets and palaces, had struck Lear with its strangeness and beauty. When he first approached it by ship on 1 August 1848, he was ill with fever and confined to his cabin, yet he still climbed on the deck at sunrise to view the great ruined walls, the white minarets and the magnificent foliage of cypress, pine and plane. He went to the Embassy at Therapia, and the Ambassador's wife looked after him and staved off his fever with tea, chicken and thin slices of bread and butter. Once well again, Lear flung himself at Constantinople, taking in the Sultan's procession, the dignitaries at the 'foot kissing ceremony' at the Seraglio, the mosques, the burial grounds, the bazaar. It was the gorgeous East, rather than a love-lorn Fatima, which appealed to Lear. *The Journals of a Landscape Painter in Albania &c.* begins when the artist left Constantinople on a steamer bound for Salonica. From there, frustrated in his first attempt to visit Mount Athos – the peninsula was cut off to avoid a spreading cholera epidemic – Lear decided to travel to Macedonia and Albania. He describes how he finally left Constantinople, steaming into the 'Sea of Marmora', and looking back at the city with its Eastern towers, and Eastern dreams.

29. Constantinople

First though let me tell you that I am immensely stronger & better – indeed quite well now; the weather is again delightful –, Monday the 28th I took a long walk, but Tuesday, the first day of the Bairum or 3 day's fete after the 28 day's fast – is the subject of this page. On returning on Monday evening – Lady Canning told me they were all going to Constantinople in their own steamer – to see the Sultan go in procession to & from the Mosque of St Sophia – & also that they were permitted (I believe the first Christians ever allowed to do so) to see the great ceremony of "foot kissing" in the second court of the Seraglio. If I could rise at 4 I would go too – & so I determined to try. Before 5 next morning – (30th) we

were all on board – & the Bosphorus – which I have quite changed my opinion about – really was delightful. I only saw it before when so ill I could not admire anything – but now the hills covered with pine & cypress – & the innumerable villas & palaces on the water's edge quite delight me. As we came near the city – it is astonishing what a beautiful effect all the snow white domes & minarets have rising from the water; there can be no place so strange & lovely. We were stunned by salutes of cannon on arriving, & too glad to get on shore – where 6 guards met us – & our own 2 – made a fierce party. The Ambassador's family never move out without one of these guards – Kwass – a state of magnificence – rather tiresome than otherwise. Constantinople is more oriental in character than Pera the Frank quarter, & the customs are more picturesque. The streets are narrow but far cleaner than I had expected. We walked up – & just outside the Seraglio walls some beautiful groves of cypress pleased me greatly. The enormous pile of building called "Seraglio" is the work of hundreds of years – & many Caliphs – it stands where the old Byzantium emperors had their palace. First we entered the court no 1. where a double line of military were drawn up in order from the gate to the Mosque, & that of the 2nd. court. All around were immense numbers of horses & grooms; the dressings & housings of the horses rich beyond description. We had only just time to rush up into a room close to the gate the Sultan returns by, when the procession began; I was close to the window & saw everything capitally. First came scores & scores & scores of officers of state – generals etc. etc. on superb horses – whose hangings of velvet & gold beat anything I ever saw. The generals themselves are in modern uniform – but with many jewels. Pages & grooms – (who spoil the effect of the procession by not keeping in line as the horses prance about,) walk by each horse, – & at intervals walk Masters of Ceremonies in scarlet & gold. After this lasted a long time – there was a space – & then came 2 by 2 on horse back – all the Pashas – (there is a great silence in all this – & it is very like a funeral for solemnity.) The Pashas have a magnificent bunch of diamonds in their scarlet caps – & their blue uniform is most richly embroidered in gold. It was very interesting to see many well known persons – such as Rifat Pasha – Halil Pasha – the Levarkier – & above all Raschid Pasha the present Grand Vizier – who rode last of all. A long space followed. Then 3 fine horses – all strapped with gold & silver – then a long space again – & dead silence; & lastly – surrounded by scarlet and gold dressed guards, with halberds or pikes, & and carrying most wonderous crescent like plumes of green and white feathers – rode the Grand Seignor himself as if he were in a grove of beautiful birds.

(EL to Ann, 27 August 1848)

The best embarking point is Tophana – & there we got a broad boat – not a Caique – & set off to the Seraglio point – which I had greatly resolved to draw. Such a strange mixture of domes, spires, towers, straight – square – round – & octogan houses, cypresses – planes – & pine trees surely never was seen! – Reflected in the water – the effect is enchanting – but it was very difficult to get the least idea of it from a boat as the current kept changing ones position. We rode afterwards all along the walls – & I got a view of Santa Sophia & the Seraglio, – & another of Sultan Achmet Mosque & St. Sophia. St. Sophia is very unlike

what I had expected – I don't know why; it is a cream colour – with reddish stripes!! & the domes are gray – & the minarets silver white!! but certainly though the square bases and round tops seem odd at first – its general appearance is wonderfully grand & light. It is under repair at present so I have not seen inside – nor much of the outside. Sultan Achmet is nearly as big – & more taking from its milk white splendour. It is the only mosque with 6 minarets. But Suleiman – bye & bye to be described is the wonder of all. Pursuing our voyage – beneath the aged & ruined walls – there is no object of interest for a long time – the vastness of the city is impressive, & that's all. – Besides I began to grow very sick as the sea got more rough – & greatly was I glad when at one o'clock we were landed at the corner of Stamboul – by the 7 towers – a huge fortress now used as a prison. – Bo! they are putting out the candles – good night. I must go to bed.
(EL to Ann, 9 September 1848)

I am silent, from much thought, and some weakness consequent on long illness: and the extra cargo in the lower deck are silent also – perhaps because they have not room to talk. At four, the anchor is weighed, and we begin to paddle away from the many domed mosques and bright minarets of Constantinople, and the gay sides of the Golden Horn, with its caiques and its cypresses towering against the deepening blue sky, when lo! we do not turn towards the sea, but proceed ignominiously to tow a great coal-ship all the way to Buyukdere, so there is a moving panorama of all the Bosphorus bestowed on us gratis, – Kandili, Baltaliman, Bebek, Yenikoi, Therapia, with its well-known walks and pines and planes, and lastly Buyukdere, where we leave our dingy charge and return, evening darkening over the Giant's Hill, Unkiar Skelessi, Anatoli Hissar, till we sail forth into the broad Sea of Marmora, leaving Scutari and the towers of wonderful Stamboul first pale and distinct in the light of the rising moon, and then glittering and lessening on the calm horizon, till they, and the memory that I have been among them for seven weeks, seem alike part of the world of dreams.
(Albanian Journal, 9 September 1848, pp. 14-15)

29. EL List:　　　Beneath the city's eastern towers
　　EL Drawing: Below the city's eastern towers,

From: ŒNONE

There lies a vale in Ida, lovelier
Than all the valleys of the Ionian hills.
The swimming vapour slopes athwart the glen,
Puts forth an arm, and creeps from pine to pine,
And loiters, slowly drawn. On either hand
The lawns and meadow-ledges midway down
Hang rich in flowers, and far below them roars
The long brook falling thro' the clov'n ravine
In cataract after cataract to the sea.
Behind the valley topmost Gargarus   10
Stands up and takes the morning: but in front
The gorges, opening wide apart, reveal
Troas and Ilion's column'd citadel,
The crown of Troas.

           Hither came at noon
Mournful Œnone, wandering forlorn
Of Paris, once her playmate on the hills.
Her cheek had lost the rose, and round her neck
Floated her hair or seem'd to float in rest.
She, leaning on a fragment twined with vine,
Sang to the stillness, till the mountain-shade   20
Sloped downward to her seat from the upper cliff.

'O mother Ida, many-fountain'd Ida,
Dear mother Ida, harken ere I die.
For now the noonday quiet holds the hill:
The grasshopper is silent in the grass:
The lizard, with his shadow on the stone,
Rests like a shadow, and the cicala sleeps.
The purple flowers droop: the golden bee
Is lily-cradled: I alone awake.
My eyes are full of tears, my heart of love,   30
My heart is breaking, and my eyes are dim,
And I am all aweary of my life....

  ... 'Dear mother Ida, harken ere I die.
He smiled, and opening out his milk-white palm
Disclosed a fruit of pure Hesperian gold,
That smelt ambrosially, and while I look'd
And listen'd, the full-flowing river of speech
Came down upon my heart.

               '"My own Œnone,
Beautiful-brow'd Œnone, my own soul,
Behold this fruit, whose gleaming rind ingrav'n   70
'For the most fair,' would seem to award it thine,
As lovelier than whatever Oread haunt
The knolls of Ida, loveliest in all grace
Of movement, and the charm of married brows."

'Dear mother Ida, harken ere I die.
He prest the blossom of his lips to mine,
And added "This was cast upon the board,
When all the full-faced presence of the Gods

Ranged in the halls of Peleus; whereupon
Rose feud, with question unto whom 'twere due: 80
But light-foot Iris brought it yester-eve,
Delivering, that to me, by common voice
Elected umpire, Here comes to-day,
Pallas and Aphrodite, claiming each
This meed of fairest. Thou, within the cave
Behind yon whispering tuft of oldest pine,
Mayst well behold them unbeheld, unheard
Hear all, and see thy Paris judge of Gods."...

  ... 'Dear mother Ida, harken ere I die.
She with a subtle smile in her mild eyes,   180
The herald of her triumph, drawing nigh
Half-whisper'd in his ear, "I promise thee
The fairest and most loving wife in Greece."
She spoke and laugh'd: I shut my sight for fear:
But when I look'd, Paris had raised his arm,
And I beheld great Here's angry eyes,
As she withdrew into the golden cloud,
And I was left alone within the bower;
And from that time to this I am alone,
And I shall be alone until I die....   190

  ... 'O mother, hear me yet before I die.
They came, they cut away my tallest pines –
My tall dark pines, that plumed the craggy ledge
High over the blue gorge, or lower down
Green-gulfed Ida, all between
The snowy peak and snow-white cataract
Foster'd the callow eaglet – from beneath
Whose thick mysterious boughs in the dark morn
The panther's roar came muffled, while I sat   210
Low in the valley. Never, never more
Shall lone Œnone see the morning mist
Sweep thro' them; never see them overlaid
With narrow moon-lit slips of silver cloud,
Between the loud stream and the trembling stars....

  ... 'O mother, hear me yet before I die.
Hath he not sworn his love a thousand times,
In this green valley, under this green hill,
Ev'n on this hand, and sitting on this stone?
Seal'd it with kisses? water'd it with tears?   230
O happy tears, and how unlike to these!
O happy Heaven, how canst thou see my face?
O happy earth, how canst thou bear my weight?
O death, death, death, thou ever-floating cloud,
There are enough unhappy on this earth,
Pass by the happy souls, that love to live:
I pray thee, pass before my light of life,
And shadow all my soul, that I may die.
Thou weighest heavy on the heart within,
Weigh heavy on my eyelids: let me die....   240

There lies a vale in Ida, lovelier
Than all the vallies of Ionian Hills.
(Œnóne)

from Mount Ida
Asia Minor.

...   'O mother, hear me yet before I die.
Hear me, O earth. I will not die alone,
Lest their shrill happy laughter come to me
Walking the cold and starless road of Death
Uncomforted, leaving my ancient love
With the Greek woman. I will rise and go
Down into Troy, and ere the stars come forth
Talk with the wild Cassandra, for she says
A fire dances before her, and a sound   260
Rings ever in her ears of armed men.
What this may be I know not, but I know
That, wheresoe'er I am by night and day,
All earth and air seem only burning fire.'

30. From Mount Ida, Asia Minor
31. *Phyle, Attica, Greece*
32. Bavella, Corsica
33. *Bavella, Corsica*

In this poem Tennyson brings together classical myth and classical lament. Allusions to Ovid and Theocritus, among other classical writers, give weight to what is mainly a dramatic monologue in blank verse. The speaker is Œnone, a nymph abandoned by Paris when he chooses to give the golden apple to Aphrodite, goddess of love. In return Aphrodite offers him the fairest wife in Greece. Paris has shown the apple to his love, Œnone, and urged her to watch him make choice

between the three goddesses. Hidden in a grove, Œnone sees Paris reject the power of Here, begs him to accept the wisdom of Pallas Athene, and recognizes her fate as he gives the apple to Aphrodite, supreme in beauty. The well-known tale is told entirely from Œnone's point of view, and her grief, well nurtured, fills the whole poem. She does not exercise the wisdom she urges on Paris: 'Self-reverence, self-knowledge, self-control', but in her long lament, she returns again and again to a death-wishing refrain: 'Dear mother Ida, hearken ere I die.' But she lives on, and decides to go down to Troy and consult the prophetess Cassandra. From her Œnone will learn of a disastrous future: of Helen and the Trojan war. But this poem ends with uncertainty – a lament for lost love which is tinged with hints of violence, hints of horror.

Œnone is narrator and chorus of her own story. But neither she, nor the other humans or gods, are given much individual character. They enact a ritual, and the nymph's sense of anger and grief does not emerge as more than part of that ritual. The individuality of the poem lies in the descriptions of Mount Ida: the highly pictorial landscapes provide a background for narrated action and lament. The woods and misty groves of the mountain, the rocks and flowing waters, the details of flowers and rich vegetation – these are the work of a skilled observer and poet of landscape. Even in his earliest poems, Tennyson could make the outward setting part of his meaning and, in 1842, he described an immense variety of natural scenes which so impressed Lear that he wanted to interpret them with different natural scenes from his own store of pictures. Tennyson took his landscapes on Mount Ida from scenery in the Pyrenees, which he had visited with Arthur Hallam in 1830. Of Lear's four illustrations one is of Mount Ida, seen on early travels in 1856, one of Phyle, Greece, and the other two of Bavella, Corsica.

The choice of Mount Ida is unusual. Lear did not often represent the actual place mentioned in a poem. Œnone's 'tall dark pines' recalled a multitude of sketches, and even a large oil painting. Lear had made an extensive tour of Corsica in 1868 and published a journal, his last, in 1870. He was no longer able to draw on the stone himself, so his fine lithography was impossible. Instead, after much difficulty, he had woodcuts made, rather cheaply, and he knew that they did not do justice to his Corsican landscapes. The great trees came out stiff and angular and the composition lacked Lear's grace of line. In this small Bavella illustration the pines have some movement, but Lear's dark, thickened lines make the foliage ponderous. The picture looks as though it has been drawn, or redrawn, at a time when Lear's eyesight was failing. Some of his surviving drawings capture the light and dark of the great trees far more effectively. And the artist's written description in the Corsican Journal beautifully evokes the high, shimmering forest of Bavella. The year after this journal was published, in 1871, Lear returned seriously to his Tennyson Illustration project. And, in this last travel journal, he quotes more lines from Tennyson's poems than in any of his other books. Œnone herself is given a part in the humorous account of Lear's night voyage to Corsica. And, more solemnly, a phrase from 'Œnone', with the verb altered to fit the context, is used to enhance the landscape artist's description. Lear's expression of wonder at the huge forest of Bavella is heightened by distant pines, 'pluming the craggy ledge'.

30. Mount Ida, Asia Minor

So on the 29th. I set off with my bed & canteen once more – Giorgio, & a guide with mules, & all the day went in going zig zag about the Trojan plain. It is by no means unlike the Campagna of Rome – but the mountains are on a far grander scale – & the trees are always beautiful feathery green pines. Towards evening, having passed the tombs of Ajax & Achilles, I came to a Greek village Jenicher, where I slept. For the life of me I cannot tell why the Turks always have good bowls of delicious milk, & the Greeks never. Next day my journey was by the Scamander a huge roaring torrent in winter but nearly dry now, & as I rode further from the mountains, the top of the range of Mt. Ida is truly exquisitely beautiful. I got one sketch on the plain with the river & willows (with great camels brousing off them,) & Ida above all, that greatly delighted me. I perceive that the landscape of Asia Minor is more simple & delicate as well as grander than any I have yet visited – & more difficult to represent. At noon I reached Bounarbashi, a little Turkish village close to the site of ancient Troy, & thither I went at once. The position is so remarkable that almost a child would hit on it for a city & castle foundation. 2 enormous Tumuli mark the tombs of Hector & Priam – & above them rises the ancient Citadel – the 2 roads up to which & the place of the gates are distinctly marked. Below runs the Scamander, & great precipices flank it 3 sides round. Had not the wind been

very high I should have drawn better – but I certainly do long to see Troy again...
(EL to Ann, 8 October 1856)

Voyage to Corsica

The night voyage, though far from pleasant, has not been as bad as might have been anticipated. He is fortunate, who, after ten hours of sea passage can reckon up no worse memories than those of a passive condition of suffering – of that dislocation of mind and body, or inability to think straightforward, so to speak, when the outer man is twisted, and rolled, and jerked, and the movements of thought seem more or less to correspond with those of the body. Wearily go by "The slow sad hours that bring us all things ill,"[1] and vain is the effort to enliven them as every fresh lurch of the vessel tangles practical or pictorial suggestions with untimely scraps of poetry, indistinct regrets and predictions, couplets for a new "Book of Nonsense," and all kinds of inconsequential imbecilities – after this sort –

Would it not have been better to have remained at Cannes, where I had not yet visited Theoule, the Saut de Loup, and other places?

Had not I said, scores of times, such and such a voyage was the last I would make?

To-morrow, when "morn broadens on the borders of the dark,"[2] shall I see Corsica's "snowy mountain tops fringing the (Eastern) sky?"

Did the sentinels of lordly Volaterra see, as Lord Macaulay says they did, "Sardinia's snowy mountain-tops," and not rather these same Corsican tops, "fringing the southern sky?"

Did they see any tops at all, or if any, which tops?

Will the daybreak ever happen?

Will two o'clock ever arrive?

Will the two poodles above stairs ever cease to run about the deck?

Is it not disagreeable to look forward to two or three months of travelling quite alone?

Would it not be delightful to travel, as J. A. S. is about to do, in company with a wife and child?[3]

Does it not, as years advance, become clearer that it is very odious to be alone?

Have not many very distinguished persons, Œnone among others, arrived at this conclusion?

Did she not say, with evident displeasure –

> *"And from that time to this I am alone,*
> *And I shall be alone until I die"? –[4]*

Will those poodles ever cease from trotting up and down the deck?

Is it not unpleasant, at fifty-six years of age, to feel that it is increasingly probable that a man can never hope to be otherwise than alone, never, no, never more?

Did not Edgar Poe's raven distinctly say, "Nevermore?"

Will those poodles be quiet? "Quoth the raven, nevermore."

Will there be anything worth seeing in Corsica?

Is there any romance left in that island? is there any sublimity or beauty in its scenery?

Have I taken too much baggage?

Have I not rather taken too little?

Am I not an idiot for coming at all? –

Thus, and in such a groove, did the machinery of thought

go on, gradually refusing to move otherwise than by jerky spasms, after the fashion of mechanical Ollendorf exercises, or verb-catechisms of familiar phrases –

Are there not Banditti?

Had there not been Vendetta?

Were there not Corsican brothers?

Should I not carry clothes for all sorts of weather?

Must THOU not have taken a dress coat?

Had HE not many letters of introduction?

Might WE not have taken extra pairs of spectacles?

Could YOU not have provided numerous walking boots?

Should THEY not have forgotten boxes of quinine pills?

Shall WE possess flea-powder?

Could YOU not procure copper money?

May THEY not find cream cheeses?

Should there not be innumerable moufflons?

Ought not the cabin lamps and glasses to cease jingling?

Might not those poodles stop worrying? – thus and thus, till by reason of long hours of monotonous rolling and shaking, a sort of comatose insensibility, miscalled sleep, takes the place of all thought, and so the night passes.

At sunrise there are fine effects of light and cloud; but, alas for my first impression of that grand chain of Corsican Alps about which I have heard so much, and which were to have been seen so long before reaching the island!

Nothing is visible at present beyond the leaden, unlovely waves, except a low line of dark gray-green coast, and above this there are glimpses from time to time between thick folds of cloud, disclosing for a moment mysterious phantom heights of far snow and rock, or here and there some vast crag dimly seen and less remote, imparting a sensation of being near a land of lofty mountains, but none of any distinctness or continuity of outline.
(Corsican Journal, 9 April 1868, pp. 2-3)

32. Bavella, Corsica

Leaving G. to oversee Peter and the horses, I wander on alone with my note-book and pencil. The colour here is more beautiful than in most mountain passes I have seen, owing to the great variety of underwood foliage and the thick clothing of herbs; forms, too, of granite rocks seem to me more individually interesting than those of other formations; and the singular grace and beauty of the pine-trees has a peculiar charm – their tall stems apparently so slender, and so delicate the proportions of the tuft of foliage crowning them. The whole of this profound gorge, at the very edge of which the road runs, is full of mountain scenes of the utmost splendour, and would furnish pictures by the score to a painter who could remain for a lengthened sojourn. Sometimes ivory-white, needle-spiry pine stems, dead and leafless, break the dark yawning chasm of some black abyss far below with a line as of a silver thread; now a great space of gray mist in the distant hollow depth is crossed by lines of black burned stems; anon the high trunk

32

my tallest pines,

My tall dark pines that plumed the craggy ledge,

(Anóne.)

Bavella.
Corsica

of a solitary tufted tree looks like a kind of giant flower on a tall stalk; and ever above are delicate myriads of far pines "pluming the craggy ledge," their stems drawn like fine hair against the sky.

At 3 the top of the pass, or Bocca di Larone, is reached; and here the real forest of Bavella commences, lying in a deep cup-like hollow between this and the opposite ridge, the north and south side of the valley being formed by the tremendous columns and peaks of granite (or porphyry?), the summits of which are seen above the hills from Sartene, and which stand up like two gigantic portions of a vast amphitheatre, the whole centre of which is filled with a thick forest of pine. These crags, often as I have drawn their upper outline from the pass I have been ascending to-day, are doubly awful and magnificent now that one is close to them, and, excepting the heights of Serbal and Sinai, they exceed in grandeur anything of the kind I have ever seen, the more so that at present the distance is half hidden with dark cloud, heavily curtaining all this singular valley; and the tops of the huge rock buttresses being hidden, they seem as if they connected heaven and earth. At times the mist is suddenly lifted like a veil, and discloses the whole forest – as it were in the pit of an immense theatre confined between towering rock-wall, and filling up with its thousands of pines all the great hollow (for it is hardly to be called a valley in the ordinary sense of the term) between those two screens of stupendous precipices. As I contemplate the glory of this astonishing amphitheatre, I decide to stay at least another day within its limits, and I confess that a journey to Corsica is worth any amount of expense and trouble, if but to look on this scene alone. At length I have seen that of which I have heard so much – a Corsican forest.

The road leads down from the Bocca di Larone to the bottom of the hollow, and, crossing it, mounts the further side, half way up which, a small white speck, is the Maison de l'Alza, and the end of my day's journey. All along the descent there are no words for the majesty and wonder of this scenery; the tremendous mystery of those cloud-piercing towers and pillars, their sides riven and wrinkled in thousands of chasms, with pines growing in all their crevices and on all their ledges and pinnacles; the waves of the forest, so to speak, stretching from side to side of the vale; the groups of ilex, mixed with pine, in innumerable pictures, massive or slender, bare-stemmed or creeper-hung, flourishing in life, or dead glittering and white.

At the end of the descent stand two small foresters' houses on the short space of level ground between the four sides of this vale of Bavella; but here, at the twentieth kilometre from Solenzaro, the clouds burst, and violent torrents of rain make shelter welcome. Yet when the storm ceases for a time, and the sun gleams out through cloud, the whole scene is lighted up in a thousand splendid ways, and becomes more than ever astonishing, a changeful golden haze illumes the tops of the mighty peaks, a vast gloom below, resulting from the masses of black solemn pines standing out in deepest shadow from pale granite cliffs dazzling in the sunlight, torrents of water streaming down between walls and gates of granite, giant forms of trees in dusky recesses below perpendicular crags; no frenzy of the wildest dreams of a landscape painter could shape out ideal scenes of more magnificence and wonder...

The sun rises cloudlessly over the world of pines, and presently forms new and glorious pictures, as point after point of the western side of the valley is lighted up, while all the eastern part of the forest is as yet in dark and solemn shadow, below the giant crags – long streams of gold and bronze widening out gradually into masses of luminous green, and a flood of glory spreading slowly up the immense granite buttresses. I set off at 5.30 A.M. down to the bottom of the valley, and crossing it, go up as far as the Bocca di Larone, M. Mathieu, on his return from Solenzaro, overtaking me by the way, of whom I took leave, with thanks, for his good-natured hospitality.

Thenceforth, all the rest of the day went in hard work, only interrupted at 11, after Giorgio's announcement, "étimon to prógevma, kýrie – Sir, breakfast is ready" – and by walking from one part to another of this never-to-be-forgotten beautiful forest, not the least of its charms being the profound silence, broken only by the cuckoo's notes echoing from the crags, and from the fulness of melody chanted by thousands of blackbirds. Other forests in Corsica are much larger than this, but surely none can surpass it in certain qualities. For, remarkable as the valley of Bavella undoubtedly is as a whole, by reason of its intense solemnity, and for the double range of apparently perpendicular barriers which close it entirely from the outer world, and admit no prospect whatever beyond its limits, it is not less so for the exquisite detail of its scenery, the brushwood or "maquis" – particularly the arbutus and great heath – being throughout of the most perfect beauty. In some spots, too, groups of large evergreen oaks standing on slopes of green sward or fresh fern, and at others, masses of isolated granite, form pictures hardly to be exceeded in grandeur.

A slowly moving black and orange lizard is a noticeable inhabitant of the forest; he waddles gravely across the road, and frequently gets crushed by the wheels of the great timber carts. For, above the Maison de l'Alza great havoc goes on amongst the stately pines, and these enormous trees, peeled and cut angularly, are carried down to the valley depth, and thence up to the Bocca di Larone, and all the way to the shore at Solenzaro – often, as I have before observed, very unpleasant loads if met at sharp turns of the road. Some of these giant trees are six feet in diameter, and require fourteen or sixteen mules to drag them up to the Bocca.

After a hard day's drawing I come up to the Maison de l'Alza before sunset. Although the wrapping mists of yesterday's cloud and storm are blown away, and what seemed the fathomless hollows and immeasurable summits are now plainly understood; yet, in spite of this, parts of the forest are still truly extraordinary, the greatest novelty of the scenery being that the great granite columns are so near to you, that here and there some of them appear literally overhead, while every imaginable beauty of detail adorns their surface; and, again, one remarks how, sometimes, multitudes of tall needle-like pine stems shine brightly off the deep-shadowed chasms in the crags, or cluster in lines of jetty black against the pallid granite.

Some of the scenes at the foot of the ascent to the Maison de l'Alza, and close to the great precipices, occupy me two or three hours – one, a narrow gorge with a perspective of spires, leading, as it were, into the very inmost heart of the mountain; another, of bold crags, dark against the sunset sky, and rising out of the most profuse vegetation – both scenes grand beyond expression in words. Nor, indeed, except by very careful study, could many of the greatest and wildest beauties of this forest be represented in a sketch, and to attempt to do so seems like endeavouring in one day to make satisfactory notes from the contents of a whole library, full of all sorts of literature. Nevertheless, I have succeeded in obtaining a few striking points of this wonderful landscape.

The wife of the guardiano did her best to procure us a dinner, though the materials of it were only potatoes in various forms; happily the Solenzaro larder was far from exhausted. A painter, however, might and should endure anything short of starvation, to see what I have seen of Bavella.

April 30. – Before the red sun glows over the eastern sea, and while yet the grand forest is in deep shade, I have risen, and having paid the expenses of Madame Guardiano, and secured a lot of pine cones and seeds for Stratton and various other English places, I leave G. to follow with disagreeable Peter and the trap, and walk on alone; strict injunctions previously given that the horses are to take their own time, since there are but six more kilometres to the top, and we shall there make a long halt.

The silence and majesty of these pine forests at this hour! the deep obscurity in dim untrodden dells! the touches of gold high up on the loftiest branches and foliage! – And as the road mounts steeply upward, how beautiful are the cushions of green, the topmost verdure of the thousands of trees on which, far below, you look down! – Generally speaking, the Corsican pine has but little lateral foliage, but sometimes on the outskirts of the forest, you meet with trees that have broad arms and dark lines of flat spreading leafage, exactly resembling some in Martin's pictures. To make small memoranda as I walk up is all I can do, though in reality there are great pictures on every side, but such as require a long time to portray.
(28-30 April 1868, pp. 91-6)

[1] From 'Love and Duty', Tennyson, *Poems* 1842.
[2] From 'A Dream of Fair Women', *Poems* 1842.
[3] John Addington Symonds who, with his family, travelled to Corsica with Lear, but did not accompany him around the island. It was for Symonds's frail young daughter, Janet, that Lear wrote 'The Owl and the Pussy-Cat' in 1867.
[4] From 'Œnone', *Poems* 1842.

30. EL List: There is a vale in Ida
    EL Drawing: There lies a vale in Ida, lovelier
                     Than all the vallies of Ionian Hills.
32. EL List: My tall dark pines that plumed the craggy ledge
    EL Drawing: my tallest pines,
                     My tall dark pines that plumed the craggy ledge,

From: THE PALACE OF ART

I built my soul a lordly pleasure-house,
    Wherein at ease for aye to dwell.
I said, 'O Soul, make merry and carouse,
    Dear soul, for all is well.'

A huge crag-platform, smooth as burnish'd brass
    I chose. The ranged ramparts bright
From level meadow-bases of deep grass
    Suddenly scaled the light.

Thereon I built it firm. Of ledge or shelf
    The rock rose clear, or winding stair.   10
My soul would live alone unto herself
    In her high palace there.

And 'while the world runs round and round,' I said,
    'Reign thou apart, a quiet king,
Still as, while Saturn whirls, his steadfast shade
    Sleeps on his luminous ring.'

To which my soul made answer readily:
    'Trust me, in bliss I shall abide
In this great mansion, that is built for me,
    So royal-rich and wide.' . . .   20

. . . Full of great rooms and small the palace stood,
    All various, each a perfect whole
From living Nature, fit for every mood
    And change of my still soul.   60

For some were hung with arras green and blue,
    Showing a gaudy summer-morn,
Where with puff'd cheek the belted hunter blew
    His wreathed bugle-horn.

One seem'd all dark and red – a tract of sand,
    And some one pacing there alone,
Who paced for ever in a glimmering land,
    Lit with a low large moon.

One show'd an iron coast and angry waves.
    You seem'd to hear them climb and fall   70
And roar rock-thwarted under bellowing caves,
    Beneath the windy wall.

And one, a full-fed river winding slow
    By herds upon an endless plain,
The ragged rims of thunder brooding low,
    With shadow-streaks of rain.

35

A huge Crag platform,
    (The Palace of Art —)

Metéora. Thessaly.
    Greece.

And one, the reapers at their sultry toil.
    In front they bound the sheaves. Behind
Were realms of upland, prodigal in oil,
    And hoary to the wind.   80

And one a foreground black with stones and slags,
    Beyond, a line of heights, and higher
All barr'd with long white cloud the scornful crags,
    And highest, snow and fire.

And one, an English home – gray twilight pour'd
    On dewy pastures, dewy trees,
Softer than sleep – all things in order stored,
    A haunt of ancient Peace.

Nor these alone, but every landscape fair,
    As fit for every mood of mind,   90
Or gay, or grave, or sweet, or stern, was there
    Not less than truth design'd.

Or the maid-mother by a crucifix,
    In tracts of pasture sunny-warm,
Beneath branch-work of costly sardonyx
    Sat smiling, babe in arm.

Or in a clear-wall'd city on the sea,
    Near gilded organ-pipes, her hair
Wound with white roses, slept St. Cicely;
    An angel look'd at her.   100

Or thronging all one porch of Paradise
    A group of Houris bow'd to see
The dying Islamite, with hands and eyes
    That said, We wait for thee.

Or mythic Uther's deeply-wounded son
    In some fair space of sloping greens
Lay, dozing in the vale of Avalon,
    And watch'd by weeping queens.

Or hollowing one hand against his ear,
    To list a foot-fall, ere he saw   110
The wood-nymph, stay'd the Tuscan king to hear
    Of wisdom and of law.

Or over hills with peaky tops engrail'd,
    And many a tract of palm and rice,
The throne of Indian Cama slowly sail'd
    A summer fann'd with spice . . . .

. . . 'From shape to shape at first within the womb
    The brain is modell'd,' she began,
And thro' all phases of all thought I come
    Into the perfect man.

'All Nature widens upward. Evermore
    The simpler essence lower lies:
More complex is more perfect, owning more
    Discourse, more widely wise.'   200

Then of the moral instinct would she prate
    And of the rising from the dead,
As hers by right of full-accomplish'd Fate;
    And at the last she said:

'I take possession of man's mind and deeds.
    I live in all things great and small.
I apart holding no form of creeds,
    But contemplating all.'

Full oft the riddle of the painful earth
    Flash'd thro' her as she sat alone,   210
Yet not the less held she her solemn mirth,
    And intellectual throne

Of full-sphered contemplation. So three years
    Throve, but on the fourth she fell,
Like Herod, when the shout was in his ears,
    Struck thro' with pangs of hell.

Lest she should fail and perish utterly,
    God, before whom ever lie bare
The abysmal deeps of Personality,
    Plagued her with sore despair.   220

When she would think, where'er she turn'd her sight
    The airy hand confusion wrought,
Wrote, 'Mene, mene,' and divided quite
    The kingdom of her thought.

Deep dread and loathing of her solitude
    Fell on her, from which mood was born
Scorn of herself; again, from out that mood
    Laughter at her self-scorn.

'What! is not this my place of strength,' she said,
    'My spacious mansion built for me,   230
Whereof the strong foundation-stones were laid
    Since my first memory?'

But in dark corners of her palace stood
    Uncertain shapes, and unawares
On white-eyed phantasms weeping tears of blood,
    And horrible nightmares,

And hollow shades enclosing hearts of flame,
    And, with dim fretted foreheads all,
On corpses three-months-old at noon she came,
    That stood against the wall.   240

A spot of dull stagnation, without light
    Or power of movement, seem'd my soul,
'Mid onward-sloping motions infinite
    Making for one sure goal.

A still salt pool, lock'd in with bars of sand,
    Left on the shore; that hears all night
The plunging seas draw backward from the land
    Their moon-led waters white.

A star that with the choral starry dance
    Join'd not, but stood, and standing saw   250
The hollow orb of moving Circumstance
    Roll'd round by one fix'd law.

Back on herself her serpent pride had curl'd.
    'No voice,' she shriek'd in that lone hall,
'No voice breaks thro' the stillness of this world:
    One deep, deep silence all!'

She, mouldering with the dull earth's mouldering sod,
    Inwrapt tenfold in slothful shame,
Lay there exiled from eternal God,
    Lost to her place and name;   260

And death and life she hated equally,
    And nothing saw, for her despair,
But dreadful time, dreadful eternity,
    No comfort anywhere;

Remaining utterly confused with fears,
    And ever worse with growing time,
And ever unrelieved by dismal tears,
    And all alone in crime:

Shut up as in a crumbling tomb, girt round
    With blackness as a solid wall,   270
Far off she seem'd to hear the dully sound
    Of human footsteps fall.

As in strange lands a traveller walking slow,
    In doubt and great perplexity,
A little before moon-rise hears the low
    Moan of an unknown sea.

And knows not if it be thunder, or a sound
    Of stones thrown down, or one deep cry
Of great wild beasts; then thinketh, 'I have found
    A new land, but I die.'   280

She howl'd aloud, 'I am on fire within.
    There comes no murmur of reply.
What is it that will take away my sin,
    And save me lest I die?'

So when four years were wholly finished,
    She threw her royal robes away.
'Make me a cottage in the vale,' she said,
    'Where I may mourn and pray.

'Yet pull not down my palace towers, that are
    So lightly, beautifully built: 290
Perchance I may return with others there
    When I have purged my guilt.'

34. *Mendrisio, Switzerland*
35. Meteora, Thessaly, Greece
36. Pentedatelo, Calabria, Italy
37. Cape St Angelo, Amalfi, Italy
38. Coast of Gozo, Malta
39. The Spercheius, near Thermopylae, Greece
40. *Near Correse below Monte Gennaro, Italy*
41. Etna, from Taormina, Sicily
42. Mount Etna, Sicily
43. Hampshire, England
44. *Near Frascati, Roma, Italy*
45. *Mount Soracte, from Nepi, Italy*
46. Ragusa, Dalmatia
47. *Telicherry, Malabar, India*
48. Mar Sabbas, Palestine
49. *Lake Lugano, Switzerland*

(N.B. 37 and 38 are reversed on the printed List).

'The Palace of Art', published in 1832, cut and revised in 1842, raised questions which were to provoke comment throughout Tennyson's career. In the 1890s, the Laureate recalled a warning given by a friend at Cambridge: 'Tennyson, we cannot live in art.' And the old poet added that 'The Palace of Art' embodied his own belief in the 'Godlike life ... with and for man.' (*Mem.* I, pp. 118-19). But how far was this based on early conviction, and how far on later rationalization? Reviewers of the 1832 *Poems* were much exercised by the problem of 'art' raised by Tennyson's friend, R.C. Trench. They were doubtful whether or not luxuriantly beautiful description, and a fine ear for metre, were enough to produce a great poet. Eleven years on, J.C. Spedding, in the *Edinburgh Review*, April 1843, was one of many critics who felt that the 1842 volumes, with their revisions and new poems, revealed Tennyson's progress:

> .... there is more humanity with less image and drapery, a closer adherence to the truth, a greater reliance for effect upon the simplicity of nature. Moral and spiritual traits of character are more dwelt upon, in place of external scenery and circumstance. He addresses himself more to the heart and less to the eye. (*Mem.* I, p. 190)

Hallam Tennyson, in his own comments in the *Memoir*, claimed that by 1842 his father's 'comprehension of human life had grown' (*Mem.* I, p. 188). These questions, about the early poems and about much of Tennyson's later work, are still being debated. 'The Palace of Art' is particularly interesting because in some ways it suggests a new 'comprehension of human life', and in some ways evades the issue.

Even in 1832 Tennyson felt the need to reply to Trench. He prefaced the poem with an apologia:

> I send you here a sort of allegory,
> (For you will understand it) of a soul
> A sinful soul possessed of many gifts ...

A thoroughly moral reading of 'The Palace of Art' proclaims the soul's sin as aestheticism. The speaker is male but the erring soul female, so it is 'she' who contemplates, without love, all beauty, goodness and knowledge. The Preface condemns the soul, but how far does the poem really explore what it is to 'live in art'?

The speaker begins with an account of the soul's 'lordly pleasure-house'. Eastern, Biblical, exotic travel and other materials, contribute to the description of the 'Palace' as it is shown rising, high on a 'crag platform', looking down on the world. It is something of a Miltonic-Victorian Pandemonium: outside, it has four great courts, dragon fountains, galleries, cloisters, spires and stained glass windows. The soul, unworried by architectural incoherence, proposes to 'abide in bliss'. Inside, the Palace offers the beauty of a series of transformation scenes, but theatrical artifice gives way, magically, to nature. Each room opens into a different natural landscape: the Palace seems not to contain, but to dissolve into the changing beauty of the natural world. The soul, enthroned, feels herself 'Lord over Nature, Lord of the visible earth' (line 179). Man appears, but distanced into myths, into ancient tales and into the great figure-heads of knowledge. Exalted, isolated, aloof 'like God' and 'contemplating all', the soul is, not surprisingly, quickly

One seemed all dark & red a tract of sand
With some one pacing there alone
Who paced forever in a glimm'ring land
Lit by a low large moon.

(The Palace of Art)

Pentedateto.
Calabria

Italy

dragged down from her supposed height. She begins to dread her solitude, to fall into despair, to see in dreams 'hollow shades' and 'white-eyed phantasms'. She contemplates no beauty, feels no power, and the Palace quickly becomes, for her, a dark and crumbling tomb.

The soul begs for 'a cottage in a vale' where she will 'mourn and pray'. Apparently she has begun to understand her cold aestheticism and her pride. But this last phase of the poem is oddly abrupt. The Palace is not destroyed, and the soul pleads: 'Yet pull not down my palace towers' (line 289). She hopes to return, 'with others', when she has purged her guilt. Does this wished for return suggest that the soul, purged and humanized, will be ready to live a 'God-like life in man'? Tennyson's ending begs the question. Is the soul, with other incorruptible and untemptable companions, to live again in the Palace of Art? The poet gives no answers.

As an artist Lear was certainly aware of the possible opposition between Art and Life. He reacted to Royal Academy exhibitions in a way which suggests that he found some of the pictures tainted with an arid aestheticism. But in his personal life, the Palace of Art seems to have signified something rather different. He feared not so much a retreat into aestheticism, but the possibility that he was forced to shut himself away only to find that creativity had failed him and his beloved art become mere drudgery. On 30 May 1871 he had nearly settled into his first home, the Villa Emily. He got up early and enjoyed his garden with its brilliant flowers and old olive

trees. He was delighted with the whole place – still new to him. But he went indoors and painted, gave a drawing lesson, painted again. He arranged and read books in his library and, later during the day in his diary quoted '"Tears, idle tears" – & indeed they are idle'. His buoyant mood had evaporated. The struggle of painting for a livelihood, the need to be indoors and isolated, even the drawing lesson – any or all of these might have prompted his next remark: 'All this "Palace of Art" work seems to me but dangerous practice' (D. 30 May 1871). Lear's use of Tennyson's title suggests that he was well aware that art might exclude life and become a burden. He had a strong sense of 'the labour, the sheer manual labour, of an Artist's life' and 'the vexations of failures of infinitely repeated experiments' (D. 6 September 1873).

The same year the artist, in Certosa to get away from the summer heat, mused over tree-shaded English places from his distant past, including Arundel Park, and the more recently known Stratton, country seat of Lord Northbrook. Lear felt it would be difficult to return to them often: they held too many memories. And some had 'ugly' or 'cold' drawbacks, but Certosa had 'few memories of sadness or affection, or tie of any sort' it was 'bald of memory', and it promised a 'picture of beauty – with no roots in the heart or any bond or tie' (D. 23 August 1871). Memory of a place and its people might bring sadness, but a beautiful place without any 'roots in the heart' risked being a mere outward show.

37

One show'd an iron coast & angry waves
    You seem'd to hear them climb & fall
And roar rock-thwarted under bellowing caves
    Beneath the windy wall.
    (The Palace of Art.)

Cape St Angelo
Amalfi.
        Italy.

38

One show'd an iron Coast, —
    (The Palace of Art,)

Coast of Gozo.
        Malta.

In his own way, Lear seems to be reacting to the dangers posed in 'The Palace of Art': aestheticism divorced from humanity.

In choosing illustrations for Tennyson's poems, Lear gathered together a number of places which had a particular hold on his memory and 'roots in the heart'. He picked out the stanzas with the 'landscape rooms' and used their pictorial detail in scenery from many of his journeys. Sixteen illustrations range over early travels in Italy, Greece, Albania and Palestine. There is one English scene, Lord Northbrook's house, and one Indian landscape. And Lear also chose Sicily, Malta and Ragusa (Dubrovnik) which appear nowhere else in his Tennyson list.

The line between beauty and humanity, the tie between observer and landscape, is never made explicit. But Lear's choice of drawings often suggests such a link. Lord Northbrook's house (given on the drawing merely as 'Hampshire'), recalled other great country houses and other possible places which might be used to illustrate the 'English home'. Lear had looked at several English houses and villages before settling on Stratton, idealizing it a little, studying trees elsewhere, and finally making this evening drawing and quoting, underneath it, the whole Tennyson verse. Lear often seems to be most attached to a scene when he quotes a whole stanza, rather than one line: poetry and topography seem to have fused completely.

Stratton was not just a fine, patrician house: it offered peace, quietness and order. It suggested a whole way of life, of hospitality and company which Lear found delightful when he felt well and bright enough to enjoy many visitors, grand dinners, and after dinner music and talk. On some of his visits to country houses, he grew depressed at the quiet, hated the clock-work regularity of life, disliked the endless 'do-nothingness'. He had to put up with cold, wet walks, with silly conversations, and with low lights and flickering candles on the dinner table, which greatly disturbed his eyes, and made him feel ill. But Stratton was a true 'English home'. There was a tie with Lord Northbrook who remained a good friend and beneficent patron to the artist and, as Viceroy, eventually invited him to India. Lear was attracted to places that seemed 'like a home', even though he was usually visiting them for a few days. The Tennysons, at Farringford, at one time seemed to offer such a 'home', and Lear once thought of settling nearby. Times changed and, in August 1872, staying at Stratton, Lear wrote: 'I went all about the gardens & avenues of Stratton – which place has more of a home feeling for me now than – I think – any other' (D. 13 August 1872).

The 'landscape rooms' in 'The Palace of Art' gave Lear a series of finely described scenes which he could translate into his own remembered landscapes. Etna (and climbing it) and Taormina are recalled from early journeys in 1842, 1847 and a later visit in 1866. These were well known sites for the hardy tourist and traveller. Meteora, Thessaly, was much less accessible. But Lear had seen the huge rocks crowned with monasteries and written about them in his Albanian Journal. One view,

39

And one, a full fed river winding slow
By herds upon an endless plain,
The ragged rims of thunder brooding low
With shadow-streaks of rain.
(The Palace of Art.)

The Spercheius.
near Thermopylæ.

Greece

lithographed for the Journal, was remembered for the 'huge crag platform' of 'The Palace of Art'. Lear sometimes kept a Tennyson line in mind – perhaps hardly consciously – and applied it to an appropriate scene. He describes a 'huge crag platform', overhung with olives, in Corfu, and another in Malta. But for his Tennyson Illustration, he returns to Meteora.

The variety of scene in the poem gave Lear opportunities to use both cliff and seascape. He hated being on board ship or boat in a rough sea, and the sweeping, curving lines of his watercolour drawings and sketches are particularly suited to depicting a calm sea, quiet bays, water rippling to the shore. But in these illustrations, besides a sinuous river, and moonlit sands, Lear has two scenes of coastal cliffs: Gozo, Malta with calm water, and Capo St Angelo, Amalfi with surging waves. In both, the careful line and striation of rock show Lear's preoccupation with geological detail. He visited Amalfi first on an early visit from Rome down beyond Naples in 1838: he did not reach Malta until 1848 and returned there, drawing all over the island, in 1865/6.

Scaled down to miniature size, there are some fine drawings among 'The Palace of Art' illustrations. It is not possible to claim that Lear had a particular 'tie' with each landscape: he visited Ragusa once and had great difficulty in finding a vantage point from which to draw it. The Roman Campagna, by contrast, he had always loved from his first to his last visit to Rome. He was attracted by Tivoli – but the picture (no. 40, with a whole verse) of reapers in the fields seems to have given him considerable trouble. He called on Frederick Thrupp, a sculptor, artist, and illustrator known from Roman days, to help with the design. The problem of the figures – the bending, leaning, moving reapers – is, of course, much more pronounced in larger versions of this illustration. In one variation Lear penned in a background of trees and hills, but the figures in the foreground remain in worked and reworked pencil.

Lear did not forget that the soul, in the poem, turns away from the view of beauty to dark places of guilt and fear. He understood well, as Tennyson did, the feeling of being lone, despairing, and 'confused with fears'. A grey and black drawing of Lugano illustrates the gloom of 'girt round / With blackness' (lines 269-70). And a dramatic composition of the ancient monastery of Mar Sabbas – a white slash across black rocks – suggests a place in Palestine which has survived the ages in its dark, bare and treeless surroundings. Is this an illustration of 'blackness', or does it endorse the soul's renewal?

The most enigmatic design in this set is the drawing for the stanza beginning, 'One seem'd all dark and red – a tract of sand / And some one pacing there alone...' (lines 65-6). The picture, which includes Pentedatelo, near the shore of Southern Calabria, goes back as far as a lithograph (not the same view) for the Calabrian Journal and an oil painting apparently begun in 1849 and finished about 1884. When Lear, who often spent years on an oil painting, finished the picture which he called 'Someone pacing there alone', he sent it to England and hoped friends might subscribe to buy it as a wedding present for Hallam Tennyson. By 1886 the picture was still not sold, and Lear wrote to Hallam saying that he and his wife were to have the painting. The last note about it in Lear's diary mentions that the picture

has reached Farringford, but is due to go to the other Tennyson house, Aldworth. Hallam wrote that he found the picture a fine illustration of the stanza. And many years later Sir Charles Tennyson recalled that the Pentedatelo looked very fine at Aldworth: he remembered many of Lear's paintings, engravings, two parrot pictures and a huge 'Enoch Arden', all hung in the poet's house.[1]

'Someone pacing there alone' seems to have begun as a moonlit scene on the sands of Sliema, Malta, in 1866. Lear drew a miniature shore and 'low large moon' in his diary. But this may have been only one stage in the gestation of a painting which Lear said he had started in 1849. On the southernmost shore of Calabria, in 1847, in a good light Lear could have looked across to Sicily. Behind him he could have glimpsed the great five-fingered rock of Pentedatelo, with its story of feuding families who destroyed each other and left a ghost town as a memorial. This was a tale with all the gothic horror and wild romance which Lear had hoped to find in Calabria. There are many versions of the design: this drawing is the smallest of the known three in monochrome. But apart from the rock – moved forward to lour over the sands – the tale remained a secret from the casual viewer, and the place seems partly remembered landscape, partly dream. The figure, sometimes cloaked, sometimes burdened, never seems to be moving fast, sometimes barely at all. It is possible that Lear was thinking, too, of another stanza:

> As in strange lands a traveller walking slow,
>   In doubt and great perplexity,
> A little before moon-rise hears the low
>   Moan of an unknown sea;   (lines 273-76)

this is an image for the soul's confusion, but the 'traveller walking slow', his terror of thunder, rocks, wild beasts and his hideous conclusion: '...I have found / A new land, but I die' (lines 279-80) may have worked on Lear's imagination as he drew his anonymous and disturbing figure 'pacing', and dark against the moonlight. This was a picture of dramatic extremes. In the oil painting Lear mentions getting in the colouring of red and black. Some of this must have been applied to the figure, and even the small monochrome suggests the brightness of the moon. The design is very much alive: in 1871 Lear sketched several minute versions of 'Someone pacing' in his diary. The 'Pentedatelo' was linked, for Lear, with Calabria in the 1840s, with Tennyson's poem and with an oil painting which finally went to the Tennyson family. The strange, open scene, with so little detail, still had its 'roots in the heart'. The figure, when darkly cloaked, might just have suggested the poet – without his broad hat. But what this scene, with its strange light, its atmosphere of dream, its pacing figure, shows us most clearly is Lear himself as the lone traveller: the artist in a landscape of the mind.

[1] Sir Charles Tennyson, *Stars and Markets* (Chatto & Windus, 1957), p. 22.

35. Meteora, Thessaly, Greece

I went very early with a villager to visit and sketch the monasteries. Truly they are a most wonderful spectacle; and are infinitely more picturesque than I had expected them to be. The magnificent foreground of fine oak and

41

And highest, snow and fire. —
    (The Palace of Art.)

Etna, from Taormina.
    Sicily.

42

And one, a foreground black with stones and slags, —
    Beyond, a line of heights; and higher,
All barred with long white clouds the scornful crags,
    And highest snow and fire.
        (The Palace of Art.)

Mount Etna.
    Sicily.

And one, an English home,—grey twilight pour'd
On dewy pastures, dewy trees,
Softer than sleep;—all things in order-stored
A haunt of ancient peace.

(The Palace of Art.)

Hampshire.
England.

detached fragments of rock, struck me as one of the peculiar features of the scene. The detached and massive pillars of stone, crowned with the retreats of the monks, rise perpendicularly from the sea of foliage, which at this early hour, six A.M. is wrapped in the deepest shade, while the bright eastern light strikes the upper part of the magic heights with brilliant force and breadth. To make any real use of the most exquisite landscape abounding throughout this marvellous spot, an artist should stay here for a month: there are both the simplest and most classic poetries of scenery at their foot looking towards the plain and mountain; and when I mounted the cliffs on a level with the summit of the great rocks of Meteora and Baarlam, the solitary and quiet tone of these most wonderful haunts appeared to me inexpressibly delightful. Silvery white goats were peeping from the edge of the rocks into the deep, black abyss below; the simple forms of the rocks rise high in air, crowned with church and convent, while the eye reaches the plains of Thessaly to the far-away hills of Agrafa. No pen or pencil can do justice to the scenery of Meteora. I did not go up to any of the monasteries. Suffering from a severe fall in the autumn of last year, I had no desire to run the risk of increasing the weakness of my right arm, the use of which I was only now beginning to regain, so the interior of these monkish habitations I left unvisited; regretting that I did so the less, as every moment of the short time I lingered among these scenes, was too little to carry away even imperfect representations of their marvels.

I had been more than half inclined to turn back after having seen the Meteora convents, but the improvement in the weather, the inducement of beholding Olympus and Tempe, and the dread of so soon re-encountering the gloomy Pass of Metzovo, prevailed to lead me forward. Accordingly, at nine A.M. I set off eastward...
(Albanian Journal, 16 May 1849, pp. 396-8)

36. Pentedatelo, Calabria, Italy

But having gained the high ground opposite, the appearance of Pentedatilo is perfectly magical, and repays whatever trouble the effort to reach it may so far have cost. Wild spires of stone shoot up into the air, barren and clearly defined, in the form (as its name implies) of a gigantic hand against the sky, and in the crevices and holes of this fearfully savage pyramid the houses of Pentedatilo are wedged, while darkness and terror brood over all the abyss around this, the strangest of human abodes. Again, a descent to the river, and all traces of the place are gone; and it is not till after repassing the stream, and performing a weary climb on the farther side, that the stupendous and amazing precipice is reached; the habitations on its surface now consist of little more than a small village, though the remains of a large castle and extensive ruins of buildings are marks of Pentedatilo having once seen better days.

I had left Ciccio and the horse below the stream, and I regretted having done so, when, as I sate making a drawing of the town, the whole population bristled on wall and window, and the few women who passed me on their way to the hanging vineyards, which fringe the cliffs low down by the edge of the river, screamed aloud on seeing me, and rushed back to their rocky fastnesses. As it is hardly possible to make these people understand ordinary Italian, a stranger might, if alone, be awkwardly situated in the event of any misunderstanding. Had the Pentedatilini thought fit to roll stones on the intruder, his fate must have been hard; but they seemed filled with fear alone. I left this wonderful place with no little regret, and rejoining Ciccio, soon lost sight of Pentedatilo, pursuing my way up the stream, or bed of the Monaca, which is here very narrow and winding, and so shut in between high cliffs, that in winter-time the torrent prevents all access from this quarter. Higher up in the ravine stands the village of Montebello; its district is famous in Calabria for the excellence of its cactus, or Indian fig, all the rocks of the neighbourhood being covered with a thick coating of that strange vegetable. The town is situated high above the river, on a square rock, perpendicular on three sides, amid wide ruins of walls and houses, betokening former times of prosperity. In the centre of this wretched little place is the house of Don Pietro Amazichi, who, though receiving me with every kindness and hospitality, was as much agitated as my acquaintances at Melito. It seems evident that coming events are casting rapidly deepening shadows, and in vain again do I try to persuade my hosts that I am not in the secret. 'It is impossible,' they said; 'you only left Reggio yesterday, it is true; but it is certain that the revolution broke out last night, and everyone has known for days past what would happen.' . . .

About two, Don Pietro accompanied me to the foot of the rock, and for some distance up the dreary fiumara; meanwhile he illustrated the history of Montebello and Pentedatilo by a tale-tragedy of the early ages of these towns, when their territories were governed respectively, the first by a Baron and the second by a Marquis.

For centuries the families of these two feudal possessors of the towns of Pentedatilo and Montebello had been deadly foes, and they ruled, or fought for, the adjoining country from their strongholds in persevering enmity. The Baron of Montebello, a daring and ferocious youth, was left heir in early life to his ancestral estates and rights, and fell in love with the only daughter of the Marchese Pentedatilo; but, although the young lady had contrived to acquaint her lover that her heart was his, her hand was steadfastly denied him by the Marchese, whom the memory of long injuries and wars hardened in his refusal. Opposition, however, did but increase the attachment of the young lady, and she at length consented to leave her father's house with her lover; an arrangement being made that on a certain night she should open a door in the otherwise impenetrable rock-fortress of Pentedatilo, and admit young Montebello with a sufficient force of his retainers to ensure the success of her elopement.

The Baron accordingly enters the castle, but finding that equal opportunity is presented him for vengeance on his feudal enemy, and for possessing himself of the object of his attachment, he resolves to make the most of both; he goes first to the chamber of the Marchese of Pentedatilo, and finds him sleeping by the side of the Marchesa, with a dagger at his pillow's head. Him he stabs, yet not so fatally as to prevent his placing his left hand on the wound, and with his right seizing his stiletto, and plunging it into the heart of the innocent Marchesa, suspecting her as the author of his death. The Baron Montebello repeating his blows, the Marchese falls forward on the wall, and his five blood-stained fingers leave traces, still shown, on part of the ruined hall, – a horrible memorial of the crime, strangely coincident with that of the form and name of the rock. (Calabrian Journal, 2 September 1847, pp. 191-6)

38. Gozo, Malta

But above, the view over the island to its west end, & Gozo beyond, is vastly grand – with the great rocks of the valley close by. (Bye the bye, the cliffs of Gozo seen above the long promontories near Miggiar, are wondrously grand: & you don't see their base, & they then seem a vast range of perpendicular hills far beyond.) (D. 1 March 1866)

41. Taormina, Sicily

Taormina is perhaps one of the most wonderful places in the world. It takes about two hours to get up to it, by a zigzag road without any parapet – sometimes hanging sheer over the sea. The views on all sides are most astonishing, particularly the ruins of the theatre, which overlook Mt. Etna, & are very perfect – Taurominium having been a celebrated Greek city. We enjoyed ourselves very much at Taormina indeed. On the 30th. we hired some mules, & set off by the coast road, – stopping at Via Paolo for two or three hours at noon – & reaching Messina – where there is an excellent hotel, by dusk. Messina is a most lovely place, & having been quite shaken down by the earthquake of 1780 looks all new. The view of the Straits over to the Calabrian mountains is very beautiful. (EL to Ann, 11 July 1847)

42. Mount Etna, Sicily

At midnight we started on mules & with a light & after two hours climbing reached the snow, beyond which it is necessary to go on foot. Here the trouble begins; fancy two hours of climbing up & slipping down, over the steepest hill of frozen snow. I never was so disgusted. Sometimes I rolled back as far as 20 minutes had taken me up. It was impossible to keep one's footing, even with a spiked stick. By the aid of the guide however, we reached the top of this horrible height & rested in another hut called Casa Anglese. Then we crossed a plain of snow which surrounds the cone, & began to climb that, an operation as difficult as the last, as it is nearly perpendicular, & made of fine ash & sulphur, into which you plunge up to your knees at each step. This however, is not the obstacle which prevents your progress – but rather the extreme rarity of the air which takes different effects on different persons. Some it stupefies, others it causes to vomit. Had it made me very ill, I should have turned back, but it only caused me to feel as if I were drowning, & made me lose my breath almost, & my voice altogether. A sort of convulsive catching was very disagreeable, & at times was so violent that for a moment or two I lost the use of the limbs & fell down. Being on the ground however, restored one's breathing, & so we got on by very slow degrees – climbing – & falling alternately. The fatigue is certainly immense, but one is amply repaid by the extraordinary scene above – where you look on the whole island of Sicily just like a great pink map in the sky – with the sea round it so blue, & the dark purple triangular shade of the mountains over that part furthest from the sun which rose just before we got to the mouth of the crater.

We did not remain long there, as you may suppose on my telling you that the sulphur we sat on burned our clothes very much, & was horribly hot – yet one was too glad to bury one's hands in it – one's body & head being wrapped up in cloaks & plaids through all which one shivered in the icy wind which blew like knives from the north. (Etna you know, is nearly as high as Mt. Blanc.) We came down ridiculously fast; you stick your heels in the ashy cone, & slide down almost without stopping to the bottom, – & with a spiked stick you shoot down the ice hill we had taken so long to surmount – in 10 minutes. We reposed & fed at Niccolosi having taken a store of bottled porter etc. with us – & by evening were once more at Catania.
(EL to Ann, 11 July 1847)

46. Ragusa, Dalmatia

Then I & G wandered – upstairs & downstairs: walls no end. few palms, vegetation generally full & lovely: in fact, Ragusa seems the Oasis of Dalmatia. But it is difficult to get any comprehensive view of the whole of its position, picturesque as it is. After endlessly poking about, we found a road above the city – but it only led down again to the Turk donkey quarter. So I went on to the high Ragusa [illegible] – road – below which are gardens down to the sea. There is a good view of the South end of Ragusa, & I drew – 7.30 – to 9.30. The female peasants are particularly clean & nice: red & yellow colours prevail. Men wear rolled red Turbans, & may or may not be Mussulmen. Everybody says – Dobra jutra. Returned to the city – then above it, & by a long walled lane all round.   5 May 1866)

48. Mar Sabbas, Palestine

On Friday the 30th – I set off to Deir Marsabbas, the very oldest monastery known; you know that all the desert west of the Jordan was full of hermits in the early Christian centuries; – among these, St. Sabbas was one of the most renowned, & after his death (about A.D. 550 I think,) his cave was built over, & by degrees frequented by other hermits, – & Justinian – later – made a strong place of it, as he did of Mt. Sinai, & of those convents I saw at Mt. Athos. Innumerable other monasteries existed in those days – but all have been more or less destroyed except this, which stands in the gorge of the Kedron – not far from the Dead Sea, & hardly 3 hours from Jerusalem. In 614, Chosroes 1st. the Persian, destroyed most of the hermits when he invaded Syria, but the building seems to have escaped; & when in 637 the Musslemen took all Palestine, Mar Saba still held its place, & to this day the fortress monastery lives in this strange wild desert – giving bread to a tribe of poor Arabs – (its resources being mainly Russian, & territories near Bethlehem) in return for which they protect the monks & all their friends when travelling to & from the building. In an hour after leaving Jerusalem, the fig gardens ceased – & we were always in one of your favourite Wadys – & a very ugly one too. We passed several camps of Arabs in their black tents – but no one took any notice of us; & in about 2 1/2 hours from setting out, came to the spot where the Kedron, (when it has water in it) runs steeply down to the Dead Sea between terrific walls of perpendicular rock. Down the sides of this – stuck against it as it were, is the monastery, fortified by immense walls – & oddly differing from my Athos acquaintances in

— a clear wall'd city by the Sea,
(The Palace of Art,)

Ragusa
Dalmatia

With blackness as a girt round *solid wall.*

Mar Sabbas.
Palestine.

(In Palace of Art.)

as much as it is all sand colour – all like the desert round
it. If it was not for the towers & the white domed church
it would hardly seem separate from the rocks. Inside, Mar
Sabbas is exactly like any other Greek monastery – & to
myself & Giorgio was really very curious – as we seemed
transported 2 years back to Athos – all the more that 2 of
the monks were from monasteries there – & knew all our
acquaintances. The Dragoman Abdel, & the Arab
Mustafa were quite in the shade, & we talked Greek all
evening. The Ighoúmenos or abbot, unluckily was not
there; he has lived at Mar Sabbas 42 years!! The monks
have some funny little gardens here & there, made with
soil brought there, & planted with lettuces etc & there are
some pomegranate trees, & one palm; & lots of birds come
& hop about. But all the rest is sandy rock, & the whole
place, even on May 1st was so like an oven that I felt as
if I should be baked, I came away (after making some good
drawings) as early as I could.
(EL to Ann, 21 May 1858)

I have been working this morning, on,
    "girt round with darkness as a solid wall."
– a scene in the gorge of Mar Saba near Jericho, which I
once saw blacker than any Hat ever yet made (by reason
of a Thunderstorm) but with the Monastery catching the
last light of sunset. Uy! my i! how black it vor!
(EL to Hallam Tennyson, 18 September 1884)

35. EL List: A huge crag platform
    EL Drawing: A huge Crag platform,
36. EL List: One show'd, all dark and red, a tract of sand

EL Drawing: One seemed all dark & red a tract of sand
              With some one pacing there alone
            Who paced for ever in a glimm'ring land
              Lit by a low large moon.

            Coast of Gozo, Malta.
37. EL List: One show'd an iron coast
38. EL Drawing: One show'd an iron Coast, –

            Cape St. Angelo.
38. EL List: One show'd an iron coast and angry waves
37. EL Drawing: One show'd an iron coast & angry waves
              You seem'd to hear them climb & fall
            And roar rock=thwarted under bellowing caves
              Beneath the windy wall.
39. EL List: And one, a full-fed river winding slow
    EL Drawing: And one, a full fed river winding slow
              By herds upon an endless plain,
            The ragged rims of thunder brooding low
              With shadow streaks of rain.
41. EL List: And highest, – snow and fire
    EL Drawing: And highest, snow and fire. –
42. EL List: And one a foreground black with stones and slags
    EL Drawing: And one, a foreground black with stones and slags, –
              Beyond, a line of heights; and higher,
            All barred with long white clouds the scornful crags,
              And highest snow and fire.
43. EL List: And one, an English home
    EL Drawing: And one, an English home, – grey twilight pour'd
              On dewy pastures, dewy trees,
            Softer than sleep: – all things in order stood
              A haunt of ancient peace.
46. EL List: A clear wall'd city by the sea
    EL Drawing: – a clear wall'd city by the sea,
48. EL List: Girt round with blackness
    EL Drawing: girt round
            With blackness as a solid wall.

THE LOTOS-EATERS

I

'Courage!' he said, and pointed toward the land,
'This mounting wave will roll us shoreward soon.'
In the afternoon they came unto a land,
In which it seemed always afternoon.
All round the coast the languid air did swoon,
Breathing like one that hath a weary dream.
Full-faced above the valley stood the moon;
And like a downward smoke, the slender stream
Along the cliff to fall and pause and fall did seem.

II

A land of streams! some, like a downward smoke,
Slow-dropping veils of thinnest lawn did go;
And some thro' wavering lights and shadows broke,
Rolling a slumbrous sheet of foam below.
They saw the gleaming river seaward flow
From the inner land: far off, three mountain-tops,
Three silent pinnacles of aged snow,
Stood sunset-flush'd: and, dew'd with showery drops,
Up-clomb the shadowy pine above the woven copse.

III

The charmed sunset linger'd low adown
In the red West: thro' mountain clefts the dale
Was seen far inland, and the yellow down
Border'd with palm, and many a winding vale
And meadow, set with slender galingale;
A land where all things always seem'd the same!
And round about the keel with faces pale,
Dark faces pale against that rosy flame,
The mild-eyed melancholy Lotos-eaters came.

IV

Branches they bore of that enchanted stem,
Laden with flower and fruit, whereof they gave
To each, but whoso did receive of them,
And taste, to him the gushing of the wave
Far far away did seem to mourn and rave
On alien shores; and if his fellow spake,
His voice was thin, as voices from the grave;
And deep-asleep he seem'd, yet all awake,
And music in his ears his beating heart did make.

50

A land of streams,—
(The Lotos-Eaters

Vodghenà.
Macedonia.

V

They sat them down upon the yellow sand,
Between the sun and moon upon the shore;
And sweet it was to dream of Father-land,
Of child, and wife, and slave; but evermore
Most weary seem'd the sea, weary the oar,
Weary the wandering fields of barren foam.
Then some one said, 'We will return no more;'
And all at once they sang, 'Our island home
Is far beyond the wave; we will no longer roam.'

CHORIC SONG

1

There is sweet music here that softer falls
Than petals from blown roses on the grass,
Or night-dews on still waters between walls
Of shadowy granite, in a gleaming pass;
Music that gentlier on the spirit lies,
Than tired eyelids upon tired eyes;
Music that brings sweet sleep down from the blissful skies.
Here are cool mosses deep,
And thro' the moss the ivies creep,
And in the stream the long-leaved flowers weep,
And from the craggy ledge the poppy hangs in sleep.

2

Why are we weigh'd upon with heaviness,
And utterly consumed with sharp distress,
While all things else have rest from weariness?
All things have rest: why should we toil alone,
We only toil, who are the first of things,
And make perpetual moan,
Still from one sorrow to another thrown:
Nor ever fold our wings,
And cease from wanderings;
Nor steep our brows in slumber's holy balm;
Nor harken what the inner spirit sings,
'There is no joy but calm!'
Why should we only toil, the roof and crown of things?

3

Lo! in the middle of the wood,
The folded leaf is woo'd from out the bud
With winds upon the branch, and there
Grows green and broad, and takes no care,
Sun-steep'd at noon, and in the moon
Nightly dew-fed; and turning yellow
Falls, and floats adown the air.
Lo! sweeten'd with the summer light,
The full-juiced apple, waxing over-mellow,
Drops in a silent autumn night.
All its allotted length of days,
The flower ripens in its place,
Ripens and fades, and falls, and hath no toil,
Fast-rooted in the fruitful soil.

4

Hateful is the dark-blue sky,
Vaulted o'er the dark-blue sea.
Death is the end of life; ah, why
Should life all labour be?

Let us alone. Time driveth onward fast,
And in a little while our lips are dumb.
Let us alone. What is it that will last?
All things are taken from us, and become
Portions and parcels of the dreadful Past.
Let us alone. What pleasure can we have
To war with evil? Is there any peace
In ever climbing up the climbing wave?
All things have rest, and ripen toward the grave
In silence; ripen, fall and cease.
Give us long rest or death, dark death, or dreamful ease!

5

How sweet it were, hearing the downward stream,
With half-shut eyes ever to seem
Falling asleep in a half-dream!
To dream and dream, like yonder amber light,
Which will not leave the myrrh-bush on the height;
To hear each other's whisper'd speech;
Eating the Lotos day by day,
To watch the crisping ripples on the beach,
And tender curving lines of creamy spray;
To lend our hearts and spirits wholly
To the influence of mild-minded melancholy;
To muse and brood and live again in memory,
With those old faces of our infancy
Heap'd over with a mound of grass,
Two handfuls of white dust, shut in an urn of brass!

6

Dear is the memory of our wedded lives,
And dear the last embraces of our wives
And their warm tears: but all hath suffer'd change;
For surely now our household hearths are cold:
Our sons inherit us: our looks are strange:
And we should come like ghosts to trouble joy.
Or else the island princes over-bold
Have eat our substance, and the minstrel sings
Before them of the ten-years' war in Troy,
And our great deeds, as half-forgotten things.
Is there confusion in the little isle?
Let what is broken so remain.
The Gods are hard to reconcile:
'Tis hard to settle order once again.
There *is* confusion worse than death,
Trouble on trouble, pain on pain,
Long labour unto aged breath,
Sore task to hearts worn out by many wars
And eyes grown dim with gazing on the pilot-stars.

7

But, propt on beds of amaranth and moly,
How sweet (while warm airs lulls us, blowing lowly,)
With half-dropt eyelid still,
Beneath a heaven dark and holy,
To watch the long bright river drawing slowly
His waters from the purple hill –
To hear the dewy echoes calling
From cave to cave thro' the thick-twined vine –
To watch the emerald-colour'd water falling
Thro' many a wov'n acanthus-wreath divine!
Only to hear and see the far-off sparkling brine,
Only to hear were sweet, stretch'd out beneath the pine.

8

The Lotos blooms below the flowery peak:
The Lotos blows by every winding creek:
All day the wind breathes low with mellower tone:
Thro' every hollow cave and alley lone
Round and round the spicy downs the yellow Lotos-dust is
    blown.
We have had enough of action, and of motion we,
Roll'd to starboard, roll'd to larboard, when the surge was
    seething free,
Where the wallowing monster spouted his foam-fountains
    in the sea.
Let us swear an oath, and keep it with an equal mind,
In the hollow Lotos-land to live and lie reclined
On the hills like Gods together, careless of mankind.
For they lie beside their nectar, and the bolts are hurl'd
Far below them in the valleys, and the clouds are lightly
    curl'd
Round their golden houses, girdled with the gleaming world:
Where they smile in secret, looking over wasted lands,
Blight and famine, plague and earthquake, roaring deeps
    and fiery sands,
Clanging fights, and flaming towns, and sinking ships, and
    praying hands.
But they smile, they find a music centred in a doleful song
Steaming up, a lamentation and an ancient tale of wrong,
Like a tale of little meaning though the words are strong;
Chanted from an ill-used race of men that cleave the soil,
Sow the seed, and reap the harvest with enduring toil,
Storing yearly little dues of wheat, and wine and oil;
Till they perish and they suffer – some, 'tis whisper'd – down
    in hell
Suffer endless anguish, others in Elysian valleys dwell,
Resting weary limbs at last on beds of asphodel.
Surely, surely, slumber is more sweet than toil, the shore
Than labour in the deep mid-ocean, wind and wave and oar;
Oh rest ye, brother mariners, we will not wander more.

50. Vodghena, Macedonia
51. Euboea, Greece
52. Philae, Egypt
53. Parga, Albania
54. *Euboea, Greece*

'Courage!' is the first word, but the need for effort is immediately cancelled by the 'mounting wave' which will inevitably roll towards the shore: 'In the afternoon they came unto a land / In which it seemed always afternoon.' Tennyson uses repetition, pauses, and a lingering Spenserian line, to create a hypnotically enticing paradise. The beauty of the landscape includes streams and rivers, mountains, forests, meadows at sunset. And the Lotos-Eaters, 'mild-eyed melancholy', bring enchanted stems of flowers and fruit; whoever eats the fruit is immediately distanced from reality, and weary of action, sinks into a half-dream. The choric song reinforces the urge to give up, to forget wedded lives and great deeds alike. And the end of the poem, focusing on the Lotos and the 'yellow Lotos-dust', again describes the mariners' toil and the apparent ideal of living 'like

Gods' in the restful Lotos-land. Tennyson brilliantly evokes a languor which is not true peace; a dream-state which does not involve real decisions. And while he describes the 'hollow Lotos-land' he allows the reader partly to experience its pleasures and yet to remain outside, to remain capable of judgement. The last line leaves out choice: 'Oh rest ye, brother mariners, we will not wander more.' But the reader can see how the speaker has been persuaded and the Lotos-eating mariners deluded.

'The Lotos-Eaters' is a poem well suited to a traveller who half wished never to return. Lear, as he set out again and again, fled the cold and the constrictions of English society. He left behind his loneliness as he briefly met new people and sketched new and beautiful landscapes. In the Khans of Albania he forgot his dismal lack of money and, as he watched birds on the Nile sandbanks, he forgot that his pictures would not sell. But Lear knew that such escapes were temporary. On Corfu once – amid the green and the flowers – he said 'This is Lotos eating with a vengeance' (D. 18 April 1866), but he knew it was a delicious moment that must end. His own melancholy temperament never quite led him towards the 'dark death or dreamful ease' of the poem: the moment he could muster his energies he started work again. His output of sketches and paintings in oil and watercolour was enormous: with these he worked through the memories of landscapes he had seen, beauty hoarded so that it came back to him when he could no longer travel himself. He needed and invented the 'toil' which Tennyson's Lotos-Eaters question. When he had settled in one place, and especially in his last years at San Remo, Lear's unremitting work was what gave him energy and a sense of identity.

All the landscapes chosen for 'The Lotos-Eaters' are serene and spacious. 'Moonlight on still waters' was the title of one of the first Tennyson landscapes in oil which Lear attempted, once he had decided on a first sequence of five. He worked on it all through 1871 and for years afterwards, sometimes concentrating on details, sometimes nearly giving up the picture completely. The design itself was reproduced as one of the monochrome illustrations and appeared in both the known completed sets. In this small picture the lines of the cliff are clumsily drawn and the water has no gleam. Lear used a thickened line because his eyesight would not allow him to work with the extremely delicate outline of his earlier years. But it is part of the travelled past, a remembrance of Philae and of a picture Lear would have wanted as part of a *Liber Studiorum*.

50. Vodghena, Macedonia

At half-past three we are in sight of Vodhena, and a more beautifully situated place can hardly be imagined, even shorn as it is just now by cloud and mist of its mountain background. It stands on a long ridge of wooded cliff, with mosques sparkling above, and waterfalls glittering down the hill-side, not unlike the Cascatelli of Tivoli, the whole screen of rock seeming to close up the valley as a natural wall.

The air began to freshen as the road ascended from the plain through prodigiously large walnut and plane-trees shading the winding paths, and as the valley narrowed, the rushing of many streams below the waving branches was most delicious; between the fine groups of dense foliage, the dark mass of the woody rock of Vodhena is irresistibly beautiful, and before we reached the dreary scattered walls and suburb lanes, by climbing for half an hour up a winding pass between high rocks, I was more than once tempted to linger and draw. From the proud height on which this ancient city stood, the combination of green wood, yellow plain, and distant mountain was most lovely, and I can conceive that when the atmosphere is clear, and all the majesty of Olympus, with the gulf of Saloniki (and perhaps Athos) also are visible, few scenes in Greece can surpass the splendour of this.

After six, we arrived at the postmaster's house in the centre of the town – one of those strange, wide-eaved, double-bodied, painted and galleried Turkish abodes which

51

They sat them down upon the yellow sand, —
(The Lotos-Eaters,)

Euboea Greece

strike the stranger with wonder; but the whole place was full of the retinue of some travelling Pasha – guards above, and horses below – a small outhouse abounding with cats and cobwebs being also full of a large party of Bulgarian merchants. So Giorgio set out to seek a lodging in some Greek tradesman's house, and I wound up the evening by a prowl through the streets of the town, in which, to all the varieties of Yenidje, is added a profusion of fountains of running water, and numerous streams half the width of its sloping streets. Tea and lodging (so called) I found prepared over a large stable – a great falling off from last night's accommodation, the floor of the barn being of that vague nature that one contemplated the horses below through various large cavities, by means of some of which one might, by any too hasty movement, descend unwittingly among them ere morning.
(Albanian Journal, 14 September 1848, pp. 38-9)

. . . Before an early "déjeûner" at ten, there was yet time to draw a street-scene, though the curiosity of half the people of Vodhena obliged me to stand on a stone in the midst of the kennel to draw. Their shouts of laughter, as I represented the houses, were electrifying: "Scroo! scroo! scroo!" (He writes it down! he writes! he writes!) they shouted. But it was all good nature: no wilful annoyance of any kind. (15 September 1848, pp. 41-2)

(Elsewhere Lear's attempts to draw in a Muslim village or town were sometimes greeted with stones, angry dervishes, and an insistence that he should put no images on paper. He usually succeeded, although sometimes the authorities had to give him an armed guard.)

51. Euboea, Greece
. . . along the coast to Oropo & so to Chalcis, that famous old city in the island of Euboea or Negropont. (Have you a map of Greece?) Chalcis delighted me, as being full of old Turkish houses & minarets, the first I had seen –; you have no idea of the picturesqueness of the people. Every group makes one stare & wonder. The houses are very full of bow windows & lattices, but the town is very wretched. All the great towns – except 3 or 4 – are quite new – having been destroyed by either Turks or Greeks, or both over & over again, in the last war. They are built on no plan & look very mean & scattered. From Chalcis we made a tour of a week all over Euboea: no such beautiful scenery can be found anywhere as the forests: you ride for days & days through whispering woods of bright green pine, – the odour of which is delightful & the branches are full of bright blue rollers. It is more like a very magnificent English park than anything else I can compare it to. The peasants – few as they are, are most obliging – simple creatures. The men wear a plain tunic, but the women dress very prettily. They bind the head with a yellow handkerchief; but plait the long hair, & then tie it on to still longer plaits of silk or horse hair till it ends in bunches of silk with silver tags; in some villages they string cowries shells all down these long tails, which are confined by a girdle. (EL to Ann, 19 July 1848)

52. Philae, Egypt
Lear spent ten days on the island of Philae during his first visit to the Nile in 1854. He wrote to Ann saying that it was 'more like a real *fairy island* than anything else I can compare it to'. Lodged in the temple of Isis with beds and luggage, the artist could survey the whole island.

It is very small, & was formerly all covered with temples, of which the ruins of 5 or 6 now only remain. The great Temple of Isis on the terrace of which . . . I now am writing, is so extremely wonderful that no words can give the least idea of it. The Nile is divided here into several channels, by other rocky islands, & beyond you see the desert & the great granite hills of Assouan. At morning & evening the scene is lovely beyond imagination. – I have done very little in oils, as the colours dry fast, & the sand injures them; water colours also are very difficult to use. But I have made a great many outlines, & I hope my journeys will eventually prove to have been of great service to me.
(EL to Ann, 7 February 1854)

In 1867 Lear visited Philae again, passing the island first and noting in his diary (19 February 1867):

The effect of these astonishing granite masses was wholly indescribable, & as we went into the pass to Mahatta:
Moonlight on still waters between walls, was wonderful
Of gleaming granite in a shadowy pass at Mahatta

The guide had not brought enough money for the ferry; while waiting, Lear records: 'So we go down to the shore opposite that lovely lovely place, & I make 2 nice drawings – tho' nothing can ever express the perfection of Philae.' Then, landing from the ferry, he showed Giorgio the temples and the little room he stayed in in 1854. When they came away Lear drew again from the boat:

'the great granite pass of gleaming rox – by moonlight they were delightfully rounded & the water was like glass – brown gray – with the least silvery sheen here and there – & the shadows of the near rox perfect, so that no line existed to shew you what was rock, what water.'

Once on shore, two donkeys were taken, but Lear soon walked along the main road to Assouan and found his Nile boat, the Zuleika, 'arrived safely – no damage done & the luggage all right.'

Beneath this Philae drawing Lear wrote: 'still waters between walls / Of shadowy granite in a gleaming pass;' but in his list he had printed 'Moonlight on still waters' and it was this misquotation that he always remembered. Tennyson's 'Lotos-Eaters' has 'night-dews on still waters' with no moonlight, no source of light at all. The lines from the choric song, bring together sound and touch: 'music' that 'softer falls'

Than petals from blown roses on the grass,
 Or night-dews on still waters between walls
Of shadowy granite, in a gleaming pass.

'Petals' touch 'grass', 'night dews' fall so softly that 'still waters' remain 'still'. 'Shadowy granite' contrasts with 'gleaming pass', but the transition is left uncertain: there is no sudden illumination. Tennyson wants to subdue sight and bring, at last, 'tired eyelids' down on 'tired eyes'. The whole song is a persuasive lullaby to sleep, to enervation. For Lear, the artist, sight was an all-important sense. He remembered the 'gleaming pass' at Philae and the moonlight on rock and water: he wanted to record, not hearing, not touching, but seeing minutely.

still waters between walls

Of shadowy granite in a gleaming pass;

(The Lotos=Eaters.)

Philæ.
Egypt.

From Tennyson's lines he has taken what his picture required and added the essential source of light. Yet with 'Moonlight on still waters' he thought he was illustrating two lines from the 'Lotos-Eaters'. His version of Tennyson's lines was usually inseparable from the Philae view. Yet Lear noted (D. 17 February 1867): 'AT's lines – "Like moonlight on still waters between walls / Of gleaming granite in a shadowy pass," – are fulfilled at the pass above Tafa, which I should like to paint some day.' Once again the effects of light on water and granite struck the artist so forcibly that he added 'moonlight' and forgot Tennyson's 'night-dews'. But even in the first Philae oil painting the combination of still water, and rounded, gleaming rock, almost defeated Lear. He had great difficulty with the painting, and his problems are not solved in the almost grotesque outlines of the small drawing. Very dark rounded cliff lines, without a hint of Lear's careful geological detail are not convincingly lit, and neither is the lifeless water beneath. The design has no delicacy, and Lear's misquotation 'moonlight on still waters' evokes the scene in words far better than the overworked drawing can do. A tiny sketch in his diary is probably more evocative of 'gleaming pass' and 'still waters' than the much worked over oil painting or the late monochrome designs. But the poor quality of this drawing shows up the astonishing range of Lear's work in these Tennyson Illustrations. For 'The Lotos-Eaters', Lear could still draw fine woods for 'Euboea' (although the figures are crude); the streams of 'Vodghena', the citadel and curved shore of 'Parga' are the work of an artist who had not lost all his skill in 'poetical topography'.

53. Parga, Albania

Long before sunrise we were away from Splantza, and taking another guide to insure certainty in reaching Parga, I bade adieu once more to the plain of the Acheron and dark Suli, as we followed the track which led us in less than two hours to the spot we had reached last afternoon, and thence for some distance along the high cliffs above the bright blue sea, through underwood of lentisk and thorn.

About nine we arrived at beautiful and extensive groves of olive, for the cultivation of which Parga is renowned; they clothe all the hills around, and hang over rock and cliff to the very sea with delightful and feathery luxuriance. At length we descended to the shore at the foot of the little promontory on which the ill-fated place and its citadel stood; alas, what now appears a town and castle consists of old ruined walls, for Parga is desolate. A new one built since the natives abandoned the ancient site, – is, however, springing up on the shore, and with its two mosques is picturesque: this with the rock and dismantled fortress – the islands in the bay, and the rich growth of olive slopes around, form a picture of completely beautiful character, though more resembling an Italian than a Greek scene; but it is impossible fully to contemplate with pleasure a place, the history of which is so full of melancholy and painful interest.

. . . In the afternoon and evening I made many drawings from either side of the promontory of Parga. From every point it is lovely, very unlike Albanian landscape in general, and partaking more of the character of Calabrian or Amalfitan coast scenery.

(Albanian Journal, 7 May 1848, pp. 372-3)

50. EL List: A land of streams
    EL Drawing: A Land of streams, –
51. EL List: They sate them down upon the yellow sand
    EL Drawing: They sat them down upon the yellow sand, –
52. EL List: Moonlight on still waters
    EL Drawing: still waters between walls
    Of shadowy granite in a gleaming pass;
[*Poems*, 1842: Of night-dews on still waters between walls
    Of shadowy granite, in a gleaming pass;]
53. EL List: To watch the crisping ripples
    EL Drawing: To watch the crisping ripples on the beach
    And tender curving lines of creamy spray;

53

To watch the crisping ripples on the beach
And tender curving lines of creamy spray;
(The Lotos = Eaters.)

Parga.
Albania

From: A DREAM OF FAIR WOMEN

I

I read, before my eyelids dropt their shade,
   'The Legend of Good Women,' long ago
Sung by the morning star of song, who made
   His music heard below;

II

Dan Chaucer, the first warbler, whose sweet breath
   Preluded those melodious bursts, that fill
The spacious times of Great Elizabeth
   With sounds that echo still.

III

And, for a while, the knowledge of his art
   Held me above the subject, as strong gales
Hold swollen clouds from raining, though my heart,
   Brimful of those wild tales,

IV

Charged both mine eyes with tears. In every land
   I saw, wherever light illumineth,
Beauty and anguish walking hand in hand
   The downward slope to death.

V

Those far-renowned brides of ancient song
   Peopled the hollow dark, like burning stars,
And I heard sounds of insult, shame, and wrong,
   And trumpets blown for wars;...

XIII

All those sharp fancies, by down-lapsing thought
   Stream'd onward, lost their edges, and did creep
Roll'd on each other, rounded, smooth'd, and brought
   Into the gulfs of sleep.

XIV

At last methought that I had wander'd far
   In an old wood: fresh-wash'd in coolest dew,
The maiden splendours of the morning star
   Shook in the stedfast blue.

XV

Enormous elm-tree-boles did stoop and lean
   Upon the dusky brushwood underneath
Their broad curved branches, fledged with clearest green,
   New from its silken sheath.

XVI

The dim red morn had died, her journey done,
   And with dead lips smiled at the twilight plain,
Half-fall'n across the threshold of the sun,
   Never to rise again.

XVII

There was no motion in the dumb dead air,
   Not any song of bird or sound of rill;
Gross darkness of the inner sepulchre
   Is not so deadly still

XVIII

As that wide forest. Growths of jasmine turn'd
   Their humid arms festooning tree to tree,
And at the root thro' lush green grasses burn'd
   The red anemone.

XIX

I knew the flowers, I knew the leaves, I knew
   The tearful glimmer of the languid dawn
On those long, rank, dark wood-walks drench'd in dew,
   Leading from lawn to lawn.

XX

The smell of violets, hidden in the green,
   Pour'd back into my empty soul and frame
The times when I remember to have been
   Joyful and free from blame.

XXI

And from within me a clear under-tone
   Thrill'd thro' mine ears in that unblissful clime:
'Pass freely thro'! the wood is all thine own,
   Until the end of time.'

XXII

At length I saw a lady within call,
   Stiller than chisell'd marble, standing there;
A daughter of the gods, divinely tall,
   And most divinely fair.

XXIII

Her loveliness with shame and with surprise
   Froze my swift speech: she turning on my face
The star-like sorrows of immortal eyes,
   Spoke slowly in her place.

XXIV

'I had great beauty: ask thou not my name:
   No one can be more wise than destiny.
Many drew swords and died. Where'er I came
   I brought calamity.'...

XXXII

I turning saw, throned on a flowery rise,
   One sitting on a crimson scarf unroll'd;
A queen, with swarthy cheeks and bold black eyes,
   Brow-bound with burning gold.

XXXIII

She, flashing forth a haughty smile, began:
  'I govern'd men by change, and so I sway'd
All moods. 'Tis long since I have seen a man.
  Once, like the moon, I made

XXXIV

'The ever-shifting currents of the blood
  According to my humour ebb and flow.
I have no men to govern in this wood;
  That makes my only woe.

XXXV

'Nay – yet it chafes me that I could not bend
  One will; nor tame and tutor with mine eye
That dull cold-blooded Cæsar. Prythee, friend,
  Where is Mark Antony?

XXXVI

'By him great Pompey dwarfs and suffers pain,
  A mortal man before immortal Mars;
The glories of great Julius lapse and wane,
  And shrink from suns to stars.

XXXVII

'That man, of all the men I ever knew,
  Most touched my fancy. O, what days and nights
We had in Egypt, ever reaping new
  Harvest of ripe delights,

XXXVIII

'Realm-draining revels! Life was one long feast.
  What wit! what words! what sweet words, only made
Less sweet by the kiss that broke 'em, liking best
  To be so richly stay'd!

XXXIX

'What dainty strifes, when fresh from war's alarms,
  My Hercules, my gallant Antony,
My mailed captain leapt into my arms,
  Contented there to die!

XL

'And in those arms he died: I heard my name
  Sigh'd forth with life: then I shook off all fear:
Oh what a little snake stole Cæsar's fame!
  What else was left? look here!'

XLI

(With that she tore her robe apart, and half
  The polish'd argent of her breast to sight
Laid bare. Thereto she pointed with a laugh,
  Showing the aspick's bite.)

XLII

'I died a Queen. The Roman soldier found
  Me lying dead, my crown about my brows,
A name for ever! – lying robed and crown'd,
  Worthy a Roman spouse.'...

XLVI

Slowly my sense undazzled. Then I heard
  A noise of some one coming thro' the lawn,
And singing clearer than the crested bird
  That claps his wings at dawn.

XLVII

'The torrent brooks of hallow'd Israel
  From craggy hollows pouring, late and soon,
Sound all night long, in falling thro' the dell,
  Far-heard beneath the moon.

XLVIII

'The balmy moon of blessed Israel
  Floods all the deep-blue gloom with beams divine:
All night the splinter'd crags that wall the dell
  With spires of silver shine.'...

LI

Th daughter of the warrior Gileadite,
  A maiden pure; as when she went along
From Mizpeh's tower'd gate with welcome light,
  With timbrel and with song....

LXIV

'Alas! alas!' a low voice, full of care,
  Murmur'd beside me: 'Turn and look on me:
I am that Rosamond, whom men call fair,
  If what I was I be.

LXV

'Would I had been some maiden coarse and poor!
  O me, that I should ever see the light!
Those dragon eyes of anger'd Eleanor
  Do hunt me, day and night.'

LXVI

She ceased in tears, fallen from hope and trust:
  To whom the Egyptian: 'O, you tamely died!
You should have clung to Fulvia's waist, and thrust
  The dagger thro' her side.'

LXVII

With that sharp sound the white dawn's creeping beams,
  Stol'n to my brain, dissolved the mystery
Of folded sleep. The captain of my dreams
  Ruled in the eastern sky.

LXVIII

Morn broaden'd on the borders of the dark,
  Ere I saw her, who clasp'd in her last trance
Her murder'd father's head, or Joan of Arc,
  A light of ancient France;

LXIX

Or her, who knew that Love can vanquish Death,
  Who kneeling, with one arm about her king,
Drew forth the poison with her balmy breath,
  Sweet as new buds in Spring.

LXX

No memory labours longer from the deep
   Gold-mines of thought to lift the hidden ore
That glimpses, moving up, than I from sleep
   To gather and tell o'er

LXXI

Each little sound and sight. With what dull pain
   Compass'd, how eagerly I sought to strike
Into that wondrous track of dreams again!
   But no two dreams are like.

LXXII

As when a soul laments, which hath been blest,
   Desiring what is mingled with past years,
In yearnings that can never be exprest
   By signs or groans or tears;

LXXIII

Because all words, tho' cull'd with choicest art,
   Failing to give the bitter of the sweet,
Wither beneath the palate, and the heart
   Faints, faded by its heat.

55. Wady Feiran, Gebel Serbal, Peninsula of Sinai
56. Civitella di Subiaco, Italy

'A Dream of Fair Women' is a strangely inconclusive poem. It was originally prefaced with some stanzas describing the poet as surveying all below him like someone taking a trip in a hot-air balloon. All this was dropped in 1842 as being too 'modern' for the subject matter of the poem. But the abandoned preface does suggest some uncertainty of tone. Tennyson has a long preamble about his reaction to Chaucer, which leads him into a description of conflicts, battles, violence of the past. It even has the poet raising his own arm, in a half-dream, to try to rescue a passing lady from a marauding knight. The main point of these sieges and incursions seems to be:

> . . . In every land
> I saw, wherever light illumineth,
> Beauty and anguish walking hand in hand
>   The downward slope to death.   (IV)

Women, or more specifically 'far-renowned brides of ancient song' are seen as victims.

   This part of the poem is linked to the rest by a beauti-

All night the splinter'd crags that wall the dell
with spires of silver shine.

(A dream of fair women.)

Wady Feiran
Gebel Serbal.
Peninsula of Sinai.

fully-crafted stanza in which the 'sharp fancies' caught in a stream of 'down-lapsing' thought, turn, by a series of images, into stone, and thus to pebbles rolling against each other, rounding, smoothing, and then coming to rest, finally in 'gulfs of sleep'. 'Fancies', 'thought', 'sleep' become stone worked on by water and 'lapsing' is both a verb for flowing water and a hint of 'lapis', stone. The conflict then ceases, and in dream the poet enters the wood of the past which has life in its 'great elm-tree-boles', and death in its 'dim red morn' which Tennyson thought 'old Turner' would have painted 'magnificently well'.[1] The forest is part 'deadly still', part live, with 'lush green grasses', flowers, and the smell of violets which bring back time remembered as 'joyful and free from blame'. The pivotal stanza of 'sharp fancies' does not lead easily into this unpeopled forest, and it is not used as a definite background for the fair women who shortly appear. The forest of the past questions and embodies both beauty and anguish, but it remains cut off from the rest of the poem.

A dramatic narrative follows in which fair women of the past tell the poet/narrator of their feelings and their fate. They pass as in a moving pageant, but they speak, quite often, with considerable vigour. Helen first, then Iphigenia: one aware of bringing calamity, the other fated to be a sacrifice. Next comes the resilient and still lively Cleopatra telling of Antony, regretting she has no man 'to govern in this world'. There is some dramatic vigour in Cleopatra's memory of her life in Egypt: she still instils love and dazzles the sense, even in a dream. Death, but not anguish, seems Cleopatra's fate. And she is followed by a dutiful and courageous Biblical figure, Jeptha's daughter, who sacrifices herself because of her father's vow. Despite the promise of her life, she dies for her God, land, and Father. Once more there is little anguish: she would do it again. From these two central figures Tennyson moves to Rosamund, Margaret Roper, Joan of Arc and Eleanor, wife of Edward I, whose deeds are briefly chronicled.

The reader, in the position of watcher and listener, now expects some distinctions or links, some weighing up of beauty and anguish, some conclusion to the dream. But the poem has the poet/narrator lingering over the glimpses given by memory and sleep. He wishes to dream again, 'As when a soul laments, which has been blest, / Desiring what is mingled with past years.' And the poem ends with the inadequacy of words to balance 'the bitter of the sweet': the heart and soul remain in anguish, but inarticulate. These last stanzas do not offer an end to 'A Dream of Fair Women', they merely raise more questions about memory, and the 'passion of the past'. The poem is not overtly lyrical about 'fair women', as in 'Eleänore' or 'Fatima', but it too is fragmented: the 'fair women' come and go. Only Cleopatra makes a really forceful impression on the reader. Tennyson, however, remained interested in fair, but also passionate and intelligent women. He tried to give them life and character in *The Princess* and succeeded brilliantly, later still, with the wayward Queen Guinevere in *Idylls of the King*.

Strange in itself, it is also an odd poem for Lear to choose. He may have been more attracted to the ideas of memory, sleep, dream and the past, than to the initial conflicts of the women. He drew nothing from the forest landscape, but, picking up 'The balmy moon of blessed Israel', he turned to Palestine and took two lines of background: 'All night the splintered crags that wall the dell / With spires of silver shine.' This is a forcefully pictorial image and Lear matches it to Wady Feiran, a place he visited early and described·to his sister Ann. The other quotation he chose spans years of his past. He always associated the line 'Morn broaden'd on the borders of the dark' with Civitella di Subiaco, a scene from early Italian travels, which became the first Tennyson oil he ever painted. He told Emily Tennyson in 1855 that he had sold the 'Morn broaden'd' to friends (William Neville and his wife), and had put a very low price on it because he needed the money. He repeated the design several times; once for Chichester Fortescue, when Lear comments on how well it has been framed. But 'Morn broaden'd', subject of a fine prose description by Lear, was a Tennyson Illustration long before he started on his first Tennyson oils in 1871. The beginning of sunrise and the darkness of rock did not produce a satisfactory small illustration. And a bare tree trunk, which crosses the picture, is hardly visible on this small scale. But the very phrase 'Morn broaden'd' Lear used for various moments of sunrise and it was always connected with Tennyson. There is no evidence that the rest of the poem entered so deeply into his consciousness.

55. Wady Feiran, Gebel Serbal, Peninsula of Sinai
Here we had fairly entered the mountains, & more magnificent scenes I have never beheld. It is not known how the Israelites came up to Mt. Sinai – but perhaps by Wady Feiran. 22nd. The whole day was passed in grand mountain passes, but we had a good deal of rain, in shower storms. Wady Mokattet is remarkable for its long rocky rides being inscribed with unknown characters; there are millions of sentences. Many suppose them to have been written by early Xtian pilgrims, & as there we see 2 or 3 on the top of Mount Serbal, this is why they fix on that Mount for Sinai. We encamped at the beginning of Wady Feiran, 23rd. After a long & tedious winding, we entered the great beautiful Oasis – the centre of Wady Feiran . . . & the most wonderful & beautiful place I ever saw. There is a city there – Pharan – in all ages – & it is believed to have been the chief city [of the] Amal & Kitar. At present there are only Arabs in huts & tents. But the great beauty of the place is that it is filled up with a forest of palm trees, & that there is a running stream in the centre. I cannot describe this place as my paper is short – but certainly the world contains not another for loveliness . . .
(EL to Ann, 16 January 1849)

56. Civitella di Subiaco, Italy
The Rock of Civitella di Subiaco – in the Apennines near Rome: – before Sunrise.

"Morn broaden'd on the borders of the Dark"
A single line written by that greatest of Word= landscape=painters, Alfred Tennyson, has placed a wellknown scene once more before me, and has made me forget the years since I last saw it, – in the almost reality of recollection, – even to the solemn horror of those black woods, and the unbroken silence of that strange hour.

When I first read the words, "Morn broaden'd on the borders of the dark", they seemed to me to describe exactly what I had so often watched in other days, – that Darkness, – edged with broadening light which I had seen through so many Summer and Autumn months during years of Italian wanderings, and most of all from the neighbourhood of Civitella, a village near Subiaco, about 40 or 50 miles from Rome.

– Instantly & vividly rose before me that Eagle's nest on the Crest of its double edged peaked rock, rising sheer out of a deep deep valley, and overlooking all the land, far & wide. Not an outline, not a detail was visible below the horizon: all seemed a profound Gulf of inky-purple gloom, in the depths of which the eye vainly sought for any object.

– Only the massive Rock, rising above the skyline, showed its Awful form, its churchtower and its houses against the clear green sky: or perhaps in the close foreground a single dead tree rather deepened than lessened the dread feeling of darkness.

Slowly the light pink cloudlets began to fleck the pure clear space above, as morn gave warning of nearer approach to the long lines of intense crimson sobered into purpler tints towards the Southern hills – and overhead, fold on fold of drapery like clouds stretched away, – each fold more deeply tinged underneath with rosy-gold as it was nearer to the horizon in the brightening East.

– "Morn broaden'd on the borders of the Dark." – (EL to Emily Tennyson, 11 November 1855)

[1] Ed. Hallam Lord Tennyson, *The Works of Tennyson* (Eversley Edition Vol. 1, 1907), p. 376.

55. EL List: All night the spires of silver shine
    EL Drawing: All night the splinter'd crags that wall the dell
                    With spires of silver shine.
56. EL List: Morn broaden'd on the borders of the dark
    EL Drawing: Morn broaden'd on the borders of the dark.

56

Morn broaden'd on the borders of the dark.
(A dream of fair Women.)

Civitella di Subiaco.
Italy.

'YOU ASK ME, WHY, THOUGH ILL AT EASE'

You ask me, why, though ill at ease,
    Within this region I subsist,
    Whose spirits fail within the mist,
And languish for the purple seas?

It is the land that freemen till,
    That sober-suited Freedom chose,
    The land, where girt with friends or foes
A man may speak the thing he will;

A land of settled government,
    A land of just and old renown,
    Where Freedom slowly broadens down
From precedent to precedent:

Where faction seldom gathers head,
    But by degrees to fullness wrought,
    The strength of some diffusive thought
Hath time and space to work and spread.

Should banded unions persecute
    Opinion, and induce a time
    When single thought is civil crime,
And individual freedom mute;

Though Power should make from land to land
    The name of Britain trebly great –
    Though every channel of the State
Should almost choke with golden sand –

Yet waft me from the harbour-mouth,
    Wild wind! I seek a warmer sky,
    And I will see before I die
The palms and temples of the South.

58

Mahatta.

I will see before I die.
The Palms and Temples of the South.
("You ask me why" &c &c)

Dôm Palms.
Mahatta. Nile
Egypt

57. *Date Palms, Sheikh Abadeh, Nile, Egypt*
58. Dom Palms, Mahatta, Nile, Egypt
59. *Cocoa Palms, Mahee, Malabar, India*
60. *Cocoa Palms, Telicherry, Malabar, India*
61. *Cocoa Palms, Avisavella, Ceylon*
62. Cocoa Palms, Alipay, Travancore, India
63. *Dondera, Coast of Ceylon*
64. Palmyra Palms, Bengal, India
65. *Areka Palms, Ratnapoora, Ceylon*
66. *Sago Palms, Ceylon*
67. *Talipat Palms, Malibar, India*
68. Paestum, Italy
69. *Segesta, Sicily*
70. *Girgenti, Sicily*
71. Bassae, Phigaleia, Greece
72. Karnak, Thebes, Egypt
73. Philae, Egypt
74. *Philae, Egypt*
75. Dendoor, Nile, Nubia
76. *Conjeveram, Madras Presidency, India*
77. Mahabalipooram, near Madras, India
78. *Tanjore, Madras Presidency, India*
79. *Trichinopoly, Madras Presidency, India*

Note: All titles and numbers above are taken from Lear's pictures. There are some differences on EL List for 59-66.

Written about 1833, this poem about British freedom reflected Tennyson's growing political interests and his reaction to the agitation over the passing of the Reform Bill. He very quickly took up the conservative attitudes of his maturity, fearing the violent changes suggested by the Polish insurrection against Russia in 1830, and the burning of hayricks by dissidents in the south of England. In the 1842 volume, among the Orianas, Marianas, and Lotos-Eaters, appeared 'You Ask Me Why', 'Love Thou the Land', and 'Of Old Sat Freedom on the Heights'. These were mildly political poems, slightly at odds with the lyrical and Arthurian pieces. Tennyson, never a locally satirical political poet, applauds the kinds of freedom which he believes to be ideally British: 'The land, where girt with friends or foes / A man may speak the thing he will.' Individual liberty, and a 'settled government' mean that 'faction seldom gathers head' and 'diffusive thought', presumably radical and destructive, has time to be worked out and slowly dispersed. The emphasis is on the survival of British freedom and solidarity.

The setting of the poem contains no landscape, although the speaker at first languishes for 'purple seas'. At the end, however, it becomes clear that if Britain were to gain great power and wealth, but lose its traditional freedoms, the speaker would at once seek a 'warmer sky'. 'Yet waft me from the harbour-mouth', he would beg, wishing to take ship for southern warmth and southern sights. This may well have attracted Lear to the poem. He kept up with the state of British politics, but increasingly as the years passed, each visit to England emphasized his rootlessness, his difficulties in selling his paintings, his dependence on friends and patrons, and the round of the country-house guest – half courted, half scorned – which brought joy in meeting friends, misery in confronting snobbish strangers. And always there was the cold which brought on asthma and bronchitis. When

Lear's sister Ann died, and his remaining sister, Eleanor, became deaf and ill, he had less family in England than in New Zealand, where several relatives had emigrated. Lear's own health needed a 'warmer sky'; as an artist he wanted a bright, clear light; and, in the end, he became a complete expatriate.

All the drawings he chose for this poem illustrate the last line. The poet adopts an explorer's voice, though Tennyson rarely moved far: the Pyrenees, Portugal, the Riviera, part of Italy, and, surprisingly, Norway. Hallam recalled the story from his mother's journal.

> Mr Lear came from Liphook...He told an excellent story...about "You ask me, why". A friend of his remarked to him: "It is a well known fact that Tennyson hates travelling." "Nonsense" answered Lear, "he loves it." "On the contrary," the friend retorted, "he hates it and he says so himself somewhere:
> 'And I will *die* before I see
> The palms and temples of the South.'"
> (*Mem.* II, p. 44-5)

By the time the artist chose the drawings for this poem his 'will see' had become 'had seen'. Lear knew the temples of Greece early in his travelling career, and Philae in Egypt he first saw in 1854. But the hoarded sketches of palms and temples in India, Ceylon and Nubia were part of his experience in the 1870s: from the British Raj he returned to the mainly expatriate community of San Remo. His great unfulfilled wish was to see his varieties of landscape, his tribute to Tennyson's verses, printed and published before his death. For one line, 'The palms and temples of the South' there are twenty-three illustrations: eleven 'Palms' and thirteen 'Temples'.

Lear's temples are, of course, recognizable (though Philae has been reconstructed on an artificial site), but his palms are equally distinct. He was exact in noting their different kinds of foliage, how they took the light, where they grew best.

58. Dom Palms, Mahatta, Nile, Egypt

...I leave the boat, wh is to sail & walk out...Coasting along the granite cliffs – just as we did last night – slowly to the village (one of the Mahattas) where I drew. A completely African scene. Doms & camels & the gt Shelaal granite rox in detail near, & in huge island walls beyond. Walking on thence, & the day was truly enjoyable, I drew twice more, & sitting in Palmshade at noon – had biscuit & orange, & heard the boat voices near. abt 12.20. coming from behind the island, lo! my Merkab – & now, at 1.p.m. I sit below a gt tree, & watch the nubians going in boat loads – apparently to pull the boat along – but the wind falls, & so by degrees they all come back again. Air lovely & dry, – the pleasantest day on the Nile for some time – beginning my 5th week. (D. 29 January 1867)

Much of Lear's Journal is in the form of short notes which give a sense of the speed, and perseverance, with which he covered huge tracts of country. They indicate too, the acuteness of his impressions.

62. Cocoa Palms, Alipay, Travancore
[On board a boat Lear seems to have slept till sunrise, but a marginal note warns that he cannot decipher his own notes!]

I will see before I die

The Palms and Temples of the South.
("You ask me why &c &c")

Cocoa Palms. Aleppay.
Travancore
India

Now, 6, the shores are golden, & we go along quickly like as in happy Nile days. G sleeps & seems pretty well. At 7 we stop to try for fowls & eggs; a long fuss, as they will take no money but 2 anna pieces. 7.40 off, very pretty scenery: the water narrower here. It seems we are all to stop for breakfast 5 miles off, which we should complete at 9.40 I suppose. 8. the Backwater is very broad: sandy edges, & remote Cocoa nut borders. 8.30, stop for breakfast, – hot sandy place, but with trees. Men ask for Toddy, refused. We sit on a topsy turvy canoe, and wait – in the shade of a mango tree. At 10.15 we go off with a sail, having had at 9.45 a very good breakfast, 3 "posty" eggs, & 2 small fowls, very tender, – with Claret & soda water. The Backwater banks here are a thick jungle to the waters' Edge, the lowest part screwpines; (& or Mangroves?) – then above them dense yellow or deep green foliage some 20 feet high; then a belt of young Cocoa nuts, with tall Cocoas above all.

[The Backwater, here, is a broad stretch of river which widens into a magnificent lake, with barely visible shores: it seems almost like a sea. But at three p.m. they reach a comparatively narrow channel].

Then – all at once, 4. PM we turned into a very narrow canal – overhung with Palms, – full of boats moving & stationary, & more exquisitely & beautifully picturesque than any canal I ever saw. The Cocoa palms & other foliage hang quite over it in places. It is now 4.30 PM – & still the canal of Aleppay, but not nearly so wondrous & interesting as it was at its entrance.
(Indian Journal, 27 December 1874)

64. Palmyra Palms, Bengal

Off in train for Arrah at 8.15. AM. Very bright & beautiful morning. These fan Palms! towering above all things, – infinitely spotting the plain, & seeming like specks against the pale hills, & over the dark masses of Mango. 8.35 Durarreh. End = ranges of Santhal hills, very pretty, green & graceful. 9 – Kujirah, – hills dwindling; still some pretty bits of broken ground here & there, – but in general the Landscape grows flat & bare, – myriads of dry squares, – (Rice beds,) being the prevailing characteristic. 9.30 Luckieserai; – curious network bridge over river... Endless flatness... Endless piled sacks of Rice... The Calcutta train comes up... 11.15 off... Candlestick Cactus. Palms on trees. Very green level of wheat, Red seemal trees....   (8 February 1874)

64

Arrah

I will see before I die

The Palms and Temples of the South.

("You ask me why &c &c.")

Palmyra Palms.
Bengal.   India

68

Pæstum.

I will see before I die

The Palms and Temples of the South.

("You ask me why &c &c.")

Pæstum.
Italy.

Lear's interest in landscape is matched by his interest in the British Raj: from vice-regal ceremony to natives bathing in the Ganges. He also notices when India seems most British and becomes an imitation of Twickenham or Bournemouth. Notes and letters hand Lear from one English administrator to another, but he usually prefers to stay in the Dak Bungalows where Giorgio (a non-European servant) will not be mistreated, and where the artist will be free to come and go. (In one huge house he thought of trying to take a bath, but could not face the miles of slippery marble steps.) Even in the train, Lear's alertness and curiosity are obvious. '1. PM. Patna. (surprisingly dressed Nepalese cove!)'.

> 2.45. Arrah, – rather a shady-seedy looking place: – but Dak Bungalow, close to Station, decidedly clean & good; nevertheless a low=hung Punkah, against the end of which I knocked my head violently, would assuredly have killed me, had I not had my hat on: – whereon I directly had it taken down. Coolies brought roba. Having arranged things, I went out & asked for Boyle-Sahib's Bangla, & everybody knew it; – an old creature showing me the way, which is for 1/4 of a mile along the high road, – where there is a magnificent border of Palmyra Palms, – & then through a park or compound to the House I wanted to see.

The house had been defended by Boyle against the rebel regiments (three thousand), the troops of a defecting Rajah (five thousand), and a further two thousand of the townspeople. With forty men, Boyle blocked up a billiard room and held it against all comers. Lear made a drawing of this 'curious historical spot': Arrah may appear commonplace and uninteresting to the passing age, but it exhibits 'a marked Episode in a great phase of English History...Boyles defence of the "House in Arrah."' Lear took in an incident of the '"Mutiny period"', drew a road scene with 'beautiful Palmyras or Toddy Fans', wrote his journal and waited for a good supper including 'Bass's beer'. By 7.0 a.m., having risen at 5.0 a.m., he was at the station again.

68. Paestum, Italy

> Next morning about 4, we started in a car for Pesto – the object of our expedition. To get there you cross this immense plain which as you approach the sea grows very desolate & lonely. The peasants have an unhealthy & melancholy air – for after June it is so dreadfully unwholesome an atmosphere – that strangers cannot stay in it – & the few poor wretches who live on in it are always ill. Eboli, standing higher is vastly healthier. – Huge herds of buffaloes you meet continually & one seldom sees any wilder scene. At last you spy the 3 temples of Pesto – once a magnificent Greek town, & of such antiquity that nobody knows anything about them: The Emperor Augustus went to see them as ruins in his time – so judge they are no chickens – notwithstanding this they are nearly perfect being of such wonderfully strong architecture – although the rest of the city is reduced to nought: the vast walls still are to be traced – with an amphitheatre etc, etc. – but only the temples are left whole. One – of Neptune – has all the outside pillars standing – & everything is as it was 2,000

71

I will see before I die

The Palms and Temples of the South.
("You ask me why" &c &c)

Bassæ. Phigaléia
Greece

I will see before I die

The Palms and Temples of the South.
("You ask me why" &c &c)

Karnak. Thebes.
Egypt.

years ago: the other 2 are minus their insides, or part of them. To describe these monstrous yet exquisitely beautiful buildings, would be impossible: they are of the simplest, earliest of architecture, & all I can say is that they leave stronger impressions on the mind than anything I ever saw – myrtle & heath & fern grow about them – vipers too are rather unpleasantly common: hundreds of jackdaws build in their summits. One is of a rich yellow – the other 2 of white marble – & this with the blue sea, sky & mountains, make a wonderful landscape. After sketching & wandering about for the whole day we returned by evening to Eboli.   (EL to Ann, 10 June 1838)

71. Phigaleia, Greece

The beauty of this part of Greece can hardly be imagined; – all the exquisite plains of the coast are seen through magnificent forests of ilex & oak. At Bassoe on the 18th. – we went to the temple of Apollo – perhaps the finest Greek ruin after the Parthenon. I never saw so beautiful a landscape as it forms part of. Then came our one wet day – 19th. – but on the 20th. it was fine again, & we got on to Mavromati, where the ruins of old Messene are very fine; all that country is more like a rich English park than anything I can compare it with. 21st. 22nd we were on the mountains again – (for each of the old states of

Greece is a plain – quite walled in by mountains,) on the 23rd. we reached Sparta. The modern town seems one of the most stirring in Greece. The landscape of Sparta is extremely grand, – a wide plain below tremendous mountains – always snow topped. 24th. – Mistra – the remains of a great Venetian town but quite destroyed by the Turks. 25th. & 26th. & 27th. – 3 day's journey to Argos – where you know Agamemnon & all those people lived. The plain of Argos is astonishingly beautiful. Ever since the rain of the 19th the ground has become literally covered with flowers; I wish you could see them; – sometimes it is quite pink with Hepaticas – scarlet & blue Anemones – Yellow Euphorbia – Cistus – & several hundred kinds of flowers I never saw before make the whole country a garden. 28th. to Nauplia & 29th. ; this was the old port of the Argive Greeks, & was made the modern capital when first King Otho came – till Athens became so. 30th. we went to Mycenae – amazing ruins – & on the 31st. came by the temple of Nemea – up to Corinth – where you know I had already been. 3 days thence brought us to Athens, & I really never remember having had so delightful a trip. We are now going to Egina, & Colonna, – to see the temples – & then return here for 2 days, when we start afresh for Delphi & Parnassus – & hope to be in Patras again by the 22nd. of April.
(EL to Ann, 4 April 1849)

73

Phile.

I will see before I die

The Palms and Temples of the South.
("You ask me why, —— .")

Philæ.
Egypt.

72. Karnak, Thebes, Egypt

. . . Extreme beauty of Theban Landscape – best of all Nile scenery. Ruins of the Temples – about wh. there are no words to be used. . . . To those who dare to think – or who cannot help thinking – Karnak as it now stands is a milestone in life. – It was 3.50 when we reached the Eastern Pylon. Many changes have been made since I was here = 1854 & in 2 ways. The ruins are more open, & also more dwellings & huts have accumulated about these parts. (D. 18 January 1867)

73. Philae, Egypt

. . . I turn off to Mahatta – a most beautiful valley, where I & G admire the palms, rox, "esplanades," houses – all. I walk on a little further, & lo! – after 13 years – Beautiful Philae once again!! – and more beautiful than ever. – I sit & draw till 2, N.B. I have never made enough of the dark gray & black=rooted granite rox in the water – always too red & yellow in my drawings. Nor have I ever made enough of the endless quantity – stones & material. The boat advances – so – 2.15., I sit in shade & eat biscuits & orange, & then wander on to Philae. The place, seeming to me, if possible more lovely than formerly; & one feels acutely how little one has done to represent such

beauty. It seems to me, my former drawings were not severe enough: & certainly, I never made enough of the grayness of local color, nor of atmosphere – nor of contrasts of almost black & green with the oker &c. The rox – so I think now – are not dark enough in my former drawings – off the sky. not tawny browny purple enough, it seems to me today – cindery. Anyhow, there is plenty of room for improvement. (D. 30 January 1867)

75. Dendoor, Nile, Nubia

Noon – great suffering, high wind, low bare sandy rocky dark hills, & a mere slip of soil, on East side, & hardly any palms. 12.30 approach rapids. Eh! how lonely is this river! – no boat! no birds! few people! hardly one living thing is seen, man, beast, or bird. 1. PM. same scenery – very severe & finely drawn, & all consistent – plain & unembellished. Queer contrast are the telegraph posts & lines amid all these wild rocks. 1.15 getting near Dendoor, & for a moment, somewhat less misery of wind . . . 2.10. Continued horrid gusts, row, and bother of changing sail. Pass Temple of Dendoor – 2.10. – At 3 – very unwell from movement so many hours . . .
(D. 31 January 1867)

Dendoor.

I will see before I die

The Palms and Temples of the South.

("You ask me why" &c &c &c)

Dendōor.
Nile. Nubia.

Mahabalipooram

I will see before I die

The Palms and Temples of the South.

("You ask me why" &c &c &c —)

Mahabalipooram,
near Madras.
India.

77. Mahabalipooram, near Madras

After midnight, awaked by the thunder & lightning, – an additional charm to this voyage! – But slept again till 5, when it began to rain in showers. Got out for 5 minutes, but now it rains harder. The Temples near seem picturesque, but it is of no use to think of drawing them in this weather, & I fancy the best thing will be to go back at once.

8.20. AM. Back at boat – after a time about 6 or so, it ceased raining, & hope revived with a good cup of tea. So, ordering cold breakfast cum tea, we set off, with a native guide, & one of our 2 men. The grandeur & lonely beauty of these strange antiquities almost overpay the beastly bore of reaching them; the Sculptures are very astonishing, – wonderful specimens of such old date. We went on – (fatiguing sand=work!) to the most southern group of temples (or whatever they may be;) all pictures; – & lastly, to the great solitary Pagoda by the sea, – a subject as interesting as any I have ever drawn in any land. Finally, I decide, at all risks & in spite of all discomfort, to stay over today, and to start about 11. AM. tomorrow; – whereon we get back to boat at 8.20. – Wash, & a mild breakfast now; & then (9.30) go out again. To the shore Temple, – certainly one of the most interesting of all the Indian Monuments I have seen.

The way thither, as far as the outskirts of the village, – runs – a broad red sandy path in many a curve, through a wood of Palmyra Palms, their crisp hard fans rattling in any breeze, & their ring'd broad columnar trunks rising from an undergrowth of young Cocoa=trees, and a sort of myrtle. – . . .

Farther on, enormous blocks of Granite open out into beautiful village bits, – the strange rock temples, and carved rock-walls being of the most striking nature. Beyond the village all is green until it gradually becomes sandy to the sea shore, where the ancient Pagoda stands in complete loneliness above the fretting waves.

Drew there till 11.30, & then crossed the sand, – the sun now shining. . . to the 5 Temples. These are very strange and curious, and might be made a good deal of: – but it grew too hot to work, & I was glad at 1.30 PM., to return to the boat, where some soda & Bdy were welcome. . .   (Indian Journal, 25 August 1874)

. . . The poetical character of this remarkably beautiful & interesting place is of a higher order than that of any I have yet seen in India, being so unique & ancient, & yet so unmixed by any sort of contamination of Modernism, still less of Anglo Saxonism.   (26 August 1874)

58-77. All quotations are the same, i.e.

EL List: I will see before I die, the palms and temples of the south

EL Drawing: I will see before I die
                      The Palms and Temples of the South

From: MORTE D'ARTHUR

So all day long the noise of battle roll'd
Among the mountains by the winter sea,
Until King Arthur's table, man by man,
Had fall'n in Lyonnesse about their Lord,
King Arthur: then, because his wound was deep,
The bold Sir Bedivere uplifted him,
Sir Bedivere, the last of all his knights,
And bore him to a chapel nigh the field,
A broken chancel with a broken cross,
That stood on a dark strait of barren land.   10
On one side lay the Ocean, and on one
Lay a great water, and the moon was full.
      Then spake King Arthur to Sir Bedivere:
'The sequel of to-day unsolders all
The goodliest fellowship of famous knights
Whereof this world holds record. Such a sleep
They sleep – the men I loved. I think that we
Shall never more, at any future time,
Delight our souls with talk of knightly deeds,
Walking about the gardens and the halls   20
Of Camelot, as in the days that were.
I perish by this people which I made, –
Though Merlin sware that I should come again
To rule once more – but let what will be, be,
I am so deeply smitten through the helm
That without help I cannot last till morn.
Thou therefore take my brand Excalibur,
Which was my pride: for thou rememberest how
In those old days, one summer noon, an arm
Rose up from out the bosom of the lake,   30
Clothed in white samite, mystic, wonderful,
Holding the sword – and how I row'd across
And took it, and have worn it, like a king:
And, wheresoever I am sung or told
In aftertime, this also shall be known:
But now delay not: take Excalibur,
And fling him far into the middle meer:
Watch what thou seëst, and lightly bring me word.'
      To him replied the bold Sir Bedivere:
'It is not meet, Sir King, to leave thee thus,   40
Aidless, alone, and smitten through the helm.
A little thing may harm a wounded man.
Yet I thy hest will all perform at full,
Watch what I see, and lightly bring thee word.'
      So saying, from the ruin'd shrine he stepp'd,
And in the moon athwart the place of tombs,
Where lay the mighty bones of ancient men,
Old knights, and over them the sea-wind sang
Shrill, chill, with flakes of foam. He, stepping down
By zig-zag paths, and juts of pointed rock,   50
Came on the shining levels of the lake.
      There drew he forth the brand Excalibur,
And o'er him, drawing it, the winter moon,
Brightening the skirts of a long cloud, ran forth
And sparkled keen with frost against the hilt:
For all the haft twinkled with diamond studs,
Myriads of topaz-lights, and jacinth-work
Of subtlest jewellery. He gazed so long

That both his eyes were dazzled, as he stood,
This way and that dividing the swift mind,   60
In act to throw: but at the last it seem'd
Better to leave Excalibur conceal'd
There in the many-knotted waterflags,
That whistled stiff and dry about the marge.
So strode he back slow to the wounded King.
      Then spake King Arthur to Sir Bedivere:
'Hast thou perform'd my mission which I gave?
What is it thou hast seen? or what hast heard?'
      And answer made the bold Sir Bedivere:
'I heard the ripple washing in the reeds,   70
And the wild water lapping on the crag.'
      To whom replied King Arthur, faint and pale:
'Thou hast betray'd thy nature and thy name,
Not rendering true answer, as beseem'd
Thy fëalty, nor like a noble knight:
For surer sign had follow'd, either hand,
Or voice, or else a motion of the meer.
This is a shameful thing for men to lie.
Yet now, I charge thee, quickly go again
As thou art lief and dear, and do the thing   80
I bad thee, watch, and lightly bring me word.'
      Then went Sir Bedivere the second time,
Counting the dewy pebbles, fix'd in thought;
But when he saw the wonder of the hilt,
How curiously and strangely chased, he smote
His palms together, and he cried aloud.
      'And if indeed I cast the brand away,
Surely a precious thing, one worthy note,
Should thus be lost for ever from the earth,
Which might have pleased the eyes of many men.   90
What good should follow this, if this were done?
What harm, undone? deep harm to disobey,
Seeing obedience is the bond of rule.
Were it well to obey then, if a king demand
An act unprofitable, against himself?
The King is sick, and knows not what he does.
What record, or what relic of my lord
Should be to aftertime, but empty breath
And rumours of a doubt? but were this kept,
Stored in some treasure-house of mighty kings,   100
Some one might show it at a joust of arms,
Saying, "King Arthur's sword, Excalibur,
Wrought by the lonely maiden of the Lake.
Nine years she wrought it, sitting in the deeps
Upon the hidden bases of the hills."
So might some old man speak in the aftertime
To all the people, winning reverence.
But now much honour and much fame were lost.'
      So spake he, clouded with his own conceit,
And hid Excalibur the second time,   110
And so strode back slow to the wounded King.
      Then spoke King Arthur, breathing heavily:
'What is it thou hast seen? or what hast heard?'
      And answer made the bold Sir Bedivere:
'I heard the water lapping on the crag,
And the long ripple washing in the reeds.'

To whom replied King Arthur, much in wrath:
'Ah, miserable and unkind, untrue,
Unknightly, traitor-hearted! Woe is me!
Authority forgets a dying king,						120
Laid widowed of the power in his eye
That bowed the will. I see thee what thou art,
For thou, the latest-left of all my knights,
In whom should meet the offices of all,
Thou wouldst betray me for the precious hilt;
Either from lust of gold, or like a girl
Valuing the giddy pleasure of the eyes.
Yet, for a man may fail in duty twice,
And the third time may prosper, get thee hence:
But, if thou spare to fling Excalibur,				130
I will arise and slay thee with my hands.'
	Then quickly rose Sir Bedivere, and ran,
And, leaping down the ridges lightly, plunged
Among the bulrush-beds, and clutch'd the sword,
And strongly wheel'd and threw it. The great brand
Made lightnings in the splendour of the moon,
And flashing round and round, and whirled in an arch,
Shot like a streamer of the northern morn,
Seen where the moving isles of winter shock
By night, with noises of the northern sea.			140
So flash'd and fell the brand Excalibur:
But ere he dipt the surface, rose an arm
Clothed in white samite, mystic, wonderful,
And caught him by the hilt, and brandish'd him
Three times, and drew him under in the meer.
And lightly went the other to the King.
	Then spoke King Arthur, drawing thicker breath:
'Now see I by thine eyes that this is done.
Speak out: what is it thou hast heard, or seen?'
	And answer made the bold Sir Bedivere:			150
'Sir King, I closed mine eyelids, lest the gems
Should blind my purpose, for I never saw,
Nor shall see, here or elsewhere, till I die,
Not though I live three lives of mortal men,
So great a miracle as yonder hilt.
Then with both hands I flung him, wheeling him,
But when I look'd again, behold an arm,
Clothed in white samite, mystic, wonderful,
That caught him by the hilt, and brandish'd him
Three times, and drew him under in the meer.'		160
	And answer made King Arthur, breathing hard:
'My end draws nigh; 'tis time that I were gone.
Make broad thy shoulders to receive my weight,
And bear me to the margin; yet I fear
My wound hath taken cold, and I shall die.'
	So saying, from the pavement he half rose,
Slowly, with pain, reclining on his arm,
And looking wistfully with wide blue eyes
As in a picture. Him Sir Bedivere
Remorsefully regarded thro' his tears,				170
And would have spoken, but he found not words,
Then took with care, and kneeling on one knee,
O'er both his shoulders drew the languid hands,
And rising bore him thro' the place of tombs.
	But, as he walk'd, King Arthur panted hard,
Like one that feels a nightmare on his bed
When all the house is mute. So sigh'd the King,
Muttering and murmuring at his ear, 'Quick, quick!
I fear it is too late, and I shall die.'
But the other swiftly strode from ridge to ridge,		180

Clothed with his breath, and looking, as he walk'd,
Larger than human on the frozen hills.
He heard the deep behind him, and a cry
Before. His own thought drove him, like a goad.
Dry clash'd his harness in the icy caves
And barren chasms, and all to left and right
The bare black cliff clang'd round him, as he based
His feet on juts of slippery crag that rang
Sharp-smitten with the dint of armed heels –
And on a sudden, lo! the level lake,				190
And the long glories of the winter moon.
	Then saw they how there hove a dusky barge,
Dark as a funeral scarf from stem to stern,
Beneath them; and descending they were ware
That all the decks were dense with stately forms
Black-stoled, black-hooded, like a dream – by these
Three Queens with crowns of gold – and from them rose
A cry that shiver'd to the tingling stars,
And, as it were one voice, an agony
Of lamentation, like a wind, that shrills			200
All night in a waste land, where no one comes,
Or hath come, since the making of the world.
	Then murmur'd Arthur, 'Place me in the barge,'
And to the barge they came. There those three Queens
Put forth their hands, and took the King, and wept. . . .

. Then loudly cried the bold Sir Bedivere,
'Ah! my Lord Arthur, whither shall I go?
Where shall I hide my forehead and my eyes?
For now I see the true old times are dead,
When every morning brought a noble chance,
And every chance brought out a noble knight.			230
Such times have been not since the light that led
The holy Elders with the gift of myrrh.
But now the whole ROUND TABLE is dissolved
Which was an image of the mighty world;
And I, the last, go forth companionless,
And the days darken round me, and the years,
Among new men, strange faces, other minds.'
	And slowly answered Arthur from the barge:
'The old order changeth, yielding place to new,
And God fulfils Himself in many ways,				240
Lest one good custom should corrupt the world.
Comfort thyself: what comfort is in me?
I have lived my life, and that which I have done
May He within Himself make pure! but thou,
If thou shouldst never see my face again,
Pray for my soul. More things are wrought by prayer
Than this world dreams of. Wherefore, let thy voice
Rise like a fountain for me night and day.
For what are men better than sheep or goats
That nourish a blind life within the brain,			250
If, knowing God, they lift not hands of prayer
Both for themselves and those who call them friend?
For so the whole round earth is every way
Bound by gold chains about the feet of God.
But now farewell. I am going a long way
With these thou seëst – if indeed I go –
(For all my mind is clouded with a doubt)
To the island-valley of Avilion;
Where falls not hail, or rain, or any snow,
Nor ever wind blows loudly; but it lies			260
Deep-meadow'd, happy, fair with orchard-lawns
And bowery hollows crown'd with summer sea,

Where I will heal me of my grievous wound.'
    So said he, and the barge with oar and sail
Moved from the brink, like some full-breasted swan
That, fluting a wild carol ere her death,
Ruffles her pure cold plume, and takes the flood
With swarthy webs. Long stood Sir Bedivere
Revolving many memories, till the hull
Look'd one black dot against the verge of dawn,   270
And on the meer the wailing died away....

80. Kleissoura, Tepedelene, Albania

'Morte D'Arthur', written in 1833-4, was the first poem of the 1842 volumes. Tennyson thus began with an ending and, despite its tone of authority and its sonorous, archaic blank verse, the ending itself is a fragment. It begins, 'So all day long the noise of battle roll'd' and ends with Sir Bedivere uncertainly pondering the future. The source is Malory, who gives much of the narrative, but we must turn to other Idylls, such as 'Guinevere' and 'Lancelot and Elaine', to fill in the details of Tennyson's recreation of the mythical King Arthur, his kingdom and his knights of the Round Table. But it is not until the *Idylls of the King* are assembled and this poem becomes part of the last piece, 'The Passing of Arthur', that we can have any complete idea of Tennyson's complex view of his Arthurian material. King Arthur is not simply an ideal King: he is naïve, out of touch with the reality of human passion and human evil. And he is to be admired as expounding a perfect way of life to which his Queen, his knights and their ladies can hardly even aspire. Their relationships, both guilty and innocent, their quarrels, contradictions, suspicions and betrayals finally undermine the Round Table and lead, indirectly, to the final Battle of the West. In the last scene of the battle, the last surviving knight, Sir Bedivere, tries to tend King Arthur who has already been given his death wound.

The poem was written after Tennyson first heard the news of Arthur Hallam's death. 'Morte D'Arthur' remains a poem based on Malory, but Tennyson's frustrated questioning of his friend's death seems to have entered into his perception of the King's death – or passing to another state. The poet leaves out all the inhabitants of Arthur's court and concentrates on one action which is a moral testing both of the King and Sir Bedivere. The last event is the mystic journey in which the wounded King, in the black barge with its weeping queens, is borne to the valley of Avilion to be healed of his wound. Before he goes he speaks of God's mysterious ways in bringing about a new order, but there is no promise of his own return. Bedivere, calm now rather than desperate, listens as the ritual wailing dies away. The end of 'Morte D'Arthur' gives no ready answers, draws no obvious conclusions.

The test in the main part of the poem brings up the question of Soul and Sense which is central to Lear's choice of Arthurian poems, and choice forms a major dichotomy throughout the *Idylls of the King*. At the King's command Sir Bedivere must throw the sword Excalibur back into the lake from which the mysterious Lady of the Lake offered it to Arthur. The King is weakening: the test for him is to retain his virtue, control

his knight, and complete a mystical, ritual act. Sir Bedivere must not swerve in his obedience to his dying King. Twice the knight fails: he cannot bear to let go of Sense, to throw away Excalibur with its beautiful hilt worked with many jewels. Material value overcomes spiritual commitment and Bedivere, after hiding the sword, returns to the King, saying he saw only wind on water. The second time, still thinking of material worth, the knight rationalizes his action by wishing to preserve some relic of the King. Only at the third attempt, with Arthur struggling to use his waning strength and impose his will upon his knight, only then does Sir Bedivere throw the sword and see the arm rise 'Clothed in white samite, mystic, wonderful'. The ritual and the testing are complete. But the poem does not swing upward into some great affirmation of ideals. The old order is passing; death and loss threaten. The Arthurian legend is left open, not tied down to a single interpretation.

This is not one of Tennyson's brilliant lyrics like 'Tears, idle tears', which Lear so often quoted in his diary. 'Morte D'Arthur' is rightly famous as a long poem in which landscape, interaction of character and deep feelings are perfectly judged. The plangent and archaic language shows no sign of strain as Tennyson re-imagined the last phase of Malory's Arthurian legend. The testing of Bedivere and the ritual of Excalibur belong to myth, but they are not relegated to that distant world. Tennyson opens up questions of moral choice which must be faced by human beings in any age: that is why his attempt to put the poem in a 'modern' frame is quite unnecessary. The problem of death, and the effect of the death of the loved, the great, the good are subjects to which Tennyson brought a depth of feeling from his own experience. The death of King Arthur, or his strange passing, encompasses other deaths and involves the reader in contemplating death not merely as ending or negation. Lear may have responded to these ideas because he felt very deeply about the death of those close to him. He commented in his diary on many deaths, and the effect they may have had on relatives, friends, and on himself. He often made an inscription – a name framed in black lines – which stands out on the diary page. Sometimes he added dates and his own memories of the dead person in years gone by. No one could take the place of his sister, Ann. He recalled the day of her death, and her goodness to him, almost until his own death. And he had to work out a consoling theory that the individual should use such deaths as 'stepping-stones' (*In Memoriam* I) from which to rise to a morally better self.

Lear took death as central to the one illustration he made for 'Morte D'Arthur': surprisingly the setting of the poem plays no part in his choice. 'The place of tombs', Kleissoura, Albania, is a drawing which dwells on a non-

Christian death in a strange land. In his journal Lear describes several tombs of dervishes and mentions cemeteries with plain upright memorial stones, but he never names Kleissoura. One description, less desolate and distant than the illustration, must serve to suggest the kind of place that Lear saw in Albania.

80. Vodghena (for Kleissoura)

By five I was out on the road to Yenidje, at a dervish's tomb, not far from the town, a spot which I had remarked yesterday, as promising, if weather permitted, a good view eastward. All the plain below is bright yellow as the sun rises gloriously, and Olympus is for once in perfect splendour, with all its snowy peaks; but the daily perplexity of mist and cloud rapidly soars upward, and hardly leaves time for a sketch ere all is once more shrouded away.

The dervish's, or saint's tomb, is such as you remark frequently on the outskirts of Mohammedan towns in the midst of wide cemeteries of humble sepulchres – a quadrangular structure three or four feet high, with pillars at the corners, supporting a dome of varying height; beneath its centre is usually the carved emblem of the saint's rank, his turban, or high-crowned hat. As these tombs are often shaded by trees, their effect is very pleasing, the more so that the cemeteries are mostly frequented by the contemplative

faithful. Often, in their vicinity, especially if the position of the tombs commands a fine view, or is near a running stream, you may notice one of those raised platforms, with a cage-like palisade, and supporting a roof, in the shade of which the Mohammedan delights to squat and smoke. There is one close by me now, in which a solitary elder sits, in the enjoyment of tobacco and serenity, and looking in his blue and yellow robes very like an encaged macaw.

(Albanian Journal, 15 September 1848, pp. 40-41)

In his diary for 16 April 1870 Lear quoted the first line of 'Morte D'Arthur' – 'So all day long the noise of battle roll'd' – using the well-known line to express his frustrations – 'i.e. the bother of doing nothingness prevailed'. He was waiting to move into his permanent home, the Villa Emily in San Remo. He was still months away from the move, but had to do much packing and sorting of pictures. He could not go out because some visitors had said they would call: he did not paint, and felt uncertain over the whole business of settling down. The quotation from 'Morte D'Arthur', in a context of everyday difficulties, re-enforces the sense that lines and phrases of Tennyson's poems were always coming into Lear's mind.

80. EL List: A place of tombs
    EL Drawing: – athwart the place of Tombs.

athwart the place of Tombs.

(Morte d'Arthur.)

Kleissoura
Tepelené,
Albania,

114

From: THE GARDENER'S DAUGHTER

... Not wholly in the busy world, nor quite
  Beyond it, blooms the garden that I love.
  News from the humming city comes to it
  In sound of funeral or of marriage bells,
  And, sitting muffled in dark leaves, you hear
  The windy clanging of the minster clock;
  Although between it and the garden lies
  A league of grass, wash'd by a slow broad stream,   40
  That, stirr'd with languid pulses of the oar,
  Waves all its lazy lilies, and creeps on,
  Barge-laden, to three arches of a bridge
  Crown'd with the minster-towers.
                   The fields between
Are dewy-fresh, browsed by deep-udder'd kine,
And all about the large lime feathers low,
The lime a summer home of murmurous wings.
    In that still place she, hoarded in herself,
Grew, seldom seen; not less among us lived
Her fame from lip to lip. Who had not heard   50
Of Rose, the Gardener's daughter? Where was he,
So blunt in memory, so old at heart,
At such a distance from his youth in grief,
That, having seen, forgot? The common mouth,
So gross to express delight, in praise of her
Grew oratory. Such a lord is Love,
And Beauty such a mistress of the world....

... And on we went; but ere an hour had pass'd,
  We reach'd a meadow slanting to the North;
  Down which a well-worn pathway courted us
  To one green wicket in a privet hedge;
  This, yielding, gave into a grassy walk   110
  Thro' crowded lilac-ambush trimly pruned;
  And one warm gust, full-fed with perfume, blew
  Beyond us, as we enter'd in the cool.
  The garden stretches southward. In the midst
  A cedar spread his dark-green layers of shade.
  The garden-glasses shone, and momently
  The twinkling laurel scatter'd silver lights.
    'Eustace,' I said, 'this wonder keeps the house.'
  He nodded, but a moment afterwards
  He cried, 'Look! look!' Before he ceas'd I turn'd,   120
  And, ere a star can wink, beheld her there.

For up the porch there grew an Eastern rose,
That, flowering high, the last night's gale had caught,
And blown across the walk. One arm aloft –
Gown'd in pure white, that fitted to the shape –
Holding the bush, to fix it back, she stood.
A single stream of all her soft brown hair
Pour'd on one side: the shadow of the flowers
Stole all the golden gloss, and, wavering
Lovingly lower, trembled on her waist –   130
Ah, happy shade – and still went wavering down,
But, ere it touch'd a foot, that might have danced
The greensward into greener circles, dipt,
And mix'd with shadows of the common ground!
But the full day dwelt on her brows, and sunn'd
Her violet eyes, and all her Hebe-bloom,
And doubled his own warmth against her lips,
And on the bounteous wave of such a breast
As never pencil drew. Half light, half shade,
She stood, a sight to make an old man young.   140
    So rapt, we near'd the house; but she, a Rose
In roses, mingled with her fragrant toil,
Nor heard us come, nor from her tendance turn'd
Into the world without; till close at hand,
And almost ere I knew mine own intent,
This murmur broke the stillness of that air
Which brooded round about her:
                        'Ah, one rose,
One rose but one, by those fair fingers cull'd,
Were worth a hundred kisses press'd on lips
Less exquisite than thine.'
                   She look'd: but all   150
Suffused with blushes – neither self-possess'd
Nor startled, but betwixt this mood and that,
Divided in a graceful quiet – paused,
And dropt the branch she held, and turning, wound
Her looser hair in braid, and stirr'd her lips
For some sweet answer, though no answer came,
Nor yet refused the rose, but granted it,
And moved away, and left me, statue-like,
In act to render thanks.
                 I, that whole day,
Saw her no more, although I linger'd there   160
Till every daisy slept, and Love's white star
Beam'd thro' the thicken'd cedar in the dusk....

81. Mount Lebanon, Syria
82. Mount Lebanon, Syria
83. *[Tivoli, Italy]*[1]
84. *[Tel El Ful, Gibeah, Palestine]*[1]

'The Gardener's Daughter' is a richly descriptive 'English Idyl', and its subtitle, 'or The Pictures', at once suggests a link with visual art. The poem is a dramatic monologue in which the narrator is an artist who is impressed by the effect of love on his fellow artist, Eustace. Eustace, newly inspired, paints a fine portrait of his Juliet, and she suggests that the narrator's painting might benefit if he were to visit the gardener's daughter, Rose. The relationships in the poem probably owe something to Tennyson's friendship with Hallam, (the narrator and Eustace), to Hallam's engagement to Tennyson's sister, Emily (Eustace and Juliet), and to Tennyson's uncertain admiration for the sophisticated and probably unresponsive Rosa Baring. The 'brothers in Art', spurred on by Juliet, set off through a lush spring countryside and discuss the power of love. They make their way to the garden, but once through the gate of this Eden, they cannot at first, see its Eve, the gardener's daughter. They soon become sentimentally enraptured by finding Rose, tending roses, posed naturally but perfectly for a portrait. A pure white gown, one arm aloft, a stream of fine brown hair, light and shadow touching form and figure: Rose appears an ideal subject for an artist and the narrator, begging a rose, immediately falls in love. But this is not a poem about a love relationship: it is a series of 'romantic' pictures that suggest Victorian genre paintings: Lovers in a Garden, a Girl at a Wicket-gate, Doves round a Dovecote, Lovers' Promises, or Lovers' Vows. The ending presents a veiled painting, a last tribute from art to love. The veil keeps out the common gaze and conceals a portrait of a young girl, loved in marriage, now dead, but alive in the memory of the ageing narrator and artist. This last moment, with its hint of Shakespeare's Hermione, rouses more feeling than the decorative, pictorial centre. As Tennyson realized, the poem suffers from a surfeit of art. Hallam records that, in working on 'The Gardener's Daughter' Tennyson said: 'The centre of the poem, that passage describing the girl, must be full and rich. The poem is so, to a fault, especially in the descriptions of nature, for the lover is an artist, but this being so, the central picture must hold its place' (*Mem.* I, p. 197). Lear loved fine English gardens and English scenery. He believed that his landscape art could complement Tennyson's descriptions and voiced no doubts about over-rich effects. But his illustrations were taken from as far away as Mount Lebanon. He chose one line with a clear-cut description of a cedar, not a tangle of English roses.

On 27 May 1858 Lear wrote a long letter to Lady Waldegrave (LEL, p. 109), in which he described the interior of Lebanon as '... wonderfully fine: – a kind of Orientalized Swiss scenery'. He wanted to explore the villages which dotted the innumerable plateaux and edges of rock, the dark ravines which wound down 'to the plains of Tripoli and the blue sea'. Sadly the extreme cold of the high mountains made him unwell; he had to come down to lower ground. But at least, he records 'having my drawing of the Cedars as a sign of my Lebanon visit.'

Lear was fascinated by the structure and foliage of these famous trees. In England, in 1860, he was working on an ambitious project: a large oil painting of 'The Cedars of Lebanon'. To complete this he pursued cedars in country-house gardens and in the grounds of Oatlands Park Hotel in Surrey, where he had the large canvas taken outside so that he could paint cedar details from life. To his great disappointment, the painting did not bring either financial reward, or artistic success. It finally sold at a lowered price; it is now lost, but several studies remain. Drawings and sketches show how attracted Lear was to these ancient, dark-layered trees and how the memories of Lebanon cedars revived in English surroundings.

Strangely, Lear's other illustration for this poem, again of cedars on Mount Lebanon, has somehow acquired a line which is not in 'The Gardener's Daughter' at all. Was it cedars, with their associations of Lebanon, which made Lear quote: 'Sighing for Lebanon'? The phrase occurs twice, once as a complete line, in *Maud* (I.xviii.615), where the context is one of love, loss and an Eden-like garden. Did Lear remember this when he transposed the line to 'The Gardener's Daughter' and had it printed for the poem in his illustrations? Whatever Lear's thought processes, he moved from an English cedar to distant Lebanon, where he had been impressed with the famous cedars and tried to draw and paint them. One illustration has 'A Cedar spread his dark green layers of shade', and the idea of Lebanon is borrowed – possibly unconsciously – from *Maud*. So the other illustration – cedars again – has inscribed below it 'Sighing for Lebanon'.

81, 82. Mount Lebanon, Syria

Lebanon is called a Mount: but it should rather be termed a great mountain district. You may as well talk of all the Westmoreland & Cumberland hills and dales as "Mount Cumberland" – or the long range of Sussex & Hampshire Downs as the Hill of Sussex. – It would be 6 or 8 days journey to go along one side of the Lebanon; – & between it & Palestine lies Antelebanon – another long range – not quite so high – but ending in a high mountain – Hermon. – Between these 2 ranges lies what was once called CoeloSyria – a wonderful cornfield days and days long – & as flat as a table: I never tired of looking at it from morning to night. [On 20 May Lear went up the mountain, a 'hardish task' because there was still some snow] ... then I came again to see what the inside of Lebanon is – So fine a view I suppose can hardly be imagined – more perhaps like one of Martin's ideal pictures: – the whole upper part of the mountain is bare & snowy, & forms an amphitheatre of heights, round a multitude of ravines & valleys – full of foliage & villages most glorious to see, and all that descends step by step to the sea beyond! – Far below your feet, quite alone on one side of the amphitheatre is a single dark spot – a cluster of trees: those are the famous Cedars of Lebanon. = Lebanon doubtless was once thickly covered with such, but now there are these only left. – I cannot tell you how delighted I was with those cedars! those enormous old trees – a great, dark grove – utterly silent – except the singing of birds in numbers. Here I staid all that day – the 20th – & all the 21st – working very hard. (EL to Ann, 26 May 1858)

81. EL List: A cedar spread his dark green layers of shade
    EL Drawing: Sighing for Lebanon
82. EL List: Sighing for Lebanon
    EL Drawing: A Cedar spread his dark green layers of shade.

On the List, the quotations for 81 and 82 are reversed.

[1] 83 and 84 are not in this set, but illustrated in the set in the Houghton Library, Harvard. 84 is an illustration to the poem 'Dora'.

81

Sighing for Lebanon ——

(The gardener's daughter.)   Mount Lebanon.
Syria.

82

A Cedar spread his dark green layers of shade.

(The gardener's daughter.)   Mount Lebanon.
Syria.

From: ST. SIMEON STYLITES

Altho' I be the basest of mankind,
From scalp to sole one slough and crust of sin,
Unfit for earth, unfit for heaven, scarce meet
For troops of devils, mad with blasphemy,
I will not cease to grasp the hope I hold
Of saintdom, and to clamour, mourn and sob,
Battering the gates of heaven with storms of prayer,
Have mercy, Lord, and take away my sin.
  Let this avail, just, dreadful, mighty God,
This not be all in vain, that thrice ten years,   10
Thrice multiplied by superhuman pangs,
In hungers and in thirsts, fevers and cold,
In coughs, aches, stitches, ulcerous throes and cramps,
A sign betwixt the meadow and the cloud,
Patient on this tall pillar I have borne
Rain, wind, frost, heat, hail, damp, and sleet, and
   snow;
And I had hoped that ere this period closed
Thou wouldst have caught me up into thy rest,
Denying not these weather-beaten limbs
The meed of saints, the white robe and the palm. 20
  O take the meaning, Lord: I do not breathe,
Not whisper, any murmur of complaint.
Pain heap'd ten-hundred-fold, to this, were still
Less burthen, by ten-hundred-fold, to bear,
Than were those lead-like tons of sin that crush'd
My spirit flat before thee.
      O Lord, Lord,
Thou knowest I bore this better at the first,
For I was strong and hale of body then;
And though my teeth, which now are dropt away,
Would chatter with the cold, and all my beard 30
Was tagged with icy fringes in the moon,
I drown'd the whoopings of the owl with sound
Of pious hymns and psalms, and sometimes saw
An angel stand and watch me, as I sang.
Now am I feeble grown; my end draws nigh –
I hope my end draws nigh: half deaf I am,
So that I scarce can hear the people hum
About the column's base, and almost blind,
And scarce can recognise the fields I know.
And both my thighs are rotted with the dew; 40
Yet cease I not to clamour and to cry,
While my stiff spine can hold my weary head,
Till all my limbs drop piecemeal from the stone,
Have mercy, mercy: take away my sin.
  O Jesus, if thou wilt not save my soul,
Who may be saved? who is it may be saved?
Who may be made a saint, if I fail here?
Show me the man hath suffer'd more than I.
For did not all thy martyrs die one death?
For either they were stoned, or crucified, 50
Or burn'd in fire, or boil'd in oil, or sawn
In twain beneath the ribs; but I die here
To-day, and whole years long, a life of death.

Bear witness, if I could have found a way
(And heedfully I sifted all my thought)
More slowly-painful to subdue this home
Of sin, my flesh, which I despise and hate,
I had not stinted practice, O my God.
  For not alone this pillar-punishment,
Not this alone I bore: but while I lived   60
In the white convent down the valley there,
For many weeks about my loins I wore
The rope that haled the buckets from the well,
Twisted as tight as I could knot the noose,
And spake not of it to a single soul,
Until the ulcer, eating through my skin,
Betray'd my secret penance, so that all
My brethren marvell'd greatly. More than this
I bore, whereof, O God, thou knowest all....

            But yet
Bethink thee, Lord, while thou and all the saints
Enjoy themselves in heaven, and men on earth
House in the shade of comfortable roofs,
Sit with their wives by fires, eat wholesome food,
And wear warm clothes, and even beasts have stalls,
I, 'tween the spring and downfall of the light,
Bow down one thousand and two hundred times
To Christ, the Virgin Mother, and the saints; 110
Or in the night, after a little sleep,
I wake: the chill stars sparkle; I am wet
With drenching dews, or stiff with crackling frost.
I wear an undress'd goatskin on my back;
A grazing iron collar grinds my neck;
And in my weak, lean arms I lift the cross,
And strive and wrestle with thee till I die:
O mercy, mercy! wash away my sin....

  Good people, you do ill to kneel to me.
What is it I can have done to merit this?
I am a sinner viler than you all.
It may be I have wrought some miracles,
And cured some halt and maim'd; but what of that?
It may be, no one, even among the saints,
May match his pains with mine; but what of that?
Yet do not rise; for you may look on me,
And in your looking you may kneel to God.
Speak! is there any of you halt or maim'd? 140
I think you know I have some power with Heaven
From my long penance: let him speak his wish.
  Yes, I can heal him. Power goes forth from me.
They say that they are heal'd. Ah, hark! they shout
'St. Simeon Stylites.' Why, if so,
God reaps a harvest in me. O my soul,
God reaps a harvest in thee. If this be,
Can I work miracles and not be saved?
This is not told of any. They were saints.

It cannot be but that I shall be saved; 150
Yes, crown'd a saint. They shout, 'Behold a saint!'
And lower voices saint me from above.
Courage, St. Simeon! This dull chrysalis
Cracks into shining wings, and hope ere death
Spreads more and more and more, and God that now
Sponged and made blank of crimeful record all
My mortal archives.
                    O my sons, my sons,
I, Simeon of the pillar, by surname
Stylites, among men; I, Simeon,
The watcher on the column till the end; 160
I, Simeon, whose brain the sunshine bakes;
I, whose bald brows in silent hours become
Unnaturally hoar with rime, do now
From my high nest of penance here proclaim
That Pontius and Iscariot by my side
Show'd like fair seraphs. On the coals I lay,
A vessel full of sin: all hell beneath
Made me boil over. Devils pluck'd my sleeve;
Abaddon and Asmodeus caught at me.
I smote them with the cross; they swarm'd again. 170
In bed like monstrous apes they crush'd my chest:

They flapp'd my light out as I read: I saw
Their faces grow between me and my book:
With colt-like whinny and with hoggish whine
They burst my prayer. Yet this way was left,
And by this way I 'scaped them. Mortify
Your flesh, like me, with scourges and with thorns;
Smite, shrink not, spare not. If it may be, fast
Whole Lents, and pray. I hardly, with slow steps –
With slow, faint steps, and much exceeding pain – 180
Have scrambled past those pits of fire, that still
Sing in mine ears. But yield not me the praise:
God only thro' his bounty hath thought fit,
Among the powers and princes of this world,
To make me an example to mankind,
Which few can reach to. Yet I do not say
But that a time may come – yea, even now,
Now, now, his footsteps smite the threshold stairs
Of life – I say, that time is at the doors
When you may worship me without reproach; 190
For I will leave my relics in your land,
And you may carve a shrine about my dust,
And burn a fragrant lamp before my bones,
When I am gather'd to the glorious saints....

85. Sta Maria di Polsi, Calabria, Italy

In his Calabrian Journal (pp. 70-76) Lear wrote of his long search for the Convent of Santa Maria di Polsi. It was a monastic foundation and famous place of pilgrimage, hidden miles up in the wooded and mountainous Aspromonte. The route began 'three miles up a torrent bed' – in one of the strange dried-out fiumaras characteristic of the Calabrian summer – and a guide was necessary as well as Lear's servant Ciccio. Lear toiled slowly upstream, noting dense woods, luxuriant ilex trees, and overhanging rocks. 'The sentiment of these scenes and solitudes – the deep, deep solitudes of those mountains! are such as neither pen nor pencil can describe!' At last they reached the highest point and began to descend deep down towards a twinkling light which was all that could be seen of the convent. Finally welcomed in, the affable Superiore was amazed at this visit: 'Wonder and curiosity overwhelmed the ancient man and his brethren, who were few in number, and clad in black serge dresses.... "Why had we come to such a solitary place? No foreigner had ever done so before!"' And he held forth knowledgeably about England 'for the benefit of his fellow-recluses'. It was, he said, thickly inhabited:

> ... about the third part of the size of the city of Rome. The people are a sort of Christians... Their priests, and even their bishops, marry, which is incomprehensible, and most ridiculous. The whole place is divided into two equal parts by an arm of the sea, under which there is a great tunnel, so that it is all like one piece of dry land. Ah – che celebre tunnel!

A simple meal was followed by a cold and windy night in two cells, but next day the scene was remarkable. The convent:

> ... stands on a rising ground above the great torrent, which comes down from the very summit of the Aspromonte, the highest point of which – Montalto – is the "roof and crown"

> of the picture. From the level of the monastery to this height rises a series of screens, covered with the grandest foliage, with green glades, and massive clumps of chestnut low down – black ilex and brown oak next in succession, and, highest of all, pines. The perpendicular character of the scene is singularly striking, the wooded rocks right and left closing it in like the side slips of a theatre; and as no other building is within sight, the romance and loneliness of the spot are complete.

There is no contrasting landscape or glimpse of the sea, only – 'close wood and mountain – no outlet, no variety – stern solitude and the hermit sentiment reign supreme.'

In adapting this scene – a lithograph in the Calabrian Journal – to the A.T. small landscape format, the perpendicular effect is lost, but not the whiteness of buildings against the dark woods. One line from the poem 'St Simeon Stylites' refers to a white convent, but it is the extraordinary and isolated Santa Maria di Polsi which seemed fitting for the strange, acerbic saint dying and complaining, on his pillar. There is no definite link – Lear does not put the figure of the saint into his picture – but the 'stern solitude' and 'hermit sentiment' can easily be associated with the saint, too arrogantly ascetic, too hard on humanity, to reach a stage of purity before death. The poem has none of the buoyancy of some of the earlier poems but it could easily have seemed to echo Lear's darker moods, his guilt over his 'demon' epilepsy, over his lack of achievement, and his sense too, of being cut off from mankind.

The line Lear extracts from the poem is used to concentrate his memory of woods and white buildings at Santa Maria di Polsi. Apart from its loneliness, that strange Calabrian monastic complex has nothing to do with St Simeon on his pillar. Yet Lear considered his chosen poems carefully. If he knew that Tennyson often read the poem with 'grotesque grimaces' and even at times 'laughed aloud' (Mem. I, p. 193 note), it would suggest the sardonic approach which Lear himself took to extravagant asceticism. St Simeon, high above the common man, scornful and pain-seeking on his pillar, might have reminded Lear of the 'miserable, mutton-hating, man-avoiding...Monx'[1] of Mount Athos whose monasteries he visited in 1856.

85. Sta Maria di Polsi, Calabria

The sentiment of these scenes and solitudes – the deep, deep solitudes of those mountains! are such as neither pen nor pencil can describe!

We were obliged to walk as fast as possible, that we might arrive at Polsi by daylight, and as we ascended, the labour was not a little severe. It was twenty-two o'clock when we reached a fountain very high up in the mountain, yet the brown-garbed guide said three hours were still requisite to bring us to our night's lodging. Clear streams, trickling down at every step to the great torrent, refreshed us, and soon we left the valley, and began to climb among oak woods, till the deep chasm, now dark in the fading daylight, was far below our feet.

A circuitous toil to the head of a second large torrent, skirting a ravine filled with magnificent ilex, brought us to the last tremendous ladder-path, that led to the "serra," or highest point of the route, wherefrom we were told we should perceive the monastery. Slowly old Ciccio and his horse followed us, and darker grew the hour. "Arriveremo tardi," quoth he, "se non moriamo prima – díghi, dóghi, dà!"[2] But alas! when we did get at the promised height, where a cross is set up, and where, at the great festas of the convent, the pilgrims fire off guns on the first and last view of this celebrated Calabrian sanctuary – alas! it was quite dark, and only a twinkling light far and deep down, in the very bowels of the mountain, showed us our destination. Slow and hazardous was the descent, and it was nine o'clock ere we arrived before the gate of this remote and singular retreat.

(Calabrian Journal, 7 August 1847, pp. 71-2)

[1] EL to Fortescue, 9 October 1856. LEL, p. 41.
[2] 'We shall arrive late, if we do not die before we get there' – EL note.

85. EL List: The white convent down the valley there.
   EL Drawing: In the white convent down the valley there

In the white convent down the valley there

(S. Simeon Stylites)

Sta Maria di Polsi,
Calabria,
Italy.

From: THE TALKING OAK

I

Once more the gate behind me falls;
　　Once more before my face
I see the moulder'd Abbey-walls,
　　That stand within the chace.

II

Beyond the lodge the city lies,
　　Beneath its drift of smoke;
And ah! with what delighted eyes
　　I turn to yonder oak.

III

For when my passion first began,
　　Ere that, which in me burn'd,
The love, that makes me thrice a man,
　　Could hope itself return'd;

IV

To yonder oak within the field
　　I spoke without restraint,
And with a larger faith appeal'd
　　Than Papist unto Saint.

V

For oft I talk'd with him apart,
　　And told him of my choice,
Until he plagiarised a heart,
　　And answer'd with a voice.

VI

Tho' what he whisper'd under Heaven
　　None else could understand;
I found him garrulously given,
　　A babbler in the land.

VII

But since I heard him make reply
　　Is many a weary hour;
'Twere well to question him, and try
　　If yet he keeps the power.

VIII

Hail, hidden to the knees in fern,
　　Broad Oak of Sumner-chace,
Whose topmost branches can discern
　　The roofs of Sumner-place!

IX

Say thou, whereon I carved her name,
　　If ever maid or spouse,
As fair as my Olivia, came
　　To rest beneath thy boughs. —

X

'O Walter, I have shelter'd here
　　Whatever maiden grace
The good old Summers, year by year
　　Made ripe in Sumner-chace:...

XVI

'And I have shadow'd many a group
　　Of beauties, that were born
In teacup-times of hood and hoop,
　　Or while the patch was worn;

XVII

'And, leg and arm with love-knots gay,
　　About me leap'd and laugh'd
The modish Cupid of the day,
　　And shrill'd his tinsel shaft.

XVIII

'I swear (and else may insects prick
　　Each leaf into a gall)
This girl, for whom your heart is sick,
　　Is three times worth them all;

XIX

'For those and theirs, by Nature's law,
　　Have faded long ago;
But in these latter springs I saw
　　Your own Olivia blow,

XX

'From when she gamboll'd on the greens
　　A baby-germ, to when
The maiden blossoms of her teens
　　Could number five from ten.

XXI

'I swear, by leaf, and wind, and rain,
　　(And hear me with thine ears,)
That, tho' I circle in the grain
　　Five hundred rings of years —

XXII

'Yet since I first could cast a shade,
　　Did never creature pass
So slightly, musically made,
　　So light upon the grass:...'

XXXVIII

O muffle round thy knees with fern,
　　And shadow Sumner-chace!
Long may thy topmost branch discern
　　The roofs of Sumner-place!

XXXIX

But tell me, did she read the name
　　I carved with many vows
When last with throbbing heart I came
　　To rest beneath thy boughs?

XL

'O yes, she wander'd round and round
　　These knotted knees of mine,
And found, and kiss'd the name she found,
　　And sweetly murmur'd thine....'

Tennyson called this long ballad 'an experiment meant to test the degree in which it was in his power as a poet to humanise external nature'.[1] The form was to be a long, humorous piece in which the ancient Oak of Sumner Chase repeated the confidences of two lovers, Walter and Olivia. Orlando's tree-messages in *As You Like It* influenced the poem, but Shakespeare's scene, with Touchstone's interventions, provide the lightness and variety that Tennyson's tree ballad often lacks. The oak is very taken with the beautiful Olivia and recalls her babyhood in stanza XX; it is both garrulous and banal; much more evocative is the description of Olivia moving near the tree in stanza XXII, where Tennyson's verse moves easily to suggest Olivia's harmony with herself and with nature. But the difficulty with the poem is that the oak has to keep up a long and fairly trivial story. Walter wishes to know from the tree, each detail of Olivia's visits: her kisses, dreams, reactions to an acorn cup – all feelings and actions transferable from oak to human lover. The end brings no surprise, no conflict, as Walter resolves to plight his troth to Olivia beside the tree, and make sure she wears a garland of oak leaves and acorns on her wedding day. The oak is to be honoured in 'prose and rhyme' more than the oaks at the Oracle of Dodona, or the famous tree that sheltered Charles I.

Three hundred lines are exchanged between Walter and the oak: the girl's voice is always reported. Olivia is never allowed to bring in her own sadness, doubt or delight. Sometimes, however, Tennyson does 'humanise' the oak so that the girl's voice and presence appear in the poem and some hint of the relationship between the two lovers is suggested. But the poet's experiment lets the oak talk for too long: the tree when 'humanised' becomes a harmless, garrulous, faintly voyeuristic bore. Tennyson is far more successful when, instead of forcing from nature a human voice, he allows the detail of nature to suggest human emotions.

This rather weak poem gave Lear the chance to reproduce an impressive English oak. His sketch adds the detail of antlers; deer are emerging from the shady fern round the tree's roots. In his country-house visits Lear often sketched trees: the great elms at Uppark, for instance, and this large oak at Blithfield, Staffordshire, seat of Lord Bagot. He notes in his diary for 29 August 1872 that he was at 'Rugby by 2.0...to Leamington by 2.25. Fly thence to Guyscliffe by 3, or so. Lunch with kind lady Charles. Then a walk with Lord & Ldy Bagot, Miss Percy & Miss Bagot.– to & about Leamington...' During his English visits Lear often went out of London to visit friends and patrons, quietly advertising his paintings, and sketching the countryside. On 25th January 1887, he wrote sadly (in San Remo), 'Lord Bagot died last week, aet. 75. born in 1811. The old days of Blithfield return to memory...' This diary entry shows that Lear lived right to the end on memories. He does not seem to have been at all close to Lord Bagot and yet, on his death, thoughts of the long past country-house visits return. Lear was never to visit England again: he died the next year, 1888.

[1] Ed. Hallam Lord Tennyson, *The Works of Tennyson* (Eversley Edition, Vol. II, 1908), p. 335.

86. EL List: Hail, hidden to the knees in fern
   EL Drawing: Hail! hidden to the knees in fern.

Hail! hidden to the knees in fern.

(The talking Oak.)

Blithfield
Staffordshire
England.

ULYSSES

It little profits that an idle king,
By this still hearth, among these barren crags,
Match'd with an aged wife, I mete and dole
Unequal laws unto a savage race,
That hoard, and sleep, and feed, and know not me.
I cannot rest from travel: I will drink
Life to the lees: all times I have enjoy'd
Greatly, have suffer'd greatly, both with those
That loved me, and alone; on shore, and when
Thro' scudding drifts the rainy Hyades   10
Vext the dim sea: I am become a name;
For always roaming with a hungry heart
Much have I seen and known; cities of men
And manners, climates, councils, governments,
Myself not least, but honour'd of them all;
And drunk delight of battle with my peers,
Far on the ringing plains of windy Troy.
I am a part of all that I have met;
Yet all experience is an arch wherethro'
Gleams that untravell'd world, whose margin fades   20
For ever and for ever when I move.
How dull it is to pause, to make an end,
To rust unburnish'd, not to shine in use!
As tho' to breathe were life. Life piled on life
Were all too little, and of one to me
Little remains: but every hour is saved
From that eternal silence, something more,
A bringer of new things; and vile it were
For some three suns to store and hoard myself,
And this gray spirit yearning in desire   30
To follow knowledge like a sinking star,
Beyond the utmost bound of human thought.

    This is my son, mine own Telemachus,
To whom I leave the sceptre and the isle –
Well-loved of me, discerning to fulfil
This labour, by slow prudence to make mild

A rugged people, and thro' soft degrees
Subdue them to the useful and the good.
Most blameless is he, centred in the sphere
Of common duties, decent not to fail   40
In offices of tenderness, and pay
Meet adoration to my household gods
When I am gone. He works his work, I mine.

    There lies the port; the vessel puffs her sail:
There gloom the dark broad seas. My mariners,
Souls that have toil'd, and wrought, and thought with
      me –
That ever with a frolic welcome took
The thunder and the sunshine, and opposed
Free hearts, free foreheads – you and I are old;
Old age hath yet his honour and his toil;   50
Death closes all: but something ere the end,
Some work of noble note, may yet be done,
Not unbecoming men that strove with Gods.
The lights begin to twinkle from the rocks:
The long day wanes: the slow moon climbs: the deep
Moans round with many voices. Come, my friends,
'Tis not too late to seek a newer world.
Push off, and sitting well in order, smite
The sounding furrows; for my purpose holds
To sail beyond the sunset, and the baths   60
Of all the western stars, until I die.
It may be that the gulfs will wash us down:
It may be we shall touch the Happy Isles,
And see the great Achilles, whom we knew.
Tho' much is taken, much abides; and tho'
We are not now that strength which in old days
Moved earth and heaven; that which we are, we are;
One equal temper of heroic hearts,
Made weak by time and fate, but strong in will
To strive, to seek, to find, and not to yield.   70

'"Ulysses"…was written soon after Arthur Hallam's death, and gave my feeling about the need of going forward, and braving the struggle of life perhaps more simply than anything in "In Memoriam".' Hallam Tennyson's note (*Mem.* I, p. 196) has done little to clarify his father's most famous dramatic monologue. Some critics, from Victorian times onward, have identified Ulysses with the poet and interpreted the poem as a decisive 'going forward' after the stagnating misery caused by Arthur Hallam's death. Other approaches consider 'braving the struggle of life' as anything but simple in a poem which displays both heroism and weariness, which demands both action and inaction.

The aged Ulysses has become a 'name', perhaps an echo of former fame, as he recollects in general terms the great events and battles of his past. He calls his mariners to follow 'this grey spirit sinking in desire', age buoyed up with hope of new lands and conquests. There is great vagueness about possible work 'yet to be done', and great rhetoric about 'sailing beyond the sunset'. Is Tennyson considering Ulysses as an old man caught in the 'maybe' of illusion, unable to brave the 'struggle of life' except by escaping from it? An ageing wife is to be left behind, and a whole Kingdom is to be the responsibility of Ulysses' son Telemachus, whose diligence is dismissed as competent bureaucracy.

Ulysses voices dreams and hopes which are undermined by the language Tennyson gives him: ''Tis not too late', 'We are not of that strength', hold suggestions of doubt, weakness, impossibility. The poem ends with a double movement: the confident infinitives 'To strive, to seek, to find', work up to the last words 'not to yield', which suggest, in spite of the negative formula, the impulse to give in. Ulysses, with no real goal, whips himself up with words which create a vision of activity and renewal, but betray a lack of hold on reality. Even as a young poet, Tennyson knew only too well that the 'struggle of life' could never be confronted with the aid of illusions. *In Memoriam* deals with many conflicting states of mind, but the poem does face, though not necessarily solve, the problems of the dark ship, of death, of loss, of the appalling difficulties of 'going forward'.

To discuss Ulysses as victim of illusion is to forget Ulysses the great classical figure. The poem may draw on Dante's Ulysses in the *Inferno*, but it also takes in the Homeric hero. In choosing such a character as speaker, Tennyson allowed into the poem Ulysses' great past adventures and achievements. What value they have, as the ageing hero imagines a future for himself, remains a matter for debate.

Lear's illustrations for this poem suggest he took a positive view of Ulysses. He respected the classical voyager, and was eager to describe Ulysses' Ithaca when he visited it. The bright jagged peaks scaled down to this small drawing suggest a fantastic, rather than a realistic mountain landscape. But the calm harbour at Ithaca

87

— among those barren Crags   Ithaca Greece,

(Ulysses.)

——— There lies the Port, ———

Thiáki.

Ithaca.

Greece.

(Ulysses -)

seems to have been quietly observed, a remembered place which waited for ships' departure and return. Grown older, Lear may have found vigour stronger than illusion in Ulysses' speeches. We cannot know. More important is Lear's association of the whole poem with memory and with the still creative use of the past. His third drawing is of a great arch in the Roman Campagna, a place he found fascinating whenever he visited it, early or late in his travels. On the picture he wrote, correctly, 'For all experience is an Arch', which for Ulysses in the poem suggests a move to the 'untravelled world' beyond. In Lear's list a misquotation changes the emphasis – 'For all remembrance is an arch' – and this is given weight as Lear's own misquotation by a diary entry for 4 August 1880, when he thinks of places, once familiar, as a 'long series of pictures seen thro' "Memory's Arch".' And on 3 May 1867, describing a journey in Italy, he remembers days of the 1840s and sudden views of the Abruzzi recall early travel; 'for all experience is a gate wherethrough...'. Lear misquotes, perhaps, because he still saw the gleam of the 'untravelled world' through the 'gate' that opens to let free memories of the past. With experience and remembrance the mind can contemplate its progress: journeys, real and imagined, now completed, and journeys still hoped for, still to come.

87, 89. Ithaca, Greece

On May 1st., I steamed away to Ithaca – where Bowen left me & returned to Corfu. I got there at dusk & dined at the officer's mess 36th. regiment. They good naturedly got me lodgings in a little house, & though I only speak a few words of Greek, yet I manage very well. Next day – 2nd. – I rose very early, & with Mr. Smith the surgeon of the regiment, & ensign Blund drew & drew & saw a great deal. Ulysses's kingdom is a little island – & charmingly quiet. I delight in it. The chief town – formed of houses entirely modern, is called Vathi – & it stands at the end of the harbour, so shut in by hills that you would think you were by a lake. In the afternoon we went to the fountain of Arethusa, – & all along the views are quite lovely – of the opposite Greek shore, & of the Ionian isles, Santa Maura, & Cephalonia. On the 3rd. May – I proposed going over to Cephalonia, so early, Smith & I went up to the ancient ruins of Ulysses's city & castle; vast walls of Cyclopian work – (like those in the first plate of my Roman book,) & sufficient left to attest the truth of the renown of old Ithaca. Coming down at noon, it was very hot, & we found an old hut where there was a great pan of fresh butter milk – but nobody to ask for it – so we drank it up & put some money in the bowl. I then took my leave of my Vathi friends & left Ithaca with the memory of 2 most pleasant days.   (EL to Ann, 14 May 1848)

88. Campagna di Roma, Italy

Meanwhile, I seem to have done and improved very little here, so much time has gone in seeing and doing nothing; – walking on that Campagna runs away with much; – I half live there now, and am continually poking about old temples which are dotted about all over the plain. I wish you could see the acqueducts! And these temples are of beautiful bright red brick – though of such extreme age – quite perfect and strong – and now used as cattle sheds;

For all experience is an Arch wherethro
Gleams the untravelled world, whose margin fades,
For ever and for ever when I move.
(Ulysses.)

Campagna di Roma
Italy)

nothing can be more beautiful than these wonderful ruins. Such bits as this are to be found by hundreds, and through these arches you see the vast yellow plains and the blue hills so beautifully. The Campagna is now covered with thousands of lambs – and as the willow trees are all quite out in leaf, we call it a real Spring. In the gardens about Rome there is no difference all the year round...
(EL to Ann, 29 March 1838)

There is a charm about this Campagna when it becomes all purple & gold, which it is difficult to tear oneself from.

Thus – climate & beauty of atmosphere regain their hold on the mind – pen – & pencil.
(EL to Ann, 27 March 1847)

87. EL List: Among these barren crags
    EL Drawing: – among those barren Crags
88. EL List: For all remembrance is an arch
    EL Drawing: For all experience is an Arch wherethro
                Gleams the untravelled world, whose margin fades,
                For ever and for ever when I move.
89. EL List: There lies the port
    EL Drawing: – There lies the Port, –

From: LOCKSLEY HALL

. . . Hark, my merry comrades call me, sounding on the   145
    bugle-horn,
They to whom my foolish passion were a target for their
    scorn:

Shall it not be scorn to me to harp on such a moulder'd
    string?
I am shamed thro' all my nature to have loved so slight
    a thing.

Weakness to be wroth with weakness! woman's pleasure,
    woman's pain –
Nature made them blinder motions bounded in a
    shallower brain:

Woman is the lesser man, and all thy passions, match'd
    with mine,
Are as moonlight unto sunlight, and as water unto wine –

Here at least, where nature sickens, nothing. Ah, for
    some retreat
Deep in yonder shining Orient, where my life began to
    beat;

Where in wild Mahratta-battle fell my father evil-   155
    starr'd; –
I was left a trampled orphan, and a selfish uncle's ward.

Or to burst all links of habit – there to wander far away,
On from island unto island at the gateways of the day.

Larger constellations burning, mellow moons and happy
    skies,
Breadths of tropic shade and palms in cluster, knots of
    Paradise.

Never comes the trader, never floats an European flag,
Slides the bird o'er lustrous woodland, droops the trailer
    from the crag;

Droops the heavy-blossom'd bower, hangs the heavy-
    fruited tree –
Summer isles of Eden lying in dark-purple spheres of sea.

There methinks would be enjoyment more than in   165
    this march of mind,
In the steamship, in the railway, in the thoughts that
    shake mankind.

There the passions cramp'd no longer shall have scope
    and breathing space;
I will take some savage woman, she shall rear my dusky
    race.

Iron jointed, supple-sinew'd, they shall dive, and they
    shall run,
Catch the wild goat by the hair, and hurl their lances in
    the sun;

Whistle back the parrot's call, and leap the rainbows of
    the brooks,
Not with blinded eyesight poring over miserable books –

Fool, again the dream, the fancy! but I *know* my words
    are wild,
But I count the gray barbarian lower than the Christian
    child.

I, to herd with narrow foreheads, vacant of our   175
    glorious gains,
Like a beast with lower pleasures, like a beast with lower
    pains!

Mated with a squalid savage – what to me were sun or
    clime?
I the heir of all the ages, in the foremost files of time –

I that rather held it better men should perish one by one,
Than that earth should stand at gaze like Joshua's moon
    in Ajalon!

Not in vain the distance beacons. Forward, forward let
    us range.
Let the peoples spin for ever down the ringing grooves
    of change.

Thro' the shadow of the globe we sweep into the younger
    day:
Better fifty years of Europe than a cycle of Cathay.

Mother-Age (for mine I knew not) help me as when   185
    life begun:
Rift the hills, and roll the waters, flash the lightnings,
    weigh the Sun –

O, I see the crescent promise of my spirit hath not set.
Ancient founts of inspiration well thro' all my fancy yet.

Howsoever these things be, a long farewell to Locksley
    Hall!
Now for me the woods may wither, now for me the
    roof-tree fall.

Comes a vapour from the margin, blackening over heath
    and holt,
Cramming all the blast before it, in its breast a thunder-
    bolt.

Let it fall on Locksley Hall, with rain or hail, or fire or
    snow;
For the mighty wind arises, roaring seaward, and I go.

90. *Kinchinjunga, Darjeeling, Himalaya, India*
91. *Darjeeling, (Himalaya), India*
92. *Khersiong, Darjeeling, (Himalaya), India*
93. *Conoor, Nilgherry Hills, Madras Presidency, India*
94. *Conoor, Nilgherry Hills, Madras Presidency, India*
95. Metapollium, Nilgherry Hills, Madras Presidency, India
96 Avisavella, Ceylon
97. *Ratnapoora, Ceylon*
98. *Adam's Peak, Ceylon*
99. Malabar, India

'Locksley Hall' has always been the subject of controversy. A reviewer in 1842 called it 'a piece of strong, full-blooded, man's writing...not unlikely to be the favourite piece of the whole collection, with most readers. It is full of daring conception, and most bitter passion, and the verse rushes on with a wild solemn flow, in splendid unison with the theme.'[1] Tennyson's friends, trying to get the poet's name on the Civil List for a pension, sent the 1842 *Poems* to the Prime Minister drawing particular attention to 'Ulysses' and 'Locksley Hall'. The latter piece was noted for its colourful and vigorous treatment of a familiar theme and its lively trochaic metre ensured immediate popularity. But opinion quickly swung against the poem: it was thought forced, and the lover almost farcical in his arrogance and assumption of superiority over his lost Amy. Even today some readers may see the hero of this poem as representing not only Byronic fervour, but also youth, strength, casting off the past and looking to a glorious future for himself, for Britain and Europe. The opposite view sees the hero as smug, self-seeking, and determined to present in the worst light possible the girl who dutifully married another. Does the narrator gloat over the details of the marriage? He certainly reminds Amy that she must tend her neglectful and drunken husband: it is her duty. And he cruelly imagines her as a widow, consoled by her baby, but later monitoring and constraining her own daughter's feelings.

The narrator sounds both bitter and superior: it is hard to believe in his initial love for the meek Amy. The trochaics of the poem pound along, suggesting forward movement, but also giving Tennyson the chance for some hollow ranting about love with an hourglass, love with a harp. The energy of 'Locksley Hall' rushes the reader on, past Amy's broken life, to the narrator's vision of future action, as a counterpart to withering despair.

In fact, the narrator has no intention of withering or despairing and immediately begins to conjure up visions of exotic commerce and to think of himself in the 'shining Orient' or some southern paradise. There he will take a native bride, but he quickly voices disgust at mating with a 'squalid savage' from a race whose 'narrow foreheads' are endowed with less brain than the 'Christian child'. Victorian attitudes to race sometimes included this conviction of total superiority, but it does rather unfortunately reinforce the hero's condescending sense of being one of a master race. The landscapes of the 'savage' paradise do at least show Tennyson's power of evocation, and it is from these that Lear drew all his illustrations. The narrator quickly casts aside ideas of paradise, realizing he must face the 'march of mind': 'In the steamship, in the railway, in the thoughts that shake

mankind.' The world must go forward, with the line Tennyson wrote, inspired by the movement of a train: 'Let the great world spin for ever down the ringing grooves of change.' Lip service is paid to knowledge, and better still, wisdom, but the narrator shows little of either as he repudiates the past, and leaves Locksley Hall to storm and thunderbolt.

At the end of 'Locksley Hall' the narrator confidently faces a challenging future. But the confidence is entirely unmerited. The long monologue leaves behind a trail of unsolved problems, unanswered questions. The hero wants to abandon his past, and ignore any of its implications for himself. He is impatient for quick solutions, never pausing in his certain judgements on others, or to consider his own behaviour. As critics have found, it is difficult to decide how far Tennyson is endorsing his hero's behaviour, but this is largely because the feelings expressed in the poem remain superficial and unassimilated.

The poet's personal problems may have compounded the difficulties of 'Locksley Hall'. He had recently been in love with Rosa Baring who was less responsive than the poem's Amy, but was also destined for an arranged marriage. The 'Locksley Hall' hero/narrator is proud, high-minded, egotistical, somewhat isolated. Tennyson himself shared all these traits, and a bitterness springing from his family's impoverished situation. His father had been passed over in favour of an uncle as far as the main inheritance was concerned. Such problems may have contributed to the emotional insistence yet incoherence of the poem.

There is no clue as to what Lear made of the narrator or his relationships in 'Locksley Hall'. His illustrations all relate to the tropical scenes which form the narrator's dream of escape from problems personal and political. All the drawings of darkly outlined trees and foliage are taken from Lear's last Indian journey. Lord Northbrook, the Viceroy, invited Lear to India, and other patrons loaded him with commissions. Feeling unwell and uncertain, Lear turned back once, but decided he must seize the opportunity in spite of indifferent health and poor sight. He set out with Giorgio in the autumn of 1873. When the ship docked, he was well rewarded with amazing sights, with 'wonderful varieties of life and dress'. Marble temples, bright foliage, bathers in the Ganges, street scenes, elephants – he was delighted with India, except for flies, rain, excessive heat and minor ailments. But on the first day he wrote from Bombay: 'The way thither drove me nearly mad with sheer beauty & wonder of foliage! O new palms!!! O flowers!! O creatures! O beauty!!' (D. 21 November 1873). These pictures give a sense of variety and density of vegetation, but they have none of the delicacy of Lear's Egyptian palm and temple scenes. Yet there are some fine watercolours and drawings done in or soon after the Indian journey, which included a short time in Ceylon. These illustrations suggest not only the problems of scaling down a large scene, but they are also late copies, several times removed even from the sketches of 1873-4. There may have been further darkening, with loss of foliage detail, when Lear prepared these drawings for different types of mechanical reproduction.

The drawings for 'Locksley Hall' are not given accurately in the printed list. (95) is listed as 'Conoor', (96)

95

Malabar

Breadths of tropic shade & palms in cluster

(Locksley Hall.)

Metapollium.
(Nilgherry Hills - Madras Presidency.
India

96

Breadths of tropic shade and palms in cluster

(Locksley Hall.)

Avisavella.
Ceylon

Summer isles of Eden, lying in dark purple spheres of sea.

(Locksley Hall.)

Malabar,
India

as 'Ratnapoora, Ceylon' and (99) as 'Calicut, Malabar, India'. The drawings themselves are inscribed (95) 'Malabar', (96) 'Ceylon' and (99) 'Beypore'. Two of the descriptions are very general: 'Malabar' was a large Western coastal area and Ceylon covered the whole island. 'Beypore' was a particular place on the Malabar coast and a Beypore river ran nearby. Descriptions from Lear's Indian Journal (in manuscript) have been chosen with the written descriptions of the pictures in mind. (95) has 'Metapollium Nilgherry Hills, Madras Presidency, India' below the picture and Lear visited the area of Metapollium and saw the distant Nilgherry hills while staying at the Malabar Club. (96) has 'Avisavella, Ceylon' beneath the picture and Lear's brief reference to 'Avisavella' has been included. (99) has 'Malabar, India', beneath the picture. Descriptions of the Beypore backwater, and of more general Malabar scenes, have been given to suggest the whole area which Lear was visiting on the Malabar Coast and slightly inland. The discrepancy between names on the list and on the drawing may be Lear's unnoticed mistakes. It is possible too, that with so many sketches of varied palm scenery, he got down a general scheme and then found that his individual pictures were of slightly different places.

95. Metapollium, Nilgherry Hills, Madras Presidency

The great plain – near the first wood, – is something too extensive & incredible even to attempt to describe, – a world of opal beaten out with a filmy horizon of light: – and the long long scheme of cloud, casting pale pearly blue shadows over great spaces of flat plain!! The infinitesimal divisions of the vast immense level! – nearer, – rivers, & the villages – towns – Metapollium, & others; – nearer still, the huge mountain of the Droog dipping step by step to the Valley below; its deep green gray purple wooded undulations & crags.! – And then the left hand middle distance of Jungle & Rocky mountain side! – & lastly, the foreground path, with the poor meagre natives in their striped blankets, – the ferns, – & the scattered Tree=ferns below!! After drawing a while, walked on through the next wood & drew again hastily. (Cries of the Jungle Fowl & many birds – also of Apes, as we came back, through the dark wood!). So, slowly back to the hotel by 6.
(Indian Journal, 13 October 1874)

96. Avisavella, Ceylon

Rose before 4. (Ow, these filthy filthy luoghi, – & this in the "principal Hotel of the Capital of Ceylon"! –). Dressed & all ready before 5. Off from the Hotel – 5.15. Distant view of Adam's Peak – at sunrise. Post. Fuss. Box. Off 5.30. Halt. Off finally 5.45. Racing – nearly upset. Crowded and very uncomfortably small coach. Bad horses at one or two changes, & at 3d change nearly upset again . . . Very beautiful foliage. Kalany(?) river exquisite, & one or two peeps of Adam's Peak. Farther on, hills, – all wooded, & inconceivably green, – some of these spots quite lovely. Reach, at 10.29 AM, the Rest House at Avisavella – 30th mile. Very neat & clean little place. Excellent breakfast. Off, 10.45 – 50. – Most beautiful "spot"!! Less pretty onwards. . . (23 November 1874)

99. Beypore, India

. . . we went in a Bullock-Bandy to the Beypore Backwater, – the picturesqueness of all the scenery about which no pen can give the least idea of. Here, after walks along the road, I inspected one of the usual passenger boats, – a long caique or canoe, [a small cabin] being the only part available for the suffering passenger, – & the whole affair so queer & rolly=polly that I decided not to go in that, but in a Bullock cart, – to Telicherry. I never certainly could draw at all in that machine, nor should I like to risk 8 hours (& some say it may be 14,) in such a boat. (25 October 1874)

Malabar Coast

Mr Hayden (a partner of Captn. Baudry?) who said – "If you want to draw fine sights, go to the Brass Pagoda." So I said to [George] "Let us go to the Brass Pagoda;" – & we set off – going along lanes for a mile or more, & frequently asking our way of schoolboys, – who generally said, – "Not know Brazen Temple, other fellows (or chaps) coming, perhaps know." – Always delighted by the exquisite lane = foliage scenery, and by the pure bright green rice-grounds, backed by distant palms & far blue mountains, we came at length in sight of a hideous barn like building, which I took for some sort of stable. Several Natives were about, & I said to George – "these do not look as if they could speak English?" – "Why not?" said a fat half naked Brahmin, – "I can speak English for one." – "Well, is this the Brass Pagoda?" – "No – it has no such name, unless among you English." – "But," – said I, "it is evidently known by that name, as 2 or 3 of you told me this lane would lead to the Brass Pagoda." "Well" said the Brahmin, – "it is the Temple of the Holy Vishnu; – but why do you want to see it? I should not like you to think me an impertinent or inquisitive person, but at the same time I should be glad to know your name, & who you are, & in what station of life, & why you come here, & where you come from, & where you are going to, and all your previous history, & all about you." – Says I, "I am an English Gentleman, & that is enough; I only want to see the outside of your temple, & have no wish to go into it." " – But you CAN'T, if you did wish ever so much!" said Fatty triumphantly. These people hereabouts are sharp enough, & aliquanto disagreable. (31 October 1874)

. . . to my very great surprise, the view was something fabulous. So very remarkable an Oriental view I have never seen nor even imagined; for although the infinite lines of low hills & higher mountains are all quite a la Claude Lorraine distance, yet the texture of Cocoa-nuttery is something quite unlike what can be seen except in this & other extended tropical Coast scenery, – myriads of small white flashes and as many myriads of deep shady dots, caused by the light & shade of the great innumerable Palm fronds. The rivers in this view are wonderfully beautiful while the sun is low, & all the colour, – changes of gray & misty lilac, and palest opal blue, – (not opal though, for that is clear, whereas here all is misty & damp,) makes a world of divinely exquisite beauty. (1 November 1874)

[1] E.F. Shannon, *Tennyson and the Reviewers* (Harvard University Press, 1952), p.62.

95. EL List: Breadths of tropic shade, and palms in cluster
    EL Drawing: Breadths of tropic shade & palms in cluster
96. EL List: Breadths of tropic shade, and palms in cluster
    EL Drawing: Breadths of tropic shade and palms in cluster
99. EL List: Summer isles of Eden
    EL Drawing: Summer isles of Eden, lying in dark purple spheres of sea.

From: THE TWO VOICES

... 'If all be dark, vague voice,' I said,   265
  'These things are wrapt in doubt and dread,
  Nor canst thou show the dead are dead.

  'The sap dries up: the plant declines.
  A deeper tale my heart divines.
  Know I not Death? the outward signs?

  'I found him when my years were few;
  A shadow on the graves I knew,
  And darkness in the village yew.

  'From grave to grave the shadow crept:
  In her still place the morning wept: 275
  Touch'd by his feet the daisy slept.

  'The simple senses crown'd his head:
  "Omega! thou art Lord," they said,
  "We find no motion in the dead."

  'Why, if man rot in dreamless ease,
  Should that plain fact, as taught by these,
  Not make him sure that he shall cease?

  'Who forged that other influence,
  That heat of inward evidence,
  By which he doubts against the sense?   285

  'He owns the fatal gift of eyes,
  'That read his spirit blindly wise,
  Not simple as a thing that dies.

  'Here sits he shaping wings to fly:
  His heart forebodes a mystery:
  He names the name Eternity....

... 'But, if I lapsed from nobler place,
  Some legend of a fallen race
  Alone might hint of my disgrace;   360

  'Some vague emotion of delight
  In gazing up an Alpine height,
  Some yearning toward the lamps of night.

  'Or if thro' lower lives I came –
  Tho' all experience past became
  Consolidate in mind and frame –

  'I might forget my weaker lot;
  For is not our first year forgot?
  The haunts of memory echo not.

  'And men, whose reason long was blind,   370
  From cells of madness unconfined,
  Oft lose whole years of darker mind.

  'Much more, if first I floated free,
  As naked essence, must I be
  Incompetent of memory:

  'For memory dealing but with time,
  And he with matter, could she climb
  Beyond her own material prime?

  'Moreover, something is or seems,
  That touches me with mystic gleams,   380
  Like glimpses of forgotten dreams –

  'Of something felt, like something here;
  Of something done, I know not where;
  Such as no language may declare.'

  The still voice laugh'd. 'I talk,' said he,
  'Not with thy dreams. Suffice it thee
  Thy pain is a reality.'

  'But thou,' said I, 'hast missed thy mark,
  Who sought'st to wreck my mortal ark,
  By making all the horizon dark.   390

  'Why not set forth, if I should do
  This rashness, that which might ensue
  With this old soul in organs new?

  'Whatever crazy sorrow saith,
  No life that breathes with human breath
  Has ever truly long'd for death.

  ''Tis life, whereof our nerves are scant,
  Oh life, not death, for which we pant;
  More life, and fuller, that I want.'

  I ceased, and sat as one forlorn.   400
  Then said the voice, in quiet scorn,
  'Behold, it is the Sabbath morn.'

  And I arose, and I released
  The casement, and the light increased
  With freshness in the dawning east.

  Like soften'd airs that blowing steal,
  When meres begin to uncongeal,
  The sweet church bells began to peal.

  On to God's house the people prest.
  Passing the place where each must rest,   410
  Each enter'd like a welcome guest....

... I blest them, and they wander'd on:
  I spoke, but answer came there none: 425
  The dull and bitter voice was gone.

A second voice was at mine ear,
A little whisper silver-clear,
A murmur, 'Be of better cheer.'

As from some blissful neighbourhood,
A notice faintly understood,
'I see the end, and know the good.'

A little hint to solace woe,
A hint, a whisper breathing low,
'I may not speak of what I know.' 435

Like an Æolian harp that wakes
No certain air, but overtakes
Far thought with music that it makes.

Such seem'd the whisper at my side:
'What is it thou knowest, sweet voice?' I cried.
'A hidden hope,' the voice replied:

So heavenly-toned, that in that hour
From out my sullen heart a power
Broke, like the rainbow from the shower,

To feel, altho' no tongue can prove, 445
That every cloud, that spreads above
And veileth love, itself is love.

And forth into the fields I went,
And Nature's living motion lent
The pulse of hope to discontent.

I wonder'd at the bounteous hours,
The slow result of winter showers:
You scarce could see the grass for flowers.

I wonder'd, while I paced along.
The woods were fill'd so full with song, 455
There seem'd no room for sense of wrong;

So variously seem'd all things wrought,
I marvell'd how the mind was brought
To anchor by one gloomy thought;

And wherefore rather I made choice
To commune with that barren voice,
Than him that said, 'Rejoice! Rejoice!'

101

In gazing up an Alpine height :—
(The two voices.)

The Matterhorn.
Switzerland.

100. *Sussex, England*

101. The Matterhorn, Switzerland

This poem, written in 1833 though begun earlier, records some of the misery felt by Tennyson after Arthur Hallam's death. Of its 'two voices', one undoubtedly speaks of hopelessness, the loss of all meaning in human life, the logic of suicide. This deadly voice has no obvious joyous counterpart. Its arguments are slowly confronted, sometimes answered, sometimes evaded, by the voice of 'I', the uncertain, undermined, yet ultimately life-affirming speaker. There is genuine tension in the poem, because the human voice is unpredictable, countering the dark voice with differing reactions, sinking into despair and then struggling again towards hope and a concept of human worth. It is not until the last part of the poem, when the 'I' has triumphed, and looks out on a bright Sunday morning scene with families going to church, that another voice sounds. Brief phrases urge the human speaker to hope and to rejoice. Is this the second of the two voices? Or can such a voice be heard only when the human being, having fought with his own doubt, allows another voice to sound within himself?

In whatever way Lear read 'The Two Voices' it echoed for him the self-doubt, misery, sense of drift, which he felt through most of his life. Lack of progress and of will power often seemed part of a lonely and hopeless existence. Yet in good moments, Lear could recognize the positive voice within himself and allow at least a moderate rejoicing. There is so little landscape description in this poem that Lear may have been moved mainly by the dilemma of the human speaker. At the very end of the poem the speaker goes out into the fields and woods; the loveliness of the natural world deepens both hope and wonder. The last triplet of the poem finally rejects the voice which urges despair. The speaker wonders how the mind can be anchored by 'one gloomy thought',

> And wherefore rather I made choice
> To commune with that barren voice,
> Than him that said 'Rejoice! Rejoice!'

For illustration Lear took 'the village yew' – its darkness a sign of death – a shadow on the village green. The other picture (seen here) is of the Matterhorn, 'an Alpine height' at which man might gaze with 'Some vague emotion of delight' even if humanity had fallen from its 'nobler place'. The yew is a recognition of death; the Alp is hope of aspiring life. Lear found two landscapes which reflect his deep interest in the conflict of Tennyson's poem.

It was during his earliest journey towards Rome that Lear first saw the Alps and marvelled, as he always did, at crags, snow and mountain splendour. He sometimes drew precipitous rocks, at Canalo, Calabria, for instance, or at Suli in Albania, but he usually preferred to use the lines and peaks of mountains as a background of distant horizontals and verticals which set off the main subject of the picture. In England again, Lear worked on several commissioned pictures; he sketched in his diary for 7 September 1861 the crudest outline of eight paintings he was working on. They included a 'Dead Sea', a 'Thebes', an 'Athos', 'La Petraia' – and also a small upright picture of the 'Matterhorn'. By 14 October the 'Matterhorn' was framed, but Lear does not speak of further work on it, or mention its future owner, Franklin Lushington. After the death of his sister Ann in March 1861, Lear had tried to distract himself from his misery by making a series of visits and moving off to Switzerland to immerse himself in drawing.

101. EL List: In gazing up an Alpine crag
     EL Drawing: In gazing up an Alpine height. –

From: THE DAY-DREAM

THE ARRIVAL

All precious things, discover'd late,
    To those that seek them issue forth;
For love in sequel works with fate,
    And draws the veil from hidden worth.
He travels far from other skies –
    His mantel glitters on the rocks –
A fairy Prince, with joyful eyes,
    And lighter-footed than the fox.

The bodies and the bones of those
    That strove in other days to pass,
Are wither'd in the thorny close,
    Or scatter'd blanching in the grass.
He gazes on the silent dead:
    "They perish'd in their daring deeds."
This proverb flashes thro' his head,
    "The many fail: the one succeeds."

He comes, scarce knowing what he seeks:
    He breaks the hedge: he enters there:
The colour flies into his cheeks:
    He trusts to light on something fair;
For all his life the charm did talk
    About his path, and hover near
With words of promise in his walk,
    And whisper'd voices in his ear.

More close and close his footsteps wind:
    The magic music in his heart
Beats quick and quicker, till he find
    The quiet chamber far apart.
His spirit flutters like a lark,
    He stoops – to kiss her – on his knee.
"Love, if thy tresses be so dark,
    How dark those hidden eyes must be!"

THE REVIVAL

A touch, a kiss! the charm was snapt.
    There rose a noise of striking clocks,
And feet that ran, and doors that clapt,
    And barking dogs, and crowing cocks.
A fuller light illumined all,
    A breeze thro' all the garden swept,
A sudden hubbub shook the hall,
    And sixty feet the fountain leapt.

The hedge broke in, the banner blew,
    The butler drank, the steward scrawl'd,
The fire shot up, the martin flew,
    The parrot scream'd, the peacock squall'd,
The maid and page renew'd their strife,
    The palace bang'd, and buzz'd and clackt,
And all the long-pent stream of life
    Dash'd downward in a cataract.

And last of all the king awoke,
    And in his chair himself uprear'd,
And yawn'd, and rubb'd his face, and spoke,
    'By holy rood, a royal beard!
How say you? we have slept, my lords.
    My beard has grown into my lap.'
The barons swore, with many words,
    'Twas but an after-dinner nap.

'Pardy,' return'd the king, 'but still
    My joints are somewhat stiff or so.
My lord, and shall we pass the bill
    I mention'd half an hour ago?'
The chancellor, sedate and vain,
    In courteous words return'd reply:
But dallied with his golden chain,
    And, smiling, put the question by.

THE DEPARTURE

And on her lover's arm she leant,
    And round her waist she felt it fold,
And far across the hills they went
    In that new world which is the old:
Across the hills, and far away
    Beyond their utmost purple rim,
And deep into the dying day
    The happy princess follow'd him.

'I'd sleep another hundred years,
    O love, for such another kiss;'
'O wake for ever, love,' she hears,
    'O love, 'twas such as this and this.'
And o'er them many a sliding star,
    And many a merry wind was borne,
And, stream'd thro' many a golden bar,
    The twilight melted into morn.

'O eyes long laid in happy sleep!'
    'O happy sleep, that lightly fled!'
'O happy kiss, that woke thy sleep!'
    'O love, thy kiss would wake the dead!'
And o'er them many a flowing range
    Of vapour buoy'd the crescent-bark,
And, rapt thro' many a rosy change,
    The twilight died into the dark.

'A hundred summers! can it be?
    And whither goest thou, tell me where?'
'O seek my father's court with me,
    For there are greater wonders there.'
And o'er the hills, and far away
    Beyond their utmost purple rim,
Beyond the night, across the day,
    Thro' all the world she follow'd him.

'oer the hills and far away,
Beyond their utmost purple rim.
(The Day Dream.)

Montenegro.

102. Montenegro
103. *Pine Forest of Pisa, (Gombo, Viareggio), Italy*

At the centre of 'The Day-Dream' lies the old tale of the 'Sleeping Beauty'. Most of the poem is divided into short stanzaic sections and the description of the Sleeping Princess was written as early as 1830. The poem was finalized in 1834 except for the prologue and epilogue which frame the whole story of the hundred years' sleep and the breaking of the spell. In 1842 a rhymed but non-stanzaic prologue first shows us a day-dreaming Lady Flora whose role is to listen to the narrator while getting on with her embroidery. She is the focus of the narrator's own day-dream which he displaces into the tale of the 'Sleeping Beauty'. He begins with the 'Sleeping Palace', then Beauty herself; the pace changes, as it always does, in this 'legend part', with 'The Arrival' as the prince breaks through to the quiet chamber and begins to kiss the Princess he finds sleeping there. 'The Revival' tells of the life which sweeps through the palace as the kiss breaks the spell of a hundred years. 'The Departure' adds some brief dialogue to the narrative as the Princess happily follows the Prince 'Across the hills, and far away'. They seem to move through a fairy-tale space, but they have a definite goal: the great court of the Prince's father. And, as they go, they exclaim delightedly on the 'happy sleep, that lightly fled!' and on the joyful awakening into life. But now time moves on again: the Princess is alive, but follows the Prince into 'the dying day'. Another twilight melts into morning, but another day ends: 'And, rapt thro' many a rosy change, / The twilight died into the dark.' The last line

is Lear's choice for illustration. He knew that travelling 'across the hills and far away' (another illustration) could ease his loneliness and put before him superb landscape for his pictures. But he knew it could not be done with the painless lack of difficulty of this fairy-tale 'Departure'. He often mourned for time past and friends dead: he recorded in detail each day, each year of his life. Thirty years of his diary survive. Was it the intrusion of passing time in the beauty of a sunset which he thought of with the dying twilight? Or was it the change from rose to dark which he loved to watch on his travels and, towards the end of his life, from the window or terrace of his villas in San Remo?

In 'The Day-Dream', the legendary Prince and Princess seem untouched by space and time. But the narrator hints to the reader that time and death must follow awakenings, however brilliant. In 'Moral' and 'Envoi' the old tale is linked to the idea of the whole world's progress in time; to the growth of science and opening of secrets of the brain, to the springing up of vast Republics, Federations, Powers. Lady Flora declines to moralize, but the narrator asks questions he cannot answer. If we could sleep and rise every hundred years would we 'learn the world'? Could we sleep through wars and wake only to 'The flower and quintessence of change'? These ideas Tennyson pursues elsewhere, especially in *In Memoriam*; the vision of mankind's onward and upward progress counterbalanced Victorian fears of man's bestial regression suggested by the new evidence of geological change and the new theories of evolution. Tennyson's elaborate approach to this allows him an excuse to bring serious, modern ideas to bear on an old tale. But despite the narrator's oblique proposal to Lady Flora in the 'Envoi', and his offering of the whole 'lay' as a tribute to her, the framing at beginning and end seem to overload the poem. The best writing is in the succinct and often comic retelling of the 'Sleeping Beauty', and in the light and lively 'Departure' scene which needs no long explanation to make clear its ambivalence.

Lear's 'O'er the hills...' illustration is a view of hills and mountains spreading into the distance, seen from above. There is no hint of human life or habitation: a landscape for dream journeys. Perhaps the artist, if not the poet, remembered the half-dreamt countries, India and Greenland, of the old song. In Gay's *Beggars' Opera* the couple's fantasy of survival depends on immediate flight 'Over the hills and far away'. In Tennyson's 'Day-Dream', the wakened Princess follows the Prince, without a moment's doubt, 'Across the hills, and far away.'

102. Montenegro

As you proceed from point to point of the promontories which make up the serpentine sides of the Bocca di Cattaro, the scenery becomes quite lakelike, & reminds you of Cormayeur in a vast wall of nearly perpendicular mountain rising above it. Quite at the end of the gulf, lies Cattaro a diminutive city nestled below stupendous precipices, those of Montenegro. The little place seems a mere speck

compared with the towering heights up wh. you see the ziggy many turning road leading (literally to day, into the clouds,) but eventually to Montenegro: & really as it ended in cloud it suggested a far more convenient and elegant ascent for the legend of Jacob's dream than the conventional ugly ladder generally used... soon I and G. went out to walk – a mile or 2 along the Lake, for so it seems. The vast semicircle of mountain crag is most striking...　　(D. 26 April 1866)

Lear visited Montenegro during a tour of the Dalmatian coast in 1866. The sketch he chose to work on for an illustration of 'Across the hills and far away' has an unreal, dream-like quality. Such a great circling of 'mountain crag' suits the fairy-tale journey of 'The Day-Dream'. And the road ending in cloud seems to produce a supernatural ascent. The legend of Jacob's ladder invokes another 'old tale', religious rather than secular. A few days later Lear talks about slowly climbing some sort of actual ladder up the rocks, so what he describes here is, by contrast, an ideal journey, a cloud fantasy.

102. EL List:　　　Across the hills and far away
　　　EL Drawing:　'oer the hills and far away,
　　　　　　　　　Beyond their utmost purple rim.
[*Poems*, 1842:　　Across the hills, and far away
　　　　　　　　　Beyond their utmost purple rim,]

ST. AGNES

I

Deep on the convent-roof the snows
  Are sparkling to the moon:
My breath to heaven like vapour goes:
  May my soul follow soon!
The shadows of the convent-towers
  Slant down the snowy sward,
Still creeping with the creeping hours
  That lead me to my Lord:
Make Thou my spirit pure and clear
  As are the frosty skies,
Or this first snowdrop of the year
  That in my bosom lies.

II

As these white robes are soiled and dark,
  To yonder shining ground;
As this pale taper's earthly spark,
  To yonder argent round;
So shows my soul before the Lamb,
  My spirit before Thee;
So in mine earthly house I am,
  To that I hope to be.
Break up the heavens, O Lord! and far,
  Thro' all yon starlight keen,
Draw me, thy bride, a glittering star,
  In raiment white and clean.

III

He lifts me to the golden doors;
  The flashes come and go;
All heaven bursts her starry floors,
  And strows her lights below,
And deepens on and up! the gates
  Roll back, and far within
For me the Heavenly Bridegroom waits,
  To make me pure of sin.
The sabbaths of Eternity,
  One sabbath deep and wide –
A light upon the shining sea –
  The Bridegroom with his bride!

104. Monastery of Pantokratora, Mount Athos

This short and unequivocally Christian poem was first printed in a small magazine, *The Keepsake*, for 1837. A critic later observed that the poem was a great popular success. It had a certain vogue, but Tennyson's friends were disappointed. 'An iced saint', said one of them, 'is certainly better than an ice cream, but not much better than a frosted tree. The original Agnes is worth twenty of her'. There was general agreement that the poem was not representative of Tennyson's best.[1]

The poet maintained that the speaker was a nun, and later changed the poem's title to 'St Agnes' Eve'. St Agnes, a martyr at thirteen, refused to marry, was raped and assaulted, but found miraculously to be a virgin at her death. The nun's monologue has to do with the legend that the virgin who prayed to St Agnes on the eve of the saint's martyrdom might see a vision of her destined lover. The 'iced saint' purity of the poem is in definite contrast to Keats's highly sensuous retelling of the same story. His lovers, once out of their magically protected warmth, as they flee confront an aged freezing world. Tennyson's chaste nun prays to her heavenly Bridegroom: the brilliance, frost, snow, starlight and white robes will lead to the ultimate whiteness – an opening in heaven where the Bridegroom waits to make her 'pure of sin'. The whole poem, a distinctly chilly prayer, projects a bright moral monotony rather than genuine innocence.

It is odd that Lear, so temperamentally drawn to matters of doubt and sin, of hope turning into despair, should have chosen 'St Agnes' for illustration. The poem, Tennyson said, was meant for a pendant to 'Sir Galahad', which tells of the quest of a pure knight for the Holy Grail. But Lear did not make this connection, and 'St Agnes' stands alone. The artist takes one line 'A light upon the shining sea', not typical of the very enclosed poem, and provides an illustration from one of the monasteries near the shore on the 'Holy Mountain', Mount Athos. In 1856 Lear drew the scenery near the monasteries with delight, but he hated the claustrophobic Christianity they represented, their centuries of inturned, unbreeding life. Is this monastery on the shining sea simply a suitable image for the nun's vision? Or is there a conscious or unconscious irony in Lear's choice? Is the bright scene, outwardly beautiful, meant as a contrast to inwardly tainted piety? Perhaps Lear's drawing of this monastery suggests a connection between Tennyson's coldly aspiring nun and the monks of Mount Athos.

104. Mount Athos

. . . the Holy Mountain, altogether the most surprising thing I have seen in my travels, barring Egypt. It is a peninsular mountain about 2000 ft. high & 50 miles long ending in a vast crag, near 7000 feet high, this being Athos. All about this bare crag is one mass of vast forest, beech, chestnut, oak, & ilex, and all around the cliffs and crags by the sea are 20 great and ancient monistirries, not to speak of 6 or 700 little 'uns above and below and around.

These convents are inhabited by, altogether perhaps, 6 or 7000 monx, & as you may have heard, no female creature exists in all the peninsula: – there are nothing but mules, tomcats, and cocks allowed. This is literally true.
(EL to Fortescue, 9 October 1856, LEL, p.40)

. . . & off I set to . . . Pantokratora. I always asked to see the churches – more to please my hosts than myself, – for I can assure you 20 Greek churches – one just like another – are a task – & I listened meekly to the dreadful nonsense stories they told me of this or that picture. One floated from Jerusalem by sea; – one cried when the Turks came; another bled at some apropos time; a 4th – a Pagan having poked his finger at him held the finger so tight it was obliged to be cut off . . . Oh those candles! & ostrich eggs! – & gold & silver & paintings!! – oh Holy Mountain! what have I not suffered to get drawings of you! – Well, Pantokratora is on the sea; & so is . . . Stavroniketes, & as they are built on rocks, & look up to the mighty peak of Athos – they make noble scenes, a lonely grandeur one hardly can understand till one has felt for days that none but these miserable solitaries occupy this strange land.
(EL to Ann, 8 October 1856)

[1] A. Waugh, *Alfred Lord Tennyson* (William Heinemann, 1902), p.60.

104.   EL List: A light upon the shining sea
          EL Drawing: A light upon the shining sea –

A light upon the shining sea —
(St Agnes' Eve.)

Monastery of Pantokratora.
Mount Athos.

TO E.L. ON HIS TRAVELS IN GREECE

Illyrian woodlands, echoing falls
  Of water, sheets of summer glass,
  The long divine Peneïan pass,
The vast Akrokeraunian walls,

Tomohrit, Athos, all things fair,
  With such a pencil, such a pen,
  You shadow forth to distant men,
I read and felt that I was there:

And trust me while I turn'd the page,
  And track'd you still on classic ground,
  I grew in gladness till I found
My spirits in the golden age.

For me the torrent ever pour'd
  And glisten'd – here and there alone
  The broad-limb'd Gods at random thrown
By fountain-urns; – and Naiads oar'd

A glimmering shoulder under gloom
  Of cavern pillars; on the swell
  The silver lily heaved and fell;
And many a slope was rich in bloom

From him that on the mountain lea
  By dancing rivulets fed his flocks,
  To him who sat upon the rocks,
And fluted to the morning sea.

105

Illyrian Woodlands, —
(To E.L. on his travels in Greece.)

near Ahkrida,
Macedonia, or Albania.

105. Near Ahkrida, Macedonia or Albania
106. The River Kalama, Epirus, Albania
107. Lake of Ahkrida, Macedonia or Albania
108. Pass of Tempe, Thessaly, Greece
109. Akrokeraunian Mountains, Albania
110. Akrokeraunian Mountains (Chimara), Albania
111. Pass of Mount Tchika, Akrokeraunian Mountains, Albania
112. Akrokeraunian Mountains, Draghiades (Khimara), Albania
113. *Mount of Tomohrit, from above Tyrana, Albania*
114. Mount Tomohrit, from Berat, Albania
115. *Mount Athos from the sea*
[**115.** *crossed out, Tomohrit*]
116. *Mount Athos from above Eriligova*
117. *Mount Athos from above Erisso or Nisboro*
118. *Mount Athos from above Karyes*
119. *Mount Athos from Karyes*
120. Monastery of Koutloumoussi, Mount Athos
121. *Monastery of Pantokratora, Mount Athos*
122. Monastery of Stavronikites, Mount Athos
123. Monastery of Karakalla, Mount Athos
124. *Monastery of Philotheo, Mount Athos*
125. *Monastery of Iviron, Mount Athos*
[**125a.** *Monastery of Laura, Mount Athos*]
126. *Monastery of Laura, Mount Athos*
127. Monastery of Laura, Mount Athos
128. Monastery of St Nilus, Mount Athos
129. *Monastery of St Paul, Mount Athos*
130. Monastery of St Dionysios, Mount Athos
131. *Monastery of St Gregorio, Mount Athos*
132. *Monastery of Simopetra, Mount Athos*
133. Monastery of Xeropotamos, Mount Athos
134. *Monastery of St Xenophon, Mount Athos*
135. *Monastery of Russikon, Mount Athos*
136. *Monastery of Dochiareion, Mount Athos*
137. Monastery of Kostamonites, Mount Athos
138. Monastery of Zographos, Mount Athos
139. *Monastery of Chiliandarion, Mount Athos*
140. *Monastery of Esphigmenu, Mount Athos*
141. *Monastery of Vatopaidhi, Mount Athos*
142. *Corfu, Greece*
[**142a.** *Naples*]
143. *Constantinople*
144. *Campagna di Roma, Italy*
145. *Mt. Kinchinjunga, from Darjeeling, Himalaya, India*

Tennyson's poems were part of Lear's concept of 'poetical topography'. From his reading of the 1842 volumes lines of poetry entered his imagination, were quoted and misquoted to help define his experience, and were marshalled into his long-lasting Tennyson Illustration project. Lear's work, on the other hand, never fired Tennyson except in the single tribute: 'To E.L. on his Travels in Greece'. Shortly after meeting the Laureate, Lear had sent his published Albanian and Calabrian Journals as a present to the Tennysons. The poem 'To E.L.' mentions some of Lear's strange Albanian places, but quickly moves to Greece and the beauties of 'classic ground'.

For Lear, the emphasis of the poem was entirely different and far more personal. Of forty illustrations, twenty-seven are given to Athos – the isolated 'Holy Mountain', the rocky peninsula thrusting into the sea in Northern Greece.

Tennyson mentions the mountain, with another, in a general description of Lear's journey, 'Tomohrit, Athos, all things fair...'. But in the Albanian journal, Lear never actually reached Athos: it remained as a distant goal. Yet Tennyson's very naming of Athos in the poem 'To E.L.', allowed Lear to focus on a landscape and an experience which moved him and disturbed him more deeply than any other place throughout his travels. He was flattered and delighted by Tennyson's poem: he wondered if he should use it to begin his illustration project and decided that might be 'too vainy-bumptious'. But the large series of drawings he made, most of them relating back to previous sketches, watercolours and some oils, concentrate on Mount Athos. Paradoxically, this place – never visited by Tennyson – has no real importance for the poet, but allows the artist to embark on his own, most remembered, 'Travels in Greece'.

Athos, the Holy Mountain, was a huge peninsula, rock-bound and rising to the peak of Mount Athos itself: it was completely cut off from the rest of civilisation. Lear set out from Constantinople in 1848, but Salonika, where he landed, was shut because of cholera, and Mount Athos had closed its gates to keep out the disease and travellers together. It was then that Lear changed plans and decided to travel through part of Turkey and into Albania. He finally reached Athos, with his servant Giorgio, in 1856.

The population consisted entirely of monks living in large monastic complexes, in smaller hermitages and a few in lone cell-caves in the rock. The large monasteries, Lavra, for instance, were often rich in paintings, icons, manuscripts and religious treasure. Smaller dwellings were sometimes miserably poor, dirty and squalid. The ancient tradition of Orthodox worship was unbroken since Byzantine times, and the lack of contact with the outside world produced an awesome display of Christianity, but also a disturbing degree of ignorance among the lesser monks and a pervading sense of desiccation, dirt, wretched food, fever and backwardness. Some of the inhabitants, Lear felt, had withered almost to death in a state of isolation and loneliness taken to its extreme limit. As letters to Ann, to Emily Tennyson and to Fortescue show, Lear was both fascinated and appalled. He felt the need to draw every monastery and to record all details he could of life in this extraordinary place.

As he travelled round, by mule, he was welcomed by highly educated and interesting monks – the Superior Fathers who ran the large monasteries and were part of the Synod which met at Karyes and organized the community's affairs. But he also met half-crazed creatures, mumbling and muttering a single prayer, subsisting on and offering a meal of dirty watermelon and fish. The bread was grimy everywhere: Lear tried to eat rice. Yet the landscapes as Lear recorded them, and as they are still to be seen, were superb. Oak-fringed and chestnut-covered slopes, the high peaked mountain, the monasteries rising from the rocks bright with domes, the light of the sun striking stone and paintwork – all these offered marvellous compositions of rock, tree and building. The whole peninsula, with its coves, inlets, tiny harbours, rock promontories, was surrounded by deep blue sea. Lear found Athos itself a paradox: beautiful yet terrible, a wonderful expanse of natural landscape, and yet a series of claustrophobic man-made, and man-chosen, retreats from human life. By tradition, which appalled Lear, no female creature was ever allowed on Athos. No woman, no female animal could enter the peninsula. Some of the large monasteries were having trouble with mice, and Lear was informed that they were about to import four hundred tom-cats from neighbouring islands. Four hundred tom-cats in a boat! For a moment the constrictions of Athos became obvious, and cheering, Nonsense.

Athos inhabited Lear's imagination. It had an importance far beyond that given to its name in Tennyson's poem, which has a strong classical frame of reference. Lear was drawn to the great beauty of the place, and yet hated the waste of life, the shadow of working Christianity which he thought he found there. The 'muttering, miserable, mutton-hating, man-avoiding, misogynic, morose & merriment-marring... Monx' seemed closer to death than life (LEL, p.41). They turned Lear's own notion of a practical, unostentatious, somewhat un-ritualistic Christianity completely upside down. Lear could joke – and did – about taking to a single cell on Mount Athos. But he dreaded the idea of loneliness which the outwardly beautiful place concealed. His vision of Athos involved some of his most ambivalent feelings: he wanted privacy and hated crowds, but he was terrified of total isolation. He sometimes wished that he felt less, reacted less to people. But when he was alone, he wrote endless letters to keep even trivial relationships going. He wanted to feel, and there were many constraints on his feelings, but sometimes the pain of feeling seemed impossible to bear. If the only way out was a kind of Athos of the heart, ultimately Lear could do nothing but reject it.

The twenty-seven drawings of Athos and its monasteries are among some of Lear's best late work. The Albanian landscapes, some of which go back as far as the lithographs made for the Journal of 1851, have a grandeur of waterfall, high rock and dark trees clinging to steep cliff. Yet the smooth lake and lightly touched-in foliage of the pictures near Ahkrida are handled with such ease that it is difficult to remember that the drawings (though probably not the designs) belong to the 1880s. One particularly successful drawing is of the Pass of Tempe, which surprised Lear by being more a gorge than a pass but which he still found impressive and full of 'legendary history'. He makes a satisfying and oddly peaceful view with gently stepped and receding vertical cliffs and a few hints of trees. In the Journal the scene is vertical, not horizontal, and the stress is on the water in the gorge and on a walking figure, with one high wall of cliff. This is an indication of Lear's skill in changing perspective in a landscape, but the pass of Canalo, from the Calabrian Journal, is perhaps less successful when eased out horizontally than when given the towering verticals of the original lithograph.

The drawings for 'To E.L.' have some of the ruggedness of Albania's 'Akrokeraunian walls'; but they vary this with the light tree foliage of Ahkrida, with a light, unoppressive view of Tomohrit, and another of the peak of Athos with a seascape given buoyancy by a few boats and a hint of white to give a blue tint to the grey wash. One half line, 'all things fair', seems to offer Lear endless possibilities. He draws a Campagna, much loved scene, a Constantinople, and a view of Mount Kinchinjunga, a scene from his last journey and an impressive but not, Lear thought, a 'sympathetic' mountain. Two further drawings seem unfinished or experimental. One is an outline of Vesuvius, the other One Gun Battery, Corfu, just sketched in, and with 'not to be autotyped' written round and across it. These weak designs suggest some confusion, or technical problems not recorded. Naples is not on the printed list at all. None of these last designs have the power of the Athos drawings – it was with those that the artist responded to the poet's 'To E.L.'.

Tennyson wrote his poem with classical interests mainly in mind. The short stanza and enclosing rhyme, which he had made so much his own in *In Memoriam*, easily accommodate Lear's distant Albanian landscapes. But Tennyson was not concerned to tread the iron paths of Akrokeraunia: he acknowledged Lear as artist and as landscape writer in the line: 'With such a pencil, such a pen'. But the poet is eager to move on:

> And trust me while I turn'd the page,
>   And track'd you still on classic ground,
>   I grew in gladness till I found
> My spirits in the golden age.

Tennyson's Gods emerging from fountain urns, and Naiads, with glimmering shoulders, have no place in Lear's illustrations. The poem moves to a spring scene – slopes 'rich in bloom' – in a golden past. Lear might have rendered this as a picture of Corfu, so often seen as an ideal Greek, flowered landscape. But Lear keeps to Athos, and Tennyson ends the poem with two pastoral figures: one feeding flocks, the other fluting 'to the morning sea'. There may be a quiet joke here about Lear's habit of annotating his drawings – 'rox' for 'rocks', 'flox' for 'flocks' – but if so this is incidental. Tennyson concentrates not on landscape, but on an ideal Greece, on pastoral classical figures in expected classical pose.

The Laureate wrote 'To E.L.' in 1851-2 and published it in 1853. He had not come close to Lear's vision of landscape in the poem. But 'I read and felt that I was there' was a tribute to be proud of; and it released, in Lear, what he had seen and felt, what he described and drew, what he could share of his inner and outer experience of Mount Athos.

107. Ahkrida, Albania

Still we began the descent toward the lake of Ochrida – a vast sheet of water glittering far below, & whose oval outline is only broken by the fort & town of Ochrida on a little promontory – where we arrived at sunset, & were housed in the Han (or Khan as you would call it.) – the best there, but bad was the best. The 21st. I passed in sketching the castle – & environs of the town – & in paying a visit to Sherrif Bey – the great man of the place to whom I had a letter. This was the first Turkish visit I had paid – but having read a description beforehand of such formalities, I knew exactly all about it; only, the squatting annoyed me dreadfully. Until today (3rd. Oct.) I had never seen a chair or table since I left Salonica – & have had to do everything on the ground, which is to me, perfectly

106

——— Echoing falls

Of Water,———

(To E L. on his travels in Greece.)

The River Kalamà.
Epirus. Albania

107

— Sheets of Summer glass,—

(To E L. on his travels in Greece.)

Lake of Ahkrida.
Macedonia— or Albania

dreadful. The Bey had about 8 servants in waiting – &
the usual routine of pipes & coffee was gone through; many
persons were in waiting on the divans, & the richness of
the dresses is really astonishing – all gold & crimson –
scarcely any blue. But as Ochrida is an exceedingly out of
the way place & as they are very violent Mahometans, I
was here obliged to take to wearing the Fez or red cap –
by means of which one may pass along the streets
unnoticed; while a hat is a signal for sticks & stones. So
you may fancy me so. – if you please. The few women
whom one sees in these places are closely veiled like those
in Constantinople – (excepting always the Xtians. – who
are here very few –) & when any of the ladies of the Turks
move from one place to another, they are carried in a sort
of van or cart – hung round with carpets, & drawn by
buffaloes – & guarded as if they were all gold. There fell
a little rain on the 21st., & I was afraid of a change of
weather – but the 22nd. was cloudless so I ordered horses
& made a day in the same mountain – Petrina – we crossed
on the 20th & the scenery of which I much wanted to
draw. We took up a large cold salmon trout – (the fish of
Ochrida are admirable.) & had a very fine day. On the
24th. we were off early from Ochrida – as soon as I have
got what I consider most worth drawing, I am too glad to
go from these places – for the Hans, have little close rooms
– only refreshed by thorough draughts – & generally dark
– so one is out of them all day as much as possible. For
the same reason, unless I am in some hotel, I travel on
Sundays, as the mind is much more at liberty on horse
back in a forest, than in a nasty hole, surrounded by staring
people – with disagreeable accompaniments. I must do the
Turks justice however, there certainly are not so many
vermin as you will find in Italy in similar places – I fear
the reason is only that there is less furniture to harbour
them – for your Han room contains no one thing in the
world – but you sweep it out & put 2 clean mats on the
floor, & there you are established. I have a wooden tubby
basin with me – & so one manages ablutions as one may.
In Ochrida, as in almost all these places, there is a sort of
piazza – where is a fountain & a Mosque – & a most
preposterously large plane tree that shades numbers of
houses; – these spots are really quite beautiful, & I hope
one day to show you my drawings of that particular one.
One of the most remarkable features in these places is the
tameness of the animals; – on the shores of the lake there
are literally millions of coots & other water fowl, who never
move as you pass close by them – nor does the beautiful
white crane – nor the gray falcon – which you may almost
take with your hand. In the streets this tameness becomes
tiresome, & you are obliged to resort to all sorts of finesses
to make a good natured buffaloe get out of your way. The
views of lake Ochrida & the plain from the castle are surely
most lovely – but I must now go on with our journey.
(EL to Ann, 21 October 1848)

Midnight, – O khans [inns] of Albania! Alas! the night is
not yet worn through! I lie, barricaded by boxes and bundles
from the vicinity of the stable, and enduring with patience
the fierce attacks of numberless fleas. All the khan sleep,
save two cats, which indulge in festive bouncings, and save
a sleepless donkey, which rolls too contiguously to my head.
The wood-fire, blazing up, throws red gleams on
discoloured arches within whose far gloom the eye catches
the form of sleeping Albanian groups. Bulky spiders,
allured by the warmth, fall thick and frequent from the
raftered ceiling. All is still, except the horses champing
straw within, and the gurgle of the rapid river chafing
without.

The principal event of the night was the donkey's walking
unexpectedly into the fireplace, thereby causing a confusion
in my nocturnal arrangements only to be remedied by a
complete decamping.
(Albanian Journal, 13-14 October 1848, pp. 183-4)

105. Near Ahkrida, Albania
107. Lake of Ahkrida, Albania

A cloudless morning, fresh and brilliant, induces me to put
in execution my plan of retracing the route to the mountain
pass by which I came hither, for the purpose of sketching
the Lake of Peupli; wherefore my armed Kawas and horses
were ready at seven, A.M. At the foot of the hills, the
little Monastery was exquisitely pretty in the clear shadows
of early morning, and an outline of it occupied me some
time; after which I began the steep ascent to the beech
forests, and in the course of the upward progress, many
were my pauses to contemplate the wide silver lake, and
its castled rock. A Government "avant-courier," blazing
in scarlet and white, his robe trimmed with fur, and his
kilt and gilt belt looking afar off like the plumage of some
tropical bird among the dark-green foliage, met us when
half-way up the mountain, and shortly afterwards the
Bey-Governor of Tyrana, with a long string of laden mules
and glittering retainers added interest to the novel and
beautiful scene. By half-past ten, we had passed the little
plain at the mountain's summit, and had reached the
solitary guardhouse.

I was glad to have devoted a day to revisiting this most
noble scene. Soothing and beautiful is that vision of the
Lake of Peupli, so dreamy and delicately azure, as it lies
below ranges of finely-formed mountains, all distinct,
though lessening and becoming more faint, till the outline
of Olympus closes the remote view. Then the nearer hills,
with their russet smoothness and pard-like spots of
clustering forest groups; – and closer, the dark masses of
feathery beech glowing with every autumnal hue! It is long
since I have tasted hours of such quiet, and all the
roughnesses of travel are forgotten in the enjoyment of
scenery so calm and lovely. Many a day – month – summer
passed among the beautiful forests of Monte Casale, amid
the steep ravines and oak-tufted rocks of Civitella di
Subiaco, in the sheltered convent and the gleaming village
of the woody Apennines; – many a recollection of the far
plains of Latium and the Volscians – of the brightness of
Italian mornings – the still freshness of its mountain noon
– the serenity of its eventide, when laden villagers wind up
the stony paths to aerial homes, chaunting their vesper
chorus, – all this, and a great deal more, flashed strongly
on my memory as I sate hour after hour on this glorious
hill-summit, when the present, by one of those involuntary
actions of thought which all must have experienced, was
thus linking itself with places and persons of the once
familiar past, with all the decision and vivacity of reality.

At half-past two, after a rural dinner of excellent cold
fish (the trout of the Lake of Akhridha are surpassingly
fine), I retraced my way westward, and was once more
at the khan before dusk.

One more day in Akhrida, and then westward and northward. There is a street scene below the castle, where a majestic plane shades bazaars rich with every sort of gay-coloured raiment. Through its drooping foliage gleams the bright top of a minaret, and below it are grouped every variety of picturesque human beings. To carry away a sketch of this was the work of half the morning; the rest was occupied in a walk on the eastern shore of the lake, an excursion I was obliged to make alone, as the protecting Kawas was sent to procure horses for to-morrow's journey. Beautiful was the castle on its rock reflected in the clear bright water; but what most amused me was the infinite number of birds which, all unsuspectingly sociable, enlivened the scene; thousands of coots fraternising with the domestic ducks and geese – white egrets performing stately tours of observation among the reeds – magpies (a bird remarkably abundant in the vicinity of Akhridha), hooded crows and daws – a world of ornithology. Far away at the end of the lake glitters a solitary white speck, which they tell me is the monastery of St. Naum, but that is out of my track for the present; so I sauntered back to the khan, lingering now and then to look at the Greek women who, with embroidered handkerchiefs on their heads and dressed in scarlet and black capotes, were washing linen in the lake, when, having watched their opportunity, and seeing me unescorted, a crowd of the faithful took aim from behind walls and rocks, discharging unceasing showers of stones, sticks, and mud. May my spectacles survive the attack! thought I, as forced into an ignominious retreat. (22-23 September 1849, pp. 72-5)

106. River Kalama, Epirus, Albania

Aurora was saluted by some score of geese who lived in the khan-yard, but there was no alacrity on her part to look pleased at the compliment, for nothing but a thick cloud could be perceived, and a mist or rain soon began to fall.

All the higher part of the landscape seems hopelessly invisible for the day, but the nearer and lower scenery clears as we proceed, and shows a rich and beautiful country through the vale of the Kalama. All the scene appears richly wooded, and abounding in forms of dell and gentle heights with innumerable charms of broken foreground. Perhaps one of the prettiest points in the morning's ride was near the falls of the Kalama (three hours after leaving Tzerovina), which not even the incessant drizzle of sleet, with bitter wind, could prevent my admiring.   (5 November 1849, p. 325)

108. Pass of Tempe, Thessaly, Greece

The early morning at Baba is more delightful than can be told. All around is a deep shadow, and the murmuring of doves, the whistling of bee-eaters and the hum of bees fills this tranquil place.

108

The long divine Penëian Pass, —
To E.L. on his travels in Greece.)

Pass of Tempe.
Thessaly.
Greece.

The village of Ambelaki is situated on the side of Mount Ossa, and thither, having heard much of its beauty and interest, I went early, before pursuing the road by the Peneus, through the gorge of Tempe. I cannot say I was so much delighted with the expedition as I expected to be, but this was mainly because heavy clouds shut out all the upper portions of Olympus, partly also from not having felt well enough to seek for the best or most picturesque points. But judging from what ought to be seen if the great mountain of the Gods had been clear, and relying on the descriptions and taste of perfectly good judges, I believe Ambelaki would well repay a long visit. On returning to the route to Tempe I met a young man dressed in the usual Thessalian garb, and on my hailing him in Greek, I was surprised to find my salutation returned in good French. At the fall of the commercial community of Ambelaki, the father of Monsieur Hippolyte, one of the richest merchants of the place, fled to France, settled and married there: this was his son, who, returning to his native place, had for some years resided on the paternal property. "Sometimes I live here," said he, "sometimes in Paris; but I come here principally for hunting." Town and country, Paris and Tempe – certainly are two points of Europe in which one might easily find pleasure and occupation.

Leaving Monsieur Hippolyte I went onward into Tempe, and soon entered this most celebrated 'vale' – of all places in Greece that which I had most desired to see. But it is not a 'vale,' it is a narrow pass – and although extremely beautiful, on account of the precipitous rocks on each side, the Peneus flowing deep in the midst, between the richest overhanging plane woods, still its character is distinctly that of a ravine or gorge.

In some parts, the Pass, (which is five or six miles from end to end), is so narrow as merely to admit the road and the river; in others the rocks recede from the stream, and there is a little space of green meadow. The cliffs themselves are very lofty, and beautifully hung with creepers and other foliage; but from having formed a false imagination as to the character of "Tempe's native vale," I confess to having been a little disappointed. Nevertheless, there is infinite beauty and magnificence in its scenery, and fine compositions might be made, had an artist time to wander among the great plane-trees on the border of the stream: a luxuriant wooded character is that which principally distinguishes it in a pictorial scene from other passes where there may be equally fine precipices bounding a glen as narrow. Well might the ancients extol this grand defile, where the landscape is so completely different from that of any part of Thessaly, and awakes the most vivid feelings of awe and delight, from its associations with the legendary history and religious rites of Greece.

(19 May 1849, pp. 408-10)

The vast Akrokeraunian walls, –

(To E.L. on his travels in Greece.)

Akrokeraunian Mountains, Albania

The vast Akrokeraunian Walls.

(To E. L. on his travels in Greece.)

Akrokeraunian Mountains.
(Chimára) *Albania*

109-112. Akrokeraunian Mountains, Albania

But it is past one, and time to set off once more, for there are four long hours to Draghiadhes, the first Khimariot village. The pathway is ever along the side of the gulf, and rises far above the blue, blue water. Anything more frightful than these (so-called) paths, along the iron rocks of Acroceraunia, it is not easy to imagine: as if to baffle invaders, the ledges along which one went slowly, now wound inward, skirting ravines full of lentisk and arbutus, now projected over the bald sides of precipices, so that, at certain unexpected angles, the rider's outer leg hung sheer over the deep sea below. To the first of these surprising bits of horror-samples of the highways of Khimara I had come all unknowingly, my horse turning round a sharp rocky point, and proceeding leisurely thence down a kind of bad staircase without balustrades; I declined, however, trying a second similar pass on his back, and at the first spot where there was safe footing, dismounted. Meanwhile the Khimariote who ever and anon kept shouting, "Kakos dromos, Signore," ['a bad road, Sir'] fired off his pistol at intervals, partly, as he said, from "allegria," and partly to prevent any one meeting us in this dire and narrow way. When we had overcome the last of the Kakos dromos – lo! a beautiful scene opened at the narrow end of the gulf, which lay like a still and dark lake below the high wall of Khimara territory. Draghiadhes, the door, as it were, of Acroceraunia, stands on a height immediately in front, while the majestic snowy peak of Tchika (the lofty point so conspicuous from Corfu, and on the southern side of which stand the real Khimariot villages), towers over all the scene, than which one more sublime, or more shut out

from the world, I do not recollect often to have noticed. At the sea-side I stole time for a short sketch, and then remounting, our party rode on over the sands to nearly the end of the gulf, whence we turned off to the left, and gradually ascended to Draghiadhes. Flocks of sheep, and most ferocious dogs abounded as we climbed higher; and Anastasio, never wearied of injunctions as to the awful character of the dogs of Khimara, especially of the two first villages. "It is true," said he, "I am responsible for your life, but at the same time you must do just as I bid you; for if you look at a dog of Khimara, there will hardly be anything but some of your largest bones left ten minutes afterwards!" which unfettered poetical flight seemed about to become a fact in the case of the pietone, who shortly had to defend himself from some ten of these outrageous beasts; they assailed him spite of all manner of missiles, and the battle's issue was waxing doubtful when some shepherds called off the enemy. As we advanced nearer to the town Anastasio's cheerfulness seemed to increase. "Mi conoscono tutti," said he, as each peasant hailed him by the title of "Capitagno." With some he stopped to laugh and converse; others he saluted after the fashion of Albanian mock-skirmishes, drawing pistols or yataghan from his girdle, and seizing their throats with many yells, and between whiles he kept up a running accompaniment of a Greek air, sung at the top of an immense voice, and varied by pistol shots at irregular intervals. We passed the village of Radima high above us, and after I had contrived to make another sketch, the scene momentarily grew finer as the descending sun flung hues of crimson over the lonely, sparkling town of Draghiadhes, and the bright peaks of the

111

The Vast Akrokeraunian Walls

(To E.L. on his travels in Greece.)

Pass of Mount Tchika
Akrokeraunian Mountains
Albania.

112

The Vast Akrokeraunian Walls —

(To E.L. on his Travels in Greece.)

Akrokeraunian Mountains
Draghiades. (Khimara.)
Albania.

huge Tchika.

Presently we came to the oak-clad hills immediately below the town, where narrow winding paths led upwards among great rocks and spreading trees worthy of Salvator Rosa, and not unlike the beautiful serpentara of Olevano. I have never seen more impressively savage scenery since I was in Calabria.   (21 October 1848, pp. 222-25)

111. Pass of Mount Tchika, Albania

Advancing nearer to the pass, the giant Tchika appeared more formidable at each approach – its pine-clad sides black in the sullen misty cloud; but as we descended the last cliff-walled abyss at the foot of the ridge or spur of the mountain which closes eastward the valley-plain of Dukadhes, driving clouds came furiously down, and thenceforth, to my great vexation, no more of the pass was visible. Toilfully we wound upwards, for an hour or more, among rocks and superb pines, now and then a cloud rolling away to disclose vistas of cedar-like firs deep below or high above in air. It would be difficult to see a finer pass even for foreground objects: such variety of crag and shrub – such huge pine-trunks slanting over precipices, or lying along the side of the path like ante-mundane caterpillars crawling out of the way of the deluge. At the top of the pass the driving fog became thinner, the "shrubless crags seen through the mist" assumed their distinct shapes, and we entered magnificent forests of beautiful pine and undergrowth of gray oak, with here and there a space of green turf and box-trees, where great black and orange lizards were plentifully crawling.
(23 October 1848, pp. 246-47)

112. Draghiadhes

"But, Signore, you could not travel here alone." And, although Anastasio certainly made the most patronizing use of his position as interpreter, guide, and guard, I am inclined to believe that he was, in this, pretty near the truth, for I doubt if a stranger could safely venture through Acroceraunia unattended. Assuredly also all the world hereabouts seemed his friends, as he boasted, for the remotest and almost invisible people on far away rocks, shouted out "Capitagno" as we passed, proving to me that I was in company with a widely-known individual.

At length we reached Draghiadhes, the houses of which were by no means pretty, being one and all like the figures of "H was a House," in a child's spelling book. Alas! for the baronial castle or the palazzo of Italy! the whole place had the appearance of a gigantic heap of dominoes just thrown down by the Titans. Sunset had given place to shadowy dusk as we passed below two of the very largest plane trees I ever beheld, where, in the centre of the village the trowser-wearing damsels of Draghiadhes were drawing water at a fountain – a strange, wild scene. Many came out to greet Anastasio, and all saluted me in a friendly manner, nor was there the least ill-bred annoyance, though I was evidently an object of great curiosity. Sending on the horses to the house we were to sleep at, we first went to one of Anastasio's friends, who would take it as a "dispetto" if he did not visit him. I sate on the steps outside and sketched: the rocks of Calabria, with figures such as are to be seen only in Albania, gathered all around – how did I lament my little skill in figure drawing, and regret having so much neglected it! The long matted hair and moustache – the unstudied and free atitude – the simple

folds of drapery – the expression of the individual – the grouping of the masses – all heighten the inconceivable originality of these scenes. Let a painter visit Acroceraunia – until he does so he will not be aware of the grandest phases of savage, yet classic, picturesqueness – whether Illyrian or Epirote – men or mountains; – but let him go with a good guide, or he may not come back again. Acroceraunia is untravelled ground, and might not be satisfactory to a solitary tourist.
(21 October 1848, pp. 227-28)

114. Mount Tomohrit, from Berat, Albania

A very break-down procession did we make, slowly plodding through quagmire and stream, when at last we were fairly under-weigh, and right glad was I when cocks crew, dogs barked, the moon faded, and gray day coldly and slowly came, unveiling "vast Tomohrit" a long way off beyond a weary expanse of plain. Yet over that have I yet to go, for Berat lies immediately at the foot of the mountain. About the third hour the journey became interesting, for Tomohrit is a noble mountain, and the multitudes of sheep scattered over the wide, shrub-dotted meadow-plain, formed beautiful features in the landscape. At length the celebrated fortress of Berat appeared – dark blue, and diminutive, on a pointed hill. Approaching the capital of Central Albania – a place I had so long desired to see – every step leads into grander scenes. The river Apsus or Beratino is repassed on a stone bridge, and the road winds over the plain on the banks of the wide stream, through a tract of country of the finest character; the high form of Tomohrit, here seen from end to end, being the principal feature throughout. I do not remember to have known a finer specimen of a simple river scene than this – it combines the broad white-channelled serpent-stream, with its broken and reed-clad banks, varied by sheep, goats, kine, and buffali; while above rises the giant mountain's single form, wrinkled into a thousand furrowed chasms, towering aloft over the uninterrupted and decided lines of the plain in grand simplicity.

Owing to the deep mud, it took us two long hours to ride from the bridge over the Beratino to that in the town; and at ten A.M. we entered this magnificently picturesque place, which, much as I had imagined of its grandeur, far surpassed my expectations.
(14 October 1848, pp. 186-87)

115-141 Mount Athos

Quarantine Island. Corfu. October 9. 1856.
My dear Mrs Tennyson,
. . . I must tell you that this sheet of paper so addressed & folded, hath travelled with me to Epirus, Thessaly, & Salonica, & all the way to Athos whence I had intended to send it to you, (& had I gone to the top of the holy mountain I meant to have written a line from it to Alfred,) & after that to Troy so the very paper has a sort of value on it from its very travels – what a place – what a strange place is that Mount Athos! – Apart from the very valuable set of drawings I have brought back, my tour there has been one of the most singular bits of my whole life. Excepting at those monasteries in Thibet of which Messrs [H..] & Gabet tell us, there is nothing in the world like the Athos peninsula for the St. Bernard & St. Gothard monasteries are placed there for a good purpose & do much to benefit others, while at Mt. Athos, many many thousand

Tomóhrit. Berat.

Tomóhrit, &c &c &c

(To E. L. on his travels in Greece.)

Mount Tomóhrit.
from Berat. Albania.

monks live on through a long long life of mere formal blank. God's world maimed & turned upside down: – God's will laughed at & falsified. Nature wounded and trampled on – that half of our species which it is the natural & best feeling of mankind to love & esteem most – ignored & forbidden – this is what I saw at Athos: – & if what I saw be Xtianity, then the sooner it be rooted out, the better for humanity. A Turk with 5 wives, a Jew working hard for little oldclo' babies, these I believe to be far nearer what Jesus Christ intended man to become than these foolish & miserable monks, what tho' they have the name of Christ written on every garment & every wall, & tho they repeat endless parrot prayers daily & nightly. Do you know the history of Athos – the ancient Acte? a long mountain narrow peninsular ridge standing up in the sea – joined at one end to the main land by a very narrow isthmus wh: once Xerxes chopped through, & its southern end rising to a pyramid 6700 feet high, strictly the Mount Athos of geography. This peak alone is bare – all the rest of the ridge is a dense world of Ilex, beech, oak, & pine. From Constantine & Justinian, who gave up the whole of Acte to Christian hermits, – to the Byzantine Emperors who

added to convents already built, & founded others, and down to Sultans as far as our own day – every ruling power in the East has confirmed the territory to the Monks as theirs, on proviso of paying £1500 per anni to the Porte. So the whole strange place has gradually grown into a large nest of monkery – there being as I said 20 large monasteries, & perhaps 5 or 600 small-hermitages or chapel=cottages holding 1 – 2 or more of the fish & watermelon eating, prayer-muttering old creatures who vegetate there, or at best, carve little wooden crosses, of which I have bought you one to put on some little table on a future day. I will not weary you by accounts of the mode of government of the monasteries – for I dare say I shall publish my doings some day or other; nor much shall I relate of Kariess the capital of the monks: – nor how my servant was ill & nearly died: & how I was afterwards very ill: nor the many other matters. But I can tell you that I never saw any more striking scenes than those forest screens & terrible crags, all lonely lonely lonely: paths thro' them leading to hermitages where these dead men abide, – or to the immense monasteries where... hundreds of these living corpses chaunt prayers nightly & daily: the blue sea dark dark against the hard iron rocks below – & the oak fringed or chestnut covered height above, with always the great peak of Athos towering over all things, & beyond all the island-edged horizon of wide ocean. The Monasteries – the large ones, are like great castles – fortified with walls & towers. Within are courtyards holding Churches, clocks, & refectories. The smaller hermitages often stand in gardens, & are gay without though filthy & mournful within. These, which often are clustered so as to seem like villages, are perhaps the saddest of all – for you think there must be some child – or a dog – or other life than those gloomy black clad men. – but no – Tomcats & mules are the only beasts allowed in the holy mountain, & crowing cocks the only birds. I solemnly declare such a perversion of right & nature is enough to madden a wise man – & many of their men are more than half foolish: they murmur & mutter & mop and mow: the greater part are utterly ignorant – only those who manage the affairs of the convents are at all intelligent. Some day perhaps I shall be able to show you the views I made of these very strange dwellings. – And so I will say no more of gloomy & terrible Athos.   (EL to Emily Tennyson, 9 October 1856)

120. Monastery of Koutloumoussi, Mount Athos

. . . I began my tour by going to Koutloumoussi – No. I – close by the town. I hardly know how to describe these astonishing places to you; as I said, they resemble a village in a box; high walls surround all; nearly all have a great tower at one end. All have a court yard more or less large – & this court contains sometimes one, sometimes 2 or 3 churches – a clock tower – a large refectory, fountains etc. etc. All have a kiosk outside the gates; also a fountain close by. Round 3 or 4 sides of the court are the cells – galleries above galleries of honeycomb arches; very frequently the abbot's house occupies one side – or his, & the strangers rooms, look out on the best view. At Koutloumoussi I made my acquaintance with the finest reception room I had seen – very large – square; a matting over the centre; low sofas & divans round 3 sides – covered with beautiful (but dirty) carpets; & a fire place somewhere about. Here they spread a bed – but I only allowed it to remain there till they were gone out of the room, when my own Capote & blankets & sheets were a better substitute. The supper in this first instance, was with the abbot – but generally alone . . . The abbot of Koutloumoussi was a jolly old man, with feet turned in, & walking with a crutch; he was one of the reasonable few I came to know – "if you like to turn Caloger," said he to me – "you may come here, but you must work; you must paint the church, & you must set up a school to teach Italian." He asked me for some needles to sew, but I had none to spare. Next day – after I had got 2 drawings – they lent me 2 mules – & off I set to No. 2 Pantokratora. I always asked to see the churches – more to please my hosts than myself, – for I can assure you 20 Greek churches – one just like another – are a task . . . oh Holy Mountain! what have I not suffered to get drawings of you! – Well; Pantokratora is on the sea; & so is No. 3 Stavroniketes, & as they are built on rocks, & look up

Athos Koutloumoussi

— Athos – all things fair

(To E. L. on his travels in Greece.)

Monastery of Koutloumoussi.
Mt. Athos.

123
122

Athos, all things fair,

(To E.L. on his travels in Greece.)

Monastery of Stavronikites.
Mount Athos.

123
124

Athos, all things fair

(To E.L. on his travels in Greece.)

Monastery of Karakálla.
Mount Athos.

to the mighty peak of Athos – they make noble scenes, a lonely grandeur one hardly can understand till one has felt for days that none but these miserable solitaries occupy this strange land.
(EL to Ann, 8 October 1856; the numbers refer to a sketch-map in the letter)

123. Monastery of Karakalla, Mount Athos

I resolved therefore to go to No. 6 (Karacallas) & get a mule on to Laura, & to return with three mules next day for Giorgio; & so – off I set. But Karacalla was an exception to all convents; they seemed very poor & filthy, & more like dead men than any I have yet seen; they would not take my letter to the abbot because he was asleep – nor did they give me even any rhum and jelly; so I set off again alone – determined to go to Laura by myself at all risks; for the matter was serious. The word "alone" in Mt. Athos has a far deeper sense than anywhere else. Oh dear! how terribly lonely I felt that place – no inhabitants near – no dogs even – scarcely a bird – & if one should meet in the 6 hour walk with a Caloyer – I knew well he would only mutter prayers & say – "how should I know?" to whatever question I asked him.
(EL to Ann, 8 October 1856)

127. Monastery of Laura, Mount Athos

At sunset I reached the huge monastery Laura – which stands on a point of high land & is beautifully situated; built to contain 800 monks, it now has barely 200 – but its courtyard full of orange & lemon trees, with the dome of the church & clock towers, is a wonderfully interesting scene. But, here I was received by Melchisedek in the kindest manner – & I long to be able to send that good man some token of remembrance for the extreme trouble he gave himself on my account. Early next morning I was set agoing back again with my 3 mules – & I got to Philotheo in the middle of the day – to find my poor servant very much worse. Judging therefore that it was better to divide the journey as much as possible, I put him on a mule & brought him to Karacalla (No. 6) for the night – & there remained. He became quite delirious – & my alarm was great. There was however no choice so next morning, I took him on the remaining 6 hours to Laura. It was not very easy to keep him on the mule – & you may suppose how glad I was to get him a room & quiet. Here for 2 days he continued to get worse – & I gave up all hope; I wrote to Lushington, begging him to tell Spero & their mother; & I wrote to you, informing you of the state of things – & how uncertain the length of my stay was, for even if Giorgio did not die, he might still remain ill for a long time – & I could not have left a good servant – (or indeed, any servant), alone in such a place. But as a last resource I bled him & gave him physic enough for 6; so that happily the fever turned, & I could give the quinine, – & thus my anxiety was lessened, though he still continued unable to rise. Meanwhile for 5 days I lounged about Laura – drawing it all round; poking about the sea shore or into the hermitage among the half witted old filthy Caloyeri; or watched the Tom cats in the galleries; or talked Greek with Melchisedek & Anthemos – smoking 5 pipes a day, & having my morning & every meal with that good dirty man; for it must be truly said that filth was at least as

127

Mt Athos A. Λαυρα

— Athos – all things fair —

(To E.L. on his travels in Greece.)

Monastery of Laura.
Mount Athos.

153

remarkable a characteristic of my friends menage as charity & kindness of his own character; I vow the table cloth daily laid was not less than 1/4 inch thick in substantial ancient dirt. U! O! A! what did I suffer! what did I not eat! – well – at least I came away – as soon as Giorgio could move, resolving to go to St. Paul's...
(EL to Ann, 8 October 1856)

128. Monastery of St Nilus, Mount Athos

One day, by the bye I saw St. Nilo – a small monastery on the cliff at the very end of the mountain; that was the queerest & saddest spot I ever beheld! 2 old men lived there – neither more than half witted; they gave me a dry fish & water melon, – but only said these words all the time I was there – "are you a Christian"? – hundreds of times over & over.   (EL to Ann, 8 October 1856)

130. Monastery of St Dionysios, Mount Athos

St. Dionysio is stupendously picturesque; it hangs with its walls & towers on the edge of the sea high on a cliff below the vast Athos, & is a terror to look at. Some of the paths to it are as high as Beachy Head above the sea, & merely projecting bits of rock 2 or 3 feet wide – like a cornice in one place there is a bit of space – & you step literally over the sea below. Here I observe the mules like particularly to scratch themselves. Though the riders outside leg is hanging over the white foam far below.
(EL to Ann, 8 October 1856)

133. Monastery of Xeropotamos, Mount Athos

I made a short move to No. 12 – Xeropotamo; – a grand

newly restored convent by the sea, with wide views towards the opposite promontory of Sithonia; here was a facetious & clever abbot – & a clean one; the rooms were clean – & he had a musical snuff box – so one felt in a civilised place, the more that he could talk rationally on various subjects. Indeed I was often obliged to try all kinds of shuffles to avoid laughing at the strange questions these monks asked; did the Queen of England speak English or Greek? What city in London was I born in? Are there any cats in England? etc. etc.   (EL to Ann, 8 October 1856)

137, 138. Monasteries of Kostamonites and Zographos, Mount Athos

16. Kostamonites is the smallest of all the convents – hidden in a deep dell of wood. 17. Zographo – a most splendid (& clean) pile of buildings in a deep valley – surrounded by high forest clad hills; its abbot was a fussy little man, & so frightfully polite I didn't know what to do.
(EL to Ann, 8 October 1856)

115-141. Mount Athos

On the morning of the 26th – I was on deck long before daylight – to see the great Mt. Athos, below which the steamer goes on her way to Cavalla. And here I made my last sketch of the Agion Oros [Holy Mountain] rising most magnificently from the calm gray sea. The sun rose as we were close to Laura – & I could see every one of the eastern monasteries, so that for an hour, it was like reading the heading of a chapter, or the index to the last 3 weeks of my life.   (EL to Ann, 8 October 1856)

128

— Athos, — all things fair —
(To E.L. on his travels in Greece.)

Monastery of St Nilus.
Mount Athos.

132
130

Mt Athos. Dionusy.

— Athos — all things fair &

(To E.L. on his travels in Greece —)   Monastery of St Dionysios
Mount Athos.

135
133

Athos. Ieropotagus.

— Athos, — all things fair &

(To E.L. on his Travels in Greece,)   Monastery of Xeropotamos.
Mount Athos.

Mt Athos. Kostamonites.

————— Athos, — all things fair, —————
(To E.L. on his travels in Greece.)

Monastery of Kostamonítes
Mount Athos.

Ζωγράφος

————— Athos, all things fair, to E ————
(To E. L. on his travels in Greece.)

Monastery of Zográphos.
Mount Athos.

105. EL List: Illyrian Woodlands
     EL Drawing: Illyrian Woodlands, –
106. EL List: Echoing falls of water
     EL Drawing: – Echoing falls
                  Of water, –
107. EL List: Sheets of summer glass
     EL Drawing: – Sheets of Summer glass –
108. EL List: The long divine Peneian Pass
     EL Drawing: The long divine Peneian Pass, –
109. EL List: The vast Akrokeraunian walls
     EL Drawing: The vast Akrokeraunian walls, –
110. EL List: The vast Akrokeraunian walls
     EL Drawing: The vast Akrokeraunian Walls.
111. EL List: The vast Akrokeraunian walls
     EL Drawing: The vast Akrokeraunian Walls
112. EL List: The vast Akrokeraunian walls
     EL Drawing: The vast Akrokeraunian walls –
114. EL List: Tomohrit
     EL Drawing: Tomohrit, &c &c &c

120. EL List: Athos
     EL Drawing: – Athos – all things fair
122. EL List: Athos
     EL Drawing: – Athos, all things fair,
123. EL List: Athos
     EL Drawing: Athos, all things fair
127. EL List: Athos
     EL Drawing: – Athos – all things fair –
128. EL List: Athos
     EL Drawing: – Athos, – all things fair –
130. EL List: Athos
     EL Drawing: – Athos – all things fair
133. EL List: Athos
     EL Drawing: – Athos, – all things fair &c
137. EL List: Athos
     EL Drawing: – Athos, – all things fair, –
138. EL List: Athos
     EL Drawing: – Athos, – all things fair &c

SIR LAUNCELOT & QUEEN GUINEVERE

A FRAGMENT

Like souls that balance joy and pain,
With tears and smiles from heaven again
The maiden Spring upon the plain
Came in a sun-lit fall of rain.
    In crystal vapour everywhere
Blue isles of heaven laugh'd between,
And, far in forest-deeps unseen,
The topmost linden gather'd green
    From draughts of balmy air.

Sometimes the linnet piped his song:
Sometimes the throstle whistled strong:
Sometimes the sparhawk, wheel'd along,
Hush'd all the groves from fear of wrong:
    By grassy capes with fuller sound
In curves the yellowing river ran,
And drooping chestnut-buds began
To spread into the perfect fan,
    Above the teeming ground.

Then, in the boyhood of the year,
Sir Launcelot and Queen Guinevere
Rode thro' the coverts of the deer,
With blissful treble ringing clear.
    She seem'd a part of joyous Spring:

A gown of grass-green silk she wore,
Buckled with golden clasps before;
A light-green tuft of plumes she bore
    Closed in a golden ring.

Now on some twisted ivy-net,
Now by some tinkling rivulet,
On mosses thick with violet
Her cream-white mule his pastern set:
    And now more fleet she skimm'd the plains
Than she whose elfin prancer springs
By night to eery warblings,
When all the glimmering moorland rings
    With jingling bridle-reins.

As fast she fled thro' sun and shade,
The happy winds upon her play'd,
Blowing the ringlet from the braid:
She look'd so lovely, as she sway'd
    The rein with dainty finger-tips,
A man had given all other bliss,
And all his worldly worth for this,
To waste his whole heart in one kiss
    Upon her perfect lips.

In Curves the yellowing river ran.

(Sir Launcelot and Queen Guinevere.)   Tepedelene.
Albania

146. Tepedelene, Albania
147. *Below Suli, Albania*

Tennyson's 1842 volumes contained several Arthurian poems, including 'The Lady of Shalott' and 'Morte D'Arthur'. Revised and changed, they were all assimilated into *The Idylls of the King.* Several Arthurian poems had been begun before 1842. This fragment 'Sir Launcelot and Queen Guinevere' may have been begun as early as 1830, but was not published until 1840. As it stands the fragment is a bright, joyous love poem set in a springtime landscape which is almost a fairy land. The problems of Soul and Sense, or Art and Life never touch the piece. It seems to be set at the moment in the legend when Sir Launcelot is bringing Guinevere to Camelot to be Arthur's Queen. But it is called 'A fragment' and a letter of 1833 explains that the poem is 'A companion to "The Lady of Shalott", called the "Ballad of Sir Lancelot".' It describes Queen Guinevere and Sir Launcelot in spring, riding through 'the forest, green, fayre, and amorous'. (This suggests that Guinevere is already Queen). They meet the ancient Merlin who tells Sir Launcelot that he is doing no good to his reputation and his fair name by riding about with his 'light o' love'. Merlin is taunted with his own misdemeanours and Sir Launcelot rides on. Putting aside the representatives of worldly prudence and worldly force, avoided by his own son Sir Galahad, Sir Launcelot, singing a 'loose song', proceeds towards 'Garde Joyeuse'.

This plan for a ballad makes the fragment, which uses the 'Lady of Shalott' stanza, far more than a simple Spring song. It is a poem of joyous Sense which avoids the problems of Soul. It is a momentary escape into a green spring of Art which forgets (although the letter's outline gives it), the winter of real life. As a fragment it celebrates the beauty and joy of the Round Table: as a whole, it would have gone on to show destruction of ideals, secrecy, rumour, shabby compromise and danger. But in the 1842 poem we have only untainted delight. Even so, the poet describes an English spring: 'The maiden Spring upon the plain / Came in a sun-lit fall of rain.' The first four lines, more than the rest of the poem, suggest a dichotomy between joy and pain. But pain is forgotten: the rain is 'sun-lit', the forest bright, the birds in song. It is the 'boyhood of the year' and Guinevere, on her white mule, seems a personification of 'joyous spring', for whom a man would give 'all other bliss'.

Did Lear wonder about the 'balance of joy and pain' in the first line? By the time he was revising his Tennyson Illustrations he would have read all the *Idylls of the King.* He was particularly impressed by 'Guinevere' published in 1859. It was not an English landscape which interested Lear, since he chose to illustrate: 'In curves the yellowing river ran' with two river scenes in remote Albania. Perhaps the 'fragment' of Arthurian legend, the beautifully described landscape, and the as yet unacknowledged dilemma of the two lovers, attracted Lear to the poem. His own loves were always to remain largely unexpressed and certainly unfulfilled. He knew, with Franklin Lushington and with Augusta Bethell, how the 'balance of joy and pain' could be contained within a relationship.

In the wild and mountainous regions of Albania, Lear was a stoic traveller. In the region of Elbassan, progress was very slow, 'either along steep and narrow paths cut in the rock, at the edge of formidable precipices, or by still narrower tracks running on the bare side of a perpendicular clay ravine'. A baggage-mule might get wedged between the huge trunks of forest trees or the small party have to take a 'tortuous path into the depths of an abyss' before climbing a 'zigzag staircase out of it'. It was 15 September 1847 and Lear had started at 5.30 a.m. What he regretted most was never securing anything like a 'finished drawing': 'Even let the landscape be ever so tempting, the uncertainty of meeting with any place of repose or shelter obliges the most enthusiastic artist to pass hastily through scenes equal or superior to any it may be again his lot to see' (Albanian Journal, pp. 84-5). Sometimes he insisted on stopping to draw some extraordinarily beautiful scene.

146. Elbassan
A most desolate and wild country does this part of Albania seem, with scarcely a single habitation visible in so great a space; stern-wrinkled hills wall in the horizon, covered midway with oak forests; but after passing another range of low hills we came to the valley of the Skumbi, and thenceforth the landscape began to assume a character of grand melancholy not to be easily forgotten. About five, the infinitely varied lines of the western heights were most glorious, their giant-rock forms receding into golden clouds as the sun sank down, while below stretched the deep widening valley of the Skumbi, a silvery stream winding through utterly wild scenes of crag, forest, and slope as far as eye could see. By six we crossed over the river on a high single arch, and shortly began to ascend the heights on the left bank...
(Albanian Journal, 24 September 1848, p. 81)

This picture of mountain and river has 'Elbassan' written clearly in the bottom left-hand corner. By the Tennyson quotation Lear has written 'Tepedelene, Albania', a transliteration of the Greek. 'Tepelene', one-time city and stronghold of the Turkish Ali Pasha, is considerably further south. Lear was moved by the melancholy ruins of the palace and buildings, destroyed in and after territorial wars between Turks and Greeks. 'Tepelene' was situated on a promontory at the junction of two rivers. In his list Lear calls this picture simply 'Tepelene'. He may have confused two river and mountain scenes – both visited years before these illustrations.

146. EL List: In curves the yellowing river ran
      EL Drawing: In Curves the yellowing river ran

From: THE VISION OF SIN

I had a vision when the night was late:
A youth came riding toward a palace-gate.
He rode a horse with wings, that would have flown,
But that his heavy rider kept him down.
And from the palace came a child of sin,
And took him by the curls, and led him in,
Where sat a company with heated eyes,
Expecting when a fountain should arise:
A sleepy light upon their brows and lips –
As when the sun, a crescent of eclipse,   10
Dreams over lake and lawn, and isles and capes –
Suffused them, sitting, lying, languid shapes,
By heaps of gourds, and skins of wine, and piles of grapes.

Then methought I heard a mellow sound,
Gathering up from all the lower ground;
Narrowing in to where they sat assembled
Low voluptuous music winding trembled,
Wov'n in circles: they that heard it sigh'd,
Panted hand-in-hand with faces pale,
Swung themselves, and in low tones replied;   20
Till the fountain spouted, showering wide
Sleet of diamond-drift and pearly hail;
Then the music touch'd the gates and died;
Rose again from where it seem'd to fail,
Storm'd in orbs of song, a growing gale;
Till thronging in and in, to where they waited,
As 'twere a hundred-throated nightingale,
The strong tempestuous treble throbb'd and palpitated;
Ran into its giddiest whirl of sound,
Caught the sparkles, and in circles,   30
Purple gauzes, golden hazes, liquid mazes,
Flung the torrent rainbow round:
Then they started from their places,
Moved with violence, changed in hue,
Caught each other with wild grimaces,
Half-invisible to the view,
Wheeling with precipitate paces
To the melody, till they flew,
Hair, and eyes, and limbs, and faces,
Twisted hard in fierce embraces,   40
Like to Furies, like to Graces,
Dash'd together in blinding dew:
Till, kill'd with some luxurious agony,
The nerve-dissolving melody
Flutter'd headlong from the sky.

And then I look'd up toward a mountain-tract,
That girt the region with high cliff and lawn:
I saw that every morning, far withdrawn
Beyond the darkness and the cataract,
God made Himself an awful rose of dawn,   50

Unheeded: and detaching, fold by fold,
From those still heights, and, slowly drawing near,
A vapour heavy, hueless, formless, cold,
Came floating on for many a month and year,
Unheeded: and I thought I would have spoken,
And warn'd that madman ere it grew too late:
But, as in dreams, I could not. Mine was broken,
When that cold vapour touch'd the palace gate,
And link'd again. I saw within my head
A gray and gap-tooth'd man as lean as death,   60
Who slowly rode across a wither'd heath,
And lighted at a ruin'd inn, and said:

'Wrinkled ostler, grim and thin!
   Here is custom come your way;
Take my brute, and lead him in,
   Stuff his ribs with mouldy hay.

'Bitter barmaid, waning fast!
   See that sheets are on my bed;
What! the flower of life is past:
   It is long before you wed.   70

'Slip-shod waiter, lank and sour,
   At The Dragon on the heath!
Let us have a quiet hour,
   Let us hob-and-nob with Death.

'I am old, but let me drink;
   Bring me spices, bring me wine;
I remember, when I think,
   That my youth was half-divine . . . .

. . . 'Drink to Fortune, drink to Chance,
   While we keep a little breath!
Drink to heavy Ignorance!
   Hob-and-nob with brother Death!

'Thou art mazed, the night is long,   195
   And the longer night is near:
What! I am not all as wrong
   As a bitter jest is dear.

'Youthful hopes, by scores, to all,
   When the locks are crisp and curl'd,
Unto me my maudlin gall
   And my mockeries of the world.

'Fill the cup, and fill the can!
   Mingle madness, mingle scorn!
Dregs of life, and lees of man: 205
   Yet we will not die forlorn.'

The voice grew faint: there came a further change;
Again uprose the mystic mountain-range:
Below were men and horses pierced with worms,
And slowly quickening into lower forms;
By shards and scurf of salt, and scum of dross,
Old plash of rains, and refuse patch'd with moss.
Then some one said: 'Behold! it was a crime
Of sense avenged by sense that wore with time.'
Another said: 'The crime of sense became   215
The crime of malice, and is equal blame.'
And one: 'He had not wholly quench'd his power;
A little grain of conscience made him sour.'
At last I heard a voice upon the slope,
Cry to the summit, 'Is there any hope?'
To which an answer peal'd from that high land,
But in a tongue no man could understand;
And on the glimmering limit far withdrawn
God made Himself an awful rose of dawn.

148. Wady Halfeh, Nile, Nubia
149. *Mount Oeta, (from Lamia), Greece*
[**150.** *Ravenna*][1]

'The Vision of Sin' begins with a vision of languorous sensuality. The narrator sees 'a child of sin' lead a youth into a palace to join a drunken, enervated and yet expectant assembly. The abandoned mood is oddly kept in check by Tennyson's choice of regular rhyming couplets. But the long last line of the first section has a near Spenserian effect of indolent hedonism as the dreaming band of 'sinners' sit or lie: 'By heaps of gourds, and skins of wine, and piles of grapes.' The next section fulfils expectancy by rousing the company to dance. The tempo quickens, and the company grows wilder, fiercer, and the dancers, 'like to Furies, like to Graces', seem partly beautiful, partly bestial until the 'nerve-dissolving melody' comes to an end in 'luxurious agony'. The dance whirls about a great fountain which was partly suggested by Turner's picture 'The Fountain of Fallacy', exhibited

151
148

The darkness, and the Cataract —
(The Vision of Sin.)

Wady Halfeh
Nile. Nubia.

in 1839 at the Royal Academy. The picture at some stage was shown with a few verses from Turner's poem 'The Fallacies of Hope'. A Turner oil entitled 'The Fountain of Indolence', and linked to Thomson's 'The Castle of Indolence', was exhibited a few years earlier in 1834. Controversy as to whether these are two paintings, or the same painting altered, has reached the point where experts, while admitting inconclusive evidence, have decided that the two 'Fountains' are one painting with alterations.[2] Tennyson could have seen either version before finishing 'The Vision of Sin', and read Turner's and Thomson's verse. The classical buildings of the picture and the effects of light, with figures playing by and in the rainbow fountain, were described by reviewers as beautiful. Tennyson certainly added more than a hint of beauty and lightness to the youthful dancers of his vision of sin. The poet's admiration for Turner may have been rather more reserved than Lear's, but occasionally it seems to have influenced his own visual description.

The pulsating music and dance, the quickening rhythm and wild costumes of the dancers build up a vision of sensuality, but never suggest a lapse into pure evil. In the last section the palace has disappeared, except for its gate. The speaker looks up to a great mountain scene where cold vapour rolls down from the heights. The landscape is supposed to symbolize 'God, the Law and the future life',[3] but the manifestation which brings day after the night's debauchery seems inexplicable: 'God made Himself an awful rose of dawn'. This is a sunrise which holds the cold warning of God's coming judgement. But speaker, and reader, move on from the young sensualists to another vision: 'A gray and gap-tooth'd man as lean as death.' The aged creature is riding across a 'wither'd heath' to a 'ruin'd inn'.

Tennyson now changes stanza and rhythm completely: a jogging ballad-like stanza takes the reader quickly through the long speech that follows. The old man talks to the 'Wrinkled ostler' and the 'Slip-shod waiter' in an inn so decayed the only possible activity is to drink and shrug off both past and present. The old man has a grim, sardonic humour which dismisses all values with cynicism. But he has a ghastly liveliness which keeps him going for a dance of death, 'Death is king, and Vivat Rex!' Ugly, bitter, ironic – this is the age to which the riotous dancers will be consigned.

At the end the old man's voice grows faint and the great mountain tract reappears. A new vision suggests man's deathly regression to earth, and moralizing voices speak of the crimes of sense and malice and the possibility of a grain of conscience. A last voice asks if there is hope for man, but is answered in a tongue no man can understand. Once again we see the distant, inexplicable sunrise which does not deny either hope or judgement: God's awful dawn.

Lear had a strong sense of sin, but of sin more subtle than sensual orgy or moral vacuity. He did have the unhappy notion that his epileptic attacks were 'sinful'. He shared the common Victorian idea that attacks were brought on by masturbation – over which the victim should exercise all possible 'self-control'. Other 'sins' Lear felt were a lack of sensibility in dealing with his Suliot servant Giorgio, and a compensatory need to help and support Giorgio's three sons. The admirable Nicola was tubercular, and the two other brothers drifted about,

always sponging off Lear and relying on him to get them out of trouble. He never gave up his generous attempts to help Giorgio's family. Lear's 'sins' were never on the scale imagined by Tennyson. He drank a little too much – especially when in pain and misery – but no one could be further from the sensualism, and aged malice and egotism of the poem. Almost morbidly self-critical, Lear was quick to take the blame himself. He believed in a Christian God, but his diaries show that he disliked ostentatious services, pomposity, anything not straight-forward. He went to church in San Remo from time to time, but writes disparagingly about fashionable fuss and bother. Prayerful thoughts for those he loves, especially his sister Ann are regularly entered in his diary: 'This day 4 years ago – died my dearest sister Ann – who is still as it were yet living: so plainly do I see her, & so clearly hear her voice' (11 March 1865). Lear sketched Giorgio's and Nicola's headstones, including the wording, remembering their lives as exemplary, (something of an exaggeration) and likely to have a good moral influence on his own.

Lear's 'visions of sin' were largely the effect of an overactive conscience. Perhaps the poem touched on imagined fears; or perhaps Lear enjoyed the speech of the horribly resilient and belligerently honest Old Man who is as outspoken and crazily confident as some of Lear's wilder Limerick characters. There is very little landscape and Lear leaves the God-as-sunrise line alone. From the third section he illustrates the mountain range – with mountains from Greece. The 'darkness and the cataract' which precede the sunrise he transformed to a desolate and yet lovely Nubian scene on the Nile from his last visit of 1867.

148. River Nile, Egypt

O lovely golden apricot sands! – borders of green & grey Trees!!! We are some 5 or 6 miles above Sabooa. The spot we were stopping at at 6 - 7 AM truly beautiful – palms, yellowgreen hawthorn like trees . . . with golden sands above, & black rocks below!! . . . The sands are really . . . positively golden: those of Egypt are pale: these, yolk of egg color, or rather apricot. 9 AM. Reports of crocodiles . . . O! the loveliness of these sands! – Pouring down all over the green lupinis – through the fluffy gray hawthorn trees . . . East side: very low sand hills, & innumerable palms. 9.38. What color! Ever the golden sand pours down & destroys the green banks . . . 10.20 on deck, more wind. What positive colour! orange – blue, green . . . 1.30 Still sailing towards the bend of the Nile – to get as near the East shore as possible. The colour (on the West side) of the sands, is absolutely apricot – (or salmon color azelea –) with the bloom on too, a sort of blush delicate pink. A mile beyond Korosko – 121 from Assouan! Neither shore very pretty just now – palms stumpy hills eccentric & lumpy . . . [They reach the West shore, land, climb up] to a gt yellow level, backed by desert sand hills. Great specimens of the posion plant – with palms & Doms sparsely placed for wonderful Nubian landscapes – Apricot sand as a foreground, & well formed "severe" dark ashy purple brown hills beyond . . . The Nile of Nubia is more condensed in character than that of Egypt . . . 3.30 we all zealously watch an object resembling a crocodile, who, as the boat sails near him, proves his crocodility by slipping into the water, & and returning as soon as the boat passes to his sandy throne. Walk on, ever over the apricot powder desert... (D. 1 February 1867)

12.30 – we get on after all, & now the hill of Wady Halfeh is in sight... 2. nearer to Wady Halfeh, & the little hill of Abou Seer is visible. – 2.20 Vultures – (those beasts hop & dance with a disgusting levity quite remote from their character & occupation). & a dead camel. How flat are these shores! Yet I had previously supposed they were like those of Philae. – at 3 – the N wind being ever violent, but we thought we should put to the shore... at 3.25 or so – really anchored at Wady Halfeh – knocking old Ali's Turban over board with a rope – (wh. they went out in a boat for to save – but found nothing,) – & settled at 3.30 PM. Feby 3 1867. – Wady Halfeh is very unlike what I had anticipated, but is not withstanding, a place of great character – topographically speaking, – & altogether Nubian or rather African in its characteristics: loneliness and extreme, – long lines of hill & river – beautiful palms – a great expanse of sand – but all length & width – no height whatever. – The paucity of people – of life amazes me – who foolishly had thought this a sort of Southern capital. Why – Denderah or Assouan are like Paris in comparison! (D. 3 February 1867)

... but as we approached Abu Seer, which is not as I imagined a wady on a far low hill, but a big rock overhanging the West shore – the scene becomes very singular & interesting – vast crowds of islands of sand, covered in parts with rocks like Coal crags & myriads of small coal as it were, so that in the distance all is an horizon of blue gray gritty substance...

As for me I made a large drawing, with a good deal of trouble – till nearly noon: the scene is surprising – & unlike any I ever saw – for its extraordinary multiplicity & detail. The rox are like infinite waggonloads of coal scattered all over innumerable sand islands – floating on a dark water but there silvered with foam. Some of the crags are large – but most are small ad infinitum, seeming so at least from the height of Abou Seer. (D. 4 February 1867)

[1] *Ravenna*, not in this set, appears on the printed list, and in the Houghton set, as an illustration to the poem 'Move Eastwards Happy Earth'.

[2] M. Butlin and E. Joll, *The Paintings of J.M. Turner* (Yale: revised edition, 1984) Vol. II, Text, pp. 204-05 and pp. 227-29.

[3] Ed. Hallam, Lord Tennyson, *The Works of Tennyson* (Eversley Edition, 1908) Vol. II, p. 353.

148. EL List: Beyond the darkness and the cataract
      EL Drawing: The darkness and the Cataract.

THE DAISY

Written at Edinburgh

O love, what hours were thine and mine,
In lands of palm and southern pine;
    In lands of palm, of orange-blossom,
Of olive, aloe, and maize and vine.

What Roman strength Turbìa show'd
In ruin, by the mountain road;
    How like a gem, beneath, the city
Of little Monaco, basking, glow'd.

How richly down the rocky dell
The torrent vineyard streaming fell   10
    To meet the sun and sunny waters,
That only heaved with a summer swell.

What slender campanili grew
By bays, the peacock's neck in hue;
    Where, here and there, on sandy beaches
A milky-bell'd amaryllis blew.

How young Columbus seem'd to rove,
Yet present in his natal grove,
    Now watching high on mountain cornice,
And steering, now, from a purple cove,   20

Now pacing mute by ocean's rim;
Till, in a narrow street and dim,
    I stay'd the wheels at Cogoletto,
And drank, and loyally drank to him.

Nor knew we well what pleased us most,
Not the clipt palm of which they boast;
    But distant colour, happy hamlet,
A moulder'd citadel on the coast,

Or tower, or high hill-convent, seen
A light amid its olives green;   30
    Or olive-hoary cape in ocean;
Or rosy blossom in hot ravine,

Where oleanders flush'd the bed
Of silent torrents, gravel-spread;
    And, crossing, oft we saw the glisten
Of ice, far off on a mountain head.

We loved that hall, tho' white and cold,
Those niched shapes of noble mould,
    A princely people's awful princes,
The grave, severe Genovese of old.   40

At Florence too what golden hours,
In those long galleries, were ours;
    What drives about the fresh Cascinè,
Or walks in Boboli's ducal bowers.

In bright vignettes, and each complete,
Of tower or duomo, sunny-sweet,
    Or palace, how the city glitter'd,
Thro' cypress avenues, at our feet.

But when we crost the Lombard plain
Remember what a plague of rain;   50
    Of rain at Reggio, at Parma;
At Lodi, rain, Piacenza, rain.

And stern and sad (so rare the smiles
Of sunlight) look'd the Lombard piles;
    Porch-pillars on the lion resting,
And sombre, old, colonnaded aisles.

O Milan, O the chanting quires,
The giant windows' blazon'd fires,
    The height, the space, the gloom, the glory!
A mount of marble, a hundred spires!   60

I climb'd the roofs at break of day;
Sun-smitten Alps before me lay.
    I stood among the silent statues,
And statued pinnacles, mute as they.

How faintly-flush'd, how phantom-fair,
Was Monte Rosa, hanging there
    A thousand shadowy-pencill'd valleys
And snowy dells in a golden air.

Remember how we came at last
To Como; shower and storm and blast   70
    Had blown the lake beyond his limit,
And all was flooded; and how we past

From Como, when the light was gray,
And in my head, for half the day,
    The rich Virgilian rustic measure
Of Lari Maxume, all the way,

Like ballad-burthen music, kept,
As on The Lariano crept
    To that fair port below the castle
Of Queen Theodolind, where we slept;   80

Or hardly slept, but watch'd awake
A cypress in the moonlight shake,
    The moonlight touching o'er a terrace
One tall Agavè above the lake.

What more? we took our last adieu,
And up the snowy Splugen drew,
    But ere we reach'd the highest summit
I pluck'd a daisy, I gave it you.

It told of England then to me,
And now it tells of Italy.　　　　　　　　　　90
　　O love, we two shall go no longer
To lands of summer beyond the sea;

So dear a life your arms enfold
Whose crying is a cry for gold:
　　Yet here to-night in this dark city,
When ill and weary, alone and cold,

I found, tho' crush'd to hard and dry,
This nurseling of another sky
　　Still in the little book you lent me,　　100
And where you tenderly laid it by:

And I forgot the clouded Forth,
The gloom that saddens Heaven and Earth,
　　The bitter east, the misty summer
And gray metropolis of the North.

Perchance, to lull the throbs of pain,
Perchance, to charm a vacant brain,
　　Perchance, to dream you still beside me,
My fancy fled to the South again.

151. *Nice*
152. *Esa*
153. *Turbia*
154. Monaco
155. *Monaco*
156. Mentone, France
157. *Vintimiglia*
158. *Bordighera*
159. Sanremo, Italy
160. Sanremo, Italy
161. *Taggia*
162. Sanctuary of Lampedusa
163. *Porto Maurizio*
164. *Finale Marina*
165. *Capo di Noli*
166. *Vado*
167. *Varegge, near Savona*
168. *Cogoletto*
169. *Genova*
170. Monte Rosa, from Varese
171. *Monte Rosa, from Monte Generoso*
172. *Lago di Orta*
173. *Lago di Como, from Villa Serbellone*
174. Lago di Como
175. Varenna, Lake of Lecco (Bellagio), Italy
176. *Varenna, Lake of Como, Italy*
177. Petra, Palestine

The daisy of this poem is a pressed flower, found in a book. It was picked on 'snowy Splugen' and releases memories of the Alps, of Italy, of 'lands of palm and southern pine'. Tennyson, staying in cold grey Edinburgh, remembers the journey he made in 1851 with his wife Emily, when they were both recovering from the funeral of their first, still-born son. The poem, written in 1853, has a relaxed, reminiscent tone. The metre is

Tennyson's own invention and is used for other verse letters. The brief moments and scenes, the quiet movement from place to place, detail of a building in Florence, of a tall agave near Lake Como – all make the reader follow out the journey. But, without complex avowals, a sense of quiet intimacy gives the poem a meaning beyond the superficially picturesque:

> O love, what hours were thine and mine,
> In lands of palm and southern pine;
> 　In lands of palm, of orange-blossom,
> Of olive, aloe, and maize and vine.

The opening lines immediately suggest a shared southern warmth and amazement at the fertility and beauty of foliage. Later there is a shared wryness over '. . . rain at Reggio, at Parma; / At Lodi, rain, Piacenza, rain.'

Tennyson's journey, and poem, go back to the early 1850s. Lear had recently met the poet. But the artist was already a determined traveller, pushing on, after early visits to Italy, to Albania, Greece, Egypt, Palestine. And, as he grew older, Lear was claimed by the 'lands of palm, of orange-blossom'. Once settled in San Remo, most of the cities and scenes of 'The Daisy' were almost home-ground. Nice, Monaco, Mentone were warm, palm-flourishing resorts along the coast. He had drawn, time and again, the cool, mountainous places near by: Esa, Turbia, Taggia and the far distant Monte Rosa. He visited Genoa and Milan on business, and went up to sketch the lakes, including Como and Lugano, in many lights and weathers. He knew every detail of citadel, promontory, cape and port along the coast near San Remo. For 'The Daisy' then, Lear was able to draw the places Tennyson describes. And this he chose to do – rather than interpret named places with remote landscapes. Artist and poet shared some travel experiences. Each had visited Switzerland, Germany,

How like a gem, beneath, the city
Of little Monaco, basking, glowed.
            (The Daisy)

France and Italy. Tennyson had been drawn to the scenery of the Pyrenees and had travelled to Portugal and to Norway. He was never a far-distant, risk-taking traveller, like Lear; in general, he remained firmly based in England and attentive to English landscapes. Lear met Tennyson and his family in England, and occasionally stayed in their houses, Farringford and Aldworth. 'The Daisy' appealed to Lear partly because it was a poem which showed that the artist and poet, had, at different times travelled the same ground.

For Lear the poem could have brought back early memories of landscape drawing in Italy and of local travels in the 1870s. From San Remo, in the 1880s, and while working on his Tennyson project, Lear could still visit some of the places in the poem which were most familiar to him. The rather weakly drawn sketch of terraced steps and flowers, with a faint view of San Remo beyond, brings Lear's own garden into his illustrations. He worked on this design from his second house, the Villa Tennyson, as late as 1885, when he wrote: 'Drew in the balcony of studio – & on the terrace – & in 2 other parts of the garden, – all for No. 160 of the ATs – being Sanremo view – No. 2' (D. 12 June 1885). Thus Tennyson's poem of travel memories touched, for Lear, on the artist's last settled home.

The poem is a record not only of a journey but of a relationship. It is also about the evocations of memory and just how much may return with a dried flower. Lear illustrates eighteen lines of the poem with twenty-seven illustrations. His own surroundings fitted 'The Daisy' exactly. But he displaces one scene, 'rosy blossom in hot ravine' and uses the line for a memory of his own: his journey to the city of Petra. The 'rosy blossom' is, for Lear, equivalent to Tennyson's daisy, releasing and vitalizing the memory. Tennyson, with Emily, was impressed by unfamiliar even exotic scenes, but the places he catalogues in his poem were mostly home ground to Lear in San Remo. Perhaps because this was so, Lear wanted to recapture his own sense of the strange journey, the unexpected landscape. Thus he recalls one of the most exciting and most dangerous expeditions he ever made. He illustrates Tennyson's gentler journey, but with one drawing shows what 'blossom' could evoke in his own memory.

Franklin Lushington published Lear's account of his visit to Petra, during which Lear's party was attacked by an alien and hostile group of Arabs, in *Macmillan's Magazine* in 1897. Lear drew and painted the astonishing rock-cut city which he finally reached in 1858. It was something of a triumph for a traveller to penetrate the secrets of this hidden, rose-coloured, ancient place, with its theatre, temples and tombs. By contrast the places of 'The Daisy', Monaco, Mentone, Ventimiglia, Bordighera, were all very near San Remo and along the coast Lear knew best. Even the beauty of Florence, was approachable and civilized in a way that Petra was not.

But Lear does not illustrate the lines about Florence, and with one exception, his drawings cover the lakes and landscapes which he knew in his San Remo years.

In 1878 Lear went up to Lake Como, remembering his other tours of the lakes in 1837 and 1867. He thought of Tennyson's much earlier visit, and of 'The Daisy', which he quoted in his diary. By the 1880s his travelling was much reduced, but he could still get up to Taggia and the Sanctuary of Lampedusa – a favourite trip to the cool heights above San Remo. Until Giorgio's death in 1883, Lear went regularly to Monte Generoso, just south of the lakes Lugano and Como. From there he could sometimes get a clear view of the outline of distant mountains: 'How faintly-flush'd, how phantom-fair, / Was Monte Rosa, hanging there' ('The Daisy' ll.65-66). 'The Daisy' was, for Lear, a poem about his own places. 'To E.L.' had been a wonderful tribute to Lear, and to his early travels: it remained for him the most important Tennyson poem on his chosen list. But 'The Daisy', record of a journey taken early in Tennyson's marriage, became for Lear, a poem of late settling down, of quiet and sometimes memory-filled excursions. But the impulse to break out still surfaced – and, moving away from the poem's places, Lear remembered the journey to Petra.

159,160. Sanremo, Italy

In December 1870, while his first villa was being finished, Lear grew doubtful about settling down at all. Much depended on the weather and his mood: 'Everything to me is sad & gloomy today: & I can't quite conceive living quietly in the Villa Emily' (D. 11 December). His last words of the day were: 'O life! O earth! O time!' (Shelley). A few days on he felt better and went to the villa to watch furniture being mended. But he had another fit of doubt when the carpenter's lad managed to get water all over the floors. Lear said he would sell the whole place. On 14 December 1870, he wrote, understandably, 'I am quite sick of houses said the Lady of Shalott'. On 16 December, however, he thought again.

G. says we could go into the new house as soon as it is done – with lots of wood fires? Rheumatic fever versus misery & melancholy from living in rooms one cant work in? – Certainly – very dim grim days. Yet, in this San Remo is a homely good feeling of security, quite curious, & only to be accounted for by the fact of the quiet industrious good characteristics of the people.
(D. 16 December 1870)

Rose at 5. The porters came at 6 – & all things were cleared off to the Villa. Till 9 I worked hard at getting things in order, & then G. gave me a capital bkft. So, in exactly a year from the day I decided on buying the ground, I am living in the house built on it!   (D. 26 March 1871)

Nobody came naturally: no letters, no nothing. But the Datura & Ipomoea flowers were there.
. . . I cant write very straight now – 7.30 P.M., because the new cat insists on sitting on my wrist.
(24 November 1872)

156

In lands of palm and orange blossom

(The Daisy)

Mentone

159

(The Daisy)   Sanremo

160

(The Daisy)   Sanremo

The garden is at its full beauty now, for tho' roses & geraniums are going – Daturas and lots of seed=flowers are coming on – the Love lies bleeding one that pleases me greatly.

... Bernardino titivated the false pergola.   (5 June 1873)

A wandering = hithery=thithery day – overlooking the terrace making &c. &c. – or visiting various gourds & Passaflorae, or enjoying the "blue" quiet – for it must be confessed, Summer in Sanremo is divine! – & so on all day – with fits of painting interspersed.   (31 July 1873)

154, 156. Monaco; Mentone, France

So I resolved to go next day to Mentone and see what I could make of that – Incordingly on Tuesday the 8th. off I set in a carriage – and certainly I had no idea the Cornice was so magnificent in scenery; Eza and Monaco are wondrously picturesque, and Mentone very pretty –; but it is too shut in and befizzled a place for me: you have to walk thro' the long only and narrow street of the town wherever you go – unless you have a carriage, or could hire a big villa.
(EL to Fortescue, 13 November 1864, LLEL, pp. 51-2)

Vintimiglia, Mentone, Monaco, Esa, all beautiful – yet somehow with scars & seams of matters past & painful.
(D. 12 June 1875)

162. Sanctuary of Lampedusa

Off by 7.45 – the sky clearing, & the color of the Autumn chesnuts & clouds lovely. – down towards Poggio... decided on going on to Taggia; – it will require all the 'wit & temper' I possess to weather through 3 or 4 winter

months, & so, even 3 or 4 days taken out of that misery is somewhat to think of... The sky cleared as we went on... & it was a real fine day on arriving at Taggia at 10. Nothing is seen in the valley, but long armed filmy foliaged olives, again driving into Taggia – narrow streets & all improviso. The Locanda didn't at all promise well outside – nor greatly inside: but improved after a bit. Luckily we had bought a fowl=remains – & there was raw ham & bread & decent wine (60 cents a bottle) & a plate of accommodated eels "anguille accommodate" – said the little girl. – At 11, set out to go to the Lampedusa Sanctuary: left town by a narrow street, & then a long bridge – almost like that of Arta – over the Taggia river – now half cut up with gardens. Beyond, a sharp stone paved road rises as rapidly as possible up the hill to Castellaro: – at first, one sees Taggia – a long outspread town, – & the river, & flat ground, once doubtless an arm of the sea in the time of Carlo 5. A precious pull up to Castellaro!! & through part of that village – of wh. – narrow & steep as are its streets one cannot but say all its people are courteous... to a great degree. A comparatively level road – paved – leads to the Chapel or Sanctuary, & that is very grandly placed though in itself nothing more than a modern white church. Going to it, found it all shut – & did not greatly regret. Drew then below it for an hour: the deep gulf of olives below is very fine.   (D. 16 October 1870)

174. Lago di Como

The people of the Como province are poor, but very honest; – and you soon get used to the barefooted people who wait on you. As for the scenery – it was quite beyond anything I had seen; the dark blue lake reflects the white houses of Domaso – and over them enormous Alps, Jiggy-Jaggy –

(The Daisy)   Sanctuary of Lampedusa

shut out the Italians from Switzerland. Being resolved to see all the district, I took a boat quite to the top of the Lake, where it is awfully grand – and walked to Chiavenna beyond which Switzerland begins. Chiavenna is just by the Pass of Splugen, and is awfully grand: some time ago, (in 1680) part of the mountain under which it stands, fell down plump and killed 500 persons – a whole village – After getting some sketches of it, I was glad to proceed Southward again – along the east side of the lake – a plan of which I place below – to Colico I tried to stop at Novate but could not, as all they had to eat was mutton and goat's flesh, half putrid, garlic – and dreadfully sour wine, and although Colico is not over comfortable, it was a good deal better. At Bellano there was a better inn and I stayed 3 days. All this part of the Lake is magnificent – it is as narrow as a wide river, so you can see the hundreds of spires and villages on the opposite side, while the Alps always form the background. Multitudes of peasants gathering grapes are on every side, and the weather was perfectly charming.   (EL to Ann, 3 November 1837)

In early summer 1867, Lear undertook a tour of seven north Italian lakes. At Como he crossed the lake by steamer and small boat: one of the boats was 'odious, small, crowded' and he was glad to find a quiet high room in Bellaggio, away from the 'gregarious rabble – & mob'. Lear was feeling distinctly irascible: he wanted quiet to remember the lake he had seen thirty years before, and revisiting Como 'freshened up' his 'fading memories'. But the 'forced society of these gregarious Hotels' he found 'truly dreadful':

"D'ye know Col. Pollimer, fresh looking man, dark eyes – dark hair – no whiskers – spot on his nose, married Miss Tobson=Lowndes who had 80,000 dollars, & their son is to be called Tobson Lowndes dropping the Pollimer name quite?" (said one American Lady to another.) "Lord! Lord! do I know Col. Pollimer! O Lord! he's my most intimate friend. But do you Ma'am know Mrs. Crewser=Stackelthwaite? tell me that!" & so on incessantly.   (D. 27 May 1867)

Como, even out of high season was 'disheartening', but Lear got some good drawings by getting up very early.

The steaming down the lake was lovely, but the delineation of mountain lines impossible – as clouds are on all. Every thing seems silver, & blue & green dark & light – the infinite sparkling of villages, the liveliness of boats, & reflections in the clear water! I would well like to pass a month or two here, but the mountain=walled & many=detailed nature of this lake makes a short stay useless. . . . I wish I could walk again all round the lake.

Instead Lear went to Varese, with

. . . its endless delicate gradation of multiplicity of verdure – slopes of green – & far away bits of level mixed with shining water, – long lines of distant blue plain – deep or faint, or grade beyond grade of more faintly delineated soft hills or more decided ridges, with Alpine snow above all! (D. 28 May 1867)

Here Lear records:

true Italian Ideal or Claude Landscapes – : the chesnut growth is superb – the tall Lombard towers – (their bells so fine in tone,) the rich green of the walnut, the almost yellow acacia, the gray willows, olives, poplars or aspens, the thick oak copses, where nightingales sing always – the smooth undulations & declivities of turf; – the cheerful

(The Daisy) "Sunsmitten Alps before me lay"   Monte Rosa from Varese

Como

(*The Daisy*)   *Lago di Como*

hayfields: the many wandering paths: the glittering villages,
& single silvery villas or cottages or chapels: the winding
bright streamlets: fig – almond – pomegranate – corn –
mulberry for foreground: – who would not rejoice in the
Landscape of the Lake Varese? even tho' it has no cliff &
rocks like the more popular Como?

In 1837 Lear described the Lake of Como enthusias-
tically, but without much subtlety. His adjectival range
does not go much beyond 'very grand'. In 1867 the lakes
soothed his worries and his temper; their scenery
brought out his mastery of landscape description. In 1878
Lear was busy with travel and, with his A.T. illustration
project in mind, tried to find entries made by Tennyson,
years before, in hotel registers. He drew a little, and
recalled the days of 1837 when, young and excited, he
was able to walk round the lake.

Got off in steamer at 8.15. – the usual giros & crossings
of the lake – & reached Bellagio by 10.30. A good steamer,
& not over bored by crowd. Omnibus up to V. Serbelloni,
by 11 where got 2 diminutive rooms – all the place rather
zitzo as G. says. Go all over gardens, which are
wonderfully interesting for distant views & foliage. Back
to lunch at 12.30. . . . Out again at 2, – drawing along at
various points till past 5. Then "dressed for dinner" at
6.30. – but the church bells & cloches are no guide here
as to time since they alter the hour according as the steamers
arrive early or late . . .   (D. 20 August 1878)

175. Varenna, Lake of Lecco (Bellagio), Italy
Find the 9.30 steamer goes to Como & not to Varenna.
– to wh. place I could not get before 11 or 12. So I am
thinking of giving up that excursion – all the more that I

should have to get into a boat. . . . But, as I wanted to get
some more drawing, & to see the gardener of the Villa –
I after all changed my mind & worked till 9. Bill dear.
Flowers in gardens beautiful. Bus at 10. . . . Steam to
Menaggio, & Varenna by 11. Wind – lake rough – &
had to get into a boat – a bore. Hotel Reale-Marcionni –
; young man Marcionni civil: garden & terrace. "one tall
Agave –" &c. Search old books for AT's name: like going
into a cemetery – Sir F. Scott – Ldy F. Harcourt – &
endless more – all now gone. Draw till 12.30 lunch – very
good. – Afterwards drew in garden – & then walked
towards Lecco & got a good drawing: – later – walk on
Colico side – recalling the days of Augt & Sept 1837 –
when I walked all round the Lake.   (D. 21 August 1878)

177. Petra, Palestine
April 13th [1858] – Clear pale sky before sunrise, with
long rosy clouds floating pennon-like round the harsh jagged
outline of Hor. A particularly early start was ordered, that
the mountain might be ascended before the hotter part of
the day; but this precautionary measure was, to say the
least, modified by the wicked camel's twisting himself
viciously against the first rocks he encountered, and
shooting all the luggage into a deep hole below. "I am quite
sick of camels," says the traveller in the East. So I walked
onwards and upwards for four hours, glad to be away from
the wearisome janglings and yells of my unpleasant suite,
and longing with increasing impatience for the first glimpse
of Petra's wonders. Every step opened out fresh interest
and beauty in the wild scenery; immense chasms and vast
views over strange boundless desert unfolded themselves at
each turn of the winding path up the steep mountain; and
at one spot the intensity of the giant-crag solitude, deepest
rifts and high pinnacles of naked rock, was more wondrous

175

— one tall Agáve —
(The Daisy.)

Varenna Lake of Lecco
(Bellaggio.)
Italy.

than anything I have ever seen except the sublimity of Gebel Musa and Sinai. About nine we reached the highest part of the mountain ascent, and passing the ridge immediately below the rocks of Gebel Haroun (Aaron's mountain), now upon our left, entered the first or upper part of Wady Mousa on its western side. But it was nearly another hour before, still descending by winding tracks, we reached the first cavern tombs and the first coloured rocks. The slow advance chills with a feeling of strange solitude the intruder into the loneliness of this bygone world, where on every side are tokens of older greatness, and where between then and now is no link. As the path wandered among huge crags and over broad slabs of rock, ever becoming more striped and glowing in colour, I was more and more excited with curiosity and expectation. And after passing the solitary column which stands sentinel-like over the heaps of ruin around, and reaching the open space whence the whole area of the old city and the vast eastern cliff are fully seen, I own to having been more delighted and astonished than I had ever been by any spectacle. Not that at the first glance the extent and magnificence of this enchanted valley can be appreciated: this its surprising brilliance and variety of colour, and its incredible amount of detail, forbid. But after a while, when the eyes have taken in the undulating slopes terraced and cut and covered with immense foundations and innumerable stones, ruined temples, broken pillars and capitals, and the lengthened masses of masonry on each side of the river that runs from east to west through the whole wady, down to the very edge of the water, — and when the sight has rested on the towering western cliffs below Mount Hor, crowded with perforated tombs, and on the astonishing array of wonder carved in

the opposite face of the great eastern cliff, — then the impression that both pen and pencil in travellers' hands have fallen infinitely short of a true portrait of Petra deepens into certainty. Nor is this the fault of either artist or author. The attraction arising from the singular mixture of architectural labour with the wildest extravagances of nature, — the excessive and almost terrible feeling of loneliness in the very midst of scenes so plainly telling of a past glory and a race of days long gone, — the vivid contrast of the countless fragments of ruin, basement, foundation, wall, and scattered stone, with the bright green of the vegetation, and the rainbow hues of rock and cliff, — the dark openings of the hollow tombs on every side, — the white river bed and its clear stream, edged with superb scarlet-tufted blossom of oleander alternating with groups of white-flowered bloom, — all these combine to form a magical condensation of beauty and wonder which the ablest pen or pencil has no chance of conveying to the eye or mind. Even if all the myriad details of loveliness in colour, and all the visible witchery of wild nature and human toil could be rendered exactly, who could reproduce the dead silence and strange feeling of solitude which are among the chief characteristics of this enchanted region? What art could give the star-bright flitting of the wild dove and rock-partridge through the oleander gloom, or the sound of the clear river rushing among the ruins of the fallen city! Petra must remain a wonder which can only be understood by visiting the place itself, and memory is the only mirror in which its whole resemblance can faithfully live. I felt, "I have found a new world — but my art is helpless to recall it to others, or to represent it to those who have never seen it." Yet, as the enthusiastic foreigner said to the angry huntsman who asked if he meant to catch the fox, – I will try.

Two small boys tending some ten or twelve goats had been descried far on in the valley as we came down into it; but these brown-striped-vested youths did not await our arrival, and were no more to be seen. My tents were pitched low down on one of the terraces near the river, about halfway between the east and west cliffs. Taking with me Giorgio and the black Feragh (that jewel among swine) I wandered on eastward through the valley, of which the spaciousness seemed to me more impressive at each step, and the mighty accumulation of ruin more extraordinary. Wonderful is the effect of the east cliff as we approach it with its colours and carved architecture, the tint of the stone being brilliant and gay beyond my anticipation. "Oh master," said Giorgio (who is prone to culinary similes), "we have come into a world where everything is made of chocolate, ham, curry powder, and salmon"; and the comparison was not far from an apt one. More wonderful yet is the open space, a portion of it cut out into the great theatre, from which you approach to the ravine of the Sik. Colour and detail are gorgeous and amazing beyond imagination. At length we reached the mouth of the Sik, the narrowing space between the loftier walls of rock becoming more overgrown with oleander and broom, and the ravine itself, into which you enter by a sharp turn on your right, seeming to close appallingly above your head. Not far from the entrance I turned round to see the effect of the far-famed Khasme or rock-fane which is opposite this end of the ravine, a rose-coloured temple cut out in the side of the mountain, its lower part half hidden in scarlet blossom, and the whole fabric gleaming with intense splendour within the narrow cleft of the dark gorge, from four to seven hundred feet in height, and ten or twelve broad. I did not penetrate further into the Sik, supposing I should have ample time in the several days I had arranged to spend at Petra, and wishing as soon as possible to obtain a general view of the valley. Retracing my steps I sat down at noon to draw, and did so uninterruptedly until it grew too dark to see the marks of my pencil or the colours I was using. First promising to call the anxious Feragh if I strayed out of sight of the tents, I worked on the whole view of the valley looking eastward to the great cliff, then in the bed of the stream among its flowering shrubs, then on one of the higher terraces where a mass of fallen columns lies in profuse confusion, not unlike the ruins of the Sicilian Selinunti, and gathered scraps and coloured effects of the whole scene from various points. And lastly at sunset I turned to draw the downward stream running to the dark jaws of the western cliff, all awful in deep shadow which threw a ghastly horror over their tomb-crowded sides, above which rose the jagged summit of Mount Hor against the clear golden sky. As the sun went down, the great eastern cliff became one solid wall of fiery-red stone, rose-coloured piles of cloud resting on it and on the higher hills beyond like a new poem-world betwixt earth and heaven. Purple and darkling the shadows lengthened among the overthrown buildings and over the orange, red, and chocolate rocks of the foreground, over the deep green shrubs and on the livid ashiness of the white watercourse. Silent and ghostly-terrible rose darker and darker the western cliffs and the heights of Aaron's burial-place, till the dim pale

— rosy blossom in hot ravine —

(The Daisy.)

Petra
Palestine

lights fading away from the myriad crags around left this strange tomb-world to death-like quiet and the gray gloom of night. Slowly I went to my tent, happy that, even if I could carry little with me as a correct remembrance of this wonderful place, I had at least seen the valley and ruins of the rock-city of Edom.

It was as I was working at my last drawing by the river-bed that Abdel came to me from the tent, and pointing to one of the higher rock-and-ruin terraces, said mysteriously (with that disdain for grammatical precision in general and prepositions in particular which characterised his utterances), "He is seeing? in the Arab from his coming in the some ten?" And truly I saw ten black images squatted in a line immediately above the tents.

"Who are they, Abdel, and what do they want?" said I.

"He is of the Arab, and is for asking from the money."

Alas! all along of those tell-tale little shepherd-boys, who saw our entrance and have alarmed their remoter friends, I perceive that the peace of this hollow Lotus-land is to suffer change. For although the council of ten behave themselves with a scrupulous and saluteful politeness almost affectionate, it is easy to see by their constant scrutiny of our tents that this is only a preliminary domiciliary visit. As the sun fell nine of the ten departed, leaving one grim savage, who sat on his hams apart. Abdel tells me that they insist on a separate gufr, or tax, beyond what I had agreed with Abou Daouk to pay to the Haweitat, and say further that the head Sheikh of the Haweitat being away from these parts they (who are

fellaheen from Dibdiba and other near villages on the hills) will not allow the Haweitat to have all the money; that in the morning fifty or sixty more fellaheen will come, and that we shall not go without paying something. To all which Abdel and the old Salah replied that the gufr is to be given to the Haweitat Sheikh, and that he will divide and dispose as he thinks proper; but as they go away threatening and murmuring, I begin to think that like many others I may have a good deal of trouble in getting the drawings I wish for, since, if surrounded by these gentry, quiet study is to me impossible.

(Macmillan's Magazine, April 1897, pp. 420-23)

154.	EL List:	How like a gem beneath, the city
	EL Drawing:	How like a gem, beneath, the city
		Of little Monaco, basking, glowed.
156.	EL List:	Lands of palm and orange blossom
	EL Drawing:	In lands of palm and orange blossom
159.	EL List:	Lands of palm and orange blossom
	EL Drawing:	[No quotation]
160.	EL List:	Lands of palm and orange blossom
	EL Drawing:	[No quotation]
162.	EL List:	High hill convent seen
	EL Drawing:	[No quotation]
170.	EL List:	Sun-smitten Alps before me lay
	EL Drawing:	"Sun-smitten Alps before me lay"
174.	EL List:	We came at last to Como
	EL Drawing:	[No quotation]
175.	EL List:	One tall Agave above the Lake
	EL Drawing:	– one tall Agave –
177.	EL List:	Rosy blossom in hot ravine
	EL Drawing:	– rosy blossom in hot ravine –

WILL

1

O well for him whose will is strong!
He suffers, but he will not suffer long;
He suffers, but he cannot suffer wrong:
For him nor moves the loud world's random mock,
Nor all Calamity's hugest waves confound,
Who seems a promontory of rock,
That, compass'd round with turbulent sound,
In middle ocean meets the surging shock,
Tempest-buffeted, citadel-crown'd.

2

But ill for him who, bettering not with time,
Corrupts the strength of heaven-descended Will,
And ever weaker grows thro' acted crime,
Or seeming-genial venial fault,
Recurring and suggesting still!
He seems as one whose footsteps halt,
Toiling in immeasurable sand,
And o'er a weary sultry land,
Far beneath a blazing vault,
Sown in a wrinkle of the monstrous hill,
The city sparkles like a grain of salt.

178. Cape St Angelo, Corfu, Greece

The high, castle-crowned rocks of Cape St Angelo,
Corfu, formed the promontory remembered from the
poet's many visits to that island. When he first went
there, Lear loved Corfu: away from the busy town, and
on the western coast, he discovered the serene and ample
bay of Palaiokastritza (see no. 16) with its blue skies and
sea, its golden fruits and lush vegetation. The enclosing
curve was balanced by this other scene of massive rocks
rising from, and reflected in, calm water. In a letter written from Corfu to Chichester Fortescue on Easter Sunday, 20 April 1862 (LEL, pp. 234-7), Lear described the
land and seascape which so moved him. Everything is a
tranquil part of a 'Paradise Island': no 'turbulent sound'
disturbs the peace of the noise-hating artist. He wonders
about 'being influenced to an extreme by everything in
natural or physical life, i.e., atmosphere, light, shadow,
and all the varieties of day and night.' Is this a blessing
or not? He decides that the best he can do is 'to make
the best of what happens':

> I should however have added "quiet and repose" to my list
> of influences, for at this beautiful place there is just now
> perfect quiet, excepting only a dim hum of myriad ripples
> 500 feet below me, all round the giant rocks which rise
> perpendicularly from the sea... far above them – higher
> and higher, the immense rock of St. Angelo rising into the
> air, on whose summit the old castle still is seen a ruin, just
> 1,400 feet above the water. It half seems to me that such
> life as this must be wholly another from the drumbeating
> bothery frivolity of the town of Corfu...

But the feeling of renewal, 'I seem to grow a year
younger every hour', did not last. Picnic parties and
'asses male and female' will come tomorrow: '. . . . and
peace flies – as I shall too'.

But Corfu's beauty remained in Lear's memory and
Cape St Angelo evolved and settled into a Tennyson
Illustration lasting into the 1880s. In the same letter Lear
mentioned his hatred of sectarian extremes, preferring
'a plain worship of God, and a perpetual endeavour at
progress'. This reminded him of 'Tennyson's little poem
"Will"', which he had been trying to translate into Greek
and sent in part to his correspondent. 'Will' had been
published in 1855, the year of Lear's first visit to Corfu.

Lear's own caption to his drawing, 'a promontory in
mid-sea', is a misquotation from Tennyson's poem which
has, in line 6, 'a promontory of rock'. But it is clear from
the context that the rock, 'citadel crowned', meets the
'surging shock' of waves 'In middle ocean'. In effect,
Lear has conflated two half-lines and this seems to be
how he remembered the importance of the poem. The
first stanza describes the man of immovable will: 'O well
for him whose will is strong!' Such a man suffers, but
stands up to the world's mockery and the shocks and
chances of life: he is steadfast as a great rock amid ocean
storms. Lear admired this power of will as he admired
Corfu's unchanging rock. Lone determination and calm
perseverance seemed to him alien to his temperament.
Self-mocking, self-deprecating, often distressed, he saw
himself as victim of lack of will, 'the seeming-genial venial fault' of the poem's second stanza. None of Lear's
dedicated work in landscape drawing and painting
brought him a lasting sense of security or achievement.
Few understood his passion for 'Poetical Topography';
few bought his pictures. He often felt, as he moved
restlessly from one country to another, like Tennyson's
traveller, 'bettering not with time': 'He seems as one
whose footsteps halt, / Toiling in immeasurable sand';
burning sand, burning heat, and the goal – the city – a
disturbingly inhuman image under the 'blazing vault'.
The traveller of the second stanza, overcome by dangers,

digression, delays – the 'seeming-genial fault' – sees his goal merge frighteningly into the unconquerable landscape. The city, creation of Tennyson's 'terrible Muse' Geology, is a crystalline grain 'sown in the wrinkle of the monstrous hill'. The traveller's loss of will has lost him his oasis: water, shade, fellow human beings. He has let himself be overrun by the lines of desert and the 'monstrous hill'.

Lear's will, like his art, was stronger than he knew. But Tennyson's poem evoked not only a Corfu seascape, but also his own most familiar inward doubts. He drew a rock to illustrate a misquoted phrase, and the misquotation led further into his own reaction to the poem. The 'promontory in mid-sea' emphasized his approval of strong will; the weak-willed are punished by their own condition and by their hopeless striving towards a dry salt city in a 'monstrous hill'. Lear's illustration of the promontory shows a stern side of the Corfu he had loved and lived on, it defines his wish for strength, for the steadfast rock: it counteracted uncertainty about his own journeying, his fear of aimlessness, of loss of will, and lack of artistic power.

Lear tried to translate Tennyson's 'Will' into modern Greek and this, in itself, suggests how important the poem must have been for him (and he quotes the line on 'strong will' twice in his diary for 1868 alone). He took Greek lessons and was proud that he could speak and write it. In his diaries it became a private language, and the translation was for Lear a curious way of coming to terms with the poem. The same letter to Fortescue gives a version of part of this translation:

> *It is needless to observe that I have not attempted to render the original. . . in verse, which, if I had done, it would have been worse. . . . Considering that little more than 6 years ago I didn't know a letter of the Greek alphabet, I think I might translate A. T.'s poems in some 10 or 20 or 50 years more.*

This idea of translating Tennyson's poems was hardly a serious one. But it shows how much Lear wanted to render his creative involvement in the poems. Drawing and painting were the artist's obvious methods of translation, and for one poem at least he added Greek words. During the second Nile journey in 1867, Lear was ill with the movement of the boat in the wind: travel became 'bitter misery'. He thought of turning back, but decided that going on would prove he had 'some resolution and enthusiasm left'. He added 'O well for him whose will &c.' (D. 25 January 1867), and his own will power steadied by Tennyson's poem, he continued, mainly with delight, his voyage on the Nile.

178. EL List: A promontory of rock
EL Drawing: – A promontory in mid-sea

— a promontory in mid-sea

(Will.)

Cape S.t Angelo.
Corfù. Greece.

From: IN MEMORIAM

I

I held it truth, with him who sings
   To one clear harp in divers tones,
   That men may rise on stepping-stones
Of their dead selves to higher things.

But who shall so forecast the years
   And find in loss a gain to match?
   Or reach a hand thro' time to catch
The far-off interest of tears?

Let Love clasp Grief lest both be drown'd,
   Let darkness keep her raven gloss:
   Ah, sweeter to be drunk with loss,
To dance with death, to beat the ground,

Than that the victor Hours should scorn
   The long result of love, and boast:
   'Behold the man that loved and lost,
But all he was is overworn.'

XV

To-night the winds begin to rise
   And roar from yonder dropping day:
   The last red leaf is whirl'd away,
The rooks are blown about the skies;

The forest crack'd, the waters curl'd,
   The cattle huddled on the lea;
   And wildly dash'd on tower and tree
The sunbeam strikes along the world:

And but for fancies, which aver
   That all thy motions gently pass
   Athwart a plane of molten glass,
I scarce could brook the strain and stir

That makes the barren branches loud;
   And but for fear it is not so,
   The wild unrest that lives in woe
Would dote and pore on yonder cloud

That rises upward always higher,
   And onward drags a labouring breast,
   And topples round the dreary west,
A looming bastion fringed with fire.

Poems written for the dead are mainly concerned with the living. *In Memoriam* commemorates and idealizes the young Arthur Hallam, Tennyson's closest Cambridge friend, who died of a brain haemorrhage in 1833. But it is the living poet's loss that most strongly informs the poem. And it is Tennyson who shaped the poem so that its lyrics form a whole, and span problems of faith, hope, doubt, man's survival – problems that reach far beyond an individual grief. The popularity of the poem was partly due to the fact that it spoke for all Victorian questioners. So many, brought up as steadfast Christians, found it difficult to confront the uncertainties of man's position suggested by the work of geologists and evolutionists such as Lyell and Darwin. From one view it seemed, Nature was not 'careful of the type': man might easily slip back into a beast. The opposite view, which clearly emerges in this poem, was that men could move upward, working out the beast, towards a life of the spirit. And around men the seasons and landscapes of the natural world pass, change, and return. Throughout *In Memoriam* nature reflects human mood yet keeps to its own cycles. Christian festivals, bound up with nature – Christmas, bells ringing in the New Year – also return, allowing a slow growth of tentative optimism, a sense of moving forward. At the end, the actual and symbolic marriage suggests a return to possibilities of human happiness, of future goals and spiritual ideals.

It is quite possible to interpret *In Memoriam* as a poem of Victorian doubt. While paying lip-service to the idea of creation moving onwards and upwards, Tennyson himself, shattered by loss, is unable to believe in a positive view of man at all. And whether or not Tennyson consciously or unconsciously endorsed the 'happy ending' of *In Memoriam*, he could brilliantly invoke moods of unbearable misery as well as moods of tempered optimism. The poem, although originally strung together from a number of lyrics, remained, at moments, intensely personal. Yet it touched on loss in a way which seemed to voice feelings for everyone whose grief had hitherto been dumb. The poem, begun sporadically and privately, made grief articulate for the general reader.

Lear was one such reader, and he responded so strongly that he and his friend Chichester Fortescue stayed up all night to read *In Memoriam* when it first came out. Lear always approved of people who read Tennyson; he sometimes came across them in his travels. In his diary for 31 August 1884 he mentions 'a family who know every line of Tennyson, *In Memoriam* &c &c.' In his own reading of the poem it was, interestingly, the first stanza that he appropriated for himself. From the 'public' poem he reinterpreted a few lines to express his own private grief. In 1858 he mentions 'stepping-stones' in a diary entry for 5 December, in 1860 he quoted 'stepping-stones' and 'higher things'. He does not seem to have developed these ideas at the time of his sister Ann's death in 1861. But the notion comes up again and is fully worked out when Lear faced Giorgio's death in 1883. At that time, Lear asked, as a kind of prayer, that he might rise to 'higher things', to a better moral self, using Giorgio's example of faithfulness and goodness and care as a 'stepping-stone'. Tennyson had written of rising on our own 'dead selves', but Lear twisted the lines so that the 'selves' belong to others from whom he should learn.

The idea of such 'stepping-stones' brought some comfort to Lear; it meant that those whom he loved when they were alive gave him the possibility of becoming a better person as he tried always to remember and learn from their example. He quoted the whole stanza (D. 30 July 1884), having just read over his account of Giorgio's death the previous year. Being a better person, Lear felt, was the only way of repaying his debt to Giorgio, and it involved taking responsibility for three Cocali sons. As two had become semi-delinquent and one was terminally ill with tuberculosis, Lear's sense of obligation was tested very hard. When the good Nicola died, Lear remembered the 'stepping-stones' again, and reminded himself of the difficulties which the Corfu Suliot family had had to face. He continued to answer appeals from Lambi and Dmitri, even as they lost, or failed to try for, job after job.

In his own way Lear applied a stanza of *In Memoriam* to his feeling of loss. And the way he read the lines suggests he was aware of the ideas of moral growth and self-knowledge inherent in the poem: 'God grant that I may indeed make my dear good Giorgio a "stepping-stone" to higher things – & that I may remember daily & hourly his goodness, & thereby render myself more fitted to leave earth!!' (D. 13 August 1883).

Lear's sense of the scope of *In Memoriam* is perhaps reflected in his choice of illustrations. Huge plains seen from mountains, a fortress on a mountain ridge, the peaks of Mount Sinai, 'A looming bastion fringed with fire'. This last drawing has dark clouds shading down into a lighter sky, then a dark, indeterminate coast merging into sea, with hinted outlines of boats; it is unlike any of Lear's other illustrations. In composition and effect, in a daring contrast of light and dark, in a disregard for the solidity of land, it suggests what Lear learned, and might have learned, by studying Turner. He had lithographs made of several Turner paintings, and when the *Liber Studiorum* was published he ordered a copy in mezzotint, and, later, one in autotype. This picture is almost abstract and, with hindsight, one might relate it to Turner's very late works. But the revolutionary approach to light, colour and form was apparent in Turner's early paintings and sketches; Lear saw some of these when he was taken to Petworth as a child and saw Lord Egremont's collection. In later years Lear looked at Turner's established paintings in London and in the Taylor Institute in Oxford. Without formal training in landscape painting, or the use of oils, Lear educated himself as he could: it is a mark of his advanced taste that Turner was his ideal. He found the paintings dazzling and tended to write simply 'O Turner'.

The drawing of the Coast of Travancore with cloud crossing half the sky and suggesting storm to come, is a picture dependent on diagonal forms: slant-wise light contrasts with dark coast, itself almost indistinguishable from dark cloud. The dark and light have no colour, no 'fringe of fire', but they make a dramatic impact even in monochrome. There is no fine outline, and the dark blurred cloud edge, which suits the design so well, is in part due to Lear's poor eyesight. But if he had been younger, and had learned more from Turner's daring and artistry, this apparently free but highly controlled technique might have been Lear's way forward as a landscape painter.

181. Coast of Travancore

Slept tolerably. At 5.50 went to see after George, – who I trust mends regularly. Travancore mountains all over cloud, & cloudier & cloudier still as we go onward, till at 1 PM. gusty squalls and rain ensue. Gave G his pill, & at 3 a Quinine powder. Tiffin at 1. – Captn. Gavin is a singularly nice man, & Mr Underwood also a pleasant fellow. But I do confess surprise at this 120th Monsoon, as poor George calls it, – sky & sea all leaden, with cool, not to say cold wind, & showers of rain! Somehow I think I shall give up my Travancore & Madura plans, for such weather as this would make the tour useless – if not odious. Remainder of afternoon uncomfortable; chilly wind & rain, – but it grew better towards 4.30, – dinner hour, – though the sky was so dark that we required candles. After dinner, saw to George, who always improves; & talked with Captn. Gavin & Mr Underwood till 7, when I came down to Sherry and Soda Water. Sky clearer, & wind less. I "revolve" in my mind whether I may not come down to see this coast as far as Cocheen.
(Indian Journal, 14 December 1874)

Rose at 5, & at 6. saw George, – who always says "Meglio." Morning beautiful, – calm & bright. Long flat shore of Travancore, & low flat hills.
(15 December 1874)

181. EL List: A looming bastion fringed with fire
       EL Drawing: A looming bastion fringed with fire. –

A looming bastion fringed with fire —
(In Memoriam)

Coast of Travancore.
India.

Three Songs from: THE PRINCESS

[III]

       . . . Many a little hand
Glanced like a touch of sunshine on the rocks,
Many a light foot shone like a jewel set
In the dark crag: and then we turn'd, we wound
About the cliffs, the copses, out and in,
Hammering and clinking, chattering stony names
Of shale and hornblende, rag and trap and tuff,
Amygdaloid and trachyte, till the Sun
Grew broader toward his death and fell, and all
The rosy heights came out above the lawns.

    The splendour falls on castle walls
        And snowy summits old in story:
    The long light shakes across the lakes,
        And the wild cataract leaps in glory.
Blow, bugle, blow, set the wild echoes flying,
Blow, bugle; answer, echoes, dying, dying, dying.

    O hark, O hear! how thin and clear,
        And thinner, clearer, farther going!
    O sweet and far from cliff and scar
        The horns of Elfland faintly blowing!
Blow, let us hear the purple glens replying:
Blow, bugle; answer, echoes, dying, dying, dying.

    O love, they die in yon rich sky,
        They faint on hill or field or river:
    Our echoes roll from soul to soul,
        And grow for ever and for ever.
Blow, bugle, blow, set the wild echoes flying,
And answer, echoes, answer, dying, dying, dying.

IV

    . . .   Then she 'Let some one sing to us: lightlier move
    The minutes fledged with music:' and a maid,
    Of those beside her, smote her harp, and sang.

    'Tears, idle tears, I know not what they mean,
Tears from the depth of some divine despair
Rise in the heart, and gather to the eyes,
In looking on the happy Autumn-fields,
And thinking of the days that are no more.

    'Fresh as the first beam glittering on a sail,
That brings our friends up from the underworld,
Sad as the last which reddens over one
That sinks with all we love below the verge;
So sad, so fresh, the days that are no more.

    'Ah, sad and strange as in dark summer dawns
The earliest pipe of half-awaken'd birds
To dying ears, when unto dying eyes
The casement slowly grows a glimmering square;
So sad, so strange, the days that are no more.

    'Dear as remember'd kisses after death,
And sweet as those by hopeless fancy feign'd
On lips that are for others; deep as love,
Deep as first love, and wild with all regret;
O Death in Life, the days that are no more.'

[VII]

   . . .   Deep in the night I woke: she, near me, held
    A volume of the Poets of her land:
    There to herself, all in low tones, she read.

    'Now sleeps the crimson petal, now the white;
Nor waves the cypress in the palace walk;
Nor winks the gold fin in the porphyry font:
The fire-fly wakens: waken thou with me.

    Now droops the milkwhite peacock like a ghost,
And like a ghost she glimmers on to me.

    Now lies the Earth all Danaë to the stars,
And all thy heart lies open unto me.

    Now slides the silent meteor on, and leaves
A shining furrow, as thy thoughts in me.

    Now folds the lily all her sweetness up,
And slips into the bosom of the lake:
So fold thyself, my dearest, thou, and slip
Into my bosom and be lost in me.'

The Princess

" The splendour falls on castle walls "

Suli, Albania

The Princess, planned in 1847, is not another 'Day-Dream'. Described as 'A Medley', it attempts to raise serious questions and yet, at times, seems to mock at seriousness. It is written in blank verse and interspersed with songs; some of these are in blank verse, including 'Tears, idle tears', one of Tennyson's finest lyrics. As in 'The Day-Dream' there is a 'frame' to the main events. The garden of a stately house, a hospitable English baronet, his daughter and a gathering of male undergraduates, are contrasted with a mass of people enjoying a Mechanics' Institute holiday within Sir Walter's grounds. Ideas of education for the masses, as liberating and as fun, come up in the somewhat surprising form of voluntary electric shocks, optical experiments and the ascent of a hot-air balloon.

All these diversions are prelude to the main educational experiment which forms the central action. It is embedded in an imaginary tale in which Lilia, Sir Walter's daughter, is cast as a 'great Princess', 'six feet high, / Grand, epic, homicidal' and the undergraduates are courtly suitors, led by a blue-eyed 'Prince', given to 'weird seizures' and odd insights. The Princess Ida and her ladies, like the *Love's Labour's Lost* courtiers in reverse, have given up the society of men and devoted themselves to the higher education of women. Dressed in 'female gear', remembering their roles as Nymphs or Goddesses in court pageants, the men infiltrate the College of Women and begin their studies. Their fears, hopes, conflicts, and their unmasking take up much of the rest of the poem. The complex plot involves a great tournament, after which the women give up their vows and tend each chivalric, wounded suitor. The College is dissolved; the Prince finally gains the Princess. The courtiers follow suit. Within this strange tale, however, the poem has much to say about the complementary nature of men and women: the conventional role of each is questioned. But the narrative turns away from the problems, back to the expectations of society: women must marry. Even the songs, which sometimes suggest the sorrow of experience in the world, endorse the exhortation, 'Come down, O maid, from yonder mountain height'. The great experiment of women's higher education has to confront not only the 'mountain height' of intellect, but also the natural instincts and the 'valley' of love.

The end of *The Princess* is marked by a return to the framing device. Princess Ida becomes Lilia again; the men resume their personalities outside the story. The day is ending and everyone, whether member of the Mechanics' Institute or guest at the great house, returns home.

Tennyson himself was rather uncertain about this poem: he felt its heroic aspirations needed rhyme rather than blank verse. This seems strange when one thinks of his blank verse in the *Idylls of the King*. But the main problem is the tone. It is very hard to tell whether or not the poem is, at any moment, slightly mocking and ironic about women, women's education and men's assumptions of superiority. And if everybody is being shown up, why does Tennyson allow for the development of genuine bewilderment and of mutual sympathy between the men and women of *The Princess*? The songs have been said to hold the poem together. Some are battle songs; some dwell on feelings of capitulation to love, as does the highly sensuous lyric which opens 'Now sleeps the crimson petal, now the white.' One song, 'Tears, idle tears I know not what they mean', suggests experiences more elusive and complex than any described in *The Princess*.

For Lear the phrase 'Tears, idle tears' exactly expressed the moods of depression and misery which he tried to avoid by dedicating himself to hard work. And he constantly looked back, relating the present to 'the days that are no more'. He often quoted that half-line in his diary, but never its beginning, 'O Death in life . . .'. But, feeling at his worst, that was what he thought of as 'the morbids', the sense that his life was utterly meaningless.

The quotations chosen from *The Princess* had to be landscape descriptions. The 'castle wall', 'the palace walk', 'A little town with towers' – such phrases come from lines which have nothing to do with the problems of women's education and marriage which seem to be Tennyson's main concerns. Nevertheless we do know something about Lear's attitude to women. He cared very deeply for Ann, the sister who had brought him up, and remembered her, with gratitude, long after her death. Yet he was capable of listing exactly what she ought to wear to make the correct impression when visiting him in Rome. Ann never made the visit. Lear was attached to Eleanor and Sarah, two of his other sisters, though he sometimes resented the fact that, as a child, he had always been fussed over by women. As an adult, Lear's personality combined deep reserve with a gently extrovert and amusing manner. He seems to have found it easy to make the acquaintance of women, and he makes shrewd comments, in his diary, about women at dinner parties or at his exhibitions. He met the old and the young, the amiable, the clever and independent, the amusing, and the cold, snobbish and silly. On his travels, he enjoyed seeing pretty women in local costume. But his lasting relationships were mainly with English women: among these, he was devoted to Emily Tennyson, admired his patroness Lady Waldegrave, and may have loved Augusta (Gussie) Bethell.

Lear's illustrations for *The Princess* consist of ten drawings, and six quotations: of these drawings, five go to one line – 'The splendour falls on castle walls' – the first line of one of the songs which punctuate *The Princess*. These lyrics are the most accomplished, and the most beautiful, pieces of writing in the long 'Medley'. Some were added in 1850 after the first appearance of the poem in 1847. Lear, long before the 1880s, had set some of these and other Tennyson lyrics to music: he sang and played the piano after dinner at countless town and country houses. He was an amateur with an affecting style, and eventually some of his Tennyson songs were transcribed for him and published.[1] Thus the main attraction of *The Princess* may have been the songs, and two other illustrations refer to lines from two songs: 'Now sleeps the crimson petal, now the white' and 'Sweet and low'. Three illustrations are to lines of scenic description from the main text of Tennyson's poem. 'The splendour falls . . .' seems to bring back mainly early memories of Italy; Lear uses sketches from his first year in Rome and his books of lithographs *Views in Rome and Environs*, 1841, and *Illustrated Excursions in Italy* (2 vols.), 1846. The influence of Claude and of standard types of composition did not stultify the young artist's work: there is a sure and vigorous use of both dark (often vegetation, especially cypresses) and light, with a wiry delicate line. Moreover, the young Lear could still see to work directly on the stone himself. The 'castle' illustrations are not late copies of these lithographs, but some relate back to sketches of that early period. The 'Villa d'Este, Tivoli' was a view drawn or painted by most topographical artists in Rome. Lear had precedents early and contemporary. One standard view, with rocks and temple, he greatly admired; other views involved the garden of the Villa with its cypresses and cascades. In March 1877 Lear took a young friend to the Villa d'Este – a visit essential to anyone being shown the sights of Rome. Although tired and out of spirits Lear remained an indefatigable guide. But he felt that he 'went through this rehearsal of Roman Sights as in a dream, or one walking among the dead.' Even the Villa d'Este, 'that glory of glories' had become 'a grave of old memories' (D. 8, 11 March 1877). In his depressed state Lear had almost forgotten the delight he felt when he first saw Tivoli nearly forty years earlier, and described it in a letter to his sister Ann.

192. Villa d'Este, Tivoli

You know how magnificent the Roman church used to be; well – about the 16th. century – Cardinal d'Este built this mansion. The house is very grand & simple in form – but it is its situation that so bewilders one. I could not believe I was awake at first. It is raised quite above all Tivoli, at the top of an extremely steep hill – all of which is turned into one exquisite garden. You come on to the upper terrace & are dumb; the most enormous trees – pines & Cypresses – are beneath you; long walks of gravel, grass & box – formally cut; fountains by hundreds of thousands – terraces; flights of stairs from the villa to the bottom of the hill – & to crown all the whole Campagna beyond. You proceed down these flights of stairs – & wonder that you have been so deceived on arriving, at the Cypress trees – which look like giants; they are the largest in the world. From the end of the long alleys you look back – & it is really like magic! I will try to give you a very little idea of this most exquisite of gardens. No. 1 may convey some notion of the place – seen from the end of the long walk; observe the vast height! – & the proportion of the little people! & think how grand these mighty black Cypresses must be! No. 2 shows you the whole house – from another Cypress walk. But this wonderful palace is all quite desolate – nobody has lived in it for a 100 years & like all palaces in Italy its beauty has a good deal of melancholy with it. Next summer I should like to pass some months at Tivoli – for although I have said so much of it, yet I can assure

189

The Princess

The splendour falls on castle walls

Celano

Celano, Abruzzi

Celano

you that it is impossible to form any idea of the extreme loveliness of the whole environment of the town. So now I have done with Tivoli. (The numbers refer to two small sketches in the letter; EL to Ann, 3 May 1838)

187. Suli, Albania

The walls of the Suliot stronghold high in the mountains of Albania seem quite at odds with the Italian castles of Lear's other four illustrations for 'The splendour falls...'. The ferocious inhabitants, as the Albanian Journal describes, fought for their territory and their freedom. The Suliots, a small, independent, Christian race, isolated in their mountainous surroundings, defended themselves against the encroaching Turks by all possible means. They were finally conquered in 1803 after fifteen years of bloody skirmishing. Lear knew their history and might have chosen Suli because of the battle in *The Princess*, but it is more likely that he was thinking of it as the native land of his servant Giorgio, although the latter was not yet in his service in 1848-9. Much of Lear's life was intermingled with that of Giorgio, who lived in Corfu and, when taken into Lear's service, kept silent for years about the existence of his wife and family. Giorgio was a near ideal servant for Lear: he coped, he travelled, he had a knack of making life comfortable for his master whether in Palestine or in San Remo. After nearly twenty-seven years his impeccable service deteriorated with age, illness, drinking and bouts of silent fury or violent temper. But Lear's servant had become, in some ways, a friend, and Lear never abandoned either Giorgio or his three difficult sons. By the end Lear tended 'good old George' as carefully as Giorgio had tended him. In his diary, especially after the Indian journey, Lear records his feelings of guilt about taking Giorgio for granted, and not helping the family enough when he discovered their existence. He was steadfast in his efforts to make up for this, by doing everything to restore Giorgio's health, and by looking after the sons. He kept reminding himself that Giorgio was a Suliot, a man from a wild, proud community, who could range mountains, but felt confined in cities. And Lear the traveller, understood such feelings. Suli is, perhaps, part of this 'Liber Studiorum' because one of its people was so important in Lear's life.

Lear's visit to the heights of Suli was fraught with difficulty. The baggage horse stumbled, losing some of its load, and the small party threaded its way along perilous rocky paths above the terrible gulf of the river called Acheron.

At sunset we reached the only approach on this side of "the blood-stained Suli" – an ascent of stairs winding up the sides of the great rocks below Avariko – and very glad was I to have accomplished this last and most dangerous part of the journey. Before me is the hollow vale of Avariko, Kiafa, and Suli – places now existing little more than in name; and darkly looming against the clear western sky stands the dread Trypa – the hill of Thunderbolts – the last retreat of the despairing Suliotes.

Here, at the summit of the rock, Ali Pasha built a castle, and within its walls I hope to pass the night. I reach it at nearly two hours after sunset, the bright moon showing me

183

193
192

A little town with towers upon a rock

(*Enid.*)

" *The cypress in the Palace Walk* "

Villa d' Este
Near ——
Tiber
Tivoli
Italy

the Albanian governor and his twenty or thirty Palikari sitting on the threshold of the gate. But as unluckily I had not procured any letter from the Turkish authorities at Prevyza, the rough old gentleman was obdurate, and would not hear of my entering the fortress. "Yok," said he, frowning fiercely, "yok, yok." And had it not been for the good-nature of a Turkish officer of engineers who had arrived from Ioannina on a visit of inspection, I must have passed the night supperless and shelterless. Thanks to him, men and horses were at length admitted to the interior of the fort.

I was ushered through several dilapidated courtyards to the inner serai or governor's house – a small building with wide galleries round two sides of it. In a narrow and low room, surrounded with sofas, the military dignitary sate down with his suite of "wild Albanians;" and to be polite, I followed their example; but the excessive smoke of the wood fire, added to that of the tchibouques, was so painful a contrast to the fresh air, that it was almost intolerable. No Greek was spoken; so Andrea was called in, and they expressed their conviction that I "looked miserable – neither eating, nor talking, nor smoking" – an accusation I willingly acceded to, for the sake of rest and fresh air, and transferred my position with all haste to the outer gallery. There I had my mattress and capotes spread, and old Andrea brought me a capital basin of rice soup. It had been a severe day's labour for a man of his years and great size, and during the passage of the gorge, he had more than once been unable to advance for some minutes; yet, with his wonted alacrity, he had not only prepared my bed as usual, but had exercised his talent for cooking withal.

I gazed on the strange, noiseless figures about me, bright in the moonlight, which tipped with silver the solemn lofty mountains around. For years those hills had rarely ceased to echo the cries of animosity, despair, and agony; now all is silent as the actors in that dreadful drama.

Few scenes can compete in my memory with the wildness of this at the castle of Kiafa, or Suli-Kastro; and excepting in the deserts of the peninsula of Sinai, I have gazed on none more picturesque and strange.
(Albanian Journal, 5 May 1849, pp. 362-4)

Lear's view of Celano for the Tennyson drawings goes back to two lithographs made for his second book, *Illustrated Excursions in Italy*, 1846, and to its preparatory note about 'a long proposed tour in the Abruzzi, or the three Northern provinces of the Kingdom of Naples.' On the first 'excursion', in 1843, Lear visited the high fortress town of Celano; its Castle was famous, so the artist relates, for a marble staircase said to cure all those who walked up it of love. (This legend could well relate to the narrative and characters of *The Princess*, but Lear never remarks on a possible connection.) In the first 1846 volume the artist describes the scenery round Celano, but without the lively particularity which he brings to his later landscape writing. The competent and attractive lithographs of the *Excursions* were necessary background work for an artist with little formal training. Such early views, however, show how far Lear was to develop his 'poetical topography', not so much in oil painting, but in the highly individual and free lines of his original watercolour drawings.

189. Celano, Italy

A lovely morning followed the tempestuous night: and as we trotted at sunrise along the road from Avezzano to Celano, – bound to no particular place, but at the mercy of the weather and our own caprices, – everything seemed fresh and delightful. Groups of peasants journeying to the market of Avezzano enlivened the way, each giving us a passing greeting. Below us on the right were fields of uninterrupted cultivation – vines and Indian corn, stretching to the Lake: to the left the yellow plain of Alba, with its town always in sight, until shut out by the hill of Paterno, on whose sides, the sunniest and most fertile in all the Marsica, the olive, an unusual guest in these parts, grows abundantly. Looking back, Serra di Sant'Antonio, the loftiest of the range of mountains guarding the valley of the Liris, towers over all the scene.

We approached Celano by stony lanes bordered with poplars, and more like watercourses than roads, for the carriage-road ceases below Paterno. Here all the scenery grows more wild and Swiss in character: vistas between mountains displayed crags with towns perched thereon; and clouds, covering many of the higher points, lent a mystery to what was beyond.

Celano, once an important fortress-town, and the head of the Marsica during the troublous times of the thirteenth and fourteenth centuries, is now remarkable only for the extreme picturesqueness of its situation: it stands below a wondrous bare precipice on a hill overlooking the whole of the Lake of Fucino, though at a considerable distance from its edge; the space between the town and the water being filled with meadows and vineyards, and watered by the clearest streams. (Illustrated Excursions in Italy, 29 July 1843, Vol. I, p.25)

[1] For a detailed account of Lear's published and unpublished Tennyson songs, see Anne Henry Ehrenpreis, 'Edward Lear Sings Tennyson Songs', *Harvard Library Bulletin*, xxvii 1979, pp. 65-85.

187. EL List: The splendour falls on castle walls
      EL Drawing: "The splendour falls on castle walls"
189. EL List: The splendour falls on castle walls
      EL Drawing: "The splendour falls on castle walls"
192. EL List: The cypress in the Palace walk
      EL Drawing: "The cypress in the Palace Walk"

From: LANCELOT AND ELAINE

... So Arthur bad the meek Sir Percivale
And pure Sir Galahad to uplift the maid;
And reverently they bore her into hall.
Then came the fine Gawain and wonder'd at her,
And Lancelot later came and mused at her,   1260
And last the Queen herself and pitied her:
But Arthur spied the letter in her hand,
Stoopt, took, brake seal, and read it; this was all.

'Most noble lord, Sir Lancelot of the Lake,
I, sometime call'd the maid of Astolat,
Come, for you left me taking no farewell,
Hither, to take my last farewell of you.
I loved you, and my love had no return,
And therefore my true love has been my death.
And therefore to our lady Guinevere,   1270
And to all other ladies, I make moan.
Pray for my soul, and yield me burial.
Pray for my soul thou too, Sir Lancelot,
As thou art a knight peerless.'
               Thus he read,
And ever in the reading, lords and dames
Wept, looking often from his face who read
To hers which lay so silent, and at times,
So touch'd were they, half-thinking that her lips,
Who had devised the letter, moved again.

Then freely spoke Sir Lancelot to them all;   1280
'My lord liege Arthur, and all ye that hear,
Know that for this most gentle maiden's death
Right heavy am I; for good she was and true,
But loved me with a love beyond all love
In women, whomsoever I have known.
Yet to be loved makes not to love again;
Not at my years, however it hold in youth.
I swear by truth and knighthood that I gave
No cause, not willingly, for such a love: ...

...   He pausing, Arthur answer'd, 'O my knight,   1315
It will be your worship, as my knight,
And mine, as head of all our Table Round,
To see that she be buried worshipfully.'

Then answer'd Lancelot, 'Fair she was, my King,
Pure, as you ever wish your knights to be.
To doubt her fairness were to want an eye,
To doubt her pureness were to want a heart –   1365

Yea, to be loved, if what is worthy love
Could bind him, but free love will not be bound.'

'Free love, so bound, were freëst,' said the King.
'Let love be free; free love is for the best:
And, after heaven, on our dull side of death,
What should be best, if not so pure a love
Clothed in so pure a loveliness? yet thee
She fail'd to bind, tho' being, as I think,
Unbound as yet, and gentle, as I know.'

And Lancelot answer'd nothing, but he went,   1375
And at the inrunning of a little brook
Sat by the river in a cove, and watch'd
The high reed wave, and lifted up his eyes
And saw the barge that brought her moving down,
Far-off, a blot upon the stream, and said
Low in himself, 'Ah simple heart and sweet,
You loved me, damsel, surely with a love
Far tenderer than my Queen's. Pray for thy soul?
Ay, that will I. Farewell too – now at last –
Farewell, fair lily. "Jealousy in love?"   1385
Not rather dead love's harsh heir, jealous pride?
Queen, if I grant the jealousy as of love,
May not your crescent fear for name and fame
Speak, as it waxes, of a love that wanes?
Why did the King dwell on my name to me?
Mine own name shames me, seeming a reproach, ...

... For what am I? what profits me my name
Of greatest knight? I fought for it, and have it:
Pleasure to have it, none; to lose it, pain;
Now grown a part of me: but what use in it?
To make men worse by making my sin known?   1405
Or sin seem less, the sinner seeming great?
Alas for Arthur's greatest knight, a man
Not after Arthur's heart! I needs must break
These bonds that so defame me; not without
She wills it: would I, if she will'd it? nay,
Who knows? but if I would not, then may God,
I pray him, send a sudden Angel down
To seize me by the hair and bear me far,
And fling me deep in that forgotten mere,
Among the tumbled fragments of the hills.'   1415

So groan'd Sir Lancelot in remorseful pain,
Not knowing he should die a holy man.

"among the tumbled fragments of the hills"

Canalo, Calabria

194. Canalo, Calabria

Tennyson's *The Idylls of the King* were over fifty years in the making. The principal source was Malory, but the poet changed and reshaped his material to create an Arthurian world of his own: its legend lay far in the past, but its characters and their relationships offered implicit moral and social comment on the present. In 1832 Tennyson published a first lyric, 'The Lady of Shalott', and in 1842 added three other Arthurian poems. In 1833 he wrote a short prose outline for an epic, and between 1833 and 1840 made a rough draft for a musical masque in five acts. Slowly Tennyson worked towards the blank verse Idylls and, contemplating the character and aims of the perfect king and his imperfect court, published the poems, one by one or in small groups, over the years. The poet's creative method, with long-drawn-out work, changes of detail, and altered views of an ending, parallels Lear's long labour at his large paintings, particularly the Tennyson oils. The varied effort and endless self-copying which went into the artist's Tennyson Illustrations – in water colour and in monochrome – again recall the poet's years of working on ideas, publishing fragments, re-dividing narratives until each Idyll had been finalized and all twelve could be brought together in the late 1880s.

'The Lady of Shalott' and 'Sir Launcelot and Queen Guinevere. A fragment' were published in 1842. Both were remembered and partially recreated in Tennyson's 'Elaine' and 'Guinevere', two of the four Idylls published together in 1859. Along with 'Enid' and 'Vivien', they represented the ideas of innocence confronted with experience and of maturity succumbing to evil. The Lady of Shalott, in her tower room, is bound by a spell which allows her to watch life passing in her mirror and lets her record it on her loom. She sees the fair and good Sir Lancelot, becomes 'half sick of shadows', breaks the mirror and the spell, only to face the outside world with an unexplained curse on her life. Lying in a boat, singing a last mournful carol, she dies as she drifts down to Camelot. The Lady is received in wonder and fear: only Lancelot offers a last blessing. This early lyric, brilliantly conceived in stanza form with a refrain, is both enigmatic and complete. Yet Tennyson, always creating and re-creating, moved on from the Lady of Shalott to the Maid of Astolat, Elaine, who also dies of love for Lancelot, who in turn is entangled in his passion for Guinevere.

'Elaine', to become 'Lancelot and Elaine', cannot have been included in Lear's early plans for illustration before its publication in 1859. On 7 June that year the artist was staying with the Tennysons at Farringford. He found the poet well, but Emily Tennyson – though 'assuredly a most complete angel' – 'ill and weary'. Lear had the rare pleasure of a 'Walk on downs with AT who recite[d] out the Lady of Astolat, – another version of Lady of Shalott: – most wonderfully beautiful and affecting – so that I cried like beans. The gulls on the cliff laughed' (D. 7 June 1859). The poem Lear heard recited was to become the Idyll 'Elaine', finally titled 'Lancelot and Elaine'. The poet's recitation must have influenced

Lear when he added 'Lancelot and Elaine' to his list. He may have been drawn, too, by Elaine's childlike innocence and faith, which caused the lily maid of Astolat to become a victim of the passions and intrigues of the Round Table. On 5 March 1866 he was thinking again of the 'Maid of Astolat'. He made a note in his diary: '. . . . & re-Read Elaine'.

At the beginning of the poem Elaine is in her tower chamber guarding and cherishing Sir Lancelot's shield. Lancelot, after a misunderstanding with Queen Guinevere, has decided to fight anonymously in the jousts which offer a great diamond as a prize. He rides to Astolat, reveals his identity, borrows a plain shield and rides to the jousts, having agreed to wear Elaine's favour in his helmet. He fights valiantly, but his own followers turn on him, not wanting this unknown knight to win in place of the absent Lancelot. Lancelot is badly wounded, wins the prize, but rides away before claiming it. Elaine's brother Lavaine, pulls the spear-head from Lancelot's side, but the knight remains grievously ill. Elaine comes to tend him until he recovers, and returns to Astolat to fetch his shield and the diamond which has been brought to the castle for him to claim. Elaine declares her love, and Lancelot does not respond. In kindness he offers her riches when she marries, but makes a point of being discourteous in not saying farewell to her when he leaves. Back at Camelot, he presents the diamond, last of a series, to his great love, the Queen. Guinevere, already jealous, throws the diamond into the river and taunts Lancelot with a new love, Elaine. Lancelot has never wavered in his guilty love for Guinevere, but the young and innocent 'lily maid' has fallen so far in love that she will have either Lancelot or death. She will not listen to her father's tale of Lancelot's passion, but, knowing her love is not returned, she sickens and pines. She asks to be put in a chariot bier in a boat manned by a dumb servant. Sadly her father and brother lay her down, putting a lily and a letter in her hand. She dies in the boat and is borne, dead, into the King's presence. Her letter, declaring her true love, is read, and after the Queen has realized that her jealousy was causeless, the King wonders why his noble knight Lancelot rejected the pure love of Elaine. Tennyson makes the irony of the situation clear, but does not labour it. The maid of Astolat is buried in splendour and the end of the poem is taken up with Lancelot's musings on Elaine's untainted love, on his own passion, guilt, doubts and remorse. One of Lear's illustrations is for a line right at the end of Lancelot's last speech. Self questioning, Lancelot wonders if he could give up his love for Guinevere – if she willed it. If even then he could not, he begs God to send an Angel to fling him '. . . deep in that forgotten mere, / Among the tumbled fragments of the hills.' After this, two lines bring a quick ending, with the promise that Lancelot will die 'a holy man'.

Lear's 'tumbled fragments' go back to his early journeys in Calabria. In his *Journal of a Landscape Painter in Southern Italy*, he describes the village of Canalo, in which he stayed, built just beneath the jutting rocks and huge broken stony pieces of the Passo del Mercante. Perhaps the 'torrent-bed', though dry, reminded Lear of Tennyson's 'forgotten mere'.

194. Canalo, Calabria

The view of Canalo from the ravine of the Novito is extremely grand, and increased in majestic wonder as we descended to the stream through fine hanging woods. Having crossed the wide torrent-bed – an impractical feat in winter – we gradually rose into a world of stern rocks – a wilderness of terror, such as it is not easy to describe or imagine. The village itself is crushed and squeezed into a nest of crags immediately below the vast precipices which close round the Passo del Mercante, and when on one side you gaze at this barrier of stone, and then, turning round, perceive the distant sea and undulating lines of hill, no contrast can be more striking. At the summit of Canalo stands a large building, the Palazzo of Don Giovanni Rosa, the chief proprietor of the place, an extremely old man, whose manners were most simple and kind. 'My grandchildren,' said he, 'you are welcome to Canalo, and all I can do for you will be too little to show you my goodwill;' and herewith he led us to the cleanest of rooms, which were to be ours during our stay, and apologised for any 'mancanza' we might find. 'You must excuse a bad fare to-day, but I will get you better to-morrow,' quoth Don Giovanni Rosa. The remainder of the afternoon we employed in wandering about the town and its most extraordinary environs, where masses of Titan rock threaten to crush the atoms of life that nestle beneath them. (Calabrian Journal, 19 August 1847, pp. 135-6)

. . . Far, far above, along the pass to the western coast, you could discover diminutive figures threading the winding line among those fearful crags and fragments! or deep in the ravine, where torrents falling over perpendicular rocks echoed and foamed around, might be perceived parties of the women of Canalo spreading out linen to dry, themselves like specks on the face of some enormous mass of stone; or groups of goats, clustered on some bright pinnacle, and sparkling in the yellow sunlight. Canalo and its rocks are worth a long journey to behold. (20 August, p. 140)

After dinner at noon, we made our last drawings in this singular place, and bade adieu to the Casa Rosa, with its clean, airy, neat rooms, its painted doors, its gardens, vines, and bee-hives, and its agreeable, kind, and untiringly merry master, old Don Giovanni Rosa. The pleasant and simple hospitality of Canalo had once more restored us to our former admiration of Calabrian life . . . (21 August, p. 140)

194. EL List: Among the tumbled fragments of the hills
       EL Drawing: "Among the tumbled fragments of the hills"

From: GUINEVERE

Queen Guinevere had fled the court, and sat
There in the holy house at Almesbury
Weeping, none with her save a little maid,
A novice: one low light betwixt them burn'd
Blurr'd by the creeping mist, for all abroad,
Beneath a moon unseen albeit at full,
The white mist, like a face-cloth to the face,
Clung to the dead earth, and the land was still.

    For hither had she fled, her cause of flight
Sir Modred; he the nearest to the King,   10
His nephew, ever like a subtle beast
Lay couchant with his eyes upon the throne,
Ready to spring, waiting a chance: for this
He chill'd the popular praises of the King
With silent smiles of slow disparagement;
And tamper'd with the Lords of the White Horse,
Heathen, the brood by Hengist left; and sought
To make disruption in the Table Round
Of Arthur, and to splinter it into feuds
Serving his traitorous end; and all his aims   20
Were sharpened by strong hate for Lancelot, . . .

. . . She half-foresaw that he, the subtle beast,
Would track her guilt until he found, and hers   60
Would be for evermore a name of scorn.
Henceforward rarely could she front in Hall,
Or elsewhere, Modred's narrow foxy face,
Heart-hiding smile, and gray persistent eye:
Henceforward too, the Powers that tend the soul,
To help it from the death that cannot die,
And save it even in extremes, began
To vex and plague her. Many a time for hours,
Beside the placid breathings of the King,
In the dead night, grim faces came and went   70
Before her, or a vague spiritual fear –
Like to some doubtful noise of creaking doors,
Heard by the watcher in a haunted house,
That keeps the rust of murder on the walls –
Held her awake: or if she slept, she dream'd
An awful dream; for then she seem'd to stand
On some vast plain before a setting sun,
And from the sun there swiftly made at her
A ghastly something, and its shadow flew
Before it, till it touch'd her, and she turn'd –   80
When lo! her own, that broadening from her feet,
And blackening, swallow'd all the land, and in it
Far cities burnt, and with a cry she woke.
And all this trouble did not pass but grew;
Till ev'n the clear face of the guileless King,
And trustful courtesies of household life,
Became her bane; and at the last she said,
'O Lancelot, get thee hence to thine own land,
For it thou tarry we shall meet again,
And if we meet again, some evil chance   90

Will make the smouldering scandal break and blaze
Before the people, and our lord the King.'
And Lancelot ever promised, but remain'd,
And still they met and met. Again she said,
'O Lancelot, if thou love me get thee hence.'
And then they were agreed upon a night
(When the good King should not be there) to meet
And part for ever. Passion-pale they met
And greeted: hands in hands, and eye to eye,
Low on the border of her couch they sat   100
Stammering and staring: it was their last hour,
A madness of farewells. And Modred brought
His creatures to the basement of the tower
For testimony; and crying with full voice
'Traitor, come out, ye are trapt at last,' aroused
Lancelot, who rushing outward lionlike
Leapt on him, and hurl'd him headlong, and he fell
Stunn'd, and his creatures took and bare him off
And all was still: then she, 'the end is come
And I am shamed for ever;' and he said   110
'Mine be the shame; mine was the sin: but rise,
And fly to my strong castle overseas:
There will I hide thee, till my life shall end,
There hold thee with my life against the world.'
She answer'd 'Lancelot, wilt thou hold me so?
Nay friend, for we have taken our farewells.
Would God, that thou could'st hide me from myself!
Mine is the shame, for I was wife, and thou
Unwedded: yet rise now, and let us fly,
For I will draw me into sanctuary,   120
And bide my doom.' So Lancelot got her horse,
Set her thereon, and mounted on his own,
And then they rode to the divided way,
There kiss'd, and parted weeping: for he past,
Love-loyal to the least wish of the Queen,
Back to his land; but she to Almesbury
Fled all night long by glimmering waste and weald,
And heard the Spirits of the waste and weald
Moan as she fled, or thought she heard them moan:
And in herself she moan'd 'too late, too late!'   130
Till in the cold wind that foreruns the morn,
A blot in heaven, the Raven, flying high,
Croak'd, and she thought 'he spies a field of death;
For now the Heathen of the Northern Sea,
Lured by the crimes and frailties of the court,
Begin to slay the folk, and spoil the land.'

    And when she came to Almesbury she spake
There to the nuns, and said, 'mine enemies
Pursue me, but, O peaceful Sisterhood,
Receive, and yield me sanctuary, nor ask   140
Her name, to whom ye yield it, till her time
To tell you' and her beauty, grace and power,
Wrought as a charm upon them, and they spared
To ask it . . . .

In January 1858 'The Parting of Arthur and Guinevere' was finished, and Emily Tennyson recorded the first impression: 'it is awe-inspiring'. The Idyll known as 'Guinevere' is central to Tennyson's Arthurian world because it works out, in painfully human terms, the Queen's fall, the parting of Lancelot and Guinevere, the Queen's retreat into a nunnery, Arthur's rejection of her, Guinevere's memories of the past and remorse over her passion for Lancelot. The poem is, perhaps, 'awe-inspiring' in its concentration on the terrible effects of the conflict between Sense and Soul and in its fears that man, forgetting Soul, can all too easily regress into a beast. The main character, Guinevere, dominated by sense, has used her great beauty to bind Sir Lancelot to her, to impress the other knights, and yet to neglect her duties, as Arthur's Queen, to encourage moral goodness and order at court and in the land. But Guinevere's fall and repentance, 'awe-inspiring' to the selfless, faithful and adoring wife of the poet, are given complex and psychologically probing treatment throughout the poem.

This is one of the most original of the Idylls and Tennyson confronts the human problems of a great but guilty love which cannot be written off as simply evil. The trials Lancelot undergoes for his faith in the Queen cannot be labelled bestial triumphs of sense. The wicked Modred, satanic betrayer, is 'hurled...headlong' by Lancelot, but that is not enough: suspicions and divisions are too deep. So by the time of Modred's betrayal, Guinevere is already taking leave of Lancelot who must ride, at her behest, back to his own lands. She flees the court, but the King comes to reject her outright, as she is living among the nuns at Almesbury. King Arthur, true to his ideals, trying to keep his city and his knights high-minded, pure, proof against human riot and sensual corruption, has to become isolated from ordinary humanity. He stands for the high innocence of Soul, and rejects the penitent Queen lying at his feet, with the vague hope they may be joined again in the next world. By now battles rage against Lancelot; Modred has taken over the Round Table, Arthur's purity stands alone in the actual and moral wreckage of the 'city built to music' – the vision of Camelot.

Much of the narrative is given through the voice of the little maid who tends Guinevere at the nunnery. Not knowing Guinevere's identity, the girl chatters on, giving fragments of what she has heard, still speaking of the great King and the good-turned-evil Queen. She remembers her father's description of the general joy at Arthur's coming, and how one man only had a darker vision:

> Yea, one, a bard of whom my father said,
> Full many a noble war-song had he sung,
> Ev'n in the presence of the enemy's fleet,
> Between the steep cliff and the coming wave...

This bard of life and death faltered and swooned; he refused to sing of what he must have foreseen: the parting of King and Queen, the terrible collapse of Arthur's Round Table. The novice's own song – of the foolish virgins – repeats 'too late, too late' and Guinevere understanding and flinching at both tale and song, knows that, partly because of her sin, it is indeed 'too late' for Arthur's Kingdom. Guinevere is one of Tennyson's most credibly human characters. Her mind twists and slides over the past, over the pleasant sin which must be forgotten. When the King rejects her, she at once begins to revalue him. He was not, after all, cold and bloodless, but a great and gentle Lord 'Who wast, as is the conscience of a saint / Among his warring senses, to thy knights' (lines 634-5). Torn by Arthur's final admonitions, accusations and rejection, Guinevere tries to admit to herself that she loved him, or should have loved him: 'We needs must love the highest when we see it' (line 655). She has greatly helped to break the 'vast designs and purpose of the King', and her only recourse is to penitence among the nuns. In the end she is made Abbess for her good deeds, as well as for her rank, and dies in peace.

What is truly 'awe-inspiring' about the Idyll is Tennyson's ability to manipulate the narrative, to move to and fro in time, and to display the strongly, recognizably human conflicts which are at the centre of the abstract struggle between Soul and Sense. Neither can stand alone in an earthly world: each human being must reach towards the right balance. Lear who was always wondering how he could use past events as 'stepping stones' to higher things, may have found Tennyson's moral stance congenial. Needless guilt dogged the artist who saw his own epilepsy as evidence of sensual sin. In reading 'Guinevere' the recognition of sexuality, of guilt, fear, and uncertain terrors may have allowed Lear an outlet for his own feelings, and a realisation that, although no part of an Arthurian past, his human problems were not his alone. But whatever Lear felt, he reacted strongly when at the Tennyson house, Farringford, at 10 p.m. he wrote in his diary: 'I read Guinevere a while: the most astonishingly lovely of all the poems AT has written' (6 June 1859). In 1860 Lear hoped for a visit from Tennyson in February, but his diary notes in Greek 'he did not come'. He did not come at the beginning of March either, but a young visitor arrived and 'I read Guinevere to him, wh. is assuredly a wondrous pome' (D. 21 March 1860). The poem perhaps compensated for the absence of the poet himself – as did 'Tithonus' which Lear read and much admired in the *Cornhill Magazine* in 1860. Tennyson was often better remembered from a distance: when Lear met him next in England the poet was disappointingly cross and querulous.

Partly misquoting 'Guinevere' for his illustrations, Lear took one English scene, Beachy Head, Sussex, England: 'Between the steep cliff and the coming sea'. Beachy Head and the great cliffs were associated with visits Lear made as a child to his sister in Sussex. Perhaps he also associated them with the downs and cliffs near Farringford where, on a walk the day after he was reading 'Guinevere', Tennyson actually recited to him another Idyll of the four published in 1859. These cliffs above the sea represent an archetypal England, like the cliffs of Dover, seen by so many returning travellers – including Lear. As such the Sussex Cliffs are part of

King Arthur's domain to which, legend has it, he will one day return. An oil painting of the white cliffs of Beachy Head exists, but the Tennyson lines printed on the picture frame are not from 'Guinevere'. For the second line Lear drew four illustrations, a 'vast plain' in Syria, India, Switzerland and Egypt. All these open out and away from England's Beachy Head, and all are concerned with Lear's past journeys, and with Guinevere's dream. As Modred spies, and Lancelot throws him in the dust, the end is coming, and Guinevere's days and nights are filled with restless guilt. If she sleeps, she dreams 'An awful dream; for then she seemed to stand / On some vast plain before a setting sun...' then her own shadow broadens, blackens until it swallows the land and burns far cities. The dream space of the great plain and the setting sun provide those quiet horizontal lines which Lear loved to draw – especially with a mountain background. The drawings relate to the one line which does not suggest the dream's horror, the demonic 'something' and the self's shadow which takes over the world. Lear's sleepless nights, the 'demon' fits, and dreams he does not have or does not describe – all these may have gone towards his decision to take a 'landscape' line and give no indication of its context.

195. Beachy Head

At 11 I set out, walking all along the coast, by the little bluffs & towers, – with Carmel-like Beachy Head afar – & the sandgirt still sea=pools, – & the Blockade man, –

& the Pevensey Marshes with the "Bullocks" dear Ann used to dread when I was 5 years old – the flox of sheep, – & the old Castle –... (D. 7 August 1859)

199. Plain of Thebes, Egypt

I wrote to you from Kenneh on the 19th. & after that, I sent a scrap on the 22nd. to say I had arrived at Luxor (Thebes). For many miles before we reached Thebes of course we were immensely interested; – what surprised me most was the extreme magnificence of the landscape, which is not unlike the Campagna of Rome, on a much larger scale. We did not pass near the great ruins, but close enough to see how wonderful they were as to extent, & to see the 2 Colossi – sitting on the plain some miles off. For my part those 2 figures struck me as the most astonishing things I had ever beheld. We stopped for an hour at Esneh on the 24th. – & I saw the temple there, a magnificent pile, but so buried in the town, as to be interesting only to the architect & historian, so I shall not stop there in returning. But Edfoo which we reached on the 26th. is perfectly sublime, & of itself well worth the journey here to see. I shall however describe nothing at present, but wait to show you the drawings I hope to make.
(EL to Ann, 28 January 1854)

On his second Nile journey in 1867, Lear was deeply impressed by the striking contrast between the wonder of Egyptian colour and light, and the sense of ancient darkness, the loneliness of desert and temple.

Denderah
. . . the intense deadness of old Egypt is felt as a weight of knowledge in all that world of utter silence – looking down on the great green valley with its modern life beyond . . . & when one peeps into those dark death-silent giant halls of columns – a terror pervades the heart & head.
(D. 16 January 1867)

Near Thebes
The evening is surely most lovely, & the golden dream

look of sunset a glorious beauty, & after the sun had gone down beyond the Theban hills – the most surprising rose purple milky color spread his-self over the East sky & was reflected below. (D. 17 January 1867)

195. EL List: Between the steep cliff and the coming sea
     EL Drawing: Between the steep cliff and the coming sea.
[*Idylls*, 1859: Between the steep cliff and the coming wave;]
199. EL List: On some vast plain before a setting sun
     EL Drawing: On some vast plain before a setting sun.

On some vast plain before a setting sun (Guinevere.)

Plain of Thebes Egypt

From: ENOCH ARDEN

...   And where was Enoch? prosperously sail'd
The ship 'Good Fortune', tho' at setting forth
The Biscay, roughly ridging eastward, shook   525
And almost overwhelm'd her, yet unvext
She slipt across the summer of the world,
Then after a long tumble about the Cape
And frequent interchange of foul and fair,
She passing thro' the summer world again,
The breath of heaven came continually
And sent her sweetly by the golden isles,
Till silent in her oriental haven.

    There Enoch traded for himself, and bought
Quaint monsters for the market of those times,   535
A gilded dragon, also, for the babes.

    Less lucky her home-voyage: at first indeed
Thro' many a fair sea-circle, day by day,
Scarce-rocking, her full-busted figure-head
Stared o'er the ripple feathering from her bows:
Then follow'd calms, and then winds variable,
Then baffling, a long course of them; and last
Storm, such as drove her under moonless heavens
Till hard upon the cry of 'breakers' came
The crash of ruin, and the loss of all   545
But Enoch and two others. Half the night,
Buoy'd upon floating tackle and broken spars,
These drifted, stranding on an isle at morn
Rich, but the loneliest in a lonely sea.

    No want was there of human sustenance,
Soft fruitage, mighty nuts, and nourishing roots;
Nor save for pity was it hard to take
The helpless life so wild that it was tame.
There in a seaward-gazing mountain-gorge
They built, and thatch'd with leaves of palm, a hut,   555
Half hut, half native cavern. So the three,
Set in this Eden of all plenteousness,
Dwelt with eternal summer, ill-content.

    For one, the youngest, hardly more than boy,
Hurt in that night of sudden ruin and wreck,
Lay lingering out a three-years' death-in-life.
They could not leave him. After he was gone,
The two remaining found a fallen stem;
And Enoch's comrade, careless of himself,
Fire-hollowing this in Indian fashion, fell   565
Sun-stricken, and that other lived alone.
In those two deaths he read God's warning 'wait'.

    The mountain wooded to the peak, the lawns

And winding glades high up like ways to Heaven,
The slender coco's drooping crown of plumes,
The lightning flash of insect and of bird,
The lustre of the long convolvuluses
That coil'd around the stately stems, and ran
Ev'n to the limit of the land, the glows
And glories of the broad belt of the world,   575
All these he saw; but what he fain had seen
He could not see, the kindly human face,
Nor ever hear a kindly voice, but heard
The myriad shriek of wheeling ocean-fowl,
The league-long roller thundering on the reef,
The moving whisper of huge trees that branch'd
And blossom'd in the zenith, or the sweep
Of some precipitous rivulet to the wave,
As down the shore he ranged, or all day long
Sat often in the seaward-gazing gorge,   585
A shipwreck'd sailor, waiting for a sail:
No sail from day to day, but every day
The sunrise broken into scarlet shafts
Among the palms and ferns and precipices;
The blaze upon the waters to the east;
The blaze upon his island overhead;
The blaze upon the waters to the west;
Then the great stars that globed themselves in Heaven,
The hollower-bellowing ocean, and again
The scarlet shafts of sunrise – but no sail.   595

    There often as he watch'd or seem'd to watch,
So still, the golden lizard on him paused,
A phantom made of many phantoms moved
Before him haunting him, or he himself
Moved haunting people, things and places, known
Far in a darker isle beyond the line;
The babes, their babble, Annie, the small house,
The climbing street, the mill, the leafy lanes,
The peacock-yewtree and the lonely Hall,
The horse he drove, the boat he sold, the chill   605
November dawns and dewy-glooming downs,
The gentle shower, the smell of dying leaves,
And the low moan of leaden-colour'd seas.

    Once likewise, in the ringing of his ears,
Though faintly, merrily – far and far away –
He heard the pealing of his parish bells;
Then, tho' he knew not wherefore, started up
Shuddering, and when the beauteous hateful isle
Return'd upon him, had not his poor heart
Spoken with That, which being everywhere   615
Lets none, who speaks with Him, seem all alone,
Surely the man had died of solitude . . . .

The last of Lear's designs is for Tennyson's narrative poem 'Enoch Arden', published in 1864. Number 200 on the printed List, this is a picture which brings together studies from Lear's visit to India and Ceylon. It combines sketches of creeper-laden trees, and details of exotic flowers grown in the artist's own garden. Poetry and topography combine in the imagined scene on a tropical island. Lear wrote appreciatively to Emily Tennyson the year that 'Enoch Arden' was published: he does not seem to have attempted a picture, and he had not yet been to India, but the poem remained in his mind. In Malta, after looking out to sea, he wrote: '... the same amazing blue & silver & absolute calm –: it is like Enoch Arden's troppicle isle – only there are no palms, & lots of sails' (D. 13 February 1866). The nonsense 'troppicle' is quite often matched, after an unsuccessful picture-selling exhibition, with the wry pun 'No sail, no sail'. It was not until 1876 that Lear started vigorously to work on 'Enoch Arden', and then he seems to have begun designs for an oil painting, because some drawings he had made for the subject suddenly reappeared. They fell out of a book Lear had been reading on board the *Sumatra*, on his way back from India in 1875 – 'The drawings I made for Enoch Arden... Jany. 12 &c 1875 – drawings so long lost' (D. 3 May 1876). Lear started at once on a new design, on a detail of flowers, on a plan for a small oil painting and, later, on a project for an enormous fifteen-foot canvas.

Lear read Tennyson's other volumes as they came out. He was delighted when Tennyson himself sent one out to San Remo. On 28 November 1880 he wrote to thank the Laureate for a volume, mentioning that he knew 'The Revenge' because he had heard Tennyson read it (under a different title) two years before. He says of 'The Voyage of Maeldune' that he wouldn't mind living on the 'Silent Isle' or the 'Isle of Flowers', but he couldn't bear the abominably noisy birds. He thinks the dedication 'to little Ally' is 'perfectly lovely', and says he has made views of Lucknow and Montenegro, so the poems with those titles may go to swell the A.T. list – 'a pleasant dream of 300 memories tied to 300 poetries'. Lear had not read the rest of the volume; his comments are courteous and pleasant, without offering any kind of critical assessment. He did irritate Tennyson over the 'Northern Farmer' pieces: he definitely disliked the dialect poems. But often, as time went on, the artist noted that he had ordered or read a volume of Tennyson's late poems or plays – and he makes no comment at all. In his burst of work on the Tennyson Illustrations in the 1880s, Lear still concentrates on lines from the 1842 poems, with the additions he had already chosen by the 1870s. 'Enoch Arden', 1864, remains the last poem, and the latest on the chronological list.

Both the poem, a long narrative, and the illustration aspire to more than they achieve. Yet 'Enoch Arden' is important in Tennyson's work as is the tropical island design in Lear's 'poetical topography'. Tennyson took up a suggestion from the sculptor, Thomas Woolner, that he should write a poem on the story of 'The Fisherman'. There were parallels and influences (such as Crabbe), but Tennyson's approach was his own. The poem was meant to be accessible, to nullify the criticism that the poet never wrote for 'the people'. The story is simple and often becomes sentimentalized.

The poem opens with a fine setting of cliff and seaside town. Three children are seen playing together on the beach. When they grow up the girl, Annie, chooses to marry Enoch, the poor fisherman, and rejects the wealthy miller's son, Philip. Enoch works to keep a home, works harder to maintain his family, but ill-luck makes his efforts unavailing. In desperation, he sets Annie up with a few oddments to sell and goes as bosun on a trading ship to the China seas. He trades well, makes money, but on the voyage home he is wrecked on a beautiful but claustrophobic island. Always watching for a sail, he exists as a prisoner, as a wretched and unwilling Robinson Crusoe.

Meanwhile Annie and the children sink into poverty and misery. The hopeful but honourable Philip, now himself the wealthy miller, offers gifts and help to educate the children. After nearly ten years, it seems certain that Enoch must be dead. The children already call the miller 'father Philip'. Annie holds out until she thinks she has been given a Biblical sign. She marries Philip, has another child, and lives happily in her new family. In the last phase of the poem Enoch is discovered on his island. Once home, he realizes what has happened in his absence, and goes up into the town to look through a window at Annie and his children at home in Philip's house. His garrulous landlady, down near the docks, tells of Annie's years of waiting and of her agonized indecision until she was convinced of Enoch's death. With great self-sacrifice, Enoch decides to leave the family alone. Soon he becomes ill and asks his landlady to tell his story after his death. The 'fisherman' dies; no gesture can touch the dead man, but, for all that, the town has never seen 'a costlier funeral'.

The poem was extremely popular: it had domesticity, adventure and pathos. The three main characters, whether poor or rich, are completely blameless and behave with great moral rectitude. A small town stands for England and for home against a terrifying and distant tropical island. In a sense, everything is too predictable: Tennyson tries to give the story coherence, but fails to sustain its energy and conflict for long. Enoch's decision to leave his family, and his suffering, produce some tension: so does Annie's slow misery. But once together, Annie and Philip are no more than ciphers. And on his return, Enoch never confronts his family or his old rival. He is not even an ancient mariner, but a self-effacing ghost. Tennyson uses a wide variety of language – colloquial, Biblical, highly ornate – but there is no overall coherence. One of the finest moments is the landscape opening, a subtle prelude to the story, with cliffs, towers, roofs, distant church and mill, and below, three children playing on the sand. This scenic focus is contrasted with another: the amazing, lonely, tropical island. This is Tennyson's dream of the kind of exotic landscape he had never seen. Yet he gives a convincing description of the density of foliage, of colour, beauty, freedom – and imprisonment.

The poet's ability to enter a landscape he had never seen was praised as proof of his command of natural description. The unseen tropics had appeared before in a Cambridge prize poem, 'Timbuctoo' and in the unpublished 'Anacaona'. But Tennyson's most evocative

The mountain wooded to the Peak -
(Enoch Arden.) Island

description of scenery remained English, adapted from the Pyrenees, or imagined in the fantasy lands of 'The Lotos-Eaters' or 'Recollections of the Arabian Nights'. At least one letter in Hallam's *Memoir* tells how Tennyson yearned to see tropical vegetation (*Mem.* II, p. 11). And in 1842, when he met Wordsworth in London, he complained of 'the old Poet's coldness'. He had, he said, endeavoured to stimulate some latent ardour by describing a tropical island where the trees, when they first came into leaf, were a vivid scarlet: ' "Everyone of them, I told him, one flush all over the island, the colour of blood! It would not do, I could not inflame his imagination in the least!" ' Tennyson revered Wordsworth, but it was an astonishing misjudgement to try to draw out the poet of the Lakes with descriptions of scarlet leaves destined to colour 'Enoch Arden's Island', twenty odd years later (*Mem.* I, p. 209).

It was not the English story but Enoch Arden on the tropical island that interested Lear. He understood the feelings of a lonely traveller, a castaway, of 'Someone pacing there alone'. He knew that beautiful landscape could not, finally, assuage loneliness. He, too, was for much of his life a wanderer, excited by his journeys, but returning to rented rooms and other people's homes. He thought of himself, when lonely, 'as melancholy as Enoch Arden' (D. 31 August 1871), even after he had achieved his own home in San Remo in 1871. Lear's first drawings for the tropical island fell out of a book in 1876: they prompted him to work on new designs. Much other work intervened and it seems that 'Enoch Arden' first emerged as a small oil study in 1881. Lear then used a tracing and went over that in pen and water. The 'tropical isle' may have been given the 'Tyrant' treatment, but, more importantly, Lear was again seeking help from Frederick Thrupp for an ideal design. In August 1881 Thrupp sent some designs for 'Enoch Arden', but they were badly packed and Lear found he had 'cut off their heads' when he unpacked them. In all, Lear seems to have received about five designs from Thrupp, none of which was exactly what he wanted. In this case Thrupp could hardly have contributed to the single figure to one side of the picture. The main feature is the central tree for which a study still exists, resembling an A.T. Illustration, which Lear was well able to place and design on his own.[1] Was it because the picture was imaginary that Lear needed help? This did not apply to 'Someone pacing there alone'. Was it because Lear planned an enormous canvas – nearly fifteen feet long – and was unsure how to manage this very large space? Possibly it was simply a matter of Lear's poor eyesight. He bought a canvas and started the picture, which he had placed in his Tennyson Gallery in the Villa Tennyson. But 'Enoch Arden's Island' remained an idea: the picture was unfinished at Lear's death. According to Sir Charles Tennyson it was eventually hung in the ballroom at Aldworth. The lonely figure gazing across the island remained fixed in an isolation impenetrable within the picture, impenetrable by the passing social world.

The tropical island became the last of the Tennyson Illustrations. In this set, the huge central tree still dominates the design. This drawing, and the nearly identical but slightly larger version in the Houghton Library set, probably show us, in miniature, the island as Lear imagined it for his fifteen-foot oil painting. In the Houghton version Lear has added a parrot beside the watching figure on the right of the picture. This detail links the figure with Robinson Crusoe and with Lear as a young ornithological artist. In his Corsican Journal (p. 141), Lear mentions a scene which reminds him 'of Robinson Crusoe's settlement as represented in beautiful Stothard drawings, those exquisite creations of landscape which made [him] when a child, long to see similar realities'. From the vantage point of his own old age, he looks back to his early painting and engraving. Lear is the watcher and the island his past. But he did not allow himself to get too 'morbid' about his design and painting for 'Enoch Arden'. He remembered Giorgio's youngest son, Dimitri, whom Lear was trying to bring up in his house. The boy was not very bright, still Lear persevered with lessons. In 1883 he noted twice in his diary (23 January, 10 April) that he had heard Dimitri reading from *Robinson Crusoe*. Progress may have been slow, but one day Dimitri called out 'Robinson Crusoe, Robinson Crusoe', and indeed, Lear remembered, there was a man dressed all in goatskins sitting on a wall (D. 29 August 1884). This was a happy memory, before the unfortunate boy began to steal, lose jobs, and expect Lear to bail him out.

The story of Robinson Crusoe is built deep into Lear's tropical island. So is the idea of the voyage to a secret place, to a country that does not appear on any map. In a letter to Emily Tennyson, 1 June 1884, Lear wrote with a touch of humorous nonsense and without a hint of melancholy:

The foreground of my large Enoch Arden picture is to be elaborately filled with all kinds of Ipomœas, Passion flowers &c. – The statistic=realistic idiot of this world will say, "Why! these flowers are of different countries! By no chance whatever do they ever grow in one place!" – On which the following discourse will occur.

E.L.   *"O yes! they do!"*

Critic   "where?"

E.L.   *"Just 43 miles from the coast Enoch Arden's ship was bound to".*

Critic   "And where then was that coast?"

E.L.   *"Exactly 43 miles from Enoch Arden's Island".*

(Critic explodes into several bits. Artist grins.)

The 'tropical isle' is beautiful, lonely, terrifying, but also teasing. In his List Lear had 'Enoch Arden's Island' printed at the end of all his real places. And the drawing leaves us to watch the lone figure watching – the obvious landscape for Tennyson's 'Enoch Arden'.

[1] Reproduced in Noakes, p. 292.

200. EL List: The mountain wooded to the peak
      EL Drawing: The mountain wooded to the Peak
On the drawing the poem's title is given, as usual, on the left below the picture: (Enoch Arden). The word 'Iland' has been added after the brackets. On the right, where all other drawings have place-names, there is a blank.

Illustrations Reproduced in Miniature

3

the day
Was sloping toward his western bower. (*Mariana.*)

Sattara.
Bombay Presidency
India

5

Imbower'd vaults of pillar'd palm.
(*Recollections of the Arabian Nights.*)

Near Tel el Kebeer.
Egypt.

6

Imbower'd vaults of pillar'd palm.
(*Recollections of the Arabian Nights.*)

Wady Feiran.
Peninsula of Mt. Sinai.

8

the solemn palms were ranged
Above, unwoo'd of summer wind;
(*Recollections of the Arabian Nights.*)

Philæ.
Egypt.

11

the Waterfall
— A pillar of white light upon the wall
Of purple cliffs
(*Ode to Memory.*)

Oeschinen See
Switzerland

14

Flowing like a crystal river
(*The Poet's Mind.*)

Platania.
Crete.

19

26

as the tree
Stands in the Sun, and shadows all beneath,
(*Love and Death.*)

The Dead Sea
Palestine.

Thunder clouds that, hung on high,
Roof'd the world with doubt and fear.
(*Eleänore.*)

Yoánnina Epirus.
Albania.

28

31

The sunset; south and north
Winds all the vale in rosy folds.
(*The Miller's daughter.*)

Narni.
Italy

Beneath yon whispering tuft of oldest pine
(*Œnone.*)

Phyle.
Attica
Greece.

33

34

My tallest pines that plumed the craggy ledge,
(*Œnone.*)

Bavella
Corsica

A huge crag platform
(*The Palace of Art.*)

Mendrisio
Switzerland.

40

44

And one, the reapers at their sultry toil.
In front they bound the sheaves. Behind
Were realms of upland, prodigal in oil
And hoary to the wind
(*The Palace of Art.*)

near Correse
below Mt. Gennaro
Italy

Or the maid-mother by a Crucifix
(*The Palace of Art.*)

near Frascati. Roma
Italy.

45

Or the Maid-Mother by a Crucifix—
(The Palace of Art—)

Mount Soracte.
from Nepi.
Italy.

47

— over hills, with peaky tops engrailed
(The Palace of Art.)

Telichery. Malabar.
India

49

first round
With blackness as a solid wall,
(The Palace of Art—)

Lake Lugano.
Switzerland.

54

Only to hear were sweet, stretch'd out beneath the pine.
(The Lotos-Eaters.)

Eu Bœa.
Greece.

57

— I will see before I die
The Palms and Temples of the South.
("You ask me why" &c)

Date Palms.
Sheikh Abadeh. Nile
Egypt.

I will see before I die
The Palms and Temples of the South.
("You ask me why —— &c)

Cocoa Palms.
Mahée. Malabar.
India

60

The Palms and Temples of the South.
— I will see before I die
("You ask me why" &c.)

Cocoa Palms.
Telichery. Malabar.
India).

61

I will see before I die
The Palms and Temples of the South.
("You ask me why" &c &c)

Avisavella Cocoa Palms
Ceylon.

63

I will see before I die
The Palms and Temples of the South.
("You ask me why" &c &c)

Dondera
Coast of Ceylon.

65

I will see before I die
The Palms and Temples of the South.
("You ask me why" &c &c)

Areka Palms.
Ratnapoora.
Ceylon

66

I will see before I die
The Palms and Temples of the South
("You ask me why — &c &c)

Sago Palms.
Ceylon.

67

I will see before I die
The Palms and Temples of the South.
("You ask me why"— &c &c)

Talipat Palms.
Malabar. India

69

I will see before I die
The Palms and Temples of the South.
("You ask me why &c &c ")

Segesta.
Sicily.

70

I will see before I die
The Palms and Temples of the south.
("You ask me why" &c &c)

Girgenti.
Sicily

74

I will see before I die
The Palms and Temples of the South.
("You ask me why" &c &c —)

Philæ.
Egypt.

76

I will see before I die
The Palms and Temples of the South.
("You ask me why" &c &c &c)

Conjeveram.
Madras Presidency.
India.

200

78

I will see before I die
The Palms and Temples of the South
("You ask me why" ⁓ ⁓ ⁓)   Madras Presidency   Tanjore   India

79

I will see before I die
The Palms and Temples of the South.
("You ask me why - ⁓ ⁓ ⁓ ")   Trichinópoly.
Madras Presidency.
India.

90

Breadths of tropic shade, and palms in cluster,
(Locksley Hall.)   Kinchinjunga. Darjeeling
(Himalaya)   India.

91

Breadths of tropic shade and palms in cluster, —
(Locksley Hall.)   Darjeeling
(Himalaya)   India

92

Breadths of tropic shade and palms in cluster,
(Locksley Hall)   Khersiong. Darjeeling
(Himalaya)   India.

93

Breadths of tropic shade and palms in cluster, —
(Locksley Hall.)   Conoor.
Nilgherry Hills
Madras Presidency   India

94

Breadths of tropic shades and palms in cluster
(Locksley Hall.)   Conoor
Nilgherry Hills. Madras Presidency.
India

97

Breadths of tropic shade and palms in cluster
(Locksley Hall)   Ratnapoora
Ceylon

98

Ratnapoora Ceylon

Breadths of tropic shade and palms in cluster   Adam's Peak
(Locksley Hall.)   Ceylon
                                                          Ratnapoora

100

Sussex. Westfield

——— Darkness in the village Yew   Sussex
(The two voices.)   England

103

And rapt thro' many a rosy change
The twilight died into the dark.
(The Day Dream.)   Pine Forest of Pisa
                                                          (Tombo. Viareggio.)
                                                          Italy.

113

Tomohrit

Tomohrit, Athos, all things fair
        With such a pencil, such a pen.
        You shadow forth to distant men,
I read, and felt that I was there.   Mount Tomohrit
        (To E.L. on his travels in Greece.)   from above Tyrana.
                                                          Albania.

114

Tomohrit. Berat.

Tomohrit, Athos, &c &c
(To E.L. on his travels in Greece.)

115
~~116~~

Mt Athos.

Tomohrit, Athos, all things fair, &c ———
(To E.L. on his travels in Greece.)   Mount Athos
                                                          from the sea.

~~116~~ ~~117~~
116

Mt Athos

Athos, all things fair,
(To E.L. on his travels in Greece,)   Mount Athos
                                                          from above Erilijova

202

117

118

— Athos, all things fair —
(To E.L. on his travels in Greece.)

Mount Athos.
from above Erissò or Nisboro

— Athos, all things fair —
(To E.L. on his travels in Greece.)

Mount Athos
from above Karyès.

119

Karyes Athos.

— Athos, — all things fair —
(To E.L. on his travels in Greece.)

Mount Athos.
from Karyès.

121

M. Athos. A.P. Pantokratoron.

— Athos — all things fair
(To E.L. on his Travels in Greece.)

Monastery of Pantokratoron.
Mount Athos.

124

Athos. A. Philothea.

Athos — all things fair
(To E.L. on his travels in Greece.)

Monastery of Philothéo,
Mount Athos.

126

125

Athos. Iviron.

— Athos, all things fair —
To E.L. on his travels in Greece

Monastery of Iviron.
Mount Athos

M. Athos. A. Laura

126

M. Athos. A. Laura.

— Athos, all things fair —
To E.L. on his travels in Greece —

Monastery of Laura.
Mount Athos.

131
129

—— Athos, all things fair ——
(To E. L. on his travels in Greece.)

Monastery of St. Paul.
Mount Athos.

133
131

—— Athos, — all things fair ——
(To E. L. on his travels in Greece.)

Monastery of St. Gregorio
Mount Athos.

134
132

—— Athos — all things fair ——
(To E. L. on his travels in Greece.)

Monastery of Simopetra
Mount Athos.

136
131.

—— Athos — all things fair ——
(To E. L. on his travels in Greece.)

Monastery of St. Xenophon
Mount Athos

137
135

138
136

141
139

—— Athos, all things fair ——
(To E. L. on his travels in Greece.)

Monastery of Chiliandarion
Mount Athos.

142
140

—— Athos, — all things fair ——
(To E. L. on his travels in Greece.)

Monastery of Esphigmenou.
Mount Athos.

~~143~~
141

— Athos, — all things fair,
(To E.L. on his travels in Greece.)

Monastery of Vatopaidhi.
Mount Athos

142

not to be used

— all things fair
(To E.L. on his travels in Greece.)

Greece

142 A

Naples

~~146~~
143

— all things fair
(To E.L. on his travels in Greece.)

Constantinople

~~147~~
144

Campagna di Roma

— all things fair

Campagna di Roma.
Italy.

— all things fair
(To E.L. on his travels in Greece.)

Mt. Kinchinjunga
from Darjeeling. Himalaya.
India

~~150~~
147

In Curves the Yellowing river ran
(Sir Launcelot and Queen Guinevere)

below Sulì.
Albania.

~~152~~
149

Uprose the mystic mountain range.
(The Vision of Sin.)

Mount Oeta (from Lamia.)
Greece.

205

150

 152

157. Nice

Esa
(The Daisy)

153

What Roman strength Turbia showed
left on the mountain road (The Daisy)

155

Ma... (The Daisy)

154

(The Daisy)   Ventimiglia

158

(The Daisy)   Bordighera

161

Taggia

(The Daisy)   Taggia

Porto Maurizio

(The Daisy)   Porto Maurizio

164

(The Daisy)   Finale Marina

165

(The Daisy)   Capo di Nole

166

(The Daisy)   Vado

167

(The Daisy)   Varegge sur Savona

168

(The Daisy)   Cogoletto

169

(The Daisy)   Genova

171

(The Daisy)   "Sunsmitten Alps before me lay"   Monte Rosa
                                              from Monte Generoso

172

(The Daisy)   Lago di Orta

173

(The Daisy)

Lago di Como
from Villa Serbellone

176

— that fair Port —
(The Daisy.)

Varenna
Lake of Como.
Italy

179

Calm and still light on that great plain
(In Memoriam.)

Mount Hermon
Syria

180

Calm and still light on that great plain
(In Memoriam.)

from Monte Generoso.
Switzerland.

182

The fortress and the mountain ridge,
(In Memoriam)

Fortress of S. Leo.
near San Marino. Italy

183

— der Sinai's peaks
(In Memoriam)

Mount Sinai

184

— silver sails all out of the west —
(The Princess)

Bombay.
India.

185

Mt. Parnassus Greece

186

The Princess   First cataract, Nile

188

"The splendour falls on castle walls"   Sermoneta, Palestine

190

The Princess The splendour falls on castle walls"   Castel San Noale
                Calabria

#192
191

(*The Princess.*)" The Splendour falls on castle walls"
           Tivoli. Bracciano . Italy

193

A little town. with towers upon a rock" Near Orte on the
                   Tiber. Italy

196

On some vast plain before a setting Sun —
(*Guinevere.*)   Damascus.
                   Syria

197

On some vast plain before a setting sun —
           Missoorie.
(*Guinevere*)   N.W. Provinces. India

198

On some vast plain before a setting sun —   Plains of Lombardy
                from Monte Generoso.
(*Guinevere*)   Switzerland.

Select Bibliography

(Place of publication is London unless otherwise stated)

1. Published Travels

Edward Lear, *Views in Rome and its Environs*, T. M'Lean, 1841.
Illustrated Excursions in Italy, 2 vols. T. M'Lean, 1846.
Journals of a Landscape Painter in Albania, &c, Richard Bentley, 1851.
Reprinted as *Edward Lear in Greece: Journals of a Landscape Painter in Greece and Albania*, William Kimber, 1965.
Journals of a Landscape Painter in Southern Calabria, &c, Richard Bentley, 1852.
Reprinted as *Edward Lear in Southern Italy: Journals of a Landscape Painter in Southern Calabria and the Kingdom of Naples*, William Kimber, 1964.
Views in the Seven Ionian Islands, pub. Edward Lear, 1863.
Facsimile edition (limited), Oldham: Hugh Broadbent, 1979.
Journal of a Landscape Painter in Corsica, Robert John Bush, 1870.
Reprinted as *Edward Lear in Corsica: The Journal of a Landscape Painter*, William Kimber, 1966.
'A Leaf from the Journals of a Landscape Painter' (Journey to Petra, with an introduction by F[ranklin] L[ushington]), *Macmillan's Magazine*, LXXV, April 1897, pp. 410-30.

Lear in Sicily (Nonsense drawings of a tour made with John Proby in 1847), introduction by Granville Proby, Duckworth, 1938.
Edward Lear's Indian Journal: Watercolours and Extracts from the Diary of E. Lear 1873-1875, ed. Ray Murphy, Jarrolds, 1953.
Lear's Corfu: An Anthology drawn from the Painter's Letters, preface by Lawrence Durrell, Corfu: Corfu Travel, 1965.
Edward Lear. The Cretan Journal, ed. Rowena Fowler, Athens & Dedham: Denise Harvey and Company, 1984.

2. Letters, Nonsense and Ornithology

Letters of Edward Lear Author of 'The Book of Nonsense', to Chichester Fortescue Lord Carlingford and Frances, Countess Waldegrave, ed. Lady Strachey, T. Fisher Unwin, 1907.
Later Letters of Edward Lear Author of 'The Book of Nonsense', to Chichester Fortescue Lord Carlingford and Frances, Countess Waldegrave and others, ed. Lady Strachey, T. Fisher Unwin, 1911.

[Edward Lear] *A Book of Nonsense* by Derry down Derry, T. McLean, 1846.
Edward Lear, *Nonsense Songs and Stories*, Frederick Warne and Co., 7th edition, 1889.
The Complete Nonsense of Edward Lear, ed. Holbrook Jackson, Faber and Faber, 1947.
Teapots and Quails, ed. Angus Davidson and Philip Hofer, Cambridge, Mass: Harvard University Press, 1953.

Edward Lear, *Illustrations of the Family of Psittacidae or Parrots*, pub. R. Ackerman and E. Lear, 1832.
Gleanings from the Menagerie and Aviary at Knowsley Hall, ed. John Edward Gray, Knowsley: privately printed, 1846.

Susan Hyman, *Edward Lear's Birds*, Weidenfeld and Nicolson, 1980.
Brian Reade, *Edward Lear's Parrots*, Duckworth, 1949.

3. Catalogues

Edward Lear 1812-1888: An Exhibition of Oil Paintings, Water-Colours and Drawings Books Prints Manuscripts Photographs and Records, introduction by Brian Reade, Arts Council of Great Britain, 1958.

Thos. Agnew and Son's 94th Watercolour Exhibition Catalogue for 1967 reproduces a number of Lear's Tennyson Illustrations identical to those of the 'eggs' reproduced here, and the correct text is cited for some..

Edward Lear 1812-1888: A Loan Exhibition of Oil Paintings, Watercolours and Drawings, Books and Prints, Nonsense Works, introduction by Vivien Noakes, Gooden and Fox Ltd, 1968.

Edward Lear: Painter, Poet and Draughtsman: An Exhibition of Drawings, Watercolours, Oils, Nonsense and Travel Books, Worcester, Mass: Worcester Art Museum, 1968.

Edward Lear in Greece: A Loan Exhibition from the Gennadius Library, Athens, introduction by Philip Hofer, Washington D.C.: International Exhibition Foundation, 1971-72.

How Pleasant to Know Mr Lear: Watercolours by Edward Lear from Rhode Island Collections, L. Candace Pezzara, Providence, Rhode Island: Museum of Art, Rhode Island School of Design, 1982.

The Travels of Edward Lear, introduction by Fani-Maria Tsikagou, Fine Art Society, 1983.

Edward Lear 1812-1888, Catalogue of Exhibition, Royal Academy of Arts, Weidenfeld and Nicolson, 1985. This Catalogue, compiled by Vivien Noakes and others, contains detailed information on Lear's ornithological and zoological illustrations, with details of the many books to which he contributed, pp. 207-10. For a selective list of Lear's Nonsense Rhymes and Stories, see pp. 210-11.

4. Books and Articles about Lear

M.R. Bruce, 'A Portfolio of Monasteries: Edward Lear's sketches of Mount Athos', *Country Life*, 8 October 1964, pp. 908-09.

Thomas Byrom, *Nonsense and Wonder: The Poems and Cartoons of Edward Lear*, New York: E.P. Dutton, 1977.

Andrew Causey, 'Landscapes to paint a poet's vision', *Illustrated London News*, 11 February 1967, pp. 18-19.

Angus Davidson, *Edward Lear: Landscape Painter and Nonsense Poet (1812-1888)*, John Murray, 1938; 2nd edition, 1968.

Anne Henry Ehrenpreis, 'Edward Lear sings Tennyson Songs', *Harvard Library Bulletin*, XXVII, 1979, pp. 65-85.

Ina Rae Hark, *Edward Lear*, Boston: Twayne Publishers, 1982.

Osbert Wyndham Hewett (ed.), '...and Mr Fortescue', John Murray, 1958. (Includes extracts from journals of Chichester Fortescue, Lord Carlingford, which refer to Lear.)

Philip Hofer, *Edward Lear*, New York: Oxford University Press, 1962.
        Edward Lear as Landscape Draughtsman, Cambridge, Mass: Belknap Press, 1967; Oxford, Oxford University Press, 1968.

John Lehmann, *Edward Lear and his World*, Thames and Hudson, 1977.

Vivien Noakes, *Edward Lear: The Life of a Wanderer*, Collins, 1968; revised edition, Fontana, 1979; revised edition, BBC Publications, 1985.

Joanna Richardson, *Edward Lear*, Writers and their Work no. 184, Longmans Green, 1965.

Bertha C. Slade (ed.), *Edward Lear on My Shelves*, New York: privately printed for W.B. Osgood Field, 1933.

Fani-Maria Tsigakou, 'Edward Lear in Greece', M.Phil. thesis, University College London, 1977. (Information on Lear's Athos paintings, sketches and Tennyson Illustrations.)

5. Alfred Lord Tennyson

The Letters of Alfred Lord Tennyson, Vol. II, 1851-1870, ed. Cecil Y. Lang and Edgar F. Shannon Jr, Oxford: Oxford University Press, 1987.
Tennyson: Poems of 1842, ed. Christopher Ricks, Collins, 1968.
Poems of Alfred, Lord Tennyson, illustrated by Edward Lear. Boussod, Valadon and Co., 1889.
The Poems of Tennyson, ed. Christopher Ricks, Longmans, 1969.
The Works of Tennyson, ed. Hallam Lord Tennyson, (Eversley Edition) 9 volumes, Macmillan, 1907-08.

Jerome Hamilton Buckley, *Tennyson, The Growth of a Poet*, Cambridge, Mass: Harvard University Press, 1974.
John Kilham, *Tennyson and the Princess*, Athlone Press, 1958.
Robert Bernard Martin, *Tennyson. The Unquiet Heart. A Biography*. Oxford: Clarendon Press & Faber and Faber, 1980.
W.D. Paden, *Tennyson in Egypt, A Study of the Imagery in His Earlier Works*, Lawrence, Kansas: University of Kansas Publications, 1942.
Christopher Ricks, *Tennyson*, New York and London: Macmillan, 1972.
Edgar F. Shannon Jr, *Tennyson and the Reviewers*, Cambridge, Mass: Harvard University Press, 1952.
Charles Tennyson, *Alfred Tennyson*, Macmillan: 1949, revised edition, 1968.
Sir Charles Tennyson, *Stars and Markets*, Chatto and Windus, 1957.
Hallam Lord Tennyson, *Alfred Lord Tennyson: A Memoir by his son*, 2 vols. Macmillan, 1897.
Lady Tennyson's Journal, ed. James O Hoge, Charlottesville: University Press of Virginia, 1981.
Alfred Waugh, *Alfred Lord Tennyson*, William Heinemann, 1902.

6. General

Martin Butlin and Evelyn Joll, *The Paintings of J.M.W. Turner*, 2 vols, revised edition, New Haven and London: Yale University Press, 1984.
Robert Byron, *The Station, Athos: Treasures and Men* (1931), Century Publishing, 1984.
Edward Malins, *Samuel Palmer's Italian Honeymoon*, Oxford: Oxford University Press, 1968.
Geoffrey Wakeman, *Victorian Book Illustration, The Technical Revolution*, Newton Abbot: David and Charles, 1973.
Gerald Wilkinson, *Turner and Landscape: The Liber Studiorum*, Barrie and Jenkins, 1982.

Victorian Printing Processes

'Also I go on irregularly at the [Alfred Tennyson] illustrations – vainly hitherto seeking a method by which I can eventually multiply my 200 designs by photograph or autograph, or sneezigraph or any other graph.'
(EL to Hubert Congreve, LLEL, p. 25)

Edward Lear lived at a time when the technology for reproducing illustrations was evolving rapidly. The following are some of the processes which were available to him.

Aquatint

An etching process, which produced a very fine reticulated pattern, the density of which could be varied, so producing shades of grey ('half-tones'). Aquatints were frequently hand coloured. Although popular at the begining of the nineteenth century, aquatints were not very often produced thereafter.

Autotype

One of the principal problems facing those who wish to reproduce illustrations mechanically is how to render shades of grey. In engravings and woodcuts the tones between black and white are produced with fine lines, the depth of tone depending on the thickness of the lines, or the distance between them. Photography offered an alternative solution, as the process depends on finding a substance that will gradually darken on exposure to light, hence producing true grey tones. The autotype process was invented by J.W. Swan, subsequently more famous for the invention of the lightbulb. The process involved a mixture of gelatine and lampblack, sensitized with bichromate of potash. This was fixed to a sheet of glass, and exposed to a photographic negative through the back. The gelatine film was removed from glass plate, and washed, the amount washed away depending on the degree of light that had fallen on that particular area. Hence the final result was of varying thickness, with the dark areas being thicker than the light.

The Autotype Company acquired the patents to the process in 1866, and appears to have continued to use the process right into the twentieth century. They produced prints on their own account, and also licensed the process to others, and published a series of handbooks. Reproductions by the process were normally of a good standard, and it is not clear why Lear was so frequently disappointed with the results the Company obtained from his drawings.

Chromolithography

The technique of producing a colour picture by printing from a number of lithographic stones, each using a different coloured ink. The individual printing surfaces were drawn by hand, making the process laborious and expensive.

Collotype

The first English patents for collotype were taken out in 1869, and it appears to have been used by the Autotype Company from about that date. The early history is confusing as the Company seems to have described prints as 'autotypes' even when they were in fact collotypes. It is therefore possible that some of the proofs that Lear obtained from the Autotype Company were done by this process. The preparation was similar to the autotype process, in that it involved a sensitized gelatine and was then exposed to a negative. In this case the effect was to cause the gelatine to develop fine reticulations where it had been exposed to light. This meant that it could be used as a printing plate; ink was rolled on and the amount transferred depended on the degree of light exposure. Hence collotype was a printing process whereas the autotype process itself was purely photographic.

Collotypes are still produced today, and for monochrome work such as reproduction of pencil drawings, they are hard to tell from the originals.

Etchings, Engravings

Both techniques were widely used for monochrome illustrations. In both processes the image is below the surface of the plate ('intaglio'). The plate is inked, and then the surface is wiped, so that the ink remains in the recesses but not on the surface. The plates were normally copper. For an etching, the plate is coated with a wax or varnish, which was then scraped away to produce the image. Acid is poured over the surface, and the plate is eaten away in the areas where the protective coating has been removed. For an engraving, the image was cut into the surface, using a sharp steel tool.

Graphotype

Invented in 1860 in America, the graphotype process involved drawing on a chalk block. The block was washed with water, with the result that a raised image was left, as the ink had the effect of rendering the requisite parts of the surface waterproof. The block itself was too fragile for printing, but could be used to make a plate. The process was attractive to artists as it was cheaper than wood engraving, and, as it did not require hand work by the blockmaker, was more likely to be true to the original drawing. Lear mentions a trial of this process (D. 23 July 1866) although not in connection with his Tennyson Illustrations.

Lithography

Lithography was invented in the 1800s and was introduced into England by Hullmandel in the 1820s. It involves drawing the required image onto a piece of smooth limestone, with a greasy crayon. The stone is damped and then inked with a greasy ink. The ink sticks to the image, but is repelled by the damp surface of the stone. A sheet of paper can be pressed against it and a print obtained.

Lear learned the technique from Hullmandel, and his first publication, *Illustrations of the Family of Psittacidae or Parrots*, was produced lithographically, and then hand-coloured by Hullmandel's assistants. He later used lithography for many of his topographical works, on occasions using two or three 'plates' to produce a coloured background.

Platinotype

A photographic process, using platinum instead of silver. It produced very good tone qualities, and was less susceptible to deterioration than other processes as platinum is very resistant to tarnishing. It was of course very expensive. Lear heard of the process, and mentions it in 1887. The American, Dana Estes, who hoped to have the Tennyson Illustrations published, took a drawing, 'Morn Broadens', to use for a Platinotype trial. It was apparently successful, but Mr Estes wrote to Hallam Tennyson that he could not embark on such an expensive project as two hundred drawings.

Wood Engraving

The most widely used printing process for illustrations in the nineteenth century, used notably by Cruikshank for his illustrations to Dickens, and also in an edition of Tennyson *Poems* published by Moxon in 1857, with fifty-five illustrations by contemporary artists. The technique involved drawing the design on a block of wood, usually box. The engraver then cut away the wood to leave the design raised. In most cases the engraver was different from the artist. Lear had wood engravings made for his Nonsense books, for which the process was admirably suited. He also had wood engravings made for the *Corsican Journal* and was justifiably unhappy with the result. He was not the only one to suffer at the engraver's hands. Rossetti was moved to write:

> These engravers! What ministers of wrath! Your drawing comes to them like Agag, delicately, and is hewn in pieces before the Lord Harry. I took more pains with one block lately than I had done with anything for a long while. It came back to me on paper, the other day, with Dalziel performing his cannibal jig in the corner, and I have really felt like an invalid ever since. As yet I fare best with W.J. Linton. He keeps stomach aches for you, but Dalziel deals in fevers and agues.

Address to Dalziel Brothers

O woodman spare that block,
O gash not anyhow!
It took ten days by clock,
I'd fain protect it now.

Chorus – Wild laughter from Dalziels' Workshop.[1]

[1] G. Wakeman, *Victorian Book Illustration*, Newton Abbot, 1973, p. 71.